"All of you are con... suming the Captain's position," Thackeray said. I gulped and tried to assume the Look of Eagles as he continued. "What we need to do today is get our own impressions of you as a person. I'd like to start by asking you why you want to go. You'll be giving up a successful life here in SpaceHome, taking your crew into some danger, perhaps, and returning to a civilization possibly hundreds of years advanced beyond your time. What's your motivation?"

Feeling somewhat like a finalist in a beauty contest, I said:

"I had the privilege of seeing the first Hexie artifact on Iapetus. Looking at it and pondering its makers gave me an indescribable feeling—an urge—which has never left me. Everything I have done since then has been pointed toward being one of the voyagers on this expedition. I don't quite understand it myself. All I know is that it is extremely important to me that mankind be able to expand itself, that the Hexies have provided a vehicle for this expansion, and that we ought to do our damnedest to be in full communication with them as soon as we can."

A LION ON THARTHEE

GRANT CALLIN

BAEN BOOKS

A LION ON THARTHEE

A Baen Books Original

Baen Publishing Enterprises
260 Fifth Avenue
New York, N.Y. 10001

First Baen printing, October 1987

ISBN: 0-671-65357-1

Cover art by Alan Gutierrez

Printed in the United States of America

Distributed by
SIMON & SCHUSTER
1230 Avenue of the Americas
New York, N.Y. 10020

To Canara

I love her.
I always will.

BOOK I

SPACEHOME

Chapter 1

Human philosophical concepts of teleology have been anthropocentric throughout most of our history. The basic premise of these is that the universe was created for man, and humans are the centerpiece of creation. The slow death of this concept began with Copernicus in the 16th century. Darwin finished it off in the mid-19th, with Huxley as his second. The funeral dirge dragged on for another half century, music supplied by the Second Law of Thermodynamics. Oratorio was by Bertrand Russell at the turn of the 20th.

But the human ego is not an animal to just lie down and die; and teleology is a world-class Phoenix. By the latter half of the 20th century, it had risen again in the form of the Anthropic Cosmological Principle.

The Weak Anthropic Principle is innocent enough; it states simply that our observations of the universe will inevitably produce data skewed by the fact that we are here to observe it. Thus, the universe must be large, because it has to be old enough to have had time to evolve second-generation stars and planets with carbon-based intelligent life. Certain physical quantities and ratios must be as they fortuitously are; carbon, oxygen, and hydrogen and water must have their unique properties; and so forth.

Toward the end of the 20th century, proposed versions of the Anthropic Principle got strong, then stronger; anthropocentric background music began to play again. The greatest 20th century evolutionists pointed out that while other complex physiological functions such as the eye evolved time after time on Earth, cognition appeared only once. (Furthermore, they said, there was no particular evolutionary reason why Man, of all the kingdoms, phyla, classes, *orders, and species, arose from the primates.) They used the now-sophisticated science of statistics to show that the evolution of life with intelligence comparable to that of humans was so improbable that it was unlikely to have occurred anywhere else in the universe.*

A few dissenting voices still remained. They said that evolution of cognition had started several times on Earth— witness the fossil records—and furthermore, the path was always via primates. Therefore, convergent primate evolution toward cognition was a robust process, distinctly and statistically possible on other planets. But these voices were drowned out by the anthropic orchestra, which by the end of the 20th century was playing that delightful old favorite: "Humans Own the Universe and Can Do with It as They Wish." And for a century of no evidence to the contrary, we danced to that tune.

Now the Hexies have the gall to exist, and now the tune is once again the Dirge for Anthropocentric Teleology. The evolutionists lost two ways: not only has cognition arisen elsewhere (and in a nearby location, for strengthened statistics), but it is primate cognition. And when our expedition returns, we will play the new convergent tune with vigor; the evolutionary similarities between the Human and Hexie species are much too remarkable to support any other score. We flatly tell the evolutionists either to sing this new tune or find a different line of work.

And we are back to the Weak Anthropic Principle, which must now remain Weak for all time. We can still claim that the local universe is tailored for carbon-based life, but allegations that humans have a special place are now so much horseshit.

> —*Badille:* Hexie White Papers, *Informal
> Prefatory Notes*

". . . remind you that all our efforts to obtain the Hexie artifacts, and the forthcoming expedition to the Hexie ship, are in actuality *archaeological* endeavors—after all, it has been nearly 4,000 years since those artifacts were emplaced. And in that context, the words that Howard Carter wrote in 1922 shortly after opening Tutankhamen's tomb are particularly apt:

" 'Archaeology under the limelight is a new and rather bewildering experience for most of us. In the past we have gone about our business happily enough, intensely interested in it ourselves, but not expecting other folk to be more than tepidly polite about it, and now all of a sudden we find the world takes an interest in us, an interest so intense and so avid for details that special correspondents at large salaries have been sent to interview us, report our every movement, and hide around corners to surprise a secret out of us.' "

I looked up from my crib sheets to the audience. It was large. It consisted of students, teachers, and other guests—plus several reporters. There were smiles as I concluded my lecture:

"And in that context, let me assure you that I am a private citizen and have no secrets worth hiding around corners to surprise out of me."

Some of the smiles turned to chuckles. "And as a final note, I will add that Carter might have complained, but he did not lack for funds and assistance in performing the monumental task of cataloging and dismantling the tomb. And that also parallels our current situation: Earth and SpaceHome have been bickering for some months over exactly how the expedition will be conducted—" I allowed time here for an artistically dramatic pause, "—but at least it is well-funded."

The chuckles were louder this time, and I tried to exit through them. But as I was collecting my notes together, a score of hands shot up throughout the audience. They belonged to polite but ignorant people; the reporters were not accustomed to such niceties:

"Dr. Whitedimple, when do you think the expedition will finally be ready to get off the—"

"—true that you've been approached to be Cap—"

"—heard that both Earth and SpaceHome are preparing secret expe—"

"—Hexie ship is really in orbit around Saturn and that we've already—"

I held up my hands and shouted them down: "Please,

ladies and gentlemen! This is supposed to be an archaeology lecture, not a news briefing." Then I looked at their faces and relented. "Oh, very well. I'll make a brief statement—but as a private citizen only. The Saturn Artifact Retrieval Team was disbanded two years ago, and I haven't been in SpaceHome's employ since then. So if I see any of those 'official sources' labels on my words, I'll make you eat 'em!"

I looked around at the smiles of relief; a lot of them were on the faces of the students and professors, as well as the reporters. Rumors that Earth and SpaceHome had just about ironed out their differences and were ready to form the expedition were rampant—but no official announcements had been made by either side. People were hungry for news; too bad I really didn't have anything new to tell them.

"First, let me assure you that the Hexie ship—if it really is out there—is not in orbit around Saturn, or anywhere else except where the message said it was. I was part of the translation team, and am as certain as anyone that it's sixty times the distance of Saturn from the Sun: 85 billion kilometers out, give or take a few.

"Second, all this negotiation time since the retrieval of the message on Saturn is the natural consequence of a certain amount of distrust between Earth and SpaceHome. Both are trying to keep the other from gaining any possible economic advantage from whatever the Hexies might have left for us to find. And with all our sophisticated instruments watching each other, I'm sure that no one here really believes that either side has even begun to mount an expedition on its own.

"And yes, I was approached with a tentative offer to be captain of the expeditionary voyage . . ." A buzz began immediately; I had to speak loudly to finish the sentence: ". . . but that was more than a year and a half ago, when I was still an exploitable political commodity."

I grinned to show them *lese rancor*. "But that was then; now the climate is a bit different. It's been well over a year since I've been contacted by the SpaceHome president, and as you may know," this drolly, "Mr. Ogumi and I are not exactly bosom buddies."

That got me my exit laugh. I looked at my watch conspicuously and thanked the audience for its attention. The applause allowed me time to take my notes from the podium and stroll offstage. I should have run. As it was dying out, a voice shouted clearly from the back of the lecture hall:

"Dr. Whitedimple, is it true that you're the bravest man in the system?"

The question was so incongruous that it stopped me cold. The voice was young—probably a freshman. He had perhaps just started high school when the first hexagonal-shaped artifact—hence the name "Hexies"—was found by two SpaceHome employees on Iapetus.

SpaceHome is not only the informal name of the collection of habitats at L4, but also the formal designation of the company which runs all big business in the Lagrangian colonies. At that time—and still today—SpaceHome President George Ogumi was trying to free the colonies from the economic hold of the large Earth conglomerates. The artifact was a message; Ogumi wanted to keep it secret until we translated it and discovered if it might bring some economic advantage. But Earth found out, and we were in a race.

I was roped into the deal to help translate the original artifact, being a professor of archaeology (the only one) at SpaceHome University who knew a little about glyphs. I won't belabor the story about how I eventually became a pilot and a leader-of-men; it's been ground to death in the media. Suffice it to say that the 40-year-old-and-going-to-pot professor (me) ended up discovering that he had a natural penchant for both. He turned his flabby belly into G-tolerant muscle; his brain parachuted out of its ivory tower into the real world. And he met and befriended one 20-year-old genius named Junior Badille, who was born and lived with his parents in a Saturn orbital research station. He looked like an old gnome, cackled like a Macbeth witch, and knew more about everything than anyone had a right to know. Junior alone made all the headaches worthwhile.

The "real" artifact—the one which contained the message the Hexies really wanted us to read—was artfully emplaced at a precise longitude and latitude on Saturn

. . . 2,000 kilometers below the cloudtops . . . where the temperature is high enough to melt mundane construction materials like iron, and the pressure is so great that it forces molecular hydrogen into the liquid state.

I ended up in a combination submarine-spaceship-balloon gondola, going down part way into that murk, so I could guide a high-pressure robot the rest of the way to make the pickup. We were in a neck-and-neck race with an Earth team, who was doing the same thing at the same time and likely to beat us to the prize. My Earth counterpart was a couple of hundred kilometers below me in a heavier vessel—but Earth had not built as well. His batteries went bad, and he was stuck and going to die, and I had to go down after him. It was a little dicey, and we almost didn't make it. Part of the deal was that I had to hyperpressurize my own vessel in order to get down to him; so I spent the next several days semi-conscious, being trundled in and out of a hyperbaric chamber with messed-up body chemistry.

So my backup pilot went down a couple of days later and made the actual pickup.

The media made a big deal of it; thus the probable adulation of the teen-ager in question. The press had stopped lionizing me—thank God!—over a year ago, but youngsters hold on to heroes longer than their elders. I should have kept right on walking as if I hadn't heard the question, but it was too late now. I turned back to the audience, swearing unprofessorlike oaths under my breath. Almost everybody was smiling. The reporters were positively grinning as they switched their recorders back on. I thought furiously before answering:

"I suppose whoever asked that is referring to my rescue of the Earther down in Saturn's atmosphere. Well, let me tell you something about that. I was unconscious when they took me out of the floater, but they told me later that my pants were wet. Now tell me how many brave people you know who wet their pants."

I got away amidst the laughter and applause. Let the reporters try to use that one!

Once out of SpaceHome University's lecture wing, I took the nearby spoke elevator directly to the hub of the

'Home III torus. I was in a hurry because Junior would be docking at SpaceHome in less than an hour; he'd been living at home for the past two years. "Home" for him was with his mother and father in the Saturn Orbiting Station, in an 80-day polar circle around the Old Man. We'd sent messages, but I hadn't been able to make it back out to see him, and he'd been too immersed in his longevity research to make the trip in-system.

Now he was coming to live in the Cube, there to work his way from the low-G hospital levels down to half a G or more. It was all part of "the Cure," as we'd come to call it.

I suited up, climbed to the inner hub, and went right to the outbound personnel cable without even bothering to check the status of the trolley. I cycled the airlock, then pushed out of it right up to the cable, hooked myself on, and announced myself to the Hub's traffic computer via my suit radio. Then, without further ceremony, I pushed off the "floor" of the 'Home III hub, activating my suit thrusters at the same time. By the time I got up to my sedate cruising speed of about 10 kilometers an hour, I was out into space heading for the Hub. I went through a familiar brief moment of disorientation as I put 'Home III behind me and became a member of the larger construct that was the Pinwheel. The Hub was still over four kilometers distant. I looked along the thick cable and saw another traveler about a kilometer ahead, and another coming back from the Hub on the inbound cable. We followed convention and waved in passing.

I let my glance slide down past the MMF—the microgravity manufacturing facility attached to the Hub by two kilometers of vibrationless umbilical. Ten kilometers farther down was the Large Cylinder, now nearing completion of its pressure shell. Next would come the enormous job of interior outfitting, then the even larger one of emplacing the megatons of crushed rock to be grown into soil. I looked at the monster with some pride of possession. I'd made an outrageous down payment for a tenth-hectare of land, and was pumping as much money as I could spare into the monthly installments. If I ever got rich, I might even put a house up. If not, I'd will the plot to my kids—not that I was bloody likely to have any. Even though I was only in my mid-forties, I was getting set in my bachelor ways.

A movement at the north end of the Hub caught my eye. It was the familiar shape of the Iapetus tug, coming in on RCS thrusters. It would be docked in five minutes. I boosted my speed a trifle. If I hurried, I could cycle through the airlock with the person in front of me. . . .

Once in the Hub, I hurried through the sliding seals into the stationary core and made my way to the north end dock. I got there just as the umbilical hookup was completed. The first thing through the hatch after pressure equalization was a pint-sized human gnome with a wizened face. He looked around quickly, spotted me, and launched himself in a perfect flat trajectory that intersected my midsection. Then his arms were around me, and mine around him, as we drifted toward the wall.

"Admiral Dimp, you old fart!"

"Hello, you little runt!"

We hit the wall and I used my elbows to steady us, then held him away from me and looked him over. Same big ears, same crooked teeth. Maybe the hair was a little sandier, maybe not.

"Well, Boy Genius, you don't look too bad for an old man of 24. Maybe you're going to make it after all."

He cackled. "Haven't aged a detectable amount since I started the Cure, Admiral. Maybe I'll even outlive you— we'll see in a few months. Thanks to what's-her-name over there. C'mon, let me introduce you." He hooked his head in the direction of the umbilical port, where a woman was watching us with a tentative smile.

I looked twice, then a third time, as we pushed off and drifted in her direction. Even in her coveralls, she was totally devastating, and I was completely taken aback.

Junior was conceived, born, and spent his early years in a close polar orbit around Saturn, before the SOS was moved out to its current (more economical) distance of 3.6 million kilometers. According to a learned paper he wrote at age six (but never published), the unique interactions of magnetic field lines, solar wind bowshock, ring spoke extensions, and a few other things all combined to wire his nervous system a bit differently from us normal peasants. It had a lot less redundancy, but a lot more efficiency.

The result of all this was a phenomenal IQ. When I first met him at age 19, it was over 300 and just starting to level off. But he was also carrying a physiological age of sixty or so—the accelerations seemed to go hand-in-hand. Junior was philosophical about it. He knew he would die in a few years, and accepted it gracefully, but I didn't. By the time we'd shared a few close scrapes together retrieving the Hexie artifacts in the Saturn system, I'd grown very fond of the little gnome. I finally extracted a promise from him that he'd put his prodigious brain to work on the aging problem. And after we retrieved the final artifact, deep in Saturn's atmosphere, he went back to SOS to do just that.

That was two years ago. Since then, we'd exchanged only a few brief, expensive messages a year. I knew that shortly into his research, he'd lured an Earth expert in biochemistry and geriatrics to come work with him. I also knew she was a female. But the only description Junior offered in his messages was that she was "a cute old bird, and plenty smart." I had her pictured as a spinster type with a pinched face, but the reality had me forming male drool in all corners of my body.

On close inspection, it wasn't that she was beautiful. Her face was pretty, but not a knockout. She was not young, by any means—I guessed her age to be mid-thirties, correcting for spending her life mostly in a one-G field. It's just that she literally *oozed* sexiness. This was not an isolated perception on my part. I could see the cargo crew staring and drooling just as I was—and for some reason, this irritated me.

"Kurious Whitedimple, I'd like you to meet Kari Nunguesser," Junior said in as formal a tone as he ever achieved.

I grabbed a nearby stanchion with one hand and used the other to shake hers. "Dr. Nunguesser, you have a ridiculous name." Don't ask me why I said that; it just popped out uninvited.

"You should talk, Dr. Whitedimple," she replied with a dazzling smile.

"Touché!" Junior said with a cackle.

I rolled my eyes. It promised to be a long year. "Let's get your stuff to the Cube and get you settled in," I said.

The Cube was really cylindrical. It got its name from the fact that its length and diameter were both 600 meters. It was the oldest habitat in SpaceHome, and the only one that was spun up to one G—and therefore, the one in which visiting Earthers lived if they wanted to keep their insurance policies in effect. It was built on fifty-two main levels, beginning at 0.993 G on the lowest residential level, just inside the cosmic ray shielding, and working up four meters at a time to the 0.3 G "colony normal" level 90 meters from the center. The central portion was reserved for low-G entertainments. It was largely empty of apartments, except for hospital recovery suites extending another 17 levels up to .073 G at the boundary of the central hub.

That highest level was where we were headed. Junior grew up in 0.06 G, and needed to work his way down slowly. In fact, there was some doubt that he'd ever be able to adapt, even to .3 G.

We installed Junior and Kari in a comfortable pair of suites, then I went down to the main lobby of the hospital to finish the paperwork. On the way back, I detoured to buy a bottle of wine. Between sips they filled me in.

". . . so after about two months of heavy reading," this was Junior talking, "I noticed that every good paper from the past dozen years or so was either written by Kari, or referenced her work." He scratched his nose, leered over the table at the woman, and took another sip. "So I invited her out to help me study me. And she came."

"It wasn't quite as simple as that, Whitey," she said. "In fact, I didn't even believe his message at first—thought it was one of my colleagues playing a practical joke. It took a couple more messages and some research into the old newspaper files to convince myself that Junior was a real phenomenon. Then it took some fancy paperwork and some heavy pressure on a friend on the committee to persuade Johns Hopkins to fork over the grant money."

However she got the grant money, she was on her way to Iapetus on the next personnel carrier, and made the transfer to SOS during its next resupply flight. She quickly found out that Junior's prodigious intellect was no joke. She also found him as well prepared as anyone could possibly be without yet having done any research. Junior had read literally everything, performed the proper critical evaluations, and had planned an initial course of experimentation, along with provisional plans for modifications, depending on initial results. He had also—with funds earned from his SART participation—set up in SOS a small but well-equipped research laboratory.

Within a week, Kari had switched from independent researcher to research partner—and had to fight gamely to keep from becoming merely a smart assistant. She was successful, and had earned Junior's respect—I could tell this from the way Junior joked about it. Kari's strengths included no mean intellect of her own, and a knowledge of the literature's pitfalls and byroads available only to one who had worked for years in the dirty-fingers lab environment. She also knew intimately everyone doing worthwhile work in the field—especially what they'd done and not yet published.

Together they plowed new ground, using Junior as a combination test subject, DNA source, and living chemical laboratory.

". . . then, when we thought we were on the right track, we took Pandora down into low Saturn orbit, and grew some very smart, short-lived rats," continued the woman. "Five of the beta-keratin derivatives showed good results, but we hit the jackpot with the gamma analog—long-lived, smart rats." She made a wry face. "Then when we got back to SOS and tried it on Junior, it hardly decelerated his baseline aging rate at all. It seems that the blood-brain barrier was stripping the molecule in such a way that the key radical . . ."

At this point Junior noticed my eyes starting to glass over, and interrupted in his sweet manner: "Hold it, Kari. I think we've just crossed the admiral's pain threshold. Put it this way, Dimp: we tried to shotgun the solution and lost. Turned out that one of those other derivatives was the right choice. So we had the cure, only it took us a couple of months longer to find out."

"So what is the cure?" I asked.

"Approximately fifty micrograms per week of delta beta-keratin," said the woman; then she flashed a dazzling smile. "Or beta keratin delta—take your pick. We were the first to synthesize it, but we haven't named it officially yet."

"Actually, Dimp," said the gnome, "a fifty-microgram dose levels me off for ten days to two weeks, depending on my mood and the phases of the moons. The once-per-week routine is just to be sure of overlap. We didn't have enough stuff in the lab to make more than a year's supply, so Kari here is going to zip over to SHU next week and make up a thousand pills—a twenty-year supply."

"This derivative is extremely stable, so far as we can tell," said Kari. "Unlimited shelf life. In fact," she gazed fondly at the little man, "I'm tempted to make up a thousand-year supply, just in case—we don't know yet just how long Junior is going to live."

"I understand that's why you're here," I said. "To find out if Boy Genius here is going to die off like us normal folk, or if we'll have to do him in after a few decades out of charity to the rest of us normal slobs. . . ."

Junior cackled. "You'll have to catch me first, Admiral. I may be halfway out of the galaxy by then."

I ignored him and plowed on: ". . . but I don't quite understand exactly how the process works. Junior's been very niggardly with message dollars recently."

Kari answered for both of them: "The only way to calibrate the aging process is in high-G, Whitey. At SOS, or any low-G environment, people age so slowly that we can't measure them against the normal population baseline established for Earth. Even at .3 G in SpaceHome, we don't really have results we can trust. . . ." She bestowed another fond glance on Junior, which caused a pang in my gut that I didn't understand. I had to force my attention back to her words: ". . . was aging so fast that he was easy to measure, even in .06 G. He would have died from nonspecific geriatric causes—old age—in six years, plus or minus two. But now—who knows? His projections all show up as 'indefinite' on the computer."

The gnome cackled and pulled at an ear. "Don't worry,

Dimp. I have no doubts that the grim march of catabolism will triumph as usual. You'll probably dance on my grave after all."

But Kari was serious with a riposte: "I'm not sure of that at all. I've studied life for more years than I care to remember, and I still don't know how biological fields function. Sometimes I think they follow their own laws and ignore what the physicists believe about space/time."

I didn't even know what a biological field was, so I nodded sagely. Junior cackled again and scratched his nose. "This is a running battle, Whitey. I *know* I'm going to kick off in a decade or three, but she says there's no way of being sure yet." He glanced sideways at her serious face. "But she won't lay money on it—and I gave her three to one."

"So," I said, "are you going to work all the way down to one G to get good data?"

Junior grimaced and shook his head. Kari smiled and nodded. "Maybe," she said. "It depends on how long he's going to live. With normal people we get reproducible results at about 0.4 G. We plan to work our way down to 0.5 and hold there while we collect data. Five days per level—" her smile became evil at this point, "—with a full daily regimen of cardiovascular exercise. We need a healthy subject for our blood samples and biopsies."

Junior rolled his eyes. (Were there tears in the corners?) "God help me," he moaned. "A hundred sixty days of aerobics, weightlifting, and treadmill tests, with my weight increasing the whole time to make it worse."

I looked professionally at the gnome. He measured a scant meter and a half, and massed maybe 40 kilos. I reached over and lifted a pipestem arm.

"You could use a little mass, pipsqueak. So how long will you have to stay at point five G?"

"Three months, maybe," he said. "Hopefully less, if I'm going to die a respectable death in a few decades." He took a final sip of wine from his squeeze bottle.

"But maybe much longer," Kari continued. "If the results are negative after three months, we'll continue on down to three-quarters G—and even further if we have to."

I looked around the room we were in. It wasn't palatial, but neither was it small. And Kari had another just like it next door. "So who's paying for all this?" I asked. "Hospital suites aren't exactly cheap."

"Johns Hopkins, of course," she replied. "We're doing the study quite carefully, with me as a control, and the results so far are quite exciting enough to justify their continuing generous grant."

"So you're taking the Cure, too," I said. "Do you expect positive results on yourself?"

"Not really," she said. I caught a fleeting, wistful look in her eyes. I didn't blame her for it—I probably had the same look myself. "Junior's body chemistry—especially across the blood-brain barrier—is different enough from ours so that I don't expect the Cure, or anything like it, to work on anyone but him." She grinned conspiratorially. "Of course, I've been wording my reports as hopefully as the truth allows—it never hurts to be politic when you're living off someone else's money."

I smiled politely, then thought of something else. "Does this substance occur naturally, or will Junior be dependent on pills for the rest of his life?"

"Well," she said, "beta-keratin occurs naturally in all of the cruciferous vegetables, so we checked all we could get from the SOS and I-Base supplies. They all showed negative except for a trace amount of the derivative in—"

"Cauliflower!" Junior finished. "Turns out that all I have to do is eat cauliflower. About 100 kilos a week. I hate cauliflower. I'll take the pills."

Exit smiling.

Chapter 2

The problem confronting the Hexies on first contact was greater than ours. How they chose to resolve it was quite understandable to us. They needed to be sure of our resolve. More importantly, they needed to be sure that we were willing to make great sacrifices for an end that in the balance was more altruistic than economic.

—Kitigawa: Hexie White Papers,
Prefatory Notes

I don't know where the next eight or nine months went; all I know is that they went there fast.

The presence of Junior in SpaceHome added a lively completeness to life that had been lacking for the previous two years. On the other hand, the presence of Kari made me distinctly uneasy, for reasons I simply couldn't fathom. I finally decided I was jealous of all the time she spent with Junior, then determined that I would not let that relationship mar my life. She was certainly fond of the little runt, and she could be in love with him for all I knew—it wouldn't be the first time that research cohorts developed a chemistry outside the lab.

I didn't think that Junior was in love with her; but just in case, I certainly was not going to stand in the way. I vowed to resist all impulses I had in her direction, and considering her almost overwhelming womanhood, it was quite a feat. I managed it by a rigorous protocol of keeping her just a little farther away than real friendship. This worked for me, but I could tell that it puzzled Junior. Kari was really a very bright and likable person, and the gnome obviously expected us to hit it off. Once in a while, I even detected a worried look in her eyes when I caught her unawares staring at me.

One thing I knew for sure: she wasn't having anything to do with other men. Many times I saw her approached; she drew men like sugar draws flies. If a man made a gentlemanly pass at her, she brushed him off gently. If the pass was boorish, she cut him down mercilessly. Within a few months, word was around that the ravishing Earther Kari Nunguesser wasn't to be had.

In the meantime, the research proceeded apace. With much grumbling, Junior began his cardiovascular conditioning. Kari followed suit with a more vigorous regimen calculated to compensate for her Earther upbringing. One of the "piggyback" papers they were doing was a landmark study of whether or not it was possible to condition a person (one Junior Badille), raised from birth in ultra-low G, to function normally in a medium- or high-G environment. "Medium G only," Junior had insisted. "We'll see," Kari had replied.

Things progressed nicely for the first two and a half months, then Junior hit a wall at .26 G, just three levels above SpaceHome normal. Up until then, he'd been gaining in endurance and body mass in a slow but satisfactory manner; but at that level, his body seemed to go on strike. He got tired more easily, and didn't do well in his exercises. They stayed there for ten days before moving down to the next level, then had to move back up when all Junior wanted to do was sleep.

I got a call from Kari at that point. She said she was at wit's end, and asked me to talk to Junior. "It might be purely physical, Whitey," she'd said, "but I'm not so sure. Junior is a very complex person, aside from his intellect, and you seem to be able to get inside him better than anyone else."

So I visited the gnome while Kari was conveniently out. We discussed the pros and cons of him joining the human race. I also mentioned the possibility of visiting the Hexies' home planet one day. "Of course, the gravity will probably be three, four times what you've got here," I said, looking around the room. "Dimp," he said with acerbity, "you have the subtlety of a hundred-kilo lead brick."

The next day I visited 'Home II—the Farm—and blew a small fortune buying what turned out to be almost an entire day's supply of cauliflower for the Colonies. I had it bundled in two large bags and delivered to Junior's suite with a note: *100 kilos, as ordered per our discussion yesterday. I hope this is more useful than lead. Love and Kisses.*

Within three weeks, Junior and Kari were residing at the Cube's base level—SpaceHome normal 0.3 G. Seems Junior climbed over that wall and was starting to gain weight again. They stayed on schedule right on down to level 15, with the gnome gaining about ten kilos in mass— all of it muscle and calcium. If I didn't know better, I'd have said that he had actually begun to enjoy doing the exercises.

When they'd been ten weeks at 0.5 G, Kari announced that Junior could be expected to live to age 49, plus or minus six years, on Earth—providing no "interruptive diseases" got him first. At SpaceHome, the figures were much cloudier, since a population baseline was not yet firmly established. Their best guess said he'd live to 70, plus or minus 15 years. And as suspected, the Cure didn't help Kari worth mentioning; her expected natural lifetime was within the noise for her current physiological age.

I thought about the political implications of all that for a day or two, then cornered Junior when Kari wasn't around. After we'd talked for a while about the Earth/SpaceHome negotiations, which were finally coming to a head, I put my speculations on the table.

"Junior, if you had started the Cure when you were much younger—say, five or six—how long would you have lived?"

"Oh, two, three hundred years, give or take a few decades." He looked carefully at me, rubbed his nose, and added: "But that's okay. Seventy is plenty—like a new lease—lots of time to have fun and kick around."

"You know that's not what I'm getting at."

He grinned evilly. "Why, Dimp, you mean my feelings aren't uppermost in your mind? I suppose you're worried about a bunch of rich people zooming off to Saturn to conceive and bear genius children who'll outlive their peers by a factor of two or three?"

"Well, something like that—or worse. It could get ugly. I'm wondering about whether or not to fudge the official results so that you don't sound so much like a dream come true."

"Not to worry, Admiral. Statistics are on our side, not to mention chromosomal complexity. We bred a lot of rats in the shadow of the Old Man, and only about fifty percent of them lived. Of those, only about a third were smart, short-lived runts. The rest appeared normal, or had complex mutations of a less pretty nature. Would you take those odds for your beloved offspring?"

"So you were a one-in-six long shot?"

"Dimp, you've got to learn about genetic statistics to appreciate what a phenomenal piece of luck we had in getting seventeen percent success. We really didn't expect that gig to produce any results at all. We would have been happy to get one viable animal in a hundred tries."

"Oh." I sipped my beer. "Well, I'm glad you were the one in six, or a hundred, or whatever."

He squinted up at me over the rim of his glass and shook his head. "I had a long hard talk with my parents after Kari and I got back to SOS from tight Saturn orbit. Mom had two miscarriages before I was born."

He was silent for a while, running a finger around the rim of his glass, then finally spoke again: "They gave up trying after the second. I was an accident—and they were in fear during the entire pregnancy until I finally popped out looking normal."

I sat and looked at the gnome for a long minute. He was more than a pal; he was the only true friend of my middle years—and the best that I'd ever known in my life. I raised my glass to him.

"Then here's to brave parents—and the mistake that wasn't. Long may he live." I drained the glass and slammed it down on the table. If there was a fireplace, I'd have thrown it in.

The little man grew a slow smile, then turned it into a crooked grin, bobbed his head up and down and raised his own glass.

"I'll drink with you, Admiral. Being is definitely more fun than not."

Besides keeping tabs on Junior, I continued my rather disjointed life style of helping Sam Sebastian turn youngsters into pilots, guest-lecturing archeo-politics at SHU, and, if the truth be known, consulting a little on the sly as an arbitrator of the Earth/SpaceHome negotiation teams. It kept me hopping around, but the combined pay was better than I could have made at my old job teaching archaeology full time at the U. Besides, I liked being my own boss. My stint as chief pilot of the Saturn Artifact Retrieval Team had spoiled me for clock-punching work.

My quasi-secret arbitration role allowed me to keep informal tabs on the process of the negotiations about the composition of the forthcoming expedition to the Hexie ship. Shortly before Kari and Junior pronounced the success of the Cure, both teams finally began to come to the ancient realization that time is money, and got down to business. Crew composition, split chain of command, conditional protocols, alternative action plans, provisioning hardware, et cetera, were worked out in detail, but nothing about the ship's captain. Every time the subject started to come up while I was performing my role, it abruptly got dropped and the teams went on to something else, so I knew that I was still a contender.

And so I was not too surprised to walk into my apartment one day and find a recording from Ogumi's secretary on my telephone. I called and set up a time for a meeting the next day. I felt sure I was going to be offered the captain's job, which was nice—especially since Junior was a shoo-in to be a crew member—and even more especially since neither of the negotiation teams had ever considered seriously the idea of allowing a mere archaeologist to use up valuable crew quarters on the expedition.

The spacious outer office of the SpaceHome Corporation's president never seemed to change. The five square meters with tasteful (and expensive) touches of wood, brass, and leather surrounded the impressive wraparound secretarial console. And as usual, the secretary was dictating a letter. She looked up and gave me a warm but reserved smile.

"Hello, Whitey. Long time."

"Hi, Andrea." She was quite pretty, and I felt a momentary twinge of sorrow that we'd broken up a year and a half ago. But we'd found out that she wanted a rising star, and I wanted as much obscurity as I could get. So we'd gently split the sheets. Now, as she activated the intercom and announced me to President Ogumi, I found myself quite unaccountably comparing her with Kari Nunguesser. Then she finished and looked back at me. Hastily, I threw out the first remark that came to mind:

"Got a pair of boxing gloves ready?"

She raised an eyebrow. "Planning on going a few rounds?"

"I hope not. But you never know."

She kept her eyebrow raised as she walked me to the door to Ogumi's office, ushered me inside, and quietly shut it as she exited.

"Hello, Whitey. It's good to see you. Please have a seat."

I took the little man's outstretched hand and looked through old-fashioned glasses, past epicanthic folds, into eyes which were cast with a generous alloy of steel.

"Hello, George." I'd earned first name rights, since I'd twice pulled SpaceHome's bacon out of the fire for him. Once reluctantly, at his connivance—for which I'd never really forgiven him. He didn't much care for me, either, since I refused to become involved in his attempts to use me as a bargaining tool with the Earthers.

He got right down to business:

"I know that you've been acting as an unofficial arbitrator for the Earth and SpaceHome negotiating teams, so I don't need to fill you in too much. The teams have taken great pains to ensure that the crew and the scientific leadership authority are split as evenly as possible between the two factions."

I nodded. At the distance of the Hexie ship, the round trip communications lag would be more than six and a half days—hardly conclusive to real-time inputs by the folks back home. If on-the-spot decisions were necessary, they would have to place their trust in the ship's organization and the people they chose to make the voyage. Therefore Ogumi's "great pains." Over two and a half years' worth.

". . . thorny problem of choosing the ship's captain," the president was continuing. "He or she will have a large part of the responsibility for the conduct of the expedition, and the negotiations have been particularly heated with respect to both the selection of the individual, and that person's sphere of authority."

I nodded, but didn't say anything. He was obviously getting around to something, but I'd be damned if I'd help him. Besides, his words were interesting, since the negotiation teams had pointedly left me out of all discussions pertaining to the captaincy.

". . . should be no surprise to you that several candidates have been discussed, and that your name is most prominent among them. I offered you that position almost three years ago, shortly after SART had been disbanded. At that time, you tentatively accepted my offer. . . ."

Tentatively, my ass! I'd accepted firmly. Not only that, I got an offer from Earth, too—the Earther I'd saved in Saturn's atmosphere had been the son of the president of one of Earth's most affluent power consortia. Ogumi knew all this perfectly well, so he was baiting me. I just looked into his eyes and waited for him to continue.

"Yes. Well, that was some time ago, but your name has certainly not been forgotten. And your subsequent lectures and public utterances to newsmen have given you a certain reputation for, umm, let us say, *impartiality*."

His thin smile was accompanied by a distinct expression of distaste. Ogumi was an almost fanatic SpaceHome chauvinist, and "impartiality" to him was tantamount to treason. But whatever my personal feelings, I couldn't deny the fact that he'd been good for SpaceHome. In the fifteen years of his tenure, he'd almost completely extricated the Lagrangian colonies from the tangled economic webs spun by the powerful energy and manufacturing cartels of Earth. And SpaceHome was now nearly free of economic bondage to the home planet. The cost of this was a growing estrangement between the Earthers and 'Homers—currently exacerbated by the fact that both factions were hoping to wrest an economic advantage from the potential inherent in the discovery of the Hexie artifacts, and what they might bring in advanced technology or trade.

". . . attitude has not been lost on the team from Earth—witness the fact that you have been called in frequently as an arbitrator. In fact," he gave me a ten-kilovolt stare, "we are both inclined to have you in that post."

He still had more to say, so I just nodded for the third time. It was great exercise for my cervical vertebrae.

"The principal question remaining is the one of authority. I have the choice of pressing for a very strong captain, a very weak one, or any of the shades of gray in between. . . ."

He proceeded to lay it on the table. He did it very cleverly, with full knowledge of my personality and leanings. He would instruct the SpaceHome team to agree on me as captain. They would further advance the notion that the captaincy must be strong, with full authority over the expedition. They would argue that these two ideas were compatible because of the demonstrated fairness and *impartiality* of Kurious Whitedimple, even though he resided in the Colonies.

My payment to Ogumi for these considerations was couched so *very* delicately. I was to enter now, in private, an agreement with Ogumi to do everything I could to advance the SpaceHome cause during the expedition. I would use my authority as necessary to try to ensure that SpaceHome would have the better chance to capitalize on whatever was discovered at the Hexie ship. Nothing specific was mentioned, but it was clear nevertheless. I was to be Ogumi's man without anyone else knowing. He even mentioned, again very delicately, that there would be an additional monetary consideration besides the captain's pay.

When he finished, he looked me in the eye and raised his eyebrows ever so slightly.

"No," I said.

"Whitey, before you walk out of here, I advise you to give it some thought. It's nothing villainous I'm asking you to do, and it is not just for the benefit of the SpaceHome Corporation—you know we're fighting for the survival of the Colonies."

"Mr. Ogumi, I've had nearly three years to think of possible conditions under which I would take the job of captain. Therefore, my answer was not ill-considered. I never have believed that the Hexies are crucial to the survival of SpaceHome. On the contrary, I think that the discovery of the Hexie artifacts, and whatever they might bring, is an event which should be a universal legacy for all humans."

"It may surprise you to know, Whitey, that privately I share your view. Unfortunately, I must daily cope with the realities of our political and economic situation—realities which underscore the fact that human nature has not been changed overnight by this discovery. There remain many people and organizations that would profit by our corporate downfall, and these also seek to gain advantage from the Hexies' existence. For instance, the Hexies apparently have the ability to temporarily overcome the local effects of gravitational fields. If the Earthers were to gain exclusive control of that ability, our advantage of the high ground would be nullified; our power and manufacturing businesses would be subject to intense competition and potential freeze-out."

I was shaking my head as he finished. I'd heard this and similar arguments from both sides. I answered firmly:

"I am thoroughly familiar with your position, Mr. Ogumi. Nevertheless, my own remains unchanged. With respect to the Hexie discoveries, I am a human first, an archaeologist second, and a SpaceHomer third. If I become captain of the expeditionary voyage, those priorities will remain intact. I will be no one's bought man. Good day, sir."

He made one more try as I was opening the door.

"You could have your land and a house in the Big Cylinder—all paid for."

He'd done his homework; that was indeed a soft spot. I sighed with regret as I turned back around and answered:

"Yes, but I don't think I'd enjoy living in it."

I exited, wondering if personal dignity was worth it. I'd probably scotched my chances for good.

Things moved rapidly after that. The negotiations seemed at last to be completed. It was announced that Earth

would supply the vessel—*High Boy*, of course, from their
ill-fated Saturn retrieval expedition. It was the only Earth
ship large enough for such a voyage. In turn, SpaceHome
would supply the fuel. The crew would number twelve: six
each from Earth and SpaceHome. The leadership would
consist of one member from each faction. Junior was
chosen as a crew member, of course; he was a natural as
computer expert and backup pilot for SpaceHome. Kari
Nunguesser was not selected, as the expedition saw no
need for a molecular biologist.

The captaincy was not announced publicly with the rest
of the crew. I heard rumors about it but little else from my
fellow pilots. Most of them thought I was a shoo-in for the
job, even though I knew differently. Obviously, the negotiation teams had not yet agreed on the particulars of
command. I nursed a small, forlorn hope in my breast.
Junior was going, and I wanted badly to go with him.

I told the tale of woe to the runt over a beer in Murphy's. Kari was there, too, but by now I trusted her
completely. I hadn't gotten closer to her, but I knew she
wasn't one for loose talk.

"Your own fault, Admiral. One little white lie and you
could've joined the party," he said with his usual sympathy.

I shook my head. "Even if I could have brought myself
to lie to Ogumi, I wouldn't want to chance getting caught
in one of his webs."

The gnome looked into my eyes. "You could handle it,
old son. You've got his measure, now—but he doesn't
have yours any more."

I shrugged. "Maybe. But if so, part of the reason is that
I won't play his games."

"Goody two-shoes," he said. There was a note in his
voice that could have been either admiration or chagrin.
Then he cackled. "But it's not over yet, Dimp. Three gets
you two that you'll get another shot at it. You're still the
fair-haired boy who pulled the chestnuts out of the fire."

I shook my head again. But he gave me hope: I'd only
known Junior to call one bet wrong in his life.

Two days later I got a call from Andrea.

"They'd like you up here if you can make it, Whitey."

"Who's 'they'?"

"No less than the full complement of both negotiation teams. They're in the visitors' conference room, as usual."

My cardiovascular system accelerated slightly. "Tell them I'll be there in half an hour."

I could hardly force myself to wait the required 20 minutes before leaving for the SpaceHome corporate offices, but it would never do to let them know I was eager.

The VIP conference complex was adjacent to Ogumi's office, but much larger. When I entered the suite, the large oval table was occupied by a complement of a dozen people, and about four tons of briefcases, recorders, and scattered paper. I recognized everyone. At one time or another I had dealt with each of them singly or in smaller groups. Ogumi wasn't present, nor were the Earth cartel heads, but I recognized Jason French, Ogumi's personal toady. If French was there, Ogumi was there.

I nodded as sweepingly as I could to the group. "Good afternoon, ladies and gentlemen."

Tuan Cao, a medium-big shot from the Chino-Arab power consortium, was the one who did the talking:

"Good afternoon, Dr. Whitedimple. I believe you know everyone here, so let us dispense with introductions." He indicated one or two remaining vacant seats. "Please, sit down if you will."

I took the chair with twenty-four eyes following me. As soon as I found Tuan's again, he began to speak.

"We asked you here for two reasons, Dr. Whitedimple. The first was to thank you for your services to this body. You, and a few others like yourself, have been invaluable in speeding the course of these negotiations. Without your skills as an arbitrator, we would still be in debate. Furthermore, your discretion with the media during these talks has been noted and appreciated."

I opened my mouth to say something—probably inane—but Tuan continued firmly:

"Therefore, this combined body has approved a check in the sum of ten thousand dollars to be added as a bonus to your consultation fees."

He pulled a small piece of plastic from his briefcase and passed it to me, then smiled and began clapping softly. The others joined him. I took the hologram and stared at

the zeros following the one while the clapping continued.
After a polite interval, they stopped. I glanced up to find
them all looking at me again. I groped uselessly for words:

"Ladies and gentlemen, I must say I am truly dumbfounded. I don't even know where to begin in thanking—"

"Please, Dr. Whitedimple, do not thank us," said Tuan,
saving me from embarrassment. "It is we who are grateful.
You have shown marvelous tact and forebearance in dealing
with this diverse collection of hard-headed people. And
we have especially appreciated your orientation that hu-
mankind, and not just certain factions, should be the ultimate benefactors of whatever legacy the Hexies might
have left us."

There were assenting murmurs around the table, into
which the Vietnamese spokesman continued:

"Which brings us to the second reason we asked you
here: we would like to offer you the position of captain of
the expeditionary voyage."

I shook off my euphoria in a hurry and looked sharply at
Cao. He was still smiling, waiting politely for a reply.

"You honor me again, sir. What are the terms of
command?"

"Your commission will start immediately. You will be
expected to arrange your in-system affairs so that you may
devote yourself full time to the job no later than three
weeks from this date. Your salary will be commensurate
with the current maximum pay scales for senior—"

"Please, Mr. Cao." It was my turn to interrupt. "I'm
sure that the salary will be adequate. I'm much more
interested in the captain's sphere of authority."

"It is spelled out in considerable detail in the contract,
Dr. Whitedimple, but the essence is this: you will have
complete decision-making authority with respect to piloting and navigation of the vessel, and in onboard emergencies. Responsibility and authority for expeditionary decisions
affecting the vessel's functioning will reside jointly with
the crew leaders from Earth and SpaceHome. . . ."

What he meant was that there would be a split command, with control of the ship much of the time in the
hands of a pair of amateurs—the road to disaster, in my
humble opinion. I saw now why Tuan gave me the bonus

first. He suspected that I might demur, and wanted to soften me up first, which meant that the teams really did prefer me as captain. I'd soon enough find out just how badly they wanted me.

"I'm sorry, Mr. Cao. I cannot accept command under such conditions."

He looked at me with regret. "Please, Dr. Whitedimple. I ask you to consider it carefully before you decline. And be assured that your input would always be weighed heavily by the crew leadership."

I shook my head. "No, sir. The captain of the vessel must assume responsibility for the safety and well-being of the expeditionary members, no matter how the contract is worded. But without commensurate authority, such responsibility is much too onerous a burden. The captain should certainly weigh the wishes of the crew leadership, but ultimate authority must be his, and his alone. Any other system is insane."

The Asiatic picked up a document from the pile in front of him. "Do you imply, then, that this contract is insane, sir?"

I looked in his eyes. They were smiling a little, thank God.

"Yes, sir, if it splits authority." I smiled, too.

He sighed. "Perhaps you are right, Dr. Whitedimple. Nevertheless, both teams have firm instructions from their principals on this issue. It is the one provision of the contract which is not subject to negotiation."

I sneaked a quick glance at Jason French, sitting across the table. He had a smug look on his face; I never did like him.

"Then I'm afraid I must refuse your inviting offer, Mr. Cao. Please believe that I am sorry to have to do so. I have more than a passing interest in the forthcoming expedition." I stood to leave. "And thank you again," I encompassed the table, "for your very generous bonus. Good day, ladies and gentlemen."

They were so impressed by my stalwart bearing and integrity that they convinced their principals to change the contract, called me back in, and gave me full authority.

Wrong. Hard-headed politics don't mix with fairy tales.
What they did was give the job to John Stevenson, the guy
who'd piloted *High Boy* during Earth's artifact retrieval
attempt at Saturn. He was a good pilot, and had the
advantage of having flown the big ship before. I didn't
think too highly of his intelligence when he said he'd take
the job, but secretly I envied him.

Chapter 3

The Hexies possess a CRF technology not much superior to that which humans have enjoyed since the Badille modifications of 2094 . . . high-G I_{sp} perhaps a few percent higher than ours, but nothing to get excited about. When I asked Keelczee why they hadn't yet developed matter-anitmatter annihilation propulsion, she told me candidly that they had, but that conversion to such a technology was not economically sound. The gain in specific impulse did not warrant the outlay for conversion of their fleet, or the enormous added cost of manufacturing the necessary quantities of antimatter . . . borne out by the off-planet ships I inspected, including the starship. However, their floater technology makes it a much easier proposition for them to obtain the fuel for their CRF fleet. . . .

—Reid: The Hexie White Papers

Installing John Stevenson as the ship's captain marked the final session of the Earth/SpaceHome negotiation team. The contracts were signed by the crew, the general TO issued, and expeditionary chains of command established. The huge vessel *High Boy* was flown from Earth orbit up to L4 and modifications begun immediately. It seemed—after nearly three years of haggling—that the powers-that-be were now in a tearing rush to have the expedition on its way. It was a classic inversion: wait, then hurry up.

The burden of pressure was on the captain, of course. He was responsible for commissioning the vessel and pronouncing it worthy for the extended voyage. All of the preliminary work had been done, but the thousand last-minute details were all in his hands, and his departure was dictated for less than two months after he first docked the behemoth at SpaceHome. In the meantime, the crew gradually mustered in the Cube as they finished closing out their domestic and business affairs.

I felt pity for the harassed captain, but during those two months, there were a thousand times I wished I were in his place. Junior, as usual, expressed a delicate empathy for my feelings.

"Don't hand me your sob story, Dimp. You had two chances to go, and blew 'em both."

Kari, Junior, and I were sitting at a table at Murphy's. The expedition was to leave tomorrow.

We all knew that—thankfully!—there was only an infinitesimal chance that actual contact would be made on this particular expedition. Most likely the team would just go, gather data, and return with it for lengthy deliberations back in Earth orbit. But there were outside chances. Decisions might have to be made on the spot. A travel team might have to be formed and leave immediately upon arrival at the vessel. There was even a slim, slim chance that one or more Hexies would be there in person awaiting us. Our knowledge of them was almost nonexistent, and who knew what comprised their code of behavior?

"Junior, what would you have done in my position?"

"I'd have taken the commission, Admiral." He tugged at an oversized ear and cackled. "But then, I don't have your sterling character." He flicked his eyes over to Kari. "Now you have to follow the Kar's example, here, and just bear the whole thing stoically."

Not only was Kari not going, but in a short while she would have to return to Earth. Her researches with Junior were essentially over, the grant money had run out, and she had commitments on Earth to report her findings in person. There was more than a small chance that we would never see her again. For reasons I couldn't quite pin down, that created an empty feeling in the pit of my stomach. I'd become used to having her around. Even though I still kept my distance, I was by now quite comfortable with her. And she had the good brain and lively wit that were requisites for sitting around a table at Murphy's. I looked over at the lovely woman and caught the tail end of a sour glare at Junior, which she smoothly changed to a smile directed at me.

"I'm on your side, Whitey. I like to think I'd have done the same thing in your shoes." She hooked a thumb at the gnome. "Don't pay any attention to Mr. Wizard, here. He's just trying to spread random noise on your doldrums."

I changed the subject through Junior's evil laugh. "When do you have to go back to Earth?"

Her smile faded to half-strength. "In about three weeks. As soon as I work my way down to the bottom of the Cube and prove to the doctors that I'm a mortal Earther again."

"Fat chance," Junior snorted. "You've spent too much time in corrupt company ever to be normal again."

"Amen," she said, then raised her glass to both of us and drained the last of her beer.

I was wondering how she meant that, when Junior pulled at my sleeve. "Listen, Dimp. You take good care of this woman when I'm gone. Keep the wolves off her back." It was hard to read the expression on his face.

I smiled. "She seems to do pretty well at that all by herself." Kari's ability to ward off advances was by now legendary throughout the Colonies.

She shook her head sadly. "Ah, Whitey, you're so young . . ." Then she cast a sharp eye over to Junior. "And *you*, my sweet unclassifiable genius, don't forget to take your pills."

"Yes, Mother," he said.

The expedition departed the next day, amidst speeches by Ogumi and assorted Earther big shots (holoed from Earth, of course). Kari and I hit Murphy's afterward and drank a toast to the gnome before we went our separate ways. I promised to give her a call and make a date when I found some free time.

The next month was a full one for me. Sam Sebastian's current class of young hopefuls was finished with their ground school and starting on RCS and CRF maneuvers, and I was pretty busy helping turn them into pilots. I only got to see Kari three times before she left for Earth. The last time was just two days before her departure. I was scheduled to take two students to the Moon on a three-day

trip for planetary landing maneuvers, and by the time I
returned, she'd be gone.

We went to Ameche's on 'Home VI for dinner, drinks,
and dancing. The prices were outrageous, but the food
was good and the scenery spectacular. It was nestled against
the flat wall at one end of the cylinder, and the wraparound windows showed views across to the opposite "floor"
one and a half kilometers "up," and down the length of the
other flat wall three kilometers away. After eating we took
the elevator up to one of the low-gravity dance floors and
went a few rounds.

I was really rusty. After the third time I stepped on her
toes, I stepped back red-faced and said, "Kari, you're a
really good dancer. I don't belong on the same floor as
you."

She gave me a devastating smile. "Sometimes the company outweighs other considerations. There's really nobody I'd rather be stepped on by." Her eyes were just
darker than china blue, with white and gold flecks radiat-
ing from dilated pupils. I almost got lost in them before
they turned impish. "Besides, it's only a tenth-G up here—
not even enough to leave a bruise."

"Yeah, but it's bruising my ego," I gulped. "How about
let's sit the next few out?"

She gave the tiniest shrug. I felt it in her shoulder
muscles, rather than saw it. "Okay."

The 500-meter ride down the elevator to the bar was
long and silent. When we got a table, she said: "Order me
a vodka-rocks. I have to go potty."

When she came back, she sat down and took a sip of the
fresh drink. "My, this is certainly a cut or two above the
stuff we get at Murphy's."

"At four dollars a shot, it better be," I retorted.

"If you're not holding, Whitey, I can help out. Been
saving my University salary, meager as it is on extended
leave."

"I'm not hurting, Kari." I found myself telling her about
the mediation bonus. Then I got lost in those eyes again
and began blurting out my hopes for a home in the Big
Cylinder. When I realized what I was doing, I blushed

and stammered to a weak halt. Kari stepped gently into the breach.

"I take back what I said a few weeks ago, Whitey. You're not young at all. You just don't know women very well."

I recovered and demanded with mock dignity what she meant. She answered my question obliquely.

"Do you realize that that was the very first time you've ever really opened up with me?"

"Well . . ."

One of my hands was on the table. She leaned forward and covered it with both of hers. "Never mind, Whitey. The last thing in the world I want to do is embarrass you."

Her smile was warm, but I still felt a flush creep up my neck. Part of it was certainly embarrassment—and part of it was from her intimate touch. I cleared my throat and changed the subject.

"Wonder what the runt is doing now?"

"Probably taking bet money from the crew and grumbling that you're not along to complain to." She flashed another smile, then faded it and cocked her head in a way I found utterly charming. "Whitey, you know you saved him back then, half a year ago, when he got himself stuck at a quarter G. I've never really had a chance to thank you."

She laughed, half to herself, then said: "I think it was that stupid hundred kilos of cauliflower that pushed him over the hump. Did you know that he actually used them for exercise? He tied those dumb sacks to the opposite ends of an aluminum rod and made a set of barbells of it. He swore that as soon as he could press the weight, he was going to break one of the bags over your head."

The picture was so ludicrous I had to laugh. "Well, did he ever make it? My head's still intact."

"Oh, yes. In fact he could lift it over his head within ten days. But then he decided to wait until we got down to half a G so he'd be able to get more force behind the blow."

She took a sip of her drink while I quieted down again, then continued. "He worked out with it every day, but kept it hidden in the closet so you wouldn't see it when you visited. Then down at about point four G, he opened the closet one day and the whole suite was filled with the most Godawful stench—seems one of the bags had broken open. You can imagine what a mass of corruption that fifty kilos of cauliflower had turned into!"

By the time I finally settled down, tears were streaming from my eyes and the customers were staring.

The rest of the night passed in a fast dream, and before I knew it we found ourselves face to face at the door to her suite.

"It was a lovely night, Whitey. One of the best in many years."

"Yes," I said. She was standing very close, face turned up to mine. Her brown-gold hair gleamed in the soft corridor light; the smell of her perfume mixed sweetly with her breath. I was frozen with desire and guilt, unable to say anything else. Then she reached a hand up to the back of my neck and pulled me down to a kiss which was several levels beyond friendly. I admit to returning it in kind.

Then it was over. She put her cheek against my shoulder and pressed me tightly for a brief, torturous moment before stepping back. "Thank you, Whitey. Thank you for many things." Then she stepped through the door and shut it behind her, and was gone.

Every ten seconds on the way back to my apartment, I wondered what would happen if I went back and knocked on her door. And I wondered how I'd feel about myself afterward.

Then, at some indefinable point, it became too late. . . .

Three months crawled by, with me wishing a thousand times that I was a part of the expedition. I established twice-weekly card-game-and-gossip sessions with Charlie Broughton, who was now Chief of Hub Communications, but all I got for my troubles was a growing cribbage debt. News dribbled in from the *High Boy* at nearly a zero rate—which was natural, considering the fact that they were doing nothing but traveling. I got an occasional brief message from Junior of the "having-a-dull-time-wish-you-were-here" ilk, but that was all.

Finally, encrypted messages began to come in. *High Boy* had arrived at the calculated point and found nothing. This was not a surprise—after all, there was a lot of nothing out there to find. But the event precipitated the first conflict between *High Boy*'s captain and the team leaders: the captain wanted to search in a 3-D spiral, but the dual scientific leadership overruled him and demanded they search along the projected orbital path of the Hexie ship. The command battle turned out to be almost academic— the search radars found the ship within the first fifteen minutes of beginning the moving sweep.

Charlie Broughton had the relative positions plotted by the big navigation computers in Hub central comm. "They were lucky," he announced to me the next evening.

"Fifteen six and a pair for eight," I said. "What do you mean 'lucky'?"

"Hey, that puts you in the stink hole," he replied. "But look at this: fifteen twelve and six are eighteen and a pair for twenty. I'm out." He punched his keyboard. My screen declared that my debt had increased by thirty cents and was now up to thirty-three dollars and fifty-five cents. He began pulling the pegs out and setting them up for another game. Charlie insisted on using a real board, even in zero G where the bottom had to be velcroed and the pegs friction-tight.

"Your deal, sucker."

I initialized the game and pushed my "deal" button. My hand was two, six, eight, ten, jack, king. I looked sourly at the older man and said, "Charlie, there's no way this computer is dealing me random cards. You've got it programmed to cheat for you." I threw the six and eight into the crib, hoping for the best. He threw his own two, then cut a four and grinned.

"I hope that hit you as well as it did me."

I groaned. "So what do you mean by 'lucky'?"

He looked at me. "This isn't for public consumption."

I looked back at him. "Charlie, what I hear from you does not pass my lips." It was a ritual we played often.

"Well," he said, "turns out that Captain Stevenson was dead right wanting to do a spiral search. If the Hexie ship had been just a hundred kilometers or so closer to the Sun, the search pattern that the so-called 'leadership team' set up wouldn't have found it for months—if ever." He pressed a key and a deuce appeared on my screen's table top. "Two."

"Four for two." I paired him and pegged my two on the board. "I take it that Stevenson sent in a protest."

"Six for six," he said gleefully, stabbing a button. A third deuce showed up on the screen and he pegged the points.

" 'Protest' is an understatement, Whitey. He sent a personal cable to the Expedition Commission, with copies to Hodgkins on Earth and Ogumi here. Said that the team leaders had no right to make navigational decisions, and he wanted their authority curtailed to scientific matters only. Mass quantities of cuss words between the lines." He looked at the screen. "You going to play?"

I punched up my jack. "Sixteen. So what came of it? Did the commission take any action?"

He paired the jack. "Twenty-six for two. They sure as hell did. Sent him a long reply back, encrypted and for his eyes only. I just finished punching it out before I came off-shift. Is that a go?"

"Yeah. So what was the message?"

He laid down a three and pegged a point. "Twenty-nine. Gist of it was to read the fine print in his contract again, and quit complaining. All very polite, of course."

I played my two remaining face cards. "Twenty for me. The time for Stevenson to read the contract was before signing it."

"Oh, that's right. You had a crack at that contract yourself, didn't you? I got fifteen four, eight's a doz, and Nobs for thirteen."

"Nineteen hand," I replied. "Yeah, I had a chance. And now I don't know whether to laugh or cry." I punched my crib onto the table top. He'd thrown a nine and a king. "Fifteen two." I pegged the meager points.

"You really lost your crib bad, Whitey."

"So what's new?"

The news that evening stated only that the search pattern devised by the expedition's leaders found that Hexie vessel within the first hour. I still didn't know whether to laugh or cry.

Now that the Hexie ship had proved to really be there, interest throughout the system picked up enormously. Literally the whole of Earth and SpaceHome were fascinated long-distance spectators to the news that came in two or three times a day. And for the most part, the encrypted messages were released without censoring by the commission.

The ship was a big one, and unusually shaped for a zero-G vessel—very long in comparison to its diameter. Even so, it could easily contain dozens of *High Boy*-sized craft. Pictures of it were awesome when the Earther vessel was included for scale. There was a clearly marked entrance, with an embossed legend that the *High Boy*'s onboard computers made quick work of—it was the same "language" used by the artifact found in Saturn. The translation said something like "Push button and stand back."

Which they did. Inside was a rather small room, with only three items of interest: an obvious computer console built into one wall; a stack of books—not magtapes, films, or anything else, just books—and a slightly-larger-than-human-sized door with a complex-looking lock mechanism. The door obviously could not be opened without knowing the code—which meant reading the books.

An initial perusal of the books showed they were not written in the same simple "language" used heretofore—some work would be required to translate them. They began without waiting for the go-ahead from Earth orbit, since they didn't want to waste the week waiting for permission (which was granted after short deliberation—with the injunction that the translation be sent back to Earth encrypted—which fact I found out only by knowing Charlie).

The translation was certainly not trivial. The books were written in a much more complex language than heretofore encountered. Thankfully, deciphering it was aided by the fact that numerous pictures were included, along with a "Rosetta Stone" document bridging the previous language with the new. Also thankfully, the new language turned out to be relatively "clean," with very few abstract concepts. But nevertheless, the chore was difficult: Junior had to begin by restructuring the translation computer architecture, and by the time the final printout was accomplished, more than three weeks had passed.

In the meantime, the Hexie ship was examined, measured, and photographed in great detail, consonant with a strict policy of nonintrusive testing. Not that there was much detail to examine. The vessel was 862 meters in length, with a diameter of 157 meters. It had a rounded, blunt nose at one end, and what appeared to be nozzles for very large CRF engines at the other. Exactly opposite the small hatch across the ship's diameter was the outline of an extremely large door, into which *High Boy* would easily fit. There was no means of opening it from the outside that the team could discern. There were also thirty-two circular and rectangular panels in the hull ranging from three to twelve centimeters in diameter. All of them were tightly fitted with coverings.

Outside of that, there was nothing. No windows, no antennas, no handholds, and no signs saying "Not an Attach Point."

In fact, the most interesting thing about the ship turned out to be the hull itself. It appeared to be nonmetallic, though quite hard. The crew, not allowed to cut a piece off for examination, jury-rigged a crude instrument and took a reflection spectrogram. Turned out that the hull material was organically based, but too unusual and complex to characterize. They left it as an unsolved puzzle, with promises to tackle it later—if they could somehow bring to bear a more sophisticated instrument.

When the translation of the "Hexie Manual" was finished, there was another altercation between the captain and scientific leadership. Stevenson thought there was absolutely no reason to censor the translation, and wanted to send it unencrypted. There was also a practical reason for doing so: the contents were so voluminous that a significant amount of message time would be saved if the data could be sent in the clear. But the dual leaders each had very pointed orders on this score, and insisted on encryption.

"They got their way, too," Charlie told me. "So the

damn translation came in at a crummy 2400 baud, net after redundancy safing—took more'n thirty hours, including the pictures. Hell, I could *read* it quicker than that!"

"So what did it say?" I asked, as casually as possible.

"Hell, Whitey, I couldn't tell you. You think I bothered to wade through that whole thing? It ran half a million words. Besides, we had special orders about 'no leaks' on that document." He leaned closer. "Frankly, almost the whole damn thing looks like an interface control document— boring stuff, unless you're a systems engineer."

I asked Sam Sebastian the next day what an interface control document was. He said it was a specification that described in detail how to mate one thing with another, and why did I want to know? I told him it came up in a conversation I overheard between two systems engineers, and I was just curious. He grunted without further comment and poured me another beer.

The day after that, Charlie Broughton was excited. "We're bringing them back!" he said. I asked him what he meant.

"Got a message hand delivered for sending this morning," he answered. "It told the crew to take all holographs and measurements necessary to verify the written documents, then return to Earth system. And it reminded the captain that no clear messages concerning the documents were to be sent on the inbound trip." He looked worried. "You'll keep that to yourself, of course, won't you, Whitey?"

"Keep what to myself?" I asked. "I didn't hear a thing."

In the final analysis, the message couldn't really be kept from the public. For one thing, the Hexies didn't really say anything worth keeping secret—it was just the reflexive habit of leaders to keep information to themselves until they'd thought of all possible angles from a political standpoint. And for another, the media simply wouldn't leave them alone until they'd divulged all.

In all honesty, Ogumi was ready to tell all as soon as he knew the text of the Hexie translation. There really wasn't any further possibility for him to gain economic advantage over Earth from the whole affair. But he honored the pact with Earth not to tell until both were in agreement to do so. So the news waited for a week while the report-

ers and public fumed. Then they released the entire set of
Hexie documents and pictures. There were three big items:
 The Hexies looked a lot like us.
 We could go in the big ship to the Hexie world.
 The round trip could take as long as 600 years.

Chapter 4

Before contact, there were two distinct schools of thought on what the physiology of an alien intelligent species would be. One said that intelligence would have no particular form, or more precisely, could have any form at all, depending on the circumstances of its evolution. The prime consideration was the ratio of brain mass to body mass. The other—the functional school—pointed to the whale and dolphin on earth and claimed that brainpower wasn't everything. Intelligence demanded the n_{th} degree of nonspecialization, implying a sensory ability to garner the maximum of information from the environment, and a manipulative ability to carry out the dictates of nonspecialization, even during the process of locomotion. These prerequisites dictated limitations of form of an intelligent species—limitations in which the human species participates. Thus, intelligent life will probably be bipedal, binocular, binaural, etc. Both factions laughed at each others' premises, and were thoroughly convinced that they were right. Until contact with the Hexies, the debate was merrily unresolvable. After contact, it was an uphill battle for the "large-brain-only" faction.

—*Prentiss:* Hexie White Papers,
Informal Prefatory Notes

The negotiations between Earth and SpaceHome began again before the expedition was a week on its way back. Within another week or so, they had zeroed in on two main questions: (1) would we expend the resources to mount the major new expedition required? and (2) if we did, who would go?

The public opinion polls from Earth and SpaceHome

both said that the majority were in favor of making the attempt—even though it would be a legacy only for their many-times-removed grandchildren. But unfortunately, the decision was not going to rest in the hands of us common people. There was no way a small private group could decide on their own to make the trip—this was an expensive proposition.

I assumed an optimistic decision, and set about to give myself the maximum chance for being selected as a crew member. The first thing on my agenda was to study the full text of the Hexie translation, drawings and pictures included. I opted to buy a hard copy of the document. No SpaceHome publishing company had yet conracted to print the thing, so I had to buy a high-resolution printout from a software bookstore. It ran 2,000 pages and cost me a hundred seventy-five dollars.

The careful reading took nearly two months of my spare time. When I'd finished I probably knew the document as well as anybody alive (with the exception of Junior, who undoubtedly memorized the text word-by-word as it erupted from his translation computer).

The Hexies didn't really look that much like us—which I knew already because their pictures were the primary focus of the media attention surrounding the document. They were apparently completely covered with short hair the color of gray leather. Their eyes were completely round and only two-thirds the size of ours, compared to the size of their faces. Their noses were rudimentary at best—if they were really noses—and almost completely flattened against their faces, with only one opening. Their mouths were considerably wider than ours, with almost nonexistent lips. And they appeared to have four ears apiece: a pair somewhat forward of where ours would be, and a smaller pair farther back. Some physiologists claimed that the rear pair might be vestigial organs, maybe not even ears at all; others speculated that the smaller pair might be for high-frequency reception. My only thought was that if all of them worked, they'd be hard to sneak up on from behind.

Yes, the Hexies were definitely a different species, but everybody understood what the media meant by the fact that the Hexies looked like us. They had two arms, two legs, and were humanoid, with everything in approximately the right place. They might be mistaken for humans in the dark. Even the body dimensions given in the pictures were in the human range—the two illustrated figures stood 1.59 and 1.61 meters.

The color picture in the document (which cost me ten dollars extra) showed two of the species together, which everyone including me interpreted as meaning they were bisexual. Not much difference was apparent between the two. Their sizes were about the same, and no sexual apparatus was visible because both figures were attired in clothing. The garb was quite different on the two beings pictured: one being wore a body suit that covered the torso and limbs, leaving only the extremities exposed; the other wore abbreviated trunks and shirt. Both garments would have passed without notice on Earth or in Space-Home, except for the fact that they were multicolored, with complex pastel shades.

A fresh-born crop of xeno-psychologists and -anthropologists sprang up with glib speculations on every aspect of the pictures—the relative equality of heights, the clothing, the fur, the physiognomy—you name it. The fact is, most people didn't really care whether they were cold-weather or warm-weather, sexist or not, had nudity taboos or not. The important thing was that they didn't look menacing; in fact, they were cute.

The second big point was that the Hexie ship was indeed a transport. It was left there to take us to their home planet. But there were no living quarters; in fact, we had no access to any part of the vessel except the little anteroom with the computer console and the adjoining "cargo hold."

But the cargo hold was huge—big enough to hold two ships the size of *High Boy*. We were expected to bring our own living quarters along. The Hexies would provide utilities: power, vacuum vent, communications with the computer, and limited quantities of oxygen and nitrogen. But they were not presumptive enough to assume our living habits. We were to provide our own enclosure, food and galleys, drinking fountains and toilets, playrooms and bedrooms, and whatever we needed to keep us sane.

They used half the document telling and showing us exactly what they were providing, and how to interface our living quarters with their utilities. So all we had to do was equip *High Boy* for a long voyage, fit it up with the appropriate umbilicals, hook into the Hexie cargo hold, close off the hatches, press the button, and wait. For about two years.

During that two years, centuries might pass on Earth. The Hexie ship was relativistic, but apparently not faster than light. Unfortunately, the translation was somewhat muddled. The computer output stated "The voyage will last approximately two years for those onboard, but more time than that will pass for those who wait behind."

Junior laughed when I asked him what the hell that meant.

"No, Dimp, the computer didn't flub it. The Hexies are being deliberately cute. They don't want us knowing in advance where their home star is. Maybe won't even let us take pictures of the sky when we get there, depending on how they interpret our sterling character." He scratched an ear. "But cheer up. They did put a limit of 300 light years on the distance. We won't time travel more'n about six centuries at the most."

"You sound pretty sure that we're going," I said sourly. The debate was still raging. Ogumi was publicly grumbling about the implied expenditures, and Earth said that the popular sentiment was not nearly as positive as it was before the discovery that the Hexie vessel was a "generation ship" (a misnomer which had somehow struck—after all, it *would* be a generation ship for everyone but those aboard). I was pretty sure that Ogumi was in favor of the venture, and that his grumblings were mostly a negotiating posture—but I wasn't so sure of the Earth moguls. The spend-money-on-the-people-and-not-on-wild-ventures faction was having a heyday with the fact that even our great-great grandchildren would see no benefit from the contact.

"We're going, Admiral. I'll give you three to two."

I think that in the final analysis, two factors combined to

seal the deal. First, there was a clear voluble majority of SpaceHomers who wanted to make contact, however long it took. This population made it quite clear that if Earth wanted out of the deal, they would coerce SpaceHome into sponsoring it alone. When this group got sufficiently powerful, Earth saw the light and decided to go halves, rather than be left out. Second—and probably even more important, if the truth be known—was the fact that the Hexies were so appealing. Turned out that we just had to find out more about them. Friends in the universe, maybe.

Emotional swings among the populace continued even after serious negotiations began—disappointment that communications would have to be in 600-year spurts, and further disappointment that the now-prominent SETI folks didn't know which direction to point their antennae. Relief that the Hexies weren't so very far in advance of us scientifically (witness that they did not have an FTL)—tempered by the fact that the (incorrectly named) antigravity implied by the 'flight of the owl' in delivering the Saturn artifact's message told of a depth in quantum technology that we did not possess.

Everything finally settled out into kind of a warm acceptance of the fact that we shared the universe with at least one other species that seemed very much like us, and a willingness to make a serious attempt at communication. There was also acceptance of the fact that we would have to progress technologically on our own, at least for the next several hundred years.

Naturally, this realization created a feeling of resolve among the entire Earth-SpaceHome population to "do better" as a species so that we could finally meet the Hexies as a proudly unified race of beings. Bullshit. What it did was to encourage the various factions that they had plenty of time to iron out their differences eventually—so they could continue to behave like jackasses for now.

But there was not nearly as much wrangling over the rules of crew selection as with the original expeditionary voyage. One reason was that the negotiation teams knew each other by now, and could work with only minor friction. Another was that there was no immediate economic

advantage at stake from the results of the voyage. The final
guidelines for selection were:
  1. Volunteers only.
  2. Bachelors only.
  3. No familial responsibilities at home.
  4. Recognized experts in important scientific or techni-
     cal disciplines.
  5. Man/woman ratio of approximately 1.
  6. Multiple skills preferred.
  7. Earther/SpaceHomer ratio of approximately 1.
  8. Crew limit of 20, including officers.
  9. Psychological compatibility.
Notes:
Number 2: Not necessarily a hard and fast rule, but
both partners of a marriage had to qualify in different
disciplines and be considered as a team. Three such couples applied—none were picked.

Number 3: This prevented "divorces of convenience"
where children were involved.

Number 4: The words "recognized" and "important"
were subject to iterative interpretation by the technical
selection committee and the negotiation teams.

Number 8: This was determined by an estimate of comfort aboard *High Boy*, whose space the crew would be
sharing for a long time.

Number 9: A catchall category that allowed the rejection
of persons that the negotiation teams considered unfit to
participate in first contact. We missed getting a biologist
because of this requirement; only three volunteered, and
all were considered "unfit." Frankly, they were all horse's
asses.

There were plenty of volunteers, especially among the
80,000 SpaceHomers. We had a high percentage of dreamers among us, and we tended to be looser in our marriage
ties than most Earther societies. And we were not so leery
of spending a couple of years in close quarters with space
all around us; after all, that was our normal habitat.

The Earthers were not nearly so unified in their enthusiasm, but on the other hand, they had a population pool
100,000 times greater than ours, which yielded up an
adequate quorum of volunteers.

As the selection process got underway, it soon became obvious that the real problem was what "experts" to pick. Almost no one was a recognized expert in more than one discipline, which left the committee with the grim job of winnowing volunteers from more than 100 contending fields down to a crew of 20. The task was iterative, lengthy, and laborious.

I had put in my application papers along with Junior. Junior claimed expertise in several fields, including piloting. He listed Maggie O'Malley as a reference in spaceship engineering design. She was a good one—her success as the leader of the Saturn Artifact Retrieval Team had moved her high into SpaceHome corporate circles. For computer technology and systems analysis he used Dr. Carl Frederickson, the Earther who had been in charge of the first expedition's translation team. He was recognized as one of the top ten solar system experts—and had ungrudgingly admitted that the Hexie translation job would have taken twice as long without Junior along. He used me as a reference for piloting ability. This was valid, since I had a teaching license now and was considered officially qualified to stand judgment. He had no references for mathematics, physics, or planetary dynamics, but if the panel contained experts in those fields, they'd be amazed at his depth.

Personally, I was thankful to be able to list archaeology and piloting.

Not much news emanated from the selection committee. They had declared a moratorium on all information regarding the selection process, including the names of the applicants. The purpose was to protect the privacy of the people involved, and to prevent pressure of any kind on the committee members doing the selecting. Only general items were released, such as the rules, and the fact that the preliminary list of applicants totaled 12,347. This list would be culled by a factor of ten or more before the interviews began.

It was also announced that the live interviews, once begun, would proceed by discipline, with disciplines being selected in alphabetical order, so I wasn't too surprised to find myself summoned about two months into the process.

The place was the SpaceHomes corporate visitors' conference room, as usual. I took great pains to get there five minutes early. When I was called in, I was also not surprised to see that the holographic conferencing facility was in full use. The Earther half of the committee and all Earther candidates would naturally remain aground. I made a mental note to watch out for the second-and-a-half time lag and pace my conversation accordingly.

"Dr. Whitedimple, my name is Philip Thackeray," said a short, dark SpaceHomer who stood up and shook my hand. "I'm the 'Homeside chairman of the selection committee, and I'll be conducting the interview today. May I present . . ." Introductions proceeded. I was surprised to discover that—in addition to the selection committee, most of whom I didn't know—almost the full negotiating team was present. I knew most of them, since I'd worked with them before.

There were three other people. ". . . also like to present Dr. Edward Allison-White . . ." A large florid gentleman with a white handlebar moustache stood up and gave the Japanese bow to equals, which was customary for holographic introductions. I returned it, somewhat surprised. Allison-White was a renowned name in anthropological circles—publisher of numerous definitive papers, some of which even I'd read. He was also universally liked and respected in the community.

". . . has been tentatively selected as the Earthside leader of the scientific crew contingent." That was a large surprise. The selection committe had announced publicly that the crew would not be chosen until all interviews had been completed. But that shock prepared me for the next introduction.

"And I believe you are acquainted with Dr. Grace Kitigawa, who will be the SpaceHome counterpart of Dr. Allison-White. Together they will constitute the scientific leadership of the crew." She was too far across the table to shake hands, so she stood and bowed. I returned it warmly. On the few occasions we'd met socially, she'd charmed my socks off. Grace was small, lithe, beautiful, and ageless. Her first paper on the uses of fractals in Lunar terrain classification had appeared more than twenty years ago in the esoteric literature of the mathematics world. Outside of Junior, she had the sharpest brain of anyone I knew. Mathematics—contrary to public opinion—is not a black-and-white science; it generates some of the most heated arguments seen in any body of literature. Grace more than held her own in this environment. She could listen demurely for half an hour while a critic harangued her over a suppositional set in a recent paper, then quietly clear her throat and in a soft voice tear the critic into strips of raw meat and feed him to the dogs. Junior had met her on the original Hexie expeditionary voyage and found her irresistable.

"She never stopped being gracious," he'd said, "and she was the only one with enough sense to laugh in all the right places. I fell in love with the twinkle in her soul." Then, with a cackle and chagrin: "But she never took a single bet I laid out. She always said something like: 'Not at those odds, Junior. A more nearly correct offering would be thirty to one, not three to two.' "

". . . final member of this board is Professor Jarwaharlal Lind . . ." I bowed with apprehension. Mixed parentage and British snobbery notwithstanding, Lind held the archaeology chair at Cambridge against all comers. He was a giant. He also flunked one graduate student for every one he passed. ". . . who will conduct the first portion of this interview. Professor Lind, will you please commence?"

"Thank you sir," the little brown man said in a cultured voice, then to me: "Dr. Whitedimple, I remember reading your dissertation *Interpretation of Pre-Etruscan Pottery Glyphs* with some admiration. It was a scholarly piece of work, and subsequent findings have validated most of your conclusions." I nodded, not trusting myself to speak. My dissertation research had been conducted in Northern Italy, some twenty-five years ago. My strongest memories of that time were of hating Earth and its gravity well, and vowing never to return. I'd kept the vow.

"Tell me, sir, have you done any field research since then?"

"No, sir, unless you count the location and interpretation of the Hexie artifacts."

"Hmmm, yes, to be sure. A special case. Not exactly

what I had in mind." He looked down at a piece of paper
he was holding. "I see that your resume includes a number of critical articles and one monograph. I recall reading
three of them. You seem to have kept up the standard of
scholarship you established with your dissertation." He
looked up and smiled thinly at me. From what I'd heard
about the man, the smile constituted just about the highest praise he was wont to give. I smiled back and began to
feel better. But not for long.

"But the last paper here is dated June of 2088. Have
you not published anything in the last seven years?"

"No, sir, I have not." In the three years previous to the
discovery of the first Hexie artifact on Iapetus, I'd been in
a lethargic funk—teaching uninspiringly to bored students.
Since then, my extracurricular activities—including learning the art of pilotry and navigation and spending considerable time with SART—had eaten up about twenty-five
hours a day. Of course, all this was irrelevant to Dr. Lind,
who was interested only in my credentials as an archaeologist. I gulped nervously as he continued.

"Hmmm, yes, very well then. In your article "Evidence
for Pre-Minoan Culture on Crete" you stated that Cooley
was drawing conclusions based on uncertain premises about
the Palace at Cnossus. I'd like to hear your rationale . . ."

The grilling went on for about forty minutes. Lind knew
very well that I was rusty, and was trying to find the depth
of rust. He wanted to see if I could still speak the language
(I could, but barely), and whether or not I'd kept up with
events in the field (I had, but only superficially). It was
pretty bad—the worst inquisition since my orals. By the
time he was finished with me, my legs were a little shaky
and a patina of sweat had broken out on my forehead. He
took notes—especially when I gave weak answers.

Finally he looked up and said: "I think that is enough,
Dr. Whitedimple. Thank you for your honest answers."
He nodded to Thackeray, who stood and said:

"Dr. Whitedimple, we'd like to continue your interview, but must take time out for private discussions. Would
you please indulge us by waiting in the outer office for a
few minutes?"

I nodded and left the room, sat down on the lounge

chair, and let my sweat dry. After the reaction began to wear off, I started wondering what the hell was going on. I could understand why the committee would want to pick the scientific crew leadership first—they could be of great service in the selection of the rest of the crew. But outside of that, it seemed only sensible to follow their advertised plan of interviewing everyone before making final selections. Yet they'd had me leave the room only temporarily, as if they were taking a vote and would tell me the results when I came back in. It didn't make sense. I waited in a stew.

"Sir, if you could come back in now, please?" I looked up with a start. The committee recorder had stuck his head through the door without my hearing him. I cudgeled my brain for his name. "Thanks, Patrick."

I wanted to see Lind's face the first thing as I walked back in; his look might tell me if I'd made it. But he was gone. I raised my eyebrows and looked at Thackeray, who was just opening his mouth to speak to the group as a whole.

"Ladies and gentlemen, we are now reconvened to consider the final candidate for captain of the expeditionary voyage to the Hexie world." He turned to me. "Please forgive us for this lengthy double interview, Dr. Whitedimple. You must understand that most of the candidates for ship's captain have listed an additional skill, and the committee feels that to be fair to the expedition, both items must be evaluated. While it is true," he smiled more warmly than I felt, "that your skill as a pilot and your leadership ability are of paramount importance, we must also find out if your outside expertise is of sufficient depth to obviate the necessity for a second authority in your scientific discipline. . . ."

He gave the speech just a little too smoothly for it to be off the cuff. I figured I was about the dozenth person to hear it—after all, Whitedimple must be pretty far down an alphabetical listing of candidates for captain. Things were clearer now. If I screwed up, I might not get a chance as an archaeologist—there must be other applicants with better archaeological credentials. I gulped silently and tried to assume a Look of Eagles as Thackeray continued.

". . . understand that the captain must be chosen very early in the process. He or she will be required to begin full-time performance of duties immediately upon selection. The captain must sit as a member of this committee, and also manage the commissioning of the expeditionary ship and the preparations to mate it with the Hexie vessel." He looked intently at me as if he were expecting me to swear a lodge oath. "So I must ask you before this interview begins if you are able to leave your current employment with a one-week notice any time from tomorrow on."

He raised a hand. "And before you answer, please take note that if you are unable to assume the duties of captain, you will still be under consideration for two other ship's officer positions."

I nodded. "I understand. And I state formally to the committee that I have no employment ties that cannot be severed immediately." I did not want to be second or third officer—but I'd settle for that if I had to.

"Very well. Please sit down." He indicated a vacant chair. "And relax as best you can." He smiled with the first touch of humanity I'd seen in him. "It's going to be a lengthy session."

When I'd gotten seated, he continued: "Please be advised that your piloting and leadership abilities are not under consideration here. Those qualities have already been judged and rated by a special joint Earth/SpaceHome committee of experts . . ."

(So *that's* what Sam Sebastian had been doing for the past six weeks! He'd unloaded most of his work on to Joe and me with the excuse that he had to work on a confidential report for Ogumi—something to do with improving the quality of the pilot fleet, he said. Hah.) ". . . hundred twenty-two applicants have been narrowed to fourteen. All of you are considered quite capable of assuming the captain's position." He smiled again. "So you are already in a select group, Dr. Whitedimple. Be advised also that this committee will strongly consider the relative ranking among you fourteen in its final selection. But what we need to do today is get our own impressions of you as a person. We are quite aware that the captain's job will be perhaps the single most important function aboard, and we intend to judge the whole man."

Again, the speech was well-practiced. I wondered if he was thankful that this was the last time he had to give it. He leaned back in his chair a bit before continuing.

"Each of the committee members will have a question or two, and I'd like to start by asking you why you want to go. You'll be giving up a successful life here in SpaceHome, taking your crew into some danger, perhaps, and returning to a civilization possibly hundreds of years advanced beyond your time. What's your motivation?"

Feeling somewhat like a finalist in a beauty contest, I said:

"I had the privilege of seeing the first Hexie artifact on Iapetus. Looking at it and pondering its makers gave me an indescribable feeling—an urge—which has never left me. Everything I have done since then has been pointed toward being one of the voyagers on this expedition. I don't quite understand it myself. All I know is that it is extremely important to me that mankind be able to expand itself, that the Hexies have provided a vehicle for this expansion, and that we ought to do our damnedest to be in full communication with them as soon as we can. And we can be very thankful that they turned out to be friendly."

One of the Earthers jumped on that one. "What makes you think they are friendly, Dr. Whitedimple? And for that matter, what makes you think they'll even be around—after all, the artifacts and ship were left here nearly four thousand years ago. In that time, we have seen many global civilizations rise and fall."

For the life of me I couldn't recall the Earther's name, so I smiled as intimately as I could and replied: "I think if they weren't friendly, none of us would be here now. Earth would be a Hexie world. And there is no doubt in my mind that they see us as potential friends. The reason for leaving the ship is so they can judge. The fact that they left it so long ago implies that their culture has attained a stability and foresightedness we can only dream about. In our present stage of development, would we even consider such an act—even assuming we had the technology?

I don't think so. In fact, I think that we might have more
to learn from them politically than technologically."

Now it was a SpaceHomer's turn: "Dr. Whitedimple,
the artifact giving directions to the Hexie ship was located
inside Saturn, at the gas/liquid interface. We had to spend
hundreds of millions of dollars, and develop a whole new
technology, which was largely useless, to retrieve it. Don't
you think that was a rather ridiculous place for the Hexies
to put it?"

"I most certainly do, sir, but I also believe it was quite
deliberate. I believe they were testing at least two things.
The first was our economic viability as a species; the
second was our resolve. . . ."

As the questions came, I formulated an ongoing strategy
based on the fact that they were "personality" questions. I
answered honestly according to my own beliefs, and gave
the committee enough emotion to let them see me as a
human being.

*Dr. Whitedimple, why do you think the Hexies chose to
communicate the location of their ship clumsily via a flying
analog of a bird, rather than more conventionally?* I suspect that they have a highly developed sense of humor,
but I will reserve judgment until I can ask them.

*Dr. Whitedimple, what in your opinion will be the cost
of outfitting the expedition?* Not too high—perhaps two or
three times that of outfitting for the expedition recently
completed.

Dr. Whitedimple, could you justify that last answer?
Yes. According to the Hexie document, there are only
seven interfaces, not including the tie-downs. All are relatively clean and well-defined. That should simplify the
engineering job enormously.

And so on.

And so forth.

*Dr. Whitedimple, in all likelihood the captain's author-
ity will be subject to override by the scientific leadership
in some circumstances. How do you propose to set up
formal procedures so that this can be handled with maximum simplicity?*

I came out of my strategy with a shock. The question
was worded so smoothly, it almost sneaked up on me. It

was Jason French who'd asked it. His face was turned up in a smile. I looked him in the eye, and let my heart beat five times before answering:

"Mr. French, ladies and gentlemen," I swept my gaze around to include them all, "I do not believe that final onboard decision authority can reside in anyone but the captain. He or she certainly must weigh the mood and wishes of others onboard, but the essence of the captain's job is to make final decisions. If any other system is implemented, the captain's authority is incomplete, and the discipline necessary for survival is weakened accordingly."

There was silence for about three seconds, then an Earther said: "Come now, Dr. Whitedimple. You said earlier that the Hexies would be friendly, and now you're talking about survival. Aren't you overdramatizing the dangers somewhat?"

"Not at all, ma'am. As a member of the human species, I do believe that the Hexies are friendly. But the captain of the expedition certainly must take into account the possibility that they are inimical. And I was not thinking only of the Hexies. Many things could threaten our survival during the two-year confinement period, from a malfunctioning computer system to a latent claustrophobic with psychotic tendencies."

At that point, Grace Kitigawa spoke up for the first time: "Dr. Whitedimple, presuming we are allowed to land and explore the Hexie world when we arrive, would you wish the captain to retain complete authority over the crew, even though we weren't aboard the ship? Don't you think that it might be prudent to relinquish authority to the scientific leadership under those circumstances?"

"No, ma'am. It would be prudent to *delegate* authority to the scientific leadership; it would be most imprudent to relinquish it."

She looked thoughtful for a moment, then nodded. Then Thackeray leaned forward and spoke: "Dr. Whitedimple, assuming that there are some minor constraints on the captain's authority, would you still be willing to accept a position as first or second officer?"

I sighed. I'm afraid it was audible. "No, sir."

He looked around the table. "Does anyone else have

any more questions?" There was a quorum of headshakes, then he turned back to me. "Dr. Whitedimple, I'd like to echo the words of Professor Lind and thank you for your honest answers."

"My pleasure, sir." I looked around the committee for the last time. "Ladies and gentlemen, my respects."

As soon as I'd shut the door behind me, my shoulders slumped. The Look of Eagles faded to black. I cursed myself for a stubborn fool. Three strikes and you're out, Whitey. I went back to my apartment in a blue funk.

Twenty-three hours later, they called me in again and commissioned me as captain of the expeditionary voyage to the Hexie world. With complete authority.

Chapter 5

Considering the selection requirements for the expeditionary crew, and especially the fact that they would have to give over their current life and come back to an unknown future, it is not surprising that we did not recruit the planet's best intellects. The highest-ranked experts were generally older and well-endowed with wealth and future security, and less inclined to relinquish their professional connexions. The ones we did get were certainly not second-rates; they were experts all. It's just that they were not, as a group, the recognized best.

What we ended up with was a first-rate collection of individualists. It was not surprising that we exhibited an eclectic array of colour. But the thing that truly gratified me was our exceptional degree of overall quality. For this (and perhaps this is a bit of a brag, since I had significant input to the selection rules), we can at least partially thank the selection committee, which weighted motivation quite heavily. Considering events which developed onboard during our long enforced confinement, this was perhaps the most important factor, for the captain's sake and for the sake of the success of the mission. . . .

> *Allison-White:* Hexie White Papers,
> *Appendix G—Scientific*
> *Leader's Journal of the*
> *Voyage*

Edward Allison-White told me some time later that my stand on the question of command authority had been a strong discriminator in the selection process.

"All of you chaps wanted very badly to go," he said. "And all but two of you advised strongly against a split command. But when pressed," he smiled at me like a proud father, "you were the only one who didn't indulge in a bit of political backpedaling."

He looked searchingly into my eyes. "That must have been extremely difficult, considering that you lost command of the first expedition over that very issue."

I smiled weakly. "You just don't know how close I was to joining the rest of the gang and backpedaling like crazy."

He was tolerant: "The proof was in the pudding, sir. Grace and I have agreed that if we have to have a tyrant, we're glad it is you."

Junior was a little less circumspect: "Those Earth/ SpaceHome yahoos had their noses rubbed in it hard enough on the first trip. If they hadn't learned by now, I wouldn't trust any officer they picked!"

By that time, though, I was already hard at work earning my captain's pay. I had two full-time jobs: sitting on the crew selection panel, and commissioning the ship. I managed to survive only by leaving the majority of the work in the hands of the experts, while I hopped around trying to maintain the Look of the Eagles in bloodshot eyes.

Since I've already started with the crew selection committee, I'll talk about that process first. Before starting on the single disciplines in alphabetical order as advertised, we dealt with the multi-discipline entries first. This enabled us to save time by eliminating several dozen applicants at the onset. The other two ship's officers were in that category: the first officer, George Petrov, was an excellent pilot and an expert linguist, being literate in Russian, Tagalog, three dialects of Chinese, Vietnamese, English, Arabic, and possibly a few others I can't remember. The report from the "expert" linguist called in for his interview stated that Petrov had an excellent grasp of comparative linguistics, language structure, and the development of idiom. Michael Prentiss, the third officer, was an amateur pianist of near-concert grade, and quite knowledgable in music theory and design of diverse musical instruments. I, of course, obviated the need for another expedition archaeologist (although I found out that my archaeological expertise alone would not have been good enough to qualify me for the expedition. Lind had told the board that I was competent enough, but he knew of at least two other applicants who would have beaten me out).

There were three other multi-discipline applicants, of which only one qualified for the expedition: Junior. The runt astonished, delighted, and confounded the committee. He held not a single degree, and had published not a single article in his own name. Yet the five experts who sat on his panel could not fault him on a single point, except perhaps a weakness on in-depth knowledge of the literature in some subjects.

After the interview, the committee's main problem was to decide how many of the sciences to let him represent. He rated as qualified in every one of the disciplines he'd listed on his application. "And God knows how many else he didn't bother to mention," remarked one of the committee members acidly, looking across the table at me. "Perhaps Whitey would like to command a crew of one—save a lot of outfitting money."

The implied question in her remark was, strictly speaking, not allowed by protocol. I had declared myself as an observer only, because of my personal ties with Junior. But I smiled and answered anyway:

"I hardly think that's what he had in mind. He'd pine away from boredom without someone to cover his bets."

In the end, they qualified him as expert in engineering design and computer sciences; they also created a job for him called "expedition synthesizer." He was required to read the reports of, and listen to, all the other onboard experts, to figure out just what the Hexies had, after it was all over. Oh, and he was also commissioned as a backup pilot to us three ordinary mortals.

After Junior's lively interview, there weren't too many highlights remaining in the selection process. The ordeal was long, tedious, and sometimes acrimonious—especially picking the Earthers, because the Earther members of the committee tended to bicker at length on the fine points of each volunteer. Finally, after endless lists were constructed and reconstructed, and after endless negotiations and iterations, the job was done. It took nearly a year, during which time I'd come to accept frustration as a way of life.

Thankfully, I was able to quote other duties as an excuse much of the time, but I felt that it was my duty to review the candidates' resumes and be there for the actual interviews. My normal procedure was to make sure the selection committee knew my opinions, then duck out when the "deliberations" began. I didn't have any authority except advisory in the final crew selection, and to be honest, I didn't press for the privilege.

We were about six months into the process when the interview schedule for organic chemistry was put in my hands. Kari Nunguesser was on the list.

She'd written an occasional letter addressed to both Junior and me, but there had been no hint of her applying for the crew. That night I asked Junior what the hell.

"Think about it, Captain," he said with a grin. "She knows you're going to be the head cheese. Didn't want to have any hint of pre-prejudice getting to the panel."

I frowned. "You did know."

"Yep. She told me right after the selection rules were posted. Asked me not to breathe a word to you."

I stared at my beer for a moment, then swirled the liquid. Junior was living in the Cube, and had worked his way down to level 30 by then, so there was plenty of G to hold the beer in the glass. The gnome was not one to keep secrets from me, so this must have been pretty important to him. I thought back to his own interview. He had woven a liberal dose of physical chemistry into one of his replies to the questions, but I could not recollect one instance in which he'd demonstrated his recently acquired mastery of organics.

"Got a bug, Dimp?"

"I was just thinking about the artful way you danced around the subject of organic chemistry in your own interview."

He gave me his evil cackle. "Well, now, maybe there was a slight tendency to avoid the subject," he said, scratching a generous nose. "But in a long voyage like this one, it's nice to be sure there's going to be at least one or two heads-up women along."

"You're sure she's going to make it, then?" I had a hint

of the answer. I'd read her application and compared it with those of the four other finalists.

"One gets you twenty, Admiral. She's a class act, and you know it."

I didn't know whether to be happy, or upset. Privately I wondered about her motivations in going, even though she'd expressed strong interest in the Hexies during her long stay with Junior in the Cube. I half-suspected that she wanted to continue whatever she might have going with Junior. I remembered our last evening together with nostalgia, then began to feel guilty about it. I renewed my vow to keep my distance and leave her to Junior, in case she made the team.

She was a class act, all right. She devastated her competition in the interviews, as far as I could tell from the esoteric questions asked by the department head of the Rockefeller Institute. And she increased the chances of her discipline being selected because she could provide a biological background for a crew which we had already decided would probably not contain a proper biologist.

After Kari's interview, there were four more months of toil for the committee and negotiating teams. We were convened for a total of 325 days, including a couple of two-week breaks which were badly needed. In the end we had a crew, for better or for worse. These were the people over which I would exert absolute authority:

Officers
George Petrov (Earth): First Officer/pilot; linguistics
Michael Prentiss (SpaceHome): Second Officer/pilot; music
Edward Allison-White (Earth): Scientific Leader; anthropology
Grace Kitigawa (SpaceHome): Deputy Scientific Leader; mathematics

Crew Members from Earth
Carl Dunsworth: particle physics
Richard Gates: botany
Michele Kimberly: social dynamics
Kari Nunguesser: organic/biological chemistry
Mayumi Sakaguchi: inorganic chemistry

Joshua Vance: theoretical physics
Hagar Zyyad: geology
Chin Wu Lin: "contact specialist"

Crew Members from SpaceHome
Junior Badille: engineering design/computers/science synthesis
Sean Davidson: life support systems
Peter Dinsworth: astronomy/cosmology
Ethel Erickson: manufacturing, materials and processing
George Korliss: medical/physiology
Georgiana Krebbs: ecological sciences
George Reid: propulsion
Anna-Marie Smith: planetology
Jason French: "contact specialist"

Yes, there were more SpaceHomers then Earthers. But that was part of the negotiations: both Sean Davidson and George Reid were considered necessary for the health of our vessel, but would not necessarily be expected to contribute substantially—especially Sean—to increasing mankind's knowledge base through exchange of information with the Hexies. And you'll notice that Earth loaded up in chemistry, physics, and social sciences, so they got what they wanted from the exchange.

The real surprise was that we ended up with 22 total crew instead of 20. The reason for this was most unpleasant: the addition of the two "contact specialists." They were last-minute additions—a "fix" that saved the negotiations from turning into a donnybrook, just when it seemed that everything was all set. I won't go into the gory details, but it was bad enough that we ended up saddled with two ringers—certified "company spies" from the word go. I didn't find out until much later what had induced them to "volunteer." They certainly didn't have the same motivations as the rest of us.

Each SpaceHome crew member was sent notification to begin physiological conditioning in the Cube immediately. This meant going through the same routine Junior and Kari had some time previously. The acceleration onboard the Hexie ship would be 1.023 G—presumably that of the

Hexie world. The Earthers were given three months to wrap up their affairs. Then they would fly to Gobwen International and make the orbital lift together from the Jamama complex in Somalia. The combined crew would then live together for three months in the Cube before climbing aboard *High Boy* and heading out.

I was thankful when the selection was finally over and the committee disbanded, with official speeches from the Earth and SpaceHome authorities. I was still deep in the throes of commissioning *High Boy* for the long voyage, and was glad to be able to put thoughts of the crew behind me for a while.

Or at least so I thought. Less than a week after the posting of the crew list, I got a call from one of my former SHU colleagues: Dr. Barbara M'Golo, leading wight of the psychology department. She'd volunteered, along with four other members of her profession, but ultimately, psychology hadn't been selected as one of the "traveling disciplines."

"Whitey, I know you're terribly busy, but I need to see you about a matter of some importance. Could you give me an hour at your convenience?"

"Sure, just a second." I covered the pickup with my hand and yelled at my secretary: "John, when's the earliest date I've got a free hour?"

He thumbed through my calendar. "Three weeks from Wednesday. Five thirty P.M."

I uncovered the speaker. "Barbara, how about dinner tonight—say, about nine?"

"That'll be fine, Whitey. We'll come to the Cube. Will your apartment be all right?"

"Sure. Who is 'we'?"

"I'm bringing along Frank Scarlatti."

I began to see the light. I didn't know Scarlatti, but he also had been a volunteer. He was an industrial psychologist specializing in long-term confinement in limited-space environments. He had a strong record and a string of recommendations from projects he'd consulted for—including Iapetus Base and the SART project on Mimas.

I prepared myself for an uneasy hour.

They had hardly come in, shaken hands, and sat down before Barbara started:

"We are quite concerned, Whitey, about the duration of the voyage. We would like to think that the crew will arrive at the Hexie world as something other than a mindless mob afraid of each other and their own shadows."

I couldn't take her seriously. "Oh, come on now, Barbara. I sat through the interviews myself. This is a fine, well-balanced group as far as I can tell. They're all highly motivated—*well, almost—not counting the contact specialists!*—"and aware of the upcoming confinement period."

She looked at her companion. "Tell him, Frank."

"Dr. White—"

"Please, call me Whitey."

"Thank you, Whitey. I am willing to admit that there is a chance that everything will go smoothly, as you now think. My best efforts at calculation put that chance at about two percent—but I must admit to a large factor of uncertainty."

This was a subject I knew little about. I groped for a reference point. "Why so uncertain, Frank? Surely there are similar situations on which you've got data. I-Base personnel are cramped into a space only about four times the volume of *High Boy*, and they spend two-year shifts. M-Base was even worse—we were jammed together like sardines."

"That's true, Whitey, but the situations are very different. I-Base personnel are half-shifted at one-year intervals—I saw to that myself!—to put new faces into place. M-Base personnel were highly goal-oriented. And in the back of every individual's mind was the knowledge that if worst came to worst, he could get out on the next available ship."

He looked worried. "Those factors do not apply to your expedition, sir. The expedition goal is indeterminate. The two-year confinement period has no ongoing purpose; it is simply a necessary evil, with an uncertain end. And in the back of everyone's mind is the knowledge that a similar confinement and uncertain future await them on the return trip."

Now Barbara spoke up: "There are other factors that aggravate the dangers, Whitey. For instance, I know you're aware that about one in forty Earthers who emigrate to the

Colonies have to give it up within the first year and return to Earth because of LEC."

I nodded. Long-term environmental claustrophobia was a well-known phenomenon in SpaceHome. After some bad experiences, a law had been enacted that Earth immigrants must live in the bottom level of the Cube for the first year, in order to stay acclimatized to one G. LEC had a nasty habit of sneaking up on its victims—and when it hit they had to get out of the Pinwheel and back to Earth's wide open spaces *now*.

". . . means that of the ten Earthers on the crew, there's nearly a twenty-five percent chance that at least one will fall victim. At the very least, that will have an unsettling effect on the rest of the crew."

"Well, I think we can safely take that number down to eight," I said. "Both George Petrov and Kari Nunguesser are proven commodities—but I take your point."

Now Scarlatti spoke up again: "Another problem that may seem trivial now could jump up and bite you before the trip is barely started. You've got a crew of all Chiefs and no Indians. These people are used to respect from their own communities, and many have probably not done mundane work in years." He looked at me and raised his eyebrows. "So who's going to clean the urinals, do the laundry, cook, and wash the dishes?"

"Well," I said. "I planned to rotate those jobs so nobody would be stuck with them permanently. Surely a highly motivated and intelligent crew such as this one can see the necessity for taking a shift at the dirty jobs."

"Perhaps, yes, at first," agreed the man. "But how about for the long haul, when the novelty has worn off. Those jobs will get to be awfully tedious—and the crew will start to see them as regular requirements, rather than as a once-in-a-while lark to perform in the spirit of cooperation. And wait until the first time Bob complains to Mary that she didn't do a good job cleaning the commode. When you get to that stage, you've got trouble!"

Now it was Barbara's turn again. "There's another thing, too, Whitey—mixed mores. Behaviors and beliefs are a basic part of individual interactions and attitudes toward one another. For instance, here in SpaceHome we tend to

be pretty loose in our sexual behavior and look with tolerance on individual foibles. But for some of the Earthers it
might be a different matter. People like Carl Dunsworth,
Mayumi Sakaguchi, Michele Kimberly, and Hagar Zyyad
were raised in widely differing cultures. They are not
likely to view each other's activities with respect—especially on the subconscious level, where they can't fight it.
And onboard ship, they will not simply be able to walk
away from it."

"Which brings us to perhaps the most important item of
all," interjected Scarlatti smoothly.

"You mean you haven't told me the worst yet?" I said
half mockingly, half serious.

"I'm afraid not," he said, without a trace of a smile.
"And it has to do with the size of the ship again." He took
a pad of paper from his briefcase (yes, he brought a briefcase) and began marking the top page with X's and Y's.
When he'd gotten to 22, he began to draw circles around
groups of two and three. Many of the circles overlapped.

"With a crew of 22, there are literally thousands of ways
for compatible individuals to interact in groups of two or
more. The trouble in a confined space is that if there are
two people who are incompatible, it cuts down their available social spheres tremendously. They have to share some
of the same friends; they have to share the same gymna-
sium, the same rec room, the same theater—even the
same bathroom."

He looked up from the circles and lines he'd been
drawing and said: "This situation has a formal title which
the social psychologists call 'forced incompatible associa-
tions.' And what it amounts to is that the *High Boy* is
simply too small for anyone to escape from someone he or
she doesn't like." He smiled his first smile; it was bleak. "I
could tell you horror stories."

Barbara was opening her mouth to speak again. I didn't
really need any more, so I headed her off. "All right,
people, you've raised my consciousness. Now make me
feel better. What can I do?"

"Please believe that we are not trying to alarm you
unduly, Whitey," said the woman. "But we are aware that
you are inexperienced in these matters. You display many

qualities we consider necessary for the expedition's success: personal courage, the ability to act quickly and decisively, the respect of almost everyone you interact with—and especially, the rare quality of being *correct* in your decisions."

"But . . ." I prompted.

"You are inexperienced in leadership under adverse conditions. Your demands to the committee for absolute authority were entirely correct. But it is one thing to have authority on paper—and another entirely to maintain it for an extended period under these conditions. We are afraid that your primarily academic background has not prepared you to do what you may have to do."

"Which is . . ." I prompted again. I suspected what she was getting at—but I wanted her to get there.

"Discipline," said Scarlatti decisively. "You must begin the voyage with firm discipline and maintain that posture throughout the entire voyage." He leaned forward to press his point. "This is a practical solution, evolved in armies and navies over a period of thousands of years, to the problem of forcing people to act together under adverse conditions—to do things they might elect individually not to do if given a choice." He put his notepad back into his briefcase and leaned back in his chair. "You must become a tyrant."

They were really serious, so I had to pay attention, at least.

"How do you think I might establish this tyranny?"

Barbara cleared her throat. "Well, we discussed this at some length before coming to see you . . ." She looked over to Scarlatti, who was carefully putting his pen back in his coat pocket. ". . . and decided that there was no rigorous set of behaviors we could definitely recommend. You'll have to find your own method and style, based on your own personality and the circumstances you'll find once you're underway."

She looked uneasy. "Probably the best thing you could do in preparation would be to undergo a series of role-playing exercises—one in which you assume the burden of being tyrant, another in which you remain aloof and delegate that authority to your first officer, and so forth. It would take some time . . ."

I shook my head firmly. "My current schedule—"

"But," she continued, "we understand that your duties are likely to keep you busy until the time for liftoff." She shrugged her shoulders. "So the best we can do is to make you aware of the potential problems you face, which I hope we have done."

She reached out and squeezed my hand. "Please don't be discouraged, Whitey," she said. "What we've been talking about are possibilities. For the most part, you appear to have a fine group of people, and with some luck and firmness you can prevent trouble. Keep your people busy. Make them work—and make them play games, too. Don't leave them entirely to their own devices—and don't try to be too nice a fellow." She let go and stood up. Scarlatti did, too.

"And if you have any questions, or even just need a hand-holding, don't hesitate to give me a call. You might need someone to talk to who isn't going to be a member of the crew. Good luck. We believe in what the expedition is doing."

I was glad to see them go. They made me nervous. they had the gall to crystallize some of the uneasy feelings I'd been having since I really sat down and tried to figure out what this command was all about.

Junior was going to be a member of the crew—but he was like no one the psychologists had in mind when they talked to me. I took him to Murphy's and put the problem to him the next night. He was quite literally no help. It was the first time I'd really ever seen him without an opinion.

"Crap, Admiral, I don't know what to say. On one hand, they sound like a couple of old mother hens." He reached up and scratched one ear. "On the other, I've never had the experience, except at M-Base—and everybody was an old hand there, and gung-ho to boot. A cramped environment is the only thing I've really ever known. Hell, the Pinwheel seems like a collection of overgrown worlds to me." He took a sip of whiskey and shuddered. "This stuff's real smooth. Must be aged five, six days."

"You still limit yourself to one ounce every other day?" I asked. I should have known that the runt couldn't help me with this one—but I still had to hide my disappointment. I guess that somehow I was counting on a little more counseling.

"Yeah," he replied. "The Cure stopped my own body from killing me off, but it sure as hell didn't give the old brain much ability to wire around dead cells." He took another sip and tapped the floor with his foot. He had to stretch to do it. "Good thing that we've got plenty of protection from cosmics here. 'Fact, I figure that every 250 days in an unprotected ship like *High Boy* takes about six points off my IQ."

"You could stand it. Fifteen years or so, and you'd be able to join the human race as just another genius." I was very glad that the Hexie documents claimed almost complete protection from cosmics inside the big vessel; otherwise, the gnome would have to think twice about coming along.

"Tell you what, Captain. I could be your crew stooge. Dig out the dirt and warn you about anything unusual coming down."

I shook my head. "Thanks, Junior. I appreciate the offer, but I wouldn't wish a job like that on anybody. It could get to be a lonely occupation—especially if people start suspecting. You'll find after a while that nobody'll talk to you." I smiled. "And if that happens, you won't find any turkeys to cover your bets."

"What then, Admiral?"

"I'm going to just have to be myself—maybe with a few minor modifications. I'll have to think about it."

Chapter 6

Although there are many variations, environmental control and life support systems generally fall into two categories: open and closed. Open systems are easy to design. You simply take along enough expendables to last the duration of the confinement, and store the waste products until you get to some closed system where they can be processed—or dump them overboard if you've achieved solar system escape velocity and feel particularly wasteful. The CRF drive, which puts any point in the system only a couple of months away from any other point, has spoiled us. We design 100 percent of our spacecraft as open systems. Closed systems, on the other hand, have rules of their own. The most important one is: the smaller the environment, the more difficult and expensive the ECLS to design. The general rule is that the cost per person is inversely proportional to habitat size. By that rule, the size of the High Boy was small, indeed; but there was no doubt that with 22 people living in it for at least two years, the system had to be closed. And with that dictum came major decisions: what measures to take for emergencies, how many backups for each system, what repair tools and machine shop equipment to take along, and so forth. Thank goodness the Hexies had provided for plenty of power to be piped into High Boy—otherwise, we wouldn't have been able to make the voyage at all. . . .

— *Davidson:* Hexie White Papers, *Appendix J, ECLS Officer's Journal of the Voyage, Prefatory Notes*

Crew selection may have been over, but my work wasn't. During that entire time, I had been wrestling with the commissioning of the *High Boy*—and there was still half a year to go. The entire 16-month effort was one I'd rather forget.

The financial negotiations between Earth and SpaceHome had ended with Earth agreeing to donate *High Boy* and SpaceHome to complete the provisioning. There was a little wrangling over this arrangement but not too much. *High Boy* was very expensive, admittedly—over a billion dollars' worth (Earth prices and wages)—and the provisioning would only cost a tenth that. On the other hand, *High Boy*'s cost was already written off by the Earth consortia, whereas SpaceHome had to come up with new money to outfit her. SpaceHome finally agreed, even though it would cost plenty. After all, that way Ogumi would get to keep the *Catcher*—the SpaceHome equivalent of *High-Boy* built for the Saturn artifact retrieval.

I understand that if the commissioning of the ship were being done in any one of several countries on Earth, there would be formal bidding, with requests for proposals issued, proposals submitted, a winner selected, negotiations, controlled procedures for cost accounting, data deliveries, and dozens of things I didn't begin to comprehend. SpaceHome was a little more unstructured—especially since the only shipfitting outfit was owned by the corporation.

What happened was that I was issued an authorization to spend money. Up to 90 million. I also got an office suite, a very competent secretary, strong advice to get a staff together quickly, and a schedule of reports due. The reports were monthly, with the first one requiring a fairly detailed schedule of work to be done, and initial estimates of expenditures. The remainder of the report asked for information to corroborate how well I was doing on the initial estimates. It all seemed straightforward enough.

I started by making a list of things I thought needed to be done, people to see, and a rough schedule of accomplishment. I started out lighthearted enough, but the more I worked, the longer the list got, and the more complex the schedule. I sweated with it for three days before I thought it was more or less complete. Then I called up the

SpaceHome Shipbuilding Company and made an appointment with the chief of the Interior Subsystems Division.

"Hello, Whitedimple. John Carling." He stood up to shake my hand. "And congratulations are in order, I believe." My appointment had just been announced, but word gets around quickly in the Colonies.

"Thanks, John. And please call me Whitey. Especially since I think I need help."

"Well, if you've got the job I think you do, that might be an understatement."

After some preliminary explanation, I showed him my list. I knew it needed some polishing and details filled in, but I was reasonably satisfied with it.

Carling took it and riffled through the papers; there were eight of them. He seemed to take in each page at a glance. Then he handed them back to me.

"What's your background, Whitey?"

"Archaeology professor. Pilot. Instructor pilot."

"No offense intended, Whitey, but I don't think you grew up in the big bad world. If you're going to spend five million dollars a month, you've got to go about it seriously. And if you want something to show for it at the end, you've got to be good."

He walked to an old-fashioned plastic whiteboard covering one wall, picked up a felt pen from the channel, and began to draw an organizational chart. "Your team'll be a lean one—only about three or four hundred. You've got to save plenty for overtime for the shops that'll be making most of the equipment, and the fitters and test conductors when it comes time to assemble, integrate, and do verification and checkout."

My name went into the top box, and from it emanated a heavy line with several more boxes attached. "Here are your second-level managers: System engineering—that'll be a heavy front-end operation. PP&C. Manufacturing—that'll include materiel. Engineering—and we'll include design, computers, software, and a significant test organization. In fact, testing might become a separate second-level function; you'll have to decide that later. But Safety and Quality Assurance will report directly to you. Normally, there would be Operations, but not in your case.

We'll need a separate training division, though—that's going to be pretty important. And Finance, of course. . . ."

As he talked and the blackboard filled, I went through several stages: irritation that he'd treated my three days' work so cavalierly; then growing embarrassment at my own naivetè; then dumbfounded awe at the scope of the job. When he paused for breath, my wayward tongue decided to show off the brain's ignorance:

"What's systems engineering?"

He walked over to his desk, pulled out his own copy of the Hexie document, and held it up.

"This thing represents a description of an overall system we have to build, but there's no way to generate a useful effort from it without specialized translation. Your systems engineers are the boys and girls who do that job. They read the document with their well-trained brains, generate a set of top-level requirements, a larger set of derived requirements, then allocate specific jobs to themselves, the technology staff, and the design engineers. Trade-off studies. Preliminary design. Long-lead procurement. Prototype development and testing. Preliminary design reviews. Critical design reviews. Interface control documents. Operational testing. And so forth."

Holy Jesus.

"Why is training important enough to warrant a separate organization?"

"Well, I imagine that you'll have two or three specialized computers aboard that you and your officers will have to run. And as many of your crew as you think desirable should learn how to operate the various subsystems—I'm thinking especially of power, communications, and life support." He smiled. "And who's going to hook *High Boy* up to the Hexie plumbing? You planning on spending the money to carry the extra round-trip crew of experts with a separate return boat? That'll be pretty expensive."

"I see your point. What's PP&C?"

"Program planning and control. There'll be quite a lot of activity going on until the job's done, and it takes several people and a good computer to lay out schedules, timelines, and so forth. At your level, you'll be looking mostly at Tier I schedules and top program problems, but they'll be

responsible for everything down through Tier IV, ensuring
that the whole program is coming along on time. They'll
develop a critical path and keep you informed on how
you're doing. In fact, you'll need a good PP&C person
right away on your preliminary team to rough out the
job. . . ."

And that's how that went. Kurious Whitedimple, archaeology professor extraordinary and Pilot-with-the-Look-of
Eagles, was reduced to a quivering mass of jelly in two
short hours. The man finally took pity on me, suggested
that I recruit a good deputy program manager—then offered me one of his top engineers for the job. I accepted,
quiveringly.

Three days later, I met my would-be savior. She bustled
into my office looking for all the world like somebody's
mother who'd been run over by the loop lorry. Her hair
was several different lengths, with various colors and split
ends. Her nose was quite generous, and right where it
met her face on the left side was a small wart. She was
wearing the dumpiest calf-length dress I'd ever seen in my
life. As she was walking toward me and I stood up to greet
her, I sneaked a look at her feet. She just *had* to be
wearing sweat socks and tennis shoes. Nope, sandals—the
paint on her toenails was chipped randomly. Finally she
was standing in front of me with an outstretched hand. I
took it.

"Curious Whitedimple? Janet Griesbaum." Her voice
sounded like gravel rolling between two boards.

"That's Kurious, Janet. *Koor*—ee—us. But please call
me Whitey."

"Gawd, I *guess*, with a name like that. Well, the boys
call me Greasy, so you can, too—though, Gawd knows,
you're no boy any more." She smiled and showed a chipped
tooth. " 'Fact, you're old enough to take me out dinin' and
dancin' once we get this program under control."

"Janet—Greasy—you get the ship under control, and
I'll take you out dancing three nights a week, meals
included."

"You got yourself a deal, Cutie," she said. In her left
hand she carried a copy of the Hexie document; she raised
it up and let it fall on my desk. "Here. I marked up a copy

of this for you to study. Be sure to read all the notes in the margins. The parts in red will be the tricky ones—the ones you'll probably have to make serious decisions about before we're through."

I leafed through the dog-eared tome. It was liberally underlined in green, with an occasional word or two in the margins, but about every ten pages was a lengthy entry to the right or left of the text. There was some red, but not an overabundant amount.

"Won't you need to keep this for yourself?"

"Gawd, no. I've lived with that thing for three days now—practically got it memorized. Besides, we're gonna be swamped with organizational details for a solid week, and gettin' out a schedule and budget after that. 'Time I get around to opening it up again, there'll be three, four kids in Jimmy's outfit who'll have it memorized better'n me."

"Who's Jimmy?"

"Jimmy Coors. One of the best systems engineers we got. I recruited him to be one of your second-level managers. He'll start tomorrow, subject to your approval. He'll have it memorized, too."

This lady was for real. I began to warm to her.

"What else have you got lined up, Greasy—subject to my approval, of course?" I smiled broadly, wishing I had a chipped tooth to show.

"PP&C. Jackie Ling. She's already read it, too, and started roughin' out a top-level schedule. It won't be too accurate for the first week, but once she starts gettin' inputs from the engineering, design, and software pukes and gets 'em into her computer—watch out! She's got an expert system that'll let you know three weeks in advance when some technician's gonna take a crap on overtime, for Gawd's sake!"

She pointed to the Hexie book still on my desk. "Open that up to the back page." I did so. There was a nearly complete organizational chart—much like the one John Carling had drawn on his wall, but more detailed.

"Lucky Ogumi's not on a spending spree this year, except for this thing; that means we got our pick of good people. Lots of things to do, of course, but I can see only one subsystem that's got a chance of bein' a show-stopper: the environmental control and life support system. So I set up an ECLS 'mission mother.' He'll have a dedicated team matrixed out of the other organizations, and gettin' that ECLS system in on time'll be the monkey on his back from day one."

"Who do you have in mind for that?"

"Best man in the solar system is John Jackson. But I got in mind the second best—still a youngster, but not far behind John and gainin' fast. Name of Sean Davidson."

"Hey, he's—"

"On your crew. Gonna be living aboard *High Boy* for a long time," she grinned. "Think maybe he'll put together a nice safe system for you, Whitey?" She sat down in the chair beside my desk, crossed her legs, and ogled me. Varicose veins wandered down her calves like rivers with multiple tributaries. I was starting to love this woman.

"Whitey, how much experience've you had in program or project management?"

I cheerfully admitted a transcending ignorance.

"Tsk, tsk. And so good-looking, too." The leer remained glued to her face. "Tell you what, lover boy. You just sit in that office for a while and look like a hero till you get your feet wet up to about your thighs. I'll do the work. When I send you somethin' to sign—sign it. If you need it explained, give me a call." I nodded. Then she raised a finger and shook it at me.

"But don't you go callin' me too much in the first couple of weeks. Gonna be busy gettin' the team together and gettin' that first cost-and-schedule report out to Ogumi's finance stooges before they bust a gut." She gave me the chipped-tooth-smile. "After that, we can have about half an hour a day together for the next few weeks." She stood up and walked toward my desk. "And after a couple of months, we'll talk for an hour or more at a time."

She reached over the top of the desk and chucked my chin. "And two, three months after that, you'll be takin' me dining and dancing." She stood back up. "And some time around then, you'll be takin' over the reins, instead of bein' a figurehead."

"So soon?" I said.

"I figure so, gorgeous," she winked. " 'What I hear, you're a man who likes to make decisions for yourself. You'll study like crazy. Won't be too long before you slip into the driver's seat.' She pointed to the Hexie book, still opened to her organizational chart in the back. "Any questions about that before I get to work?"

"I notice you don't have a third-level manager for computer systems yet. Got anybody in mind?"

She laughed. "I asked Jeff Albert to do it; just about the best man in the Colonies. He said he'd be glad to, but that I ought to consider a funny little runt by the name of Junior Badille. Said he was the shit-hottest analyst to come along in a generation—knew hardware, software, and microprogramming like nobody else. Maybe you know somethin' about this little guy, eh, Whitey?"

I was already laughing myself. There was no doubt in my mind that she knew all about my friendship with Junior. "Tell you what, Greasy. Badille won't take the job, so go ahead and get Jeff Albert—then tell him to recruit Junior. The little runt will be glad to work for him."

She cocked her head. "Whitey, if you're planning on takin' over this early, you'd better let me sit in your lap and keep you out of trouble."

I threw up my hands. "Heaven forbid! I just have specialized knowledge. Please, by all means, go and ask him. But you'll get an answer like: 'Naw, let old Jeff take the job. I'll just kind of look over his shoulder once in a while.' "

Her smile came back. "You seem to be pretty sure about that, Whitey. But I'll check it out. Like to meet this little genius, anyway."

I nodded. "He's worth the visit, Greasy. But he avoids responsibility like the plague."

"Just like my third husband—but that man was no genius. When I split the sheets with him he had to get a job as a waiter—didn't know how to do anything else."

She headed toward the door. "Gotta run, sweetie. Just 'cause you're sexy and fun to talk to, don't mean that those deadlines're gonna wait for us." She blew me a kiss for her exit.

So Greasy began to run the show, and I humped like

hell to catch up with what she was doing and how she was doing it. Two weeks later, while I was still trying to find the towel to start drying behind my ears, the first cost and schedule report was laid on my desk. There was a copy to me, and three copies for Ogumi's SpaceHome Finance Division, complete with all the lower-level concurrences and sign-offs, with my signature block the only thing left blank.

The computer printouts were beautiful—schedules down to Tier IV. Task flows. Critical path. Work breakdown structure, with costs collected by WBS number. Organizational charts to two levels, with almost every name filled in. Manning levels. Narrative text outlining the job and each task. Preliminary parts lists. Long-lead purchase items.

I decided that it was true love I had for Greasy. I signed SpaceHome's copies, sent them off, and buckled down to study my own. After a couple of hours, I made a phone call.

"Greasy, it looks like you've got the whole job costed at just under 72 million, except for something called MR that costs 18 million. What the hell is MR?"

"Management reserve, sweetie. Twenty percent. I've put these yahoos on a tight but workable budget. Any of 'em come cryin' to you about needin' more money to meet their schedule, tell 'em nix, then send 'em to me and I'll chew 'em out. You hang onto that money for dear life— you'll need it before the end."

"A whole 18 million? Whatever for?"

"If I knew, I'd quit this job and get rich playin' the stock market. In general, two things: changes, and surprises. Changes happen when you thought that somethin' would work and it doesn't—so you gotta go back to the drawin' board. Surprises are when some cargo handler with a hangover drops a finished piece of flight hardware. Then he's out of a job, and you're out four million dollars. Too many surprises and your project folds."

"Thanks, Greasy. I'll hang on to the money."

"If we're lucky, by the time you have to spend some of it, you'll be smart enough to make the decisions yourself."

"I'm beginning to wonder."

The weeks and the months passed. *High Boy* was flown

from Earth orbit and officially dedicated to Contact, as the expedition was coming to be known in the media. After the speeches were over, the big vessel was connected to the south end of the Hub, where SpaceHome's shipbuilding facilities resided.

The largest cargo umbilical we had—the one built originally to outfit the *Catcher*—wasn't long enough, so we had to add a few links—$147,000 worth. SpaceHome also charged us $800 a day for the use of the cargo hatch, plus another $500 for atmosphere and utilities. It was all SpaceHome's money, but they had to keep the books straight. And those expenses were not surprises; they were in the cost model. My pricing team was on the job.

We started working on *High Boy* as soon as she was docked. The simple stuff: internal decking and partitioning. Living and playing space for 20 people. Three decks for crew quarters, theater, lounge, galley, dining room, and gym. Then below those, utilities, maintenance, and food storage. Then below that, fuel storage, which took 40 percent of the entire volume.

Much of the outfitting consisted of just modifying and adding to what had already been put there for the original expedition to the Hexie ship. That first voyage had only 14 crew. We weren't to be so lucky. Not only would there be six more of us, but we had to carry food to last through two years each way in the Hexie ship, the four months getting to and from the Hexie ship, and an unknown amount of time to be spent in the Hexie solar system itself.

In the end, we settled on a six-year supply for 20 people. "We" were the project dietician, ecological engineer, chief systems engineer, Greasy, and myself. I was included because how much food to carry was a judgment call, with the health of the crew at stake. Then, after deciding on six years, came the hard part. Typical dialogue follows:

C: So how much weight are we talking?

D: Dry weight is about half a kilogram per person per day. For six years—call it 22,000 kilograms.

C: Well, that's not so bad, we were initially figuring on—

D. Plus another 30 percent for packaging.

C: That seems rather excessive . . .

G: Remember, Lover, you got dehydrated food that's gotta be kept dry up to six years. Let any moisture creep in and you've ruined your supply and killed your crew. For safety, you've got to seal the food in individual meal-sized packages and—

S: Those packages have to be much more securely designed than anything currently in use. Probably the best way is to triple-pack them—

D: In nitrogen atmosphere, of course. But an all-dehydrated diet is not a healthy one, Whitey. The gastro-intestinal tract needs roughage, or else you develop all kinds of long-term problems. Of course, you can supplement with psillium mucillant or other appropriate dry cereals—

E: —but humans get awfully depressed eating nothing but reconstituted food. We've all heard the stories about the early colonists, Frank.

C: So what do we need to do, and how much is it going to cost?

D: I think the minimum we can get away with is an additional kilogram of whole food per week per crew member. Preferably fresh.

S: Fresh is expensive; requires a big hydroponics setup to produce three kilograms a day. Power. Volume. Fertilizer. If you use night soil you've got to modify the toilets to collect it. Gets messy. And if your crops die for any reason, you're out of luck. Besides, you can't grow meat.

D: Of course, frozen would do, also.

S: Frozen is expensive. Power. To guarantee sustained quality for six years you'd have to flash-freeze and hold the food at fifty below, at least. We've built small ones that can do that, but you're talking about six or seven kilotonnes. And the cook would have to get into it at least once a week, which decreases the safety factor for the remaining food . . .

And on it went for another half an hour before we drove out all the issues. We finally decided on several freezers, the number to be determined later by a trade study taking into account weight, power, volume, and safety.

As I became more aware of the details of the project, I grew more and more respectful of the system engineers—and of the smart subsystem designers who had to take many things into account. Everything was related to everything else, and everything traced back to either the interfaces with the Hexie ship, or the requirement for a long-term confinement in the *High Boy*.

I got more tied up in the project management job as time progressed, and more eager for the crew selection to be finished so I could devote full time to this effort. As it was, about four hours of every working day was taken up with sitting in on interviews and making recommendations to the committee. I knew better than to burn myself out by trying to spend another eight on the project, but I sneaked in six, then caught up by working Saturdays. During this time, my secretary, John Halvorsen, was a wonder. He kept me supplied with all the right details for anything I was working on at the moment, and worked my hours, besides. I cheerfully paid him a healthy salary, with time-and-a-half for overtime and double on weekends. He got rich during that hectic year and a half—but he deserved it.

As I got smarter, my project working hours also became more and more infused with the two big design drivers: power and safety.

With CRF ships, we don't think too much about power. We have an almost unlimited supply tappable at will when the engine is firing—all it costs is a little reduction in specific impulse. But we would not be able to fire up the CRF once onboard the Hexie ship; we had to take the power they supplied us through one of their interfaces. It amounted to about ninety kilowatts nominal—about eighty-five after we got through conditioning it to the voltage and frequency we needed and running all the lines, circuit breakers, switches, and other controls.

I would have thought that was plenty—until I ran up against the myriad pumps, valves, air conditioners, lights, controllers, stoves, coffeepots, refrigerators and freezers, radios, disk players, holo sets, and other paraphernalia required to sustain and nurture the crew during their confinement. We were constantly trading off power versus budget. CRF had spoiled us there; we did not have a technology geared toward minimum-power flight equipment. And if we wanted to make something use less power than the standard model, we had to redesign—with all the costs for development and testing to pay.

The other issue—safety—seemed self-evident at first. Just make a top-level decision: the odds you want to give the crew for survival for six years, say point nine nine nine nine. Then design all the subsystems around that number. It seems straightforward enough, if a little cold-blooded. It was complicated by the interaction between subsystems. If power went, for instance, so did everything else. And we also had to work with the fact that safety numbers are multiplicative. For instance, if you've got a thermal control system and an ECLS and a power system that are all four nines safe, your overall safety is not four nines—it's only point nine nine nine seven. To get it back up to four nines, you've got to spend more money. I found out that for developing new systems, a good rule of thumb is that each nine you want to tack on costs you about ten times more.

There were ways around this, backups being the cheapest. Also, our vessel was big enough to carry plenty of spare parts. And even more important, we had an onboard machine shop. I decided that the SpaceHome half of the crew, anyway, would thoroughly know all the subsystems— and at least three of the crew would be expert machinists. It cost me extra training money—almost two hundred thousand from my reserve—but it made me feel one nine better.

All except for the ECLS system.

"I'll give you two nines, Whitey. That's the best I can do with twenty million."

That was Sean Davidson talking. It was several months into the project. By then I was pretty smart. Smart enough to know that Sean had done all the trades, considered backup systems, and knew we'd have a machine shop and that he'd be aboard, and also knew that the Hexie document promised enough oxygen and pressurization nitrogen to last about four months, if everything else failed. Nevertheless:

"Is that figured on six years?"

"No," he said. "Two and a half. If the Hexies won't help us when we get there, we're probably dead anyway."

I nodded. Sean was young, but nobody's fool. He was in his early thirties, and had that tow-headed, boyish look of second-and third-generation colonists. Junior had described him aptly as "just young enough to know everything there is to know about ECLS."

"Okay, Sean, talk to me."

"The Colonies and CRF have spoiled us. The habitats are so large that we can use ecological biosystems for life support. And if anything goes wrong, they act as big capacitors to slow things down until we can get it in hand. Oh, we control toxic substances, manufacturing processes, and so forth. But that's old hat—almost ingrained into us. CRF means that spaceships are never more than a couple of weeks away from help. We can carry plenty of throwaway emergency supplies—oxygen and CO_2 scrubbers—on every trip, even for the big personnel carriers. Hell, we've got an ECLS standard of five nines per voyage for all SpaceHome ships."

He frowned a boyish frown. "So we've got a technology that's been essentially static for fifty years. Oh, sure, we've got tried-and-true water electrolysis systems and can recover all the body water and laundry. But those off-the-shelf systems have to be factory overhauled every 18 months or the reliability figures go to hell."

He ran a hand through his light-blond hair. "And they're not really designed for field maintenance. One craps out on a short hop, you switch to the backup. If the second one goes, you switch to the emergency O_2 supply or the lithium hydroxide canisters and hotfoot it for home. Hell, we don't even save our feces except for very short flights; we just wait until we've reached solar system escape velocities, then vent all of our solids and brine overboard."

"What did you do for the original expedition? That lasted a year."

"We beefed up some off-the-shelf stuff, put in three backups for every system, and took four nines reliability. That included an emergency plan to blast for home at half a G if we lost the second backup. But we're a little short of space and a little long on time for this one. Emergency plan for our trip is to die."

I chewed a lip and thought about it, then said: "Would you fly with two nines?"

He grinned. "Personally, yes. I think the game's worth it. But if I were in your shoes, I'd never agree to risking twenty people in a one percent chance."

So I finally asked the question he wanted me to ask: "How much to tack another pair of nines on to our system?"

"Thirty to forty million, if you want to get it on schedule. If you're willing to wait an extra year, you can cut that ten percent."

I whistled. I'd known Sean was coming, because Greasy had called me with the warning. She'd told me that in the first place, I was now smart enough to handle this one alone; and in the second place, this was a decision she'd never make for me—because I was the one who had to live with its consequences.

"How much for one extra nine?"

"Ten to twelve million."

I thought a while longer, juggling budget and policy. I made my decision, then added a silent proviso that I'd talk to each of the crew members in private before I asked them to fly with me.

"Tie down that number for the three nines option. I want work-around schedules, and hard dollar estimates within two weeks. I take it you've got a pretty good idea about what you need to do, or you wouldn't have such a good handle on the cost."

He grinned; it made him look about fifteen years old. "I'll have it on your desk in six days."

So much for the management reserve. I called Greasy.

"How much did he stick you for?" she asked.

"Eleven million, give or take—just to get three nines reliability. And I still don't have the odds. I'm going to have to talk to each of the other crew members and offer them an out."

"Gawd. Better think twice about that one, Whitey. It might be better if they just didn't know. Not many of 'em have engineering heads, anyway."

"No. I won't play politics on this one, Greasy. I doubt

any of them will back out—but they have a right to know, and choose without pressure."

"You're the boss. Well, you've had your first big change. Let's hope the rest of 'em are tiny ones."

"Hear, hear."

But there was another big one in store—a surprise and change combined. Half a year later when the negotiation teams added those extra two "contact specialists," we had to do a redesign, tear out a lot of interior work that was already in place, increase our supplies and storage space by ten percent, completely reallocate the power budgets, and a couple of other annoying things. The ECLS system had been designed with a fifty percent duty cycle margin, so that didn't need redesign—but that margin dropped to 36 percent, and the overall reliability went down to .996.

Before that I'd used up only fifteen million of my reserve and was beginning to convince myself that we'd come in on time and budget. Now I had to go to the well for ten million more—the "well" being Ogumi. He put up a good front—surprised, irritated, reluctant—and insinuated that I wasn't doing my job properly if I couldn't handle a little change like that within budget.

But I could tell that he wasn't surprised. I pointed out that it was not the greatest idea in the world to redesign a large effort like this after it was nine-tenths finished. I brought along a copy of my recommendations to the Committee on the subject—which stated in no uncertain terms that the inclusion of two extra bodies on the expedition would entail a great deal of additional expense and threaten our departure schedule. I further told Ogumi that he was welcome to have my resignation, but that if I were to remain in charge of the outfitting program, I'd need that ten million.

He gave it to me. Not only that, he got sixty percent of it from the Earth authorities—based on complex negotiations that were above my pay grade.

The bitterest pill I had to swallow, though, was Junior. The last bet I'd made with him was several years ago, and by a lucky fluke I'd won. I kept that five dollar bill framed and hanging conspicuously on my office wall. I was the only known living being who'd won a bet with Junior

Badille. It gained me a lot of respect from the smart engineers who knew the gnome.

But then, about two months before, Junior had tempted me once again. He bet me even money—that five on my wall against another one in his pocket—that I wouldn't bring the project in for the original 90 million. I thought very hard about it, ran over all the costs and schedules in my head, ticking off mentally which groups were ahead, and which were behind. The work was almost all done, the show-stoppers behind us. Many groups were under-running—one by almost $100,000—and the worst group was overrunning by only $25,000. And I had three million left in my reserve. I took the bet.

Then the abovementioned lightning struck.

When I returned to my office from Ogumi's, flush with the easy victory in getting the extra ten million, Junior was waiting for me. He pointed to the framed five on the wall.

"Let's have it, Admiral."

I sighed, pulled it off the hook, and handed it to him. His cackle of glee would have done credit to the opening scene of Macbeth.

"That'll teach you to wager with your betters, Dimp."

And then the little runt had the gall to go hang it in his own office—right where everybody could see it!

I swear to this day he had inside information that I didn't—and I was on the selection committee!

BOOK II

OUTBOUND

Chapter 7

I knew that an anthropological study of the Hexies
would be a difficult undertaking. Our profession's field
work is generally performed under carefully controlled
conditions: isolated cultures, small samples, static condi-
tions, and so forth. Observing the Hexies would be an
extremely ambitious undertaking, especially if our stay
was to be anything less than ten years. To sharpen my
mind I worked on the crew during our outbound voyage.
It was a small sample but dynamic, confronted with a
threatening environment, and required to adapt to evolv-
ing circumstances and cultural situations. This turned out
to be a crucial step in my process. My understanding of
the Hexies was ultimately augmented tenfold by observing
their reactions to the behaviors of the crew. So it was well
that I had learned the crew behaviors and interactions
before contact with the Hexies. This learning process was
complex, the crew fascinating. . . .
                                    —*Kimberly:* Hexie White Papers,
                                                Prefatory Notes

Once the excitement from the final big surprise died
down, our work-around schedules were tightened, and the
program back on track, there weren't many weeks left
until departure. I'd set that departure date almost a year
ago, and I worked hard to keep it: it was Remembrance
Day, the most universal holiday on Earth and SpaceHome,
because Christian and non-Christian alike celebrated it.
And this year of 2097 was the hundredth anniversary of
that day when Deborah Champion sacrificed her life to
orbit the enormous terrorist device and save the industri-
alized world from holocaust and nuclear winter.

I chose it because I wanted to remind the peoples of Earth and SpaceHome that we were not going to the Hexies as two groups with disparate opinions on how the solar system should be managed; we were going as humans, and we'd better stick together when the time came for meeting this alien race.

The Earther contingent arrived three months before the scheduled takeoff and took up residence in the Cube. The lead time was deliberate. It was to give the entire crew a chance to live together and get to know one another. By then most of the SpaceHomers had worked their way down to level 43. They were now closing out their affairs in the Colonies and would begin to train with the Earthers.

During that final three months, I should have been able to spend time getting to know the crew. But that last big change scotched my plans. Greasy and I were busy trying to be three or four people and get the program back on schedule, so I didn't have too much time with the crew. I was living down at the bottom level, but spending most of my time in the office, or floating around in *High Boy* keeping track of progress on the modifications.

Sean Davidson was also heavily occupied. He not only had to train the rest of the crew in the operation of the ECLS system (my earlier orders to increase safety), but also to oversee the exhausting series of qualification and operational tests of his hardware. He taught classes during the day, then sneaked over to *High Boy* to check on the testing at night. He was getting haggard, and not adjusting well to the higher gravity regime imposed by moving down in the Cube. He was behind in his acclimation, and getting more so. Finally, I got Greasy on the phone and asked her if she could get John Jackson for a few weeks.

"How much you got left in your reserve, sweetie?"

"Enough, and even if I didn't, I'd pay him out of my own wages. I need Sean healthy when this trip starts."

"Just order him off the testing site, boss. Gawd knows you're the man can do it. Those test teams are plenty smart—they know what they're doin'."

"That doesn't cut ice with Sean, Greasy. If I did that, he'd just worry himself to death. He knows he's got 22 lives riding on the ECLS, and he's not about to let anyone less qualified than himself write down those check marks."

"I take your point, Cutie-pie. The boy's young and conscientious—needs a little balance, though. Well, if you can pay Jackson's outrageous consultant fees, he'll come. John's semi-retired, growin' a pot belly, dandlin' his grandchildren on his knee—and hatin' it about half the time."

The next day I called Sean into my office between classes. There were dark circles under his eyes unbecoming to one of his age—even counting the fact that he was now living at nearly nine-tenths G.

"Morning, Whitey. What's up?" He was laboring to look relaxed.

"Hello, Sean," I said. "Can you handle it all right down here at full G?"

"Oh, sure. I'm down to level 40 now. I'll have it licked in no time—well, in time for Remembrance Day, anyhow. Uh, say, what did you want to talk about?" He looked at his watch.

"Sit back and relax, Sean. I've canceled your next class; the crew is being informed right now. In fact, I'm cutting your teaching load to fifty percent starting today. That order will be in effect until we leave."

"Whitey, you can't really mean that. These people still have a lot to learn in diagnosis and repair. What if the expert maintenance system craps out during the trip?"

"If they aren't up to snuff when we take off, then you can keep drilling them during the outbound trip," I answered. "Now tell me: what's our current number for thirty-month reliability?"

"Still holding at point nine nine seven. The tests are going pretty well."

I looked him in the eye. "Tell me the number if you're not along with us to baby that equipment."

He sat back in his chair, chewed his lip for a moment. "Lower. But I'm going to be along, so the question's not relevant."

"Yes, you are," I said, "because I'm going to make sure you don't flunk the physical. I'm taking you off the test program in three days."

"You can't do that, Whitey!" he said, jumping out of his

seat. "None of those technicals knows enough about the integrated system verification procedures. Even Jonsey's weak in—"

"Hold it!" He stopped and looked at me accusingly. I smiled. "John Jackson is taking your place. He's reporting in tonight to take over the protoflight qual program. You've got three days to get him up to speed, then you're off the job. After that, I'll give you half an hour a day to go over there and keep tabs on what's happening—but I've asked John to keep a stopwatch on you." I grinned at the young man. "And he's got strict orders to throw you out if you stay a minute longer. When the qual tests are over, you go back on the job for installation and checkout—but that's six weeks away. In the meantime, you're going to relax, sleep eight hours a day, and put some muscle on. Right now even Junior could pin your shoulders to the mat in ten seconds flat."

He thought it over, then smiled sheepishly. "Well, I *could* use a little more sleep. . . ."

"Damned right. And I'm also putting you on a high-protein, high-calcium diet." I picked up his medical report and waved it in the air. "Doctor's orders. And you're going to start working out with the rest of the SpaceHomer crew immediately. Take it easy at first, but within three weeks, I want to see you doing the full hour, along with the rest of them."

He took a deep breath. "Okay, boss. Captain."

"That's right. I'm both," I smiled.

I told Junior the bones of it that evening. He grinned. "The kid was pushing himself too hard. You did good, Admiral."

We were sitting around a small table at the Earthlight Bar, a place that until a few months ago had catered almost solely to Earthers. (What SpaceHomer in his right mind would want to drink at one G?) Kari was back with us, and had resumed testing with Junior to get a "longer baseline."

"Now all you have to do," continued the runt, "is to take the same advice for yourself."

"It's not that bad," I said. "After all, I'm fully acclimatized. I've been living down here for three months now."

"Yes, but you've got a nice set of bags under your own eyes," chipped in Kari. "When you live in a one-G field, you've got to get your beauty sleep—that's a lesson well known to us poor Earthers over thirty." She flashed that knee-weakening smile.

"Well, I'll do what I can," I promised insincerely.

When I got back to my apartment, I looked in the mirror. I *did* have bags. But there wasn't too much I could do about it. I'd taken control of the program from Greasy a year ago, and there was no turning back the clock—especially with the new modifications. We had to get the job done a month before Remembrance Day, in time for all us pilots to give *High Boy* her trial runs before the crew boarded for the long trip.

So I was busy. I didn't get to see nearly as much of the crew as I would have wished, but according to what the psychologists had told me, perhaps that was for the better: the role of the Distant Captain was one of the things they'd suggested as a possibility. But by then I'd at least met them all and had had chances for casual conversation—and they were a good group. The earlier seeds of doubt planted by that well-meaning deputation had now all but disappeared. I would be approachable.

There was one rule I had made for myself: no involvements. To my way of thinking, it would be disastrous to show any kind of favoritism on this voyage. Almost everyone knew of my friendship with Junior—and now with Kari we made a threesome—but I resolved to try to give equal time to the rest of the crew as soon as we got cooped up together.

The last three months raced by. As hard as Greasy and I and the outfitting and checkout crews worked, we still ended up two weeks behind schedule, but I wouldn't postpone the departure date. What that meant was that George Petrov, Mike Prentiss, Junior, and I did double duty on the checkout schedule. George was quite familiar with *High Boy*, but there were changes in the manual navigation and landing systems that he had to learn, too. So for that entire two weeks, we took practice maneuvers in six-hour shifts. The simulator was very good, but there is nothing like the real thing for learning the real thing.

Added to my grief during that time was the relentless attention of the newspeople. Media interest ran in cycles during that entire year and a half. It peaked right after selection of me as captain, then a year later on announcement of the crew list, then three months before departure when the Earthers arrived at SpaceHome. Then, naturally, when *High Boy* began its trials—right when I didn't have a minute to spare for another story of my life and times.

I'd set up a public relations office, which handled most of it for me. But the reporters with pull somehow managed to get through all of the barriers. And I learned from them, and their stories, the somewhat disquieting fact that we were being written off as "time travelers." It was disquieting because I didn't want this trip to be forgotten, no matter how long we were gone. Every time one of them made it into my office, I stated bluntly that if Earth and SpaceHome didn't remember us after a few years, they ought to have a cerebral enema to clean their brains out. The role of Contact was extremely important, even if it was a centuries-long process.

And finally, Remembrance Day was upon us. The crew was mustered in the Hub, looking just like any other tourist group returning to Earth—except for the dignitaries and media hovering over us. Even if we were written off the books an hour after we left, we were news then. So we answered the reporters' questions one last time, and listened to speeches by Ogumi and the holoed image of the Earther consortium representative. They were pretty, wishing us Godspeed and reminding us gently to be good ambassadors for humanity.

They even put me in front of the microphones (telling me in whispers beforehand that I had to hold it to five minutes) for an acceptance and thank-you speech. I took thirty seconds: I told them never fear, we'd be good representatives of humanity, and reminded them gently that Earth and SpaceHome needed to get together and back our play when the time came. I think they were glad when I got off the microphone.

Then the speeches were over and we boarded. Our large ration of luggage had been loaded some time before, thank God. The crew was to sit in the theater during takeoff, strapped into 19 of the 22 available seats. It was the high point of my day to see this gaggle of dignified personnel acting like kids on a holiday outing. Most of the Earthers hadn't been in *High Boy* since the modifications, and many of the 'Homers had never been onboard.

Everybody wanted to see his or her "room" before going to the theater, and I obliged. After all, we weren't on a very tight schedule—it was a holiday and traffic was light. We had a two-hour window to get to the fifty-kilometer standoff point and light the CRF. And if we dawdled enough, it might throw off the schedules of the network coverage—a cheering thought.

An hour and a quarter later I was sitting in *High Boy's* control room in the right seat, watching Petrov do the work. He'd been through the RCS checkout and was now preparing to take the monstrous vessel away from the Hub. I let George do it because I hadn't had much chance to see him in action during the compressed training schedule. I knew Mike Prentiss was good because I'd flown with him before; he'd even been helping Sam Sebastian with pilot training classes during my enforced absence from the school. But I needed to learn more about how Petrov behaved with steel under his fingers.

He was smooth, confirming my earlier impressions. He handled the new nav computer and the relatively unfamiliar SpaceHome departure procedures with the confidence of an old pro.

". . . confirm vector four eight at rotation nine zero degrees. RCS maneuvering will commence thirty seconds from my mark. CRF plume in twenty-eight minutes, plus-or-minus five. Mark, over."

Confirm your mark at Zulu 1657:02:09. No further transmissions necessary except for deviations. Hub control ten-ten. Good luck and Godspeed, High Boy.

"Understand no further transmissions, Hub. *High Boy* ten-ten, out. . . . "

Petrov's competence was beyond question. As he instructed the nav computer and maneuvered us to the Hub's 90-degree radian, I relaxed and studied him while pretending to watch his board. He knew I was doing it—a

good pilot knows everything happening in his control room—
but it didn't seem to make him the least bit self-conscious.
He remained phlegmatic during the entire procedure.

I had Petrov's dossier, of course, and had studied it
thoroughly, along with those of the other crew members.
His was more thorough than most; the Russians tend to
work that way.

George Petrov was born to White Russian parents in (of
all places) the Philippines. He'd grown up speaking Russian, Spanish, and Tagalog, along with standard English.
His parents were life members of the diplomatic corps.
When George was 13 they were transferred to a post in
China. The boy fought the move and shed a great many
tears over losing his Filipino friends—the last tears anyone
had ever seen from him.

In a world where everyone outside the English-speaking
countries grew up learning at least two languages, George
was somewhat of a prodigy. During three years in Beijing,
he mastered Mandarin, Cantonese, and one or two other
dialects of Chinese. Then, when his parents were stationed in Hanoi for another brace of years, he picked up
the more difficult five-toned tongue of the Vietnamese.
During this time he never allowed himself the luxury of a
close peer friendship. According to the notes of the psychologists who'd put the appendix in his profile, the departure from the Philippines had traumatized him to the
extent that he was unwilling ever again to form close ties
with anyone. This spilled over into his love life. He had
affairs with several women, but let none of them get close.

His parents returned to Moscow, where George entered
the Soviet military academy and excelled physically and
mentally. His high class standing allowed him to opt for
space pilot training. Ten percent graduated from that rigorous course, and he was at the top. In the meantime, his
parents had been assigned to Iraq. During furloughs from
schools and post-academic duties, he visited. And, of course,
he learned quite passable Arabic from his parents' new
friends.

It was his acquisition of Arabic, in fact, that was his real
ticket to space. The military space roles of all Earther

countries were severely limited by the Treaty of 2002—but the commercial consortia were something else.

No one understood quite how it happened, but after Petrov's eighth visit to his parents, the Soviet Space Ministry received a formal request to detach him from duty for reassignment as a commercial pilot for Svioto-Iraq, the giant Arab-Russian communications/power combine. Svioto-Iraq had about ten times the clout of any Soviet government agency. Within five years, Petrov became the top pilot of the combine, and recognized as one of the tops on Earth.

When the Hexie artifacts were discovered and Earth mounted its two abortive ventures to grab the bacon from SpaceHome, Petrov had to be content with backup crew status. He was too good to be left out altogether, but politics were involved also. Svioto-Iraq was too powerful for the Cartel Alliance to chance having that organization's loyal top pilot getting the artifacts under his control. Therefore, others were chosen: Mike Jacobs for the ill-fated Earther expedition to the Iron Maiden in Saturn's rings; John Stevenson for the equally ill-fated expedition in *High Boy* to retrieve the final artifact in Saturn's atmosphere. And John Stevenson again when I opted out of the command role for the original expeditionary voyage to the Hexie ship.

But Petrov's superior ability, his bachelor status, and his aptitude with languages made him a natural for the long voyage. There was never much doubt that he'd be high on the list—and politics didn't count for so much since this was to be a "generation" voyage.

"Begin RCS primary burn on vector four eight."

As the gentle tenth-G thrust pushed us back into our seats, I wondered if Petrov resented being backup again. He shouldn't have any reason to believe he was a better pilot than me. Even though I was a relative newcomer, my record was, in all modesty, beyond question. But Petrov was very close with his emotions; I'd probably never know.

At 38 years of age, he was in trim shape for an Earther—187 cm and 79 kilos. His light brown hair showed no touch of age, and his complexion was fair; he'd lost his

Earther tan during his three months in SpaceHome. He had regular features—even handsome—except for a torn ear that he wouldn't talk about and refused to let a plastic surgeon touch. His good looks and soft voice were a challenge to some women, but his coolness turned most off. His emotional energy seemed to be channeled to his profession, and an occasional monologue in comparative linguistics.

"RCS cutoff. Fifty meters per second. Zero G for fifteen minutes, forty seconds. Crew will please remain strapped in."

He thumbed off the intercom and turned to me as we floated out toward the kickoff point. "Orders, Captain?"

"Go ahead and stay in the left seat, George," I said. He nodded and turned back to set up the CRF trajectory on autonav. He was finished in less than ten minutes. His apparent unflappability caused me to ask a question I really didn't want to broach until later:

"What do you really think about this growing economic conflict between Earth and SpaceHome, George?"

He answered me matter-of-factly, as if I'd asked the time of day:

"I do not know how others feel, and cannot answer for them. Myself, I believe that SpaceHome is trying to swallow a bite too large to chew. To have a small company and less than 100,000 people controlling valuable resources needed by ten billion is wrong. I believe that the proper forum for making such decisions is within the councils of the Earth consortia; they must ultimately be responsive to the needs of the billions."

He spoke English without any trace of the gutturals I'd learned to expect from Russians—yet I'd heard him conversing in colloquial Russian on a voice link to his parents. I'd really become a believer, though, while listening to him speak fluent Arabic to Hagar Zyyad—then change to Cantonese in mid-sentence to address a remark to Chin Wu Lin. It is unusual for one so gifted in languages to be as phlegmatic as Petrov—it usually requires an outgoing personality to take the emotional risks of mimicking new sounds and risking ridicule. That made Petrov all the more enigmatic. All of these were side thoughts as I asked the key question—the one I would eventually ask everyone on board:

"Do you think that the Earth-SpaceHome differences should be a background for how we deal with the Hexies?"

He turned to look at me with an unreadable expression. "No. I believe that those differences are out of context in dealing with the Hexies, and that we should be humans only. But what I learn from the Hexies I shall use for the benefit of Earth when we get back—that is, if it makes any difference any more. History is moving rapidly in the solar system, and it is quite likely to be beyond our comprehension when we return."

I nodded, having found out what I wanted. I thought Petrov was naive if he believed that the Earth consortia were any more concerned about the ten billion than SpaceHome, but he was also likely to be incorruptibly honest. I felt I could trust him not to attempt to sway the crew to an Earther viewpoint, and to do his job to the best of his ability.

"RCS maneuvers in ten seconds." His voice cut into my reverie, and I felt a momentary spasm of guilt, having been caught in the act of judging him. Not that he was likely to care one way or the other.

The thrusters spun us around, pushed us back for fifty seconds, then stopped. We were nearly dead still with respect to the Pinwheel fifty kilometers away. Petrov keyed in the long-distance nav program, then made his last announcement to Hub control:

"*High Boy* to Hub. Information message only. CRF maneuvering to commence in ten seconds, out."

"*Confirm*, High Boy. *Please switch to Hub communications frequency for further transmissions. Out.*" That was Marge Whitcombe on the Hub traffic comm. Normally, she'd have been a lot looser, but Petrov's formality apparently had turned her prim and proper.

The attitude control thrusters slewed us back around and tilted the nose up thirteen degrees out of the plane of the Earth-Moon system. If we'd been on any other mission, I'd have stabbed the abort button. Then the CRF lit off and we were riding a one-G tail of lively quarks. George instructed the central computer to perform a complete functional check of all onboard systems again, then watched the screens as they flashed their messages. He was a proper human backup for the nearly infallible system diagnostics.

I looked at the mission clocks, now twitching merrily to count the seconds between events for us poor humans. It proudly declared our elapsed flight time of 8 seconds, and informed us that our ETA at the Hexie ship was 5,914,368 seconds hence. I growled at some unnamed test technician and punched the "change display" button, upon which the numbers obligingly changed to 68d 10h 52m 45s . . . 44s . . . 43s . . . 42s. The time to turnover was 34d 4h 26m, etc. I sighed inwardly. I suppose I should have been thinking great thoughts about motherhood and humanity at this momentous instant in time. Instead, I was wondering what my gin and cribbage losses would amount to before we even boarded the Hexie vessel. . . .

"All onboard systems nominal, Captain." Petrov's quiet voice cut into my calculations. "Do you wish to take command?"

"No," I said, then looked over my shoulder and addressed Prentiss: "Mike, take the left seat for a couple of hours until we're well out of Earth orbit and up off system plane."

Then I thumbed the intercom button and spoke to the crew: "You may unstrap, ladies and gentlemen, but please remain in your seats for a few more minutes. I'm coming down for an in-person talk." I switched off and turned back to my first officer. "George, would you please come with me?"

I quieted the chatter in the theater by stepping up to the podium—but if the crew thought I was going to make a big speech, they were wrong. I just wanted to take command, which I hadn't really done yet in their eyes.

"Ladies and gentlemen, you are now a crew for the first time together. Your job and mission for the next two years is to form a ship's company for the purpose of bringing your collective knowledge into contact with the Hexie culture. It is my function as captain to see that you perform that job properly. Therefore, as of this moment, you are all on ship's discipline, and will remain so until the end of this voyage. This trip will have few rigors except those of boredom. Your routines will not be harsh or demanding, and my orders will be few and far between. Nevertheless, I will expect compliance when they are given.

"Right now, I would like you to spend the next hour unpacking your gear and moving into your quarters. Then we will observe an hour for Remembrance Day. After that, your duties will commence. You'll find them in Mr. Petrov's 'read only' directory in the file named 'Roster.' Mr. Petrov will be in charge of this operation, and in general, the day-to-day functioning of *High Boy*. For the first week, the assignments as given will stand without changes; after that, you may negotiate swaps with your compatriots and Mr. Petrov. I ask your cooperation in making his job as easy as possible.

"There will be a meeting of the ship's officers and Drs. Allison-White and Kitigawa in my conference room in 45 minutes. That's all for now. Thank you for your attention."

I don't know what they expected, but that was what I gave them. Just before they dispersed, I took a gestalt of the small sea of upturned faces. Almost all were serious. Junior, of course, grinned and winked. I hoped no one saw him.

My "conference room" was pretty cramped with five people in a one-G field. I hoped it would never have to contain us all again; but for this one time I needed to have them all together, in private, on my own turf.

"We are it." I smiled at them, but not too warmly; I wanted them to take me seriously. "It falls upon us five to keep the ship functioning and the crew sane and happy, for at least the next two years. I say 'us,' because there's no way I can do it alone. I'll be relying heavily on George and Michael to make sure the ship and crew stay healthy, and to parcel out official duties and other orders when necessary. I must similarly rely on you, Grace and Edward, to provide moral and emotional leadership in nonofficial arenas. In fact, your jobs might be the most important ones in the long run. And they will perhaps be more difficult, because in order to stay in tune with the crew, you'll have to lead by persuasion and example—even though you will be delegated authority in many areas.

"I don't intend to hold myself inaccessible. I believe this complement is too small to institute a formal chain of command. I'm going to announce an open door policy. But," I tried to eyeball them all at the same time, "if people start coming to me with minor complaints, I'm going to suspect that you aren't doing your jobs. I'll expect at least ninety percent of the onboard problems to be resolved before they get to my office."

I turned my attention to the two officers. "George and Mike, I'm putting the physical well-being of the ship and crew into your care. I'll watch over your shoulders, but you've got the monkey on your backs. Work with Sean Davidson to get everyone up to snuff on learning the ECLS. And George Korliss will help you set up a reasonable physical exercise routine for all of us.

I turned to the other two. "Edward and Grace, you have the tougher assignment of keeping our crew from boredom. We officers can keep them busy for only an hour or so each day on the average. You're going to have to find out how to balance the rest of their time between work and play. It won't be so bad for the first few months; things will be new, and they'll still be learning their job rotations. But once we settle into the long haul aboard the Hexie ship, your job is going to be extremely important. I'll take ideas from anyone, but it's going to be up to you two to implement them and elicit the crew's support."

I smiled again—leave 'em happy. "I know we've got a lot of planning to do, but right now I'd like to just spend a week or so getting used to the closed environment. We're all more or less amateurs at this business; we need the time to get smarter. Mike, could you stay for a second? George, take a check on the conn, would you, before you set up your quarters? Thank you all."

After the others left, I looked Prentiss in the eye. He was an excellent pilot with potential leadership qualities. Short, dark, and good-looking, he had liquid brown eyes that were almost irresistible to women. And when he played the piano, even those who were "only attracted to tall

men" slobbered all over him. There's something charis-
matic about a class performer.

But he was young.

"Michael, do you understand what I'm trying to do
here?"

He smiled, looking all of 18 years old. "I think so,
Whitey—Captain."

I smiled approval. "Whitey is just fine as long as we're
alone, Mike. I think our big problem is going to be finding
the right balance between too much and too little discipline. If this were a crew of kids, I'd go all out for discipline, but we've got a small, motivated group of mature
adults here. We try to do too much play-acting, and they
just won't buy it; but we have to keep subtle reminders in
front of them all the time."

He digested it for a moment, then nodded. "I think I
see what you're driving at."

"What if Petrov and I were suddenly out of the picture,
for whatever reason. Do you think you could pull it off
alone?"

That one took longer. "I'm not sure, sir."

"Think about it—about how you'd go about it right from
the start. It's not bloody likely to happen—but you are
third in command, with many lives in your hands. My way
might not be yours, but you've got to give it enough
thought to act decisively if the time comes." I smiled—
warmly this time. "Okay, end of lecture."

As he was leaving I added one last shot: "One thing you
might do is grow a moustache. That'll help put some years
on your face. Get your looks and abilities in synch." I held
up my hand as he opened his mouth. "Not an order—not
even a strong suggestion. Just something to think about."

He left thoughtful, and that was good.

Chapter 8

On discovering that the Hexies appeared to have little interest in grand unified theory, I was at first acutely disappointed, then unbelieving. It was not until Czeenveer showed me the historical record that I truly believed that they had lost interest in pushing the limits of high-energy research several thousand years ago. By then, they had achieved only a factor of ten above what we could do when the expedition left Earth. Why they have not continued still remains somewhat of a mystery to me, although it might have something to do with their perception of long-term economic payoff. This notion is foreign to me. I have been taught to believe that basic research always pays off in the long run. This belief extends even to the multi-billion-dollar high-energy accelerators in Europe, America, China, and Russia. . . .

          —*Dunsworth:* Hexie White Papers

"Zero G in ten seconds, stand by . . . 3 . . . 2 . . . 1 . . . CRF cutoff. Ladies and gentlemen, we are now traveling at an estimated velocity of 29,406 kilometers per second with respect to Sol—the highest such velocity ever achieved by human or probe. The previous expedition to the Hexie ship turned over at a mere 15,866 kilometers per second relative.

"We will be in free fall for two hours only, while we get a state vector update. Please leave all equipment battened down, and refrain from going to the john if at all possible. Mr. Davidson has activated only one zero-G toilet for our use. Keep an eye on the countdown clock. At the end of our update, we'll flip ship and begin decelerating. Out."

I turned the con over to Mike and headed to the ship's

bar, where I had authorized a restrained party, zero-G style. The bar was really the rec room, but soon after the voyage started it had been informally named "Ethanol Ethel's" on the first of our weekly alcohol nights.

Our total alcohol ration was 400 liters, which I ordered broken out at two liters per week. That was plenty, since the stuff was 200 proof. Saturday night was normally the only drinking night, except for special occasions such as this.

After making the rules, I had put Ethel Erickson in charge of the whole business. She was a perfect choice because (1) she was a crusty old gal who wouldn't take crap from anybody; and (2) she was a confirmed teetotaler. She kept the only key to the locker, brought the ration out every week, mixed and distributed the drinks—and kept unerring track of who had had how many. She'd used a tally sheet the first week, but didn't need it after that. Her own ration went to whom she pleased. It wasn't in the form of extra drinks, but when she picked out her target for the night, she'd double the alcohol in his or her drinks to fifty grams.

"What'll you have, Captain?" she said in her gravelly voice.

"Just orange juice, Ethel." It was a kindness to call the powdered stuff orange juice.

Ethel was an expert in zero-G operations. Her second home in the Colonies had been the microgravity manufacturing facility two kilometers south of the Hub. She'd already prepared the mixers in their individual squeeze bottles—ice included—and had only to transfer the alcohol. For mine, she just reached a long arm into the recesses of one of her sphincter boxes, pulled up a cold bottle, and handed it to me.

"Try not to get stoned on that terrible stuff, Whitey."

I grinned my thanks and floated over to my target table. It contained Junior, Kari, Mayumi Sakaguchi, and an empty seat. It was standard practice to maintain the pretense of gravity. All tables and chairs were bolted to the floor fittings, and straps had been installed for the party.

"Welcome, Admiral. Pull up a seat belt and join us." The runt was relaxed, as he'd been ever since we departed. The last-minute work on *High Boy* had involved him, too. Now he had little more to do than help Sean teach ECLS theory, operation, maintenance, and repair to selected members of the crew.

"Thanks." I levered myself into the vacant chair and strapped in loosely.

"Who's running the ship while you're down here, Captain?" asked Mayumi. She was short, plump, and always slightly dumpy looking, even dressed up in a single jump suit as she was now. She'd not been picked for a world-class brain, but rather for extensive knowledge of inorganic chemistry. She'd also done a dozen years' work in the chemistry of geological formations, and had done much to educate the expert ecological computer systems on Earth. High-pressure, high-temperature chemistry was an esoteric subject, and she was one of its masters.

She laughed readily, and was easy to get along with. Almost everyone in the crew liked her; no one viewed her as a threat.

"George Petrov," I answered. "He volunteered; said he didn't feel the need to party a day before the real one."

"He's a cold fish," said Kari. She was devastating, as usual, even with neck and face puffy from lack of gravity.

"Yes," laughed Mayumi, "but awfully good-looking."

"And an awfully good second-in-command," I added absent-mindedly.

"A penny for 'em, Admiral." Junior noticed that my mind wasn't on the conversation.

I smiled wistfully. "I was thinking about another state vector update we did together. Things were a little different."

He returned the smile. "Our north polar traverse of Saturn. Times were a little hairier back then, Captain. What was that—six, seven years ago?" He squeezed some screwdriver into his mouth. "Back when we still had a bit of growin' up to do."

Mayumi remained blank through the interchange; she had no referent. She knew only what the Earth authorities had told the general population about the Battle of the Iron Maiden. And since Earth had ended up with egg on its face, that hadn't been much. Anyway, it was old history now, and best forgotten by the mixed crew.

But of course Kari knew. Enough to be wistful herself:

"I wonder how far in the universe we'd have to travel to see as beautiful a sight as that," she said. She and Junior had done the traverse many times, duplicating the orbit in which Junior had been conceived and born. I felt a small pang of jealousy, then suppressed it immediately. I couldn't afford it. I couldn't even afford the guilt I felt about that last night Kari and I had spent together in SpaceHome when Junior was gone—so I suppressed that, too. I wondered how long I'd have to live seeing Kari every day before she didn't remind me of things I'd rather forget.

"Do you think the Hexies will have a Saturn?" Mayumi asked Junior.

"Not bloody likely," answered the gnome, scratching his nose. "In the first place, it takes a low probability collision to create the ring material; and in the second, the half life of a gaudy system like that is only a few million years. Humans lucked out. I'll bet the Hexies were jealous when they first saw it."

". . . two . . . one . . . CRF cutoff. Stand by for RCS maneuvers." I checked the radar. We had matched orbits almost perfectly, and were drifting only a few cm per second relative to the big vessel. I flipped *High Boy* one-eighty and looked at the Hexie ship. It was easily visible. It was hard to believe that it was fifty kilometers away; I had to remember that it measured nearly a kilometer in length.

I was in the left seat this time. I wanted to handle the approach myself. I used the radar and nav computer to figure my RCS profile, but flew us in on manual. I was rusty, and wanted to get the feel of *High Boy* again.

Half an hour later we were stopped fifty meters away from the high-contrast sign marking the small personnel hatch. The full size of the monster was awesome. I wondered about a civilization that could leave such a machine on the off chance that we'd be able to use it to visit them.

I checked the proximity readouts. We were closing with respect to the big vessel at .001 cm per second. That would increase due to gravitational attraction, but not quickly enough to make any difference. The big ship was in a very slow tumble referenced to the background, but not enough to cause problems. I'd already matched it, and our Earth communications antenna handled it quite well.

"RCS maneuvers completed. Tie-line crew, begin your work. Interfacing crews, suit up and prepare to carry out your tasks. Everyone else is free to move around, but stand by for further instructions and possible maneuvering." I glanced at the mission clock. "The final message from Earth is scheduled in seven and a half hours. I'd like to be finished with phase one by then. Out."

I turned to Prentiss, who was sitting in the right seat. Petrov was in charge of the first EVA. "It's yours, Mike. I'm going to suit up and nose around, make myself a nuisance."

He nodded and moved to the left seat. I made my way down to the ready room. By that time Petrov had attached the guide line to a tie-down embedded just inside the Hexie personnel hatch, and George Reid was horsing the heavy-duty cable across. By the time I was suited up, the takeup reel had removed the slack. On cue, Prentiss's voice came into my helmet on the override frequency:

"All crew stand by. I'm instituting RCS tension program in ten seconds. Grab on to something. Three . . . two . . . one . . . burn." A tiny lurch as the balancing program adjusted nose and stern thrusters to apply a smooth constant tension of 100 kilograms-force on the cable. "Resume activity. Please note that *High Boy* nose and tail areas are now off limits. Out."

Petrov and Reid were now cycling the airlock again, so I had to wait to go over to the big ship. By the time they were pressurized, the initial prep team—Davidson, Erickson, Krebbs, and Dinsworth—was standing by with its paraphernalia. Petrov didn't bother to unhook his helmet. He had a word for us as he re-entered the ready room:

"One person on the line at a time, please. And please wait for me to join you before cycling the lock." He turned his head toward me. "Are you going over, Captain?"

"Yes." There was ample room in *High Boy*'s intermediate airlock for six plus equipment.

He nodded, drifted through the ready room hatch, and was back carrying a small package before we were finished crowding into the airlock. As the lock was cycling, he addressed me again:

"Any orders, Captain?"

"No," I replied. "I'm just going to look it over. I'll stay out of your way and let you do your assigned jobs."

I was last across. I hooked my belt loop to the cable and pushed with my legs to give me momentum, rather than activate the suit thrusters. As I entered the "small" hatch—it was not really very small at two meters by four—I felt like Jonah.

The "personnel hold" was about six meters square and four high. Its only features were a medium-complex computer console and another two-by-four hatch into the main hold; otherwise, the walls were all blank. Petrov was the only person in there. He was busy affixing labels and instructions in English to the console. These were principally for unexpected use. We'd programmed the onboard translation computer for every situation covered in the Hexie manual. It would take our verbal or written commands and turn them into the appropriate binary-coded strings, with on and off voltages and intervals as specified by the Hexies. The communications link was one of the interface hookups in the large bay.

The only thing not linked via the communications channel was the abort switch. If tripped any time after the voyage started, it would turn the ship back and deposit us where we started. But once it was used, the voyage was over; there was no second chance. We would be deposited back near the solar system, be given several hours to get out of the ship, then the vessel would be gone—whether by leaving or self-destructing we knew not. I didn't intend to find out. It was clear that the Hexies didn't want this being tripped by accident. It consisted of two toggles high up on the wall near the console. They had to be tripped in sequence, with a timed wait between the first and second—during which a message translating as "ARE YOU SURE?" appeared on the screen and through the communications link.

Our TO called for super-gluing a double-bend piece of

angle-iron on the wall underneath it to protect the toggles from accidental activation. Petrov finished his labeling tasks as I watched and proceeded to apply the glue. I drifted through the open inner hatch without bothering to say anything; he knew his job perfectly well.

I'm used to large, enclosed spaces, and I knew the dimensions of the Hexie "cargo hold." Nevertheless, after taking several seconds to get used to the scale, I headed toward what must have been George Reid's group, about 80 meters away against a wall.

The three were busy hooking flexible fittings up to the Hexie onboard interfaces: power, thermal, pressure, vent, comm, clock, and alarm. The other ends would plug into *High Boy*. We could have waited until our vessel was moved into the Hexie hold, but the plan was to make sure we had the interfaces right while we were still in contact with Earth.

"How's it going, Sean?"

"No sweat, Captain. The first two are well within tolerances. With luck, we'll be finished up here within an hour and a half."

"Good."

I looked around for Ethel. She was a tiny bug on a far wall, putting up a large yellow sign. By the time I made my way over to her, she almost had the thing up. There was a modest-sized Hexie poster on the wall, about one meter by two. It had a thick line with asterisks on one side and symbols on the other.

What Ethel was doing was a translation—in style. Our own version of the sign was three meters by nine: it was a huge black arrow, with huge black words declaring "DOWN" at the tip of the point. She was struggling with the thing, but almost had it pasted in place.

I noted her helmet number and voice-activated a private channel into her suit. She was mumbling, and the words were not polite. I broke into her diatribe:

"Now, Ethel, you know it has to be big; I'm getting old and my eyes aren't what they used to be."

"I'll give you 'old,' you young whippersnapper. Sir." Her voice managed to keep its gravel, even when turned tinny by the small headset speakers. "You let them put this ridiculous procedure in the TO, the least you can do is give a helpless old woman a hand carrying out the farce." Ethel Erickson was just about the least helpless person I knew in zero G.

So I gave her a hand. Just about the time we got the fourth sign posted, Junior came in with a surveying instrument and navigational markings for the placement of *High Boy* on the "floor." I waved goodbye and checked back in with Sean's group. They'd finished five out of the seven hookups with no problems, and were working industriously on the heat transfer cold plates. Everybody would be done in plenty of time for the final message from Earth.

"... *message. You have already said your private goodbyes individually to your loved ones. This one is for all of us. We now give you your final commission: be the best representatives you can for our species. Our goodwill will follow you* ..."

It was several hours later. The speeches were coming in—almost done, in fact. I surreptitiously checked over the crew, especially the members from Earth. Michele Kimberly was stifling a yawn. I didn't blame her—the speeches were trite and boring. Hagar Zyyad was reading something. Two seats from her, Dick Gates was writing in a notebook. Edward Allison-White sat patiently with a blank, interested look on his face, as he must have sat through hundreds of such ordeals. Carl Dunsworth, who was an avid pro-Earther, had a hard look on his face. Chin Wu Lin sat expressionless. No signs of tears or regrets, except possibly from Jason French. Most of the 'Homers looked eager to get on with it. I appraised us as a healthy crew.

"... *so goodbye, good luck, and Godspeed.*"

I took the podium. "Fellow crew members, I feel obligated to say a word or two for our goodbye to the solar system. Does anyone want anything in particular in the message?"

After a pregnant pause, Allison-White said: "Go ahead, Captain. You speak for all of us."

I thumbed the transmission button and told the solar system (1) Goodbye, and (2) They'd better be ready for our return. The crew cheered. By the time the message was received, we'd be well on our way, if the Hexies built well. I was sure they did.

"All right, everyone. Suit up and take your posts."

Half an hour later, I moved *High Boy* around to the other side of the Hexie vessel. One hundred percent of the crew were in micropore suits, and would remain so until the Hexie vessel was underway and all systems thoroughly checked out. Prentiss was in the right seat with me in the control room; Junior and Petrov were stationed at the Hexie control console, standing by. Junior was there because he was the expert translator; he knew eidetically every symbol and symbol combination of the artificial Hexie language, and would act as real-time interpreter if the need arose. Petrov was there because I wanted the second in command outside the ship at this critical time; he was also good with the Hexie language.

I looked at the mission clock. It was time for Junior to instruct the Hexie vessel to open the cargo hatch.

The Hexies were superb machinists. From inside, it was obvious that the huge door would pull itself inward and slide to one side; but on the strange hull material there was only the finest hairline crack to mark its outline. As I watched, that monstrous piece of hull—big enough to admit the solar system's largest vessel with plenty of room left over—sank into the vessel, then began to move to my left. I shook my head—partly in relief, partly in awe. After all these years, the Hexie ship was going to let us in.

"—rov to *High Boy*, Petrov to *High Boy*, communications check, over." The opening of the large hatch reestablished radio contact.

"I read you five by, George. Any unforeseen developments from the Hexie message center, over?"

"No, sir. Just a reiteration of the original instructions. We have 6^6 heconds to order the hatch closed and begin acceleration profile; otherwise, an unknown event will occur."

A "hecond" was about eight-tenths of a second; 6^6 heconds equaled exactly one Saturn rotation.

"Thank you." I thumbed the open frequency and talked to everyone:

"The Hexie cargo hatch has opened, and we are going in. RCS maneuvers commencing."

I took *High Boy* in on manual. The operation was too delicate to do otherwise, even with the ladar reflectors we'd planted on the cargo deck. I used very small thrust increments to avoid possible damage to the interior. Even though there was ample room inside, I had to position our vessel very accurately on the deck—otherwise, the umbilicals wouldn't reach their interfaces.

It wasn't quite the challenge of putting the *Catcher* down on Titan—not even a G field to liven things up.

"Perfect, Captain. All your landing jacks are dead on the marks."

"Thank you, Mr. Petrov. Please perform initial tie-down."

Five minutes, then: "Completed, Captain."

"Thank you, Mr. Petrov." I turned off the 100 kilograms of balanced RCS thrust pushing *High Boy* against the deck and shut down the navigation board. "RCS off. CRF total shutdown. Systems to internal battery power."

I let out my breath; we were close to being committed. Once inside the Hexie vessel we didn't dare run the CRF, even on standby mode just to provide power. There was no way to lose the excess heat to space. And once the big hatch closed, we were completely at the mercies of the Hexies and their technology. If the ship didn't go anywhere, and the abort switches didn't work, we had a slow death ahead: we'd last only as long as the interfaces and our onboard systems continued to work. I forced myself to continue:

"Tie-down crew out first. Hook-up crew stand by and follow them outside. I want preliminary system checkout in three hours. Crew members report to me individually after trial and re-hook of each of your PRQD's. Captain out."

The positive-release quick-disconnects were my idea—my one personal spending spree as program manager. All umbilicals would hold firmly, even through heavy lurching of the Hexie vessel—yet one person could disconnect all seven lines in less than twenty seconds. The development of those disconnects—especially the tricky ones like the vacuum vent—was expensive. I paid the half million from my manager's reserve without a qualm—I wanted the insurance. During the entire time the Hexie cargo hatch was open and there was a chance to get *High Boy* out in case of emergency, there would be someone standing by those disconnects, and I would be in the control room ready to scoot us out of here. It wasn't much, but I was doing what I could to cover all bets.

"All right if I go out and take a look around, sir?" asked Prentiss from the right seat. He'd been stuck in the control room since the CRF cutoff.

"Sure, Mike. And on your way, go casually through the theater and case the crew. I'd like your impression of their mood; I'm especially interested in worried faces." All of the Earthers except Kari Nunguesser and George Petrov were still in *High Boy*. As a matter of policy, I was letting only experienced zero-G hands work the hookups.

I forced myself to sit quietly and monitor the control board as sounds of scraping and clanking came through the hull. Petrov's tie-down crew was attaching twelve heavy cables from *High Boy* to various of the utilitarian lugs spotted on all six walls of the cargo hold. Eventually they would all be hand-tightened, with midline ratchet wheels, to 650 kilograms tension. The quick disconnect for this setup consisted of an electrical system onboard that retracted the cross-pins set in the eyepads on *High Boy*'s hull. I didn't intend to test it; those cables would whip.

"First four tie-downs attached. Applying fifty kilos tension." Within ten seconds a mild creaking sounded throughout the hull as Petrov's four workers coordinated their efforts.

"Communications attached. PRQD tested and functional." That was Anna-Marie Smith's voice.

"Thank you. Testing," I replied. I activated the translation computer. The screen said: TIME REMAINING: 9H 7M 23S. It jerked downward in uneven increments as it translated heconds into the human clock. Junior's post was still the Hexie console; I switched to his private frequency.

"What do you have on your screen out there, Junior?"

"I just got an indication that the communications channel is opened and transmitting. Outside of that, it's giving us the time limit, as advertised, Captain. I make it a shade over nine hours and seven minutes." Junior was limited to the speed of chemical processes in his brain, but for a simple calculation like that he was not very distinguishable from a computer.

"Thanks, Wonder Boy. Keep watching for surprises; cut in if you have to."

"I know my knitting, Mother. Don't go Nervous Nellie on me." Junior showed proper respect for the captain with witnesses present. On the private channel, he felt free to be his normal nasty self.

"Captain's privilege. Lump it and out."

"Power umbilical tested and re-hooked." I glanced at the screen; it confirmed the hookup and zero power transmission. I echoed the confirmation over clear channel.

"Second four tie-downs. Applying 50 kilograms."

"Alarm cable tested and re-hooked."

"Vacuum vent tested and re-hooked."

The reports came in fast and furious. By the time the clock had counted down to 8 hours 20 minutes, we had confirmed hookups on all seven umbilicals, and were tied down with full tension on all twelve cables.

"Power switchover." George Reid and Sean Davidson were down in the utility deck performing final acts. The control panels didn't even flicker as the Hexie vessel took over the power load and our own ship's batteries went on standby. I glanced at the translation screen. It was now broken into eight windows, showing the status of the seven umbilicals and the time remaining. We were using 48 kilowatts.

"Confirmed. Forty-eight kilowatts," I announced. "Go ahead and test the vent." I noticed the small power surge as he did so.

"Works fine, Captain."

"Thank you, Mr. Davidson." I took a deep breath. "Are you ready, Mr. Petrov?"

"Yes, Captain." Petrov was one of two outside the hull of *High Boy*. He was my emergency umbilical disconnect officer. The other outside was Junior, still at the Hexie console in the small room. Not only did I want him standing by the abort switch, but the Hexie manual said that the voyage must also be started at the console itself, rather than through the communications link.

"Are you ready, Mr. Badille?"

"Aye, Captain." I took a very deep breath. I was about to commit, and now that it came right down to it, I was afraid. I didn't give myself time to think.

"Close the hatches."

"Activated."

I forced myself to sit in silence as the huge cargo hatch slid closed and shut off the stars.

"Hatches closed. Seal confirmed by message."

I started and looked at the screen; it was telling me the same thing.

"Begin the journey." I said it without thinking. It was too late to turn back; Junior wouldn't hesitate.

"Activated."

The first sounds began to come from the Hexie ship. They were familiar and expected.

"Pressurizing. Seventy-nine twenty-one, as advertised."

The screen confirmed. Nitrogen and oxygen were pouring into our space. It took several minutes; there was a lot of volume to fill. I sat still, not talking to Mike in the right seat.

I jumped when the alarm tones began to sound. We had tested them softly, then adjusted the volume up to emergency levels afterward. The Hexies supplied a warning wire pair that carried tones of 6, 36, 216, 1296, 7776, and 46656 Hz all mixed together in equal strengths. The human ear frequency response is such that 1296 dominated—but the mixture sounded weird, anyway.

Six short tones at one-hecond intervals, then a silent interval of six heconds, then five tones with a five-hecond interval, then four tones, and so forth. It was the maneuvering countdown. We were committed, until and unless we slapped the abort toggles.

The final beep sounded, then nothing. No, something. I heard through *High Boy*'s hull sounds that could be solenoids activating, then what might have been electric motors whirring. Then scrapings. Then we moved. The Hexie ship still seemed to work, at least partly. Then nothing.

I calmed fears by deducting what must be happening.

The first sounds were probably RCS thrusters being pushed out of the protective hull. The first movement was probably to still the vessel with respect to the background stars, in which case, we were now doing a state vector update. So depending on the elegance of their optics and the speed of their computer, we might wait anywhere from a few minutes to several hours—or even days—before starting.

"Sir," Mike broke into my thoughts, "if they're doing a state vector update, it could take quite a while. Perhaps we should let the crew—"

He was interrupted loudly by the first six warning tones from the intercom. I had been thinking exactly what he had; I smiled at both of us.

"They do state vector updates faster—" pause for five weird tones "—than we do." I finished in time for the next five; then added: "Probably a very large onboard computer." Four beeps. Three. I was almost choking with excitement, or apprehension; I couldn't figure out which. The final tone.

The vessel did a slow dance in three dimensions. Simultaneously a very low humming started, more felt than heard. If they had a CRF or equivalent, it had now come to life.

We waited a minute, then two. Then the beeps started again. I wondered if humans would ever be able to build such a complex mechanism to last as many centuries and still function. Of course we would. According to Ethel, we were only a generation or so away from "never break" technology—that would be the next scientific revolution. By the time we got back, *High Boy* would be an obsolete, accident-prone piece of junk.

The beeps ended as I was daydreaming. The hum grew louder—almost audible—and then acceleration began. We were underway. We added G slowly. According to the manual, it would be a 36-hecond buildup.

With adrenaline running high, the mind plays tricks. About halfway through the profile, I thought sure we were going to go well over one G. I had to look at the nav readouts from *High Boy* to reassure myself. Point six, point seven. Through the pervasive hum I could hear metal creaking softly as strain shifted on the tie-down cables. Point nine, nine five. One point zero. One point zero two three. No change. No change. I looked up from the board. Mike was grinning, looking like a sinister kid with his new pencil-thin moustache.

"We're on our way, Captain."

"I do believe you're right, Mike. Why don't you talk to our nav computer and find out where we're heading, while I secure us from standby."

"Aye, aye, sir."

I activated Junior's frequency. "What does it look like out there?"

"All quiet on the console, Admiral. Just the seven status messages, and the one telling us we've got a year to change our minds and abort."

I glanced at my repeater screen. "Actually, it's just a little over 357 days."

"Don't pick my nit and I won't pick yours."

"Okay, you can secure from station and come on in."

"Gladly. My feet are killing me, and micropore suits get sweaty in pressure."

I hadn't noticed my own sweat until then. All of a sudden, I couldn't wait to get unsuited myself. I switched to the all-hands frequency.

"Ladies and gentlemen, we appear to be safely under way, with no anomalous readings or messages from the Hexie console. You are now free to resume normal ship's routine. Mr. Petrov, you may secure from standby. Please remember that even though we have safe breathing air outside *High Boy*'s hull, the airlock doors will remain closed as a matter of policy. Captain out."

I unsnapped my helmet and looked over to Prentiss.

"Well, Mike, where are we headed?"

"Well, sir, as near as the 'puter makes it, we're heading out about 16 degrees north of the ecliptic in the general direction of the top edge of Orion. Of course, with no outside referents, our accuracy is none too good. And it'll get worse the longer we travel without them."

"Maybe when we get there we can ask them where we are."

Chapter 9

On arrival at the Hexie World, I found that our "short" lives were just as much of a mystery to them as their "long" lives were to us. To try to understand this phenomenon, I began at the beginning. The total number of heartbeats in the individual geriatric lifetimes of recently evolved Earth fauna is roughly constant at about 10^9, humans included. I collected sufficient data from phylogenetically equivalent fauna on Tharthee to become reasonably certain of two facts: (1) there exists a "total heartbeat" constant, just as on Earth; and (2) this constant is roughly 10^{10} (see supporting data in Addendum B, this section). Thus, the planetary fauna themselves demonstrate that the Hexie "long" life is a genetic consequence of the phylum in which they evolved. . . .

　　　　　　　　　　　—Nunguesser: Hexie White Papers

"Come in, Mr. Chin. Please, sit down." I stood as Chin Wu Lin entered my conference room.

"Thank you, Captain. You honor me."

"Not at all."

As the elderly Chinese gentleman arranged his formal kimono and folded his body into the chair across from my desk, I studied him carefully. Of all the people on board, he was the one about whom I knew least. Yet in his quiet way, he was one of the most renowned—and certainly the richest—person on the expedition.

He had power—power enough to keep his dossier skimpy. He was Earth's premiere "deal-maker." He was a professional arranger of meetings, usually between heads of state or consortia, wherein fabulous transactions took place. His fees were also fabulous. He was born and lived in Hong

Kong, and therefore nominally a citizen of the People's
Republic of China. But he owned estates, and was *persona
grata*, in nearly every major country on Earth.

When it became evident that Earth and SpaceHome
would be sending along watchdogs under the euphemism
of "contact specialists," Earth had the usual problem of
choosing one from among several opposing factions. Then,
at the last minute, Chin's name had been put forth—a
seemingly miraculous occurrence. His reputation for neu-
trality and integrity was beyond question; his fortune was
founded on it.

He was also hard as nails beneath that bland exterior.
He endured my scrutiny with no sign of discomfort. I had
called him in, and had to speak first.

"I'm sure you know, Mr. Chin, that I'm in the process
of conducting private interviews with all crew members.
The object is to catch up on my homework, which I
neglected sadly during the final stay at SpaceHome and
the voyage out to the Hexie ship. I would like to get to
know each crew member better, and to have everyone
know me as well as possible."

My formal tone was almost forced; somehow, Chin's
presence demanded it. He merely nodded at my statement and waited for me to continue. He was an acknowledged master at establishing relationships, and it seemed
that he was trying his damnedest now to establish the
upper hand in ours.

"I'd like to ask you a question I'm sure you are tired of
hearing: Why in the world did you agree to come on this
voyage?"

He smiled, but his eyes didn't. "Captain, for many years
I have been in the business of arranging liaisons. I have
had ample success. But I regard this contact between
species as the most important meeting humanity has ever
undertaken. To be of assistance in its undertaking will
bring a man of my profession rewards that cannot be
measured."

Very smooth. Too smooth. I shook my head once to let
him know. "Please, Mr. Chin. I am not a youngster.
Certainly your reasons are more complex than that."

He raised his thinning eyebrows a fraction of a millimeter, perhaps feigning surprise at my perspicacity.

"Professional challenge though it might be, I did not agree to undertake this job without compensation. My Earth properties are being guaranteed by several governments with covenants-in-perpetuity. I have hidden substantial assets in places from which only I can recover them. And I asked and received a fee of fifteen million dollars, which I am carrying with me in the form of rare coins and *objets d'art*. Their value alone, increasing during the centuries of our voyage, will more than triple my current fortune."

He smiled again. "I hate to admit to simple greed, rather than more complex reasons, sir, but at my age, it is one of the few motivations left to the flesh."

"But three times infinity is still just infinity," I said.

"I beg your pardon?"

"Forgive me, Mr. Chin, but I still have a hard time understanding. You left behind more wealth than anyone could spend in a hundred lifetimes, to embark on a tedious voyage with almost no luxuries and an uncertain outcome. And perhaps just as astounding, you left behind a life of respect and power to spend a precious five years in a subordinate and unloved position at the very bottom of a small chain of command." I shook my head again. "To talk of allowing simple greed to place you in this position stretches credibility."

This time his eyebrows didn't move. He just looked at me with that bland expression for fifteen seconds while I waited. When he finally spoke, there might have been the hint of a sigh in his voice.

"How old are you, Captain? It is difficult to tell with you Colonists."

"Forty-six."

He shook his own head. "On Earth you would be mistaken for a man in his late twenties—or early thirties at the most. I still make mistakes of judgment in dealing with Colonists, based on a lifetime of reading callowness into smooth skin, and wisdom into wrinkles."

"You are certainly not the first," I said.

"No, but reading people is part of my profession; to

make mistakes hurts professional pride. Your courage has
been demonstrated in the past, and on this voyage you
have shown that you possess at least the rudiments of
leadership ability. But you have not heretofore behaved in
such a way that I could read much depth in your mind."

He paused again; I waited.

"How old do I look to you?" He raised a hand. "You
know I'm seventy-three, but how old do I look?"

"Like an Earther in his mid-sixties," I said. "But if you
were a Colony-born man, I couldn't say. We don't have
any natives that looks as old as you. Perhaps a hundred."

"Yes. I am in excellent health for a septuagenarian;
witness that I easily passed the physical examination to
embark on this voyage. But I have studied geriatrics; it has
been a hobby of mine for several years. Organ cloning and
other expensive biotechniques are available to one of my
wealth. I can keep my body running in good health for
perhaps forty more years.

"But with all our knowledge, we cannot keep the mind
alive. The DNA has a built-in death wish. Some of it is
because of gravitational stress—you may have perhaps ten
or twenty more years of mental health than I. But the
neurons die and cannot be replaced. The inevitability of
this is difficult for me to accept."

"That's an unusual attitude for a person of your heri-
tage," I said.

"Yes," he replied. "A devastating mind set I picked up
from the western culture. And one shared most strongly
by that woman you are so interested in, but so carefully
avoid," he showed teeth, "Miss Nunguesser." I guess it was
only fair for him to try to get back at me, since I was
putting him through the wringer. I tried not to betray my
surprise.

"Yes, but she hides it almost as well as do you," I said
with a straight face.

He nodded. "I followed her researches on your Mr.
Badille with a great deal of interest. I was quite disappointed to find out that the little man was a genetic sport,
and that his cure entailed techniques inapplicable to normal humans."

"So you're taking a gamble on this trip," I said.

"Yes. I'm wagering five precious years of my life—and perhaps all of it, if things go wrong—that the fruits of this voyage will contain seeds of long life." He shrugged. "Perhaps a foolish gamble from your standpoint, but there are two chances to win.

"The first is the Hexies themselves. I am convinced that they enjoy a much longer lifespan than us, and there is an obvious similarity in form and function. It is not beyond the bounds of reason that their chemistry is similar to ours, and that they have developed artificially a long-life technique which they might share with us. And the second, of course, is that this voyage of ours is essentially time travel. We could very well come back to a future in which old age is delayed or conquered.

"With both of these possibilities, I have assessed my chances at nearly fifty percent of achieving a significantly longer life by embarking on this voyage than if I had never attempted it. To me, this is well worth a five-year investment."

"Long life, and wealth to enjoy it," I said. "Very old dreams of mankind." There might have been something else he wasn't telling me, but I wasn't sure.

"Now, Captain," he said, "we have established your strong personality and my weak one. Is the interview over, then?"

"No," I said, ignoring the sarcasm. "I'd like to know your views of the job you have during this voyage. What are you really supposed to do?"

"Look out for the interests of Earth, naturally," he replied. "I am to make sure that whatever wealth is to be obtained from this voyage does not come solely to Space-Home."

"I understand that," I said. "But exactly what do you intend to *do* on the trip? What will be your method of carrying out your task?"

"Captain Whitedimple, I do not think it is your business to inquire how I am to go about my job."

"On the contrary, Mr. Chin, it is very much my business." I put as much hardness as I could into my voice. "The very presence of yourself and Mr. French onboard this vessel is a threat to the unity of my crew. I must know what you intend to do, and have assurances that your methods will not foment trouble. So I ask you again, how do you intend to carry out your function?"

"By observation. By learning greeds, corruptibilities, strengths and weaknesses. In short, by getting to know the crew so well that if I think SpaceHome is getting an upper hand, I'll have the leverage to stop it. It is something I do very well, Captain, without seeming to do it."

"In fact," he added, "our jobs are very much the same in this respect. We must make the same observations and each know the crew equally well to perform our functions properly. The only difference is that you have the option of using a formal method such as these interviews, whereas I must remain informally in the background."

I didn't rise to the ploy. "Nevertheless, I am quite certain that you will learn many things that I do not, Mr. Chin. And I must tell you now that I intend to regard you just as I would any other specialist crew member. If I ever need your unique knowledge to bring this ship out of danger, I will expect you to cooperate fully in divulging it—whatever the personal cost to yourself."

"That is reasonable," he said.

"I also expect you to volunteer information, if you think there is something which threatens the well-being of the ship or crew," I added.

"That, too, is reasonable," he said. Neither reply was a commitment, but it was probably all I would get from him.

"Very well," I said. "Now I'd like to find out if you have any gripes so far about your crew status or duties. Do you have any problem with your current jobs as cook and dishwasher four days a week?" From sublime to mundane with a change of subject.

"Not at all. My first employment in the early '40's was as a dishwasher in a Vietnamese restaurant in Hong Kong. I learned to cook during that time, and it has been a hobby ever since."

I smiled. "Well, I'm afraid you won't find too many varieties of spice aboard to liven up the dried food which is our staple. But after four months onboard, we all know that.

"Mr. Petrov will maintain the policy of rotating jobs to avoid stagnation and resentment. I encourage you to go with this policy, rather than trying to trade back to cook with anybody who is willing."

He nodded without replying.

"The scientific leaders, Mr. Allison-White and Miss Kitigawa, will be announcing the formation of a school next month," I continued. "We are all going to learn as much as we can about each other's specialities. The obvious reason for this is as another measure to forestall boredom. There is another not so obvious. We do not know what our situation will be on the Hexie world, and any single crew member might find himself alone in circumstances which may require scientific insight to evaluate. So the more diverse our knowledge base, the better chances we have of taking advantage of whatever circumstances might arise."

"I'm afraid I will not be of much use in such a scheme, Captain."

"Nonsense. It is true that you will probably not be asked to teach, but you are perfectly capable of learning one or more of the disciplines to be offered. In any case, you will be strongly encouraged to undertake several courses of study, and even to specialize in one if you show particular aptitude."

He nodded without commitment.

"I am also announcing soon a standing order that everyone keep a full personal record of his or her findings and observations during this entire venture. The principal output of this voyage will be a collected set of White Papers— one from each of the crew members. We will use it to deduce as much as we can about the Hexies and their technology. Each of the crew will be required to open a private access file in the onboard data management computer, and add to it daily, even if it's a negative statement. You alone are to view your file, and are not to discuss its contents with any other crew member. The object is to maintain strict observational independence, which will enormously strengthen any correlations we find when the files are opened at the end of the trip.

"You are also encouraged to keep a private diary, handwritten and secured in your personal locker. It may or may not be published, at your request. But in case of great need, it may be used to resolve debates about onboard happenings, so I request that if you begin one, you date it always by the onboard mission clock."

Again the expressionless nod, leaving me in the middle of a flat monologue. I gave up.

"That's all that I have to say, Mr. Chin. Now, is there anything you'd like to talk about?"

"Not at the moment, Captain."

"Very well. Please feel free to come to this office whenever you need. And thank you for your time."

I stood up as he rose from his chair and exited. Then I sat back down to collect myself. After a full fifteen minutes of candid talk, I wasn't sure that he'd told me the full truth, and he hadn't committed to a single thing. Mr. Chin was a powerful personality—at least as strong as Ogumi—and nobody's fool. If he ever became an opponent, he'd be a deadly one. I hoped it would never happen.

Chapter 10

The existence of Vazteer as a global retreat from the pressures of civilisation (see Appendix B, subsection "Happy Hunting Ground") cannot be underestimated in importance. Hexies evolved from the same relatively simple survival-oriented environment as did humans, and their current society is every bit as complex as our own. Yet their incidence of neuroses and psychoses is, for all intents and purposes, zero. Perhaps an important reason for this is that every Hexie knows that if the complex pressures become too great, this retreat is available. Within the millions of hectares of Vazteer, no technology higher than bow and arrow is permitted, and there are no pressures extant more complex than individual or tribal survival within a relatively benign environment.

—Allison-White: Hexie White Papers

". . . but the only one I've really heard talking about it is that creep French. That guy should be gagged and stuffed in a closet."

The speaker was Peter Dinsworth, SpaceHome's expert in astronomy and cosmology. He and his "twin," Carl Dunsworth, were sitting with Junior and me at a table in Ethanol Ethel's. I would not give up socializing with Junior; we were best friends and had dedicated ourselves long ago to doing this trip together. But I also had to maintain social discipline as captain, so I tried to make sure that whenever I sat with the runt, there was at least one other at the table.

We were seven months into the voyage, and traveling at an estimated 180,000 kilometers per second relative to the solar system. For every eight seconds by the ship's clock, ten were passing back home. I'd heard talk—just a rumor, actually—that "people" were contemplating asking me to initiate the voyage abort. It was only five months to the halfway point, then it would be too late.

"What do you think, Carl?" I asked. Dunsworth was Earth's particle physics expert. He'd started the trip as an avid anti-SpaceHomer, but was mellowing somewhat— mainly due to his close friendship with Pete.

"You know that, Captain. I told you in our interview six months ago. I have the strongest possible desire to meet the Hexies and find out where they are in grand unified theory. If we can bring back a valid GUT, it will be our own key to the universe. Even if they've just gotten back to 10-^{41} second, that should be all we need."

"Wouldn't mind that myself, Carl," said Pete. "But I'm afraid the rest of the folks around here would like to get their hands on some more practical technology. Like how to do the A-G trick."

"Toys," replied the Earther. "Just toys. If we could . . ."

My head swiveled back and forth as I watched the two converse. Of all the friendships that had sprung up among the crew, theirs was the most unlikely. Carl Dunsworth was quiet, intense, and tended not to fraternize. He had come to the Cube with a huge pro-Earth—or rather, antiSpace-Home—chip on his shoulder. He'd been one of the leading wights of the venerable CERN accelerator complex, whose power over the past four generations had inched up and up until now it was only a few magnitudes shy of achieving the energy level of the embryonic universe at Planck time— 10^{43} seconds—when all the forces were unified.

But recently, an important modification had fallen through. The reason given to the scientists by the European authorities was that SpaceHome had pulled out of the joint Saturn Artifact Retrieval Project, and now Earth had to fund it on its own. Dunsworth had become very bitter, but that didn't stop him from applying for the Hexie voyage. His thirst for knowledge was even greater than his antipathy toward SpaceHome—and now it looked as if the Hexies might be the best chance to get it.

Peter Dinsworth's personality was nearly opposite to Carl's. He was friendly, easygoing, and tended to look on the Earth-SpaceHome conflict with a relatively unbiased and amused resignation. Perhaps that was because he spent a great deal of his time on the backside of the Moon—figuratively, anyway. He was one of the principal investigators who remotely controlled the seven-meter Lunar Darkside Telescope; his mind was mostly far away.

The friendship had begun by circumstantial whimsy: their similarity in last names. During the selection process, they'd been mistaken for one another by "officialdom"—in the form of a not-too-alert data entry operator, who had convinced the personnel computer that they were the same person, with the name of Carl Peter Dunsworth. Then, when they began to live in the Cube together, the confusion was continued by baggage handlers, mail deliverers, and even fellow crew members. As a consequence, they'd struck up a defensive friendship, while exchanging various articles of mail and belongings sent to the wrong rooms. It turned out also that they were in the same business, from opposite ends. Carl looked into the nuclear particles to go backward in time; Peter looked to the red-shift horizon to accomplish the same purpose.

During their tenure together, Pete had gently laughed off most of Carl's naive viewpoints regarding the "greedy ogres" of the SpaceHome Corporation. He was able to get away with it because (1) he did it without malice; and (2) he was totally honest in not trying to bias Carl toward SpaceHome. Although he was quick to point out how Carl had been brainwashed by the Earth authorities, he was also truthful enough to point out the realities of Ogumi's tight policies, and to compare them with those of Earth as he saw them. For Carl, Pete represented living proof that the Colonists were human, and free to criticize their own administration.

". . . be a long time before technology could catch up to a complete unified field theory," Pete was replying. "What do you think, Junior?" When it came to a question of intergrating science with technology, literally everyone on board deferred to the gnome.

"Sorry, Petey. You're wrong and Carl's right." Junior was always delicate in expressing his opinions. "Our technology's just about at the point where we could really use some new math, and a decimal or two tacked onto our best measurements."

"What would it buy us, Junior?" I asked, interested.

"At least two biggies," he said. "First, the final step up from CRF technology—safe reaction drives with matter-antimatter annihilation. Second, 'never-break' technology. We need to completely understand the nuclear glue before we get to third base." He took a sip of his drink and grimaced. "This raspberry flavor is awful. Last time I'll take that old bat's advice about how to mix my poison." It was Saturday night, and Ethel was presiding at the bar as usual.

"I heard that, you ungrateful brain-stuffed brat!" she said loudly from behind the counter. "So why don't you put your God-blessed grand unified theories to work to try and figure out how to make the orange and grapefruit flavors last for five years when nobody likes strawberry or raspberry!"

It was well known that Ethel could keep track of at least ten conversations simultaneously on Saturday night. As we laughed, I made a mental note to pump her discreetly about the crew's desire to abort the mission. If it were a true groundswell of opinion—even a small one—I had to meet it head on; but that would be a dangerous tactic if it was just one person, such as French, trying to stir up trouble.

Just then Kari walked into the room talking animatedly to Dick Gates, the tall, shy Earther botanist. When she saw us, she turned to him with a quick word and came over to our table. Dick retreated to the bar.

"Hello, fellows, what's happening?" She was cheerful.

The other three greeted her in kind. She turned to me. "And how's our erstwhile captain?"

"In fair shape," I replied. "But I don't think we can say the same for poor Dick, over there. You seemed to have left him in the lurch."

She showed a hurt look for a microsecond, then came back breezily: "Oh, that's all right. We weren't really a date. He just met me in the hallway and we walked in together."

"Well," I said, "I'm not sure he shares your opinion.

Looks like he just lost his last friend. You ought to at least go have a drink with him."

She looked at me long and hard. "Very well." She swept the table with her gaze. "Excuse me, gentlemen," then looked into my eyes again. "Goodbye, Captain White-dimple." Then she turned on her heel and headed toward the bar.

I found confused looks on the faces of Carl and Pete, but Junior was downright acid: "Dimp, what the hell you got against that woman?"

"Absolutely nothing," I answered truthfully.

He snorted, got up, walked over to where she was now drinking with Gates, and joined their conversation. I didn't miss the hurt look in his eyes.

I wasn't worried about Junior's friendship; that was too close to be broken so easily. But I wondered about that obvious hurt he'd taken. It couldn't have been because Kari was his lover. Junior had disabused me of that notion one acerbic evening just after the voyage started. After I'd asked an artless question, he'd informed me bluntly that he had no romantic interest in Kari, never had, and that she'd never been interested in him except as a friend—and what the hell had I been thinking of, anyway?

I finally decided that it was because he thought I'd slighted a good friend. I had tried to be as warm as I could early in the voyage, while still keeping the captain's distance. Then the interview with Chin had thrown cold water on me. If he was of the opinion that I had a crush on Kari, then so might others of the crew. I didn't dare let anything like that develop; if it did, I was sure to lose some of my tenuous authority. So from then on, I'd tried to keep my distance. It was hard. Many times I'd caught myself thinking of her when I was alone in my cabin. Then I'd kick myself as a horny fool—I hated to have to classify myself with all the other drooling men in her life.

Well, this incident was apparently the last straw of some kind. Somehow, I was sure that for the rest of the voyage, she'd cut me cold. Perhaps it was for the better; in fact, I was certain of it. But somehow, that didn't help take away the empty feeling I had in the pit of my stomach.

Later that night, Junior sought me out after I'd retired to my cabin—something he did very rarely.

"What the hell's gotten into you, Dimp? The last few months, you've been going out of your way to be cool to Kari. And tonight you put her down so bad she might never speak to you again."

"Really?" I said. "I didn't think it was all that big a deal."

He snorted with disgust. "Come on. What's happening? I've never seen you act like this before. I know she's never done anything to hurt *you*."

So I told him about my need to keep above familiarity and favoritism with the crew, the interview with Chin, and my fears about it, my worries about the tenuous thread of discipline.

"Hmmp," he said, after I'd poured it all out. "Leadership is out of my league; you've got to do what you think best." He looked me in the eye. "Have you told Kari about any of this?"

"No," I admitted.

"Well, why not? It sure as hell would make things easier on the woman."

"It's kind of a catch-22," I answered. "I don't dare see her alone to tell her. That would make the situation even worse."

"Rot. It would only take a minute or two; you could make it look completely casual."

"Well, I, I'm afraid that somehow it might bring us closer together," I said in a rush, then finished lamely, "I know it sounds crazy."

He looked at me for a long second, then asked: "Admiral, are you in love with Kari? Was our shifty Mr. Chin right?"

I sat and looked down at the floor. "I don't know. Maybe."

"Well," he said. "Looks like you're saddling yourself with all kinds of problems that're out of my pay grade." He reached up and scratched an ear. "But it seems to me that if you're in love, you're going about it the damnedest way I ever heard of. . . ."

* * *

"Okay, talk to it."

Sean Davidson and I were down in the maintenance level, below the living quarters. There were only 180 centimeters between the deck and the overhead here, and we were both stooping slightly. I'd received a first-level warning from the control room computer that there was an incipient failure in the number three carbon dioxide removal system. I'd gone after Sean without paging him, found him in the gym, and told him about it. He looked concerned, then said we should go down and ask the local expert system what was wrong with it.

"Activating."

He punched keys on the console in front of us. Down here it was too noisy for voice recognition—besides, it had saved money to exclude it from the local troubleshooters. The screen came to life, showing a diagram of the two-bed molecular sieve. A portion of the diagram was illuminated in red, with the letters "IFD" flashing beside it.

"It's showing the number one bed heater," he said. "It won't localize it any further than that. Might have a hot spot in the heating element." He frowned. "Highly unusual."

I thought about it for a minute. We had four mole sieve units on line. Any three could handle the CO_2 load without degrading air quality, as long as the crew was not overly active. There were three backups, already plumbed into the system and ready to be activated at any time. There was also a six-month emergency supply of $LiOH$, but I didn't want to think about that right away.

"If we warm up one of the backup units and put it on line, how soon can you have this one apart and diagnosed?"

"By tomorrow afternoon, at the latest. Tonight, if you let Anna-Marie help me." Anna-Marie Smith was Sean's star pupil in ECLS. She also tended to talk freely.

I shook my head. "I'd rather keep this among just you and the officers for now. If we find out that it's serious, then it's time to talk to the crew, but as far as we know now, it's just a single anomaly."

He nodded. "I understand, sir."

He came into my office late the next morning holding up a small loop of metal. It was about the size of a long pencil and had been bent into a "U" with both ends attached to a small flat plate.

"Here it is, Captain. The simplest low-tech item in the whole damn subsystem. A good old-fashioned Calrod heating element. The ceramic covering's intact. Only way I could tell it was bad was by replacing it with a spare; then the IFD indication went away when I put the sieve back on line."

I took my mind back a year and a half. "Don't these heaters have a mean-time-between-failure rating of 50 years?"

"Yes, sir," he nodded. "In fact, the real MTBF is probably twice that, but 50 is the highest number we're allowed to enter in the computer." He frowned. "As far as I know, only two things can go wrong with one of these. First, you might accidentally crack the ceramic covering, in which case, you'd eventually get a spectacular short. That's not the problem here. Second, you could get a spot of high resistance in the NiChrome heating wire underneath. That's still a common problem on Earth, where they don't get as good an alloy mixing control as we do in zero G."

I took the element and looked it over. "What are the chances that this is an isolated event?"

"I'd say pretty good, sir," he shrugged. "The heating element's made from off-the-shelf stock down in the MMF. We've never had any problem with the stuff."

I activated my line to Ethel Erickson's quarters, hoping she was in and that I wouldn't have to page her.

"This is Ethel."

"Ethel, this is the captain. Could you come up to my office for a minute, please?"

"Be right there, boss."

I turned back to Davidson. "Sean, for the life of me, I can't remember: how many spare heating elements did we stock?"

"Four."

I did some quick arithmetic in my head. With only eight months down and sixteen to go, I didn't particularly care for the answer.

"Do we have any way to manufacture or jury-rig any more of these things?"

"I'm afraid not, sir. They were way down on the criticality list because of their inherent reliability. In fact, we're damned lucky to have four spares."

"Damn. Well, let's wait to hear what Ethel says."

"Did I hear my name being called in vain?" Erickson said, coming through the door.

I explained the situation. If anyone on board could give me an off-the-cuff answer, it was Ethel. She'd spent forty-seven years on Earth becoming a top materials and processes engineer, then a manufacturing expert, before moving to the Colonies in 2080. Since then, she'd worked her way up to the top of the SpaceHome ladder in the Microgravity Manufacturing Facility. I looked hopefully at her wrinkled face.

But she frowned and said: "That shouldn't have happened." Then she thought about it for ten more seconds while the frown deepened.

"Can I use your 'puter for a second?"

"Sure." I got up from my desk and waved her into my seat. "Be my guest."

She sat down. "Sean, where d'you keep the pedigree for the mole sieve subsystems?"

"Directory ECLS, sub MOLE, file PED."

She punched the keys and played with the mouse. It didn't seem to bother her that she was using my console and couldn't voice activate it. In a couple of seconds she was scanning a spreadsheet on the screen.

"Jesus."

She moved the cursor to a second place, then swore again. Then to a third. She mumbled under her breath.

"What did you say, Ethel?"

"I said I'm gonna kill somebody! Every damn Calrod we got for the mole sieves was made with a batch of NiChrome that was mixed and extruded on the graveyard shift on July 15, 2095."

"Isn't that rather common, that they'd make our special order out of the same batch?" I asked.

"Yeah, but not that batch! It should have been remelted and remixed. . . ."

Seems that July 14 being Bastille Day, a group of eight people of French origin had celebrated a bit too much for

their better senses. At three o'clock in the morning they
decided to have a two-kilometer "tube race," and so had
opened all of the vibration-damping doors in the umbilical
connecting the MMF with the Hub. After which, they had
had their merry chase, bumping the walls and partitions
with the robust painlessness of their analgesic condition.

"Those yahoos got put on half-pay for three months to
pay for damages," she finished, "and we had to condemn
everything that was in process on that shift. Gravity waves
you wouldn't believe—some of them peaked at a hundredth G!"

She waved disgustedly at the screen. "And now we've
got an old ghost on board. I'll bet it was that damned Gus
Gooch. NiChrome isn't on the critical list, and he probably sneaked that batch of wire off and hid it away so he
could use it later. That asshole'd sell his own children to
increase his productivity rating. I'm gonna kill him!"

"He'll be long dead by the time we get back," I said.
"But right now it's that ghost we've got to worry about.
What're the chances that the rest of the heaters will hold
up?"

"Close to zero," she said, dashing my hopes. "You'll
probably find hot spots all through 'em. You'd've done
better to buy a batch from Earth."

"Can you take a wag at the MTBF, Ethel?" asked Sean.

"Nine, ten months, maybe," she replied. "But since
you've had only one failure, your guess is as good as mine.
All I can tell you for sure is that it's bloody likely that
that," she pointed at the element, "won't be your only
failure."

"Okay, thanks, Ethel," I said. "And I'd appreciate it if
you'd keep quiet about this until I break it to the crew."

"Sure thing, Boss." She left.

Sean looked at me as he was going out the door.

"You going to tell the crew right away, Captain? After all,
it's still only a single event, and we might luck out."

"Maybe, but we both doubt it. And the crew has a right
to know. I'm also putting it into the captain's log and the
open log. This is an annoyance, certainly, but not a danger. My main hope in this thing is not to have to use the
lithium hydroxide, because that's our second-to-last backup."

*   *   *

". . . come to ask you on behalf of the crew to throw the abort switch and take us back home. We're only nine months into the voyage as yet, and Dr. Vance says that our current time compression is only two to one, so if we turn back now, we'll experience very little time differential when we return."

Jason French had made an appointment and was now spending my time.

In my initial interview with him, I'd forced some things out which I'm sure he didn't want to divulge. His dossier also had a special entry by Ogumi that was most enlightening. As far as I knew, he was the only person who hadn't really wanted to be on this voyage in the first place.

French was medium height and medium overweight. For years, he'd been the one minion of Ogumi disliked by nearly everyone. He had raised false bonhomie to a fine art, and fooled almost nobody with it. He was also a master of innuendo. Ogumi used him for necessary hatchet work that would make other people morally squeamish. He in turn used Ogumi to climb the power ladder. All even. His ultimate goal was a seat on the SpaceHome Corporation Board of Directors.

When Earth forced on Ogumi the requirement to place a "political observer" aboard *High Boy*, the president called French into his office and used him for the last time. Gave him two choices: take the job, and have a promised seat on the board of directors when he returned, or refuse the job, and find honest work somewhere else in the Colonies or on Earth. Thus French had come—apparently eager, but emotionally reluctant.

He'd never liked me—partly because Ogumi didn't like me, and partly because I often bucked Ogumi and got away with it. But Ogumi at least respected my abilities; I do not believe that French ever did.

Now the man had been agitating ineffectively for months to get crew support for activating the abort sequence. It was the only way he knew to fulfill his end of the contract and still go back to a familiar world.

"Just which members of the crew do you speak for, Mr.

French? And what are your reasons for wanting to abort a mission we've worked so hard to initiate?"

"Why? Because this whole voyage is ridiculous in the first place. It will bring no benefits to our current society, or even to our immediate descendants—only our many-times-great-grandchildren, if at all. And besides, we now have serious problems with our life support system. We should turn back while we still have adequate reserves."

"Mr. French, the crew has discussed the problem with the molecular sieve at some length. It is an annoyance, certainly, but the situation is nowhere near dangerous. There are many options open to us. We can almost certainly finish the final fifteen months without even touching the reserves the Hexies have provided us."

"And that's another thing," he said agitatedly. "How do we know there even *are* any reserves. And for that matter, how do we even know the trip will be over in fifteen months? We really don't know the Hexies' intentions at all."

"I think there are many more reasons to believe the Hexies than to disbelieve them, Mr. French. But in any case, we all came along on this voyage with our eyes open, and nothing has happened to alter our views."

"Yes, but I speak for a large contingent of the crew, who think it's better, in view of the circumstances, to hit the emergency abort and go back home. We can say that we gave it a go, but trouble with the life support system forced us back."

"Mr. French," I said sternly, "that's the second time you've said that you speak for the crew. I would like to know the exact nature of your representation. Just who on the crew do you speak for?"

"A sizable contingent. They do not wish to be named, but want their voices heard anyway."

"In that case, Mr. French, you are officially representing only yourself. Nevertheless, your voice has been heard. This conversation has been recorded into the captain's log, and will also be entered in the open log if you so wish. I will take your request under consideration. If I decide to act positively upon it, I will announce that decision to the assembled crew. Good day, sir."

"Damnit, Whitedimple, you can't just dismiss me like that! I want an answer and I want it now!"

"Mr. French," I said coldly, "for the remainder of this voyage, you will address me as 'captain' or 'sir.' If you need an immediate answer, I will give it to you: request denied. If you wish to make further comments, do so in the open log. I am required by policy to read that file daily, and will duly note any further real evidence you put forth. Now leave this office at once."

He left. I was not proud of browbeating French, but I had to make him understand that he would never be allowed to show me open disrespect. Then a thought struck me. I called Petrov's quarters.

"First officer."

"George, would you please get with George Reid and rig a locked cover for the mission abort switch over the Hexie console? Set it to open only with two keys used simultaneously. Make just three keys, one for each officer."

"Right away, Captain."

"What do you make of this, Junior? The nav system accelerometer has been drifting downward for the past several months." I indicated the acceleration readout, which now stood just barely above 8.8 meters per second squared.

"Not surprised, Admiral. That's an off-the-shelf laser gyroscope system. Cheap and effective—but only inside the calibration window, which is forty-five days." He pulled at his nose. "Normal use, the nav computer software does an automatic recalibration during state vector updates. No sweat; only one trip in a thousand accelerates longer than forty-five days." He grinned. "And this is the one."

"But why would it be off that much?"

"Dimp, do you know anything about the accelerometer algorithm?"

I admitted ignorance.

"Hmm, still a few holes in your education. Well, basically, it works like this: within the calibration period, this little puppy," he hooked a thumb at the readout, "stays good to seven or eight significant figures. After that, all bets are off. Which direction it heads in depends on the residuals left over from the last update, but once it starts going, it goes fast. And the longer it goes without calibration, the worse it gets."

"Do they ever stay accurate longer than forty-five days?"

"Sure. Sometimes they can go for years and keep good to three, four significant figures. On the other hand, they might go totally whacko a few weeks after the forty-five days are up. It's all in the residuals, Admiral."

"Well, why do I feel lighter?"

He cackled. "Hell, Admiral, if I were looking at that readout every day, I'd start to feel lighter, too. C'mon, let's go see Josh to ease your brain."

Joshua Vance was one of Earth's large crop of premiere theoretical physicists. He was short, heavyset, and completely above any possible Earth-SpaceHome conflict. To him, data were data, and he didn't care where they came from. Now in his mid-fifties, he'd been married twice—both times to physicists. Divorces had followed when his mates had discovered that he loved his craft more than them. He had plenty of brains. He could talk shop with Dunsworth, Dinsworth, Kitigawa—but he was perfectly content with a pencil and paper.

"Captain! Badille!" He greeted us ebulliently, rising from a large tablet on his desk covered with incomprehensible integrals, curls, dels, and matrices. "What a pleasant surprise. What can I do for you?"

"We just came down to find out where you've got us," I said.

"When, you mean," he smiled. "We're almost eleven months on the road now, and the calculations are beginning to differ significantly from special relativity. But," he stuck a forefinger up into the air, then pointed it dramatically at his desk console, "as near as this stupid little computer and I can figure, we will reach a three-to-one time compression day after tomorrow, ship's time. Then, for the next two months or so—ship's time—during maximum velocity, turnaround, and beginning of deceleration, we will be in a realm most difficult to characterize without external measurements. Pity. I'm trying to make do with pencil and paper," he waved deprecatingly at the Greek-filled tablet, "but it's a poor substitute for red-shift observations."

Junior wandered to his desk and casually looked over the physicist's scribblings.

"What figure are you using for acceleration?" I asked.

"The one we started out with, of course," he said. "One point oh-two-three-oh-oh-seven standard G. One thousand three point two-two-seven-one-six centimeters per second squared."

"I was wondering," I continued, "because, according to the navigation computer accelerometer, we're down to about point nine G."

"No," he shook his head. "That calibration is absolutely no good any more—hasn't been for months. Wouldn't dream of using it. Besides," he added, "I don't think even the Hexies would program this vessel to change accelerations in mid-flight. The relativistic navigation would simply be too difficult."

"Hey, Josh," said Junior, "what are you doing with a negative sign in front of your partial of epsilon here?"

The chubby physicist peered at the spot on the tablet to which Junior was pointing. "Why, I discussed that with Talmidge before leaving Earth. He was of the opinion, and I agreed, that it was appropriate to use the negative when applying it to this matrix expression at tau below point one. It's an approximation only, of course. Becomes important only in the last hour or so before turnaround."

"Dammit, Josh, you expand that tensor that way, and you're going to pick up several hundred extra years of dilation during turnaround. Here, let me show you. . . ."

I quietly slipped out of the room.

As I was making my way from Vance's quarters back to the control room, the door to Chin Wu Lin's apartment opened and he beckoned me inside. I raised my eyebrows and stepped in.

"Forgive me for asking you in here so casually, Captain, but I did not wish to call attention to myself with a formal interview."

"That's perfectly all right, Mr. Chin." I looked with interest at the layout of his quarters. It was decorated in traditional Chinese, as much as possible with the limited weight allowance given each crew member. The one exception was a "crazy clock" of the kind popular in the last two decades of the century. Five or six steel pellets at regular intervals were conveyed up to the top of a drop, from whence they rolled down inclines, through tubes and channels, and eventually struck an escapement that marked a unit of time. The instrument was totally out of keeping with the rest of the decor.

"Does my clock interest you, Captain? It was given to me by the Society of the Preservation of Space for Earth, as one of the three crew members who most closely adhere to the ideals of the Society. The other two recipients, naturally, were Messrs. Petrov and Dunsworth."

As I watched the mechanism, fascinated, he waved a deprecatory hand. "I display it every once in a while, to remind myself of the feeblemindedness of mankind. It was a totally useless gesture. The very principles on which the Society thrives will probably not even be remembered by the time we get back. Even now it keeps time which has no relevance to that passing on the planet of its construction. I believe Mr. Petrov and Mr. Dunsworth keep theirs hidden away in their lockers. They do not appreciate the humor of the situation.

"But," he continued in a different tone of voice, "in a way, it is about time that I wish to speak to you briefly. As the time for turnover draws closer, my erstwhile colleague, Mr. French, seems to become more and more agitated."

"I have noticed that, Mr. Chin. But I do not think he has been very effective in enlisting the crew to his point of view."

"That is true," the old man said. "But now I believe he may become more than just a nuisance. I do not think he is entirely stable." He raised a hand before I could answer. "I hesitated quite some time before approaching you. I feared that his official position in opposition to myself would tend to cast doubt on any observations I might make. Now, however, I am sufficiently concerned to bring it to your attention, to take whatever measures you think appropriate."

"Thank you, Mr. Chin," I said.

"Thank you, Captain, for listening."

When I got back to my own quarters, I sat down on my

bed and thought for a minute. The fact that Chin had
volunteered that information was highly telling. His instinct for self-preservation was honed by a seventy-year
background of survival and intrigue.

I unlocked my private locker and fished out something
that I had only reluctantly agreed to carry along: a hand-
gun. It was the only one aboard; all luggage and supplies
had been inspected carefully to ensure that. I loaded it
with the magazine of five-mm low-velocity shells. They
would not be lethal unless they hit a vital organ, but I'd
been assured they packed a nasty wallop. I hated guns,
but had practiced with it dutifully, reminding myself that
it was just another piece of insurance.

I put the safety on, threw the thing on my desk, and
buzzed Petrov and Prentiss for a conference call.

"Gentlemen, I have reason to believe that Mr. French
might try to cause some devilment before turnaround. I
would like you to keep as close an eye on him as possible
without being obvious about it. I would also like for each
of you to auto-patch the 'hatch open' indicator into your
quarters as an alarm. If someone goes into the Hexie hold,
I want at least one of us to be along. Any questions?"

"No, sir."

"Yes, sir." That was Prentiss. "Why don't we just lock
him up until turnaround? God knows he's given us enough
excuse. The stuff he's been spreading around would be
tantamount to treason in a military ship."

"I understand that, Mike. But unfortunately, this is not
a military command. The only real authority we officers
enjoy is bestowed on us by the crew. The crew members
are largely academic; they're used to hearing dissenting
opinions. To them, French may be annoying—even silly—
but not unusually aberrant. So if we take the easy way out
and restrain him forcefully, we might do more harm than
good, by setting ourselves up as a repressive dictatorial
regime. So let's do it my way. But be on the alert for the
next six weeks."

"I understand, sir."

After signing them off, I sat and thought. Could I do
anything else? Not really. What I'd told Mike was the
truth. I stood up and put the gun into one of my pants

pockets. It made a godawful bulge. I snorted and threw it into the top drawer of my dresser. Chin or no Chin, I wasn't going to panic the crew by starting to tote a sidearm.

"Ladies and gentlemen, I've called this meeting to update you on the current situation with the ECLS." I smiled confidently and kept my voice firm. A second heating element had failed now, and a third had just shown up as an IFD item, but we were nowhere near a panic situation. I was choosing my words carefully to make sure the crew understood that. Nevertheless, I did not want to delay Davidson's work in rigging an LiOH scrubber. He might very well have developmental problems, and need the extra time to get it right.

"—and to let you know about that Godawful racket coming from the machine shop today. I don't mean the pounding on metal; I'm referring to Mr. Davidson's habit of swearing as he works."

Dramatic pause for nervous chuckles. I caught Junior's face near the back of the auditorium; he rolled his eyes with a disgusted look. French was also in the rear, in the other corner.

As French moved his head slightly, the overhead lights reflected off a patina of sweat on his forehead. I didn't think about it consciously at the time; but the auditorium was distinctly cool, and I remember having a sudden pang of uneasiness. However, the chuckles were dying down and I had to continue:

"In the nine weeks since we last discussed this annoying problem, we've put two of our four spare heating elements into the on-line mole sieve units. The other two will probably have to be installed within the next couple of months.

"So the arithmetic tells us this: we'll probably be switching over to the three backup units before the trip ends. And there is some chance that we'll be running on just those when we arrive in the Hexie home system. Those three can be run at a slightly inefficient overload and easily carry the whole ship for the little time remaining until we reach the Hexie world. We can finish the voyage without touching our secondary lithium hydroxide backup supply. If we do have to dip into it, we have a four-month reserve without drawing on our final backup, which is another four-month supply of oxygen and nitrogen provided by the Hexies."

I smiled confidently. "But Mr. Davidson is building us a third insurance policy. He is constructing a pressurized high-temperature oven assembly to bake out the LiOH. That way, if we need to, we can use the LiOH cannisters indefinitely.

"We are going to give it a trial run this week. Day after tomorrow we will put an LiOH cannister in the ECLS system ducting and leave it until it's saturated with CO_2 —that'll take about eight hours. Then that night, we'll bake it out. This will cause you some inconvenience, I'm afraid: your evening power budgets will be cut by 30 percent, to 140 watts.

"The reason for conducting the trial so long before any possible need is to give us plenty of developmental lead time. Even Sean's design may have a few bugs that need to be worked—"

"This is outrageous!" French suddenly yelled from the back of the theater.

I was stunned for a second, then realized that French must have been working himself into a fever pitch the whole time I'd been talking.

"What is outrageous, Mr. French?" I said calmly and firmly.

"You've been talking about all these so-called backups without once mentioning the most sensible option we have—aborting this mission. We've got to turn back while we still have air to breathe!"

I started to make a sharp reply, then noticed something that checked my resolve: among the embarrassed faces of the crew, there were some who showed what seemed to be genuine concern. French might have touched subconscious claustrophobic fears with his remark about having air to breathe. I had to put those fears to bed once and for all.

"Mr. Davidson, would you please stand up and give us your honest estimate of the danger we're in from the current situation?"

"Begging your pardon, Captain," the young man said, rising, "but 'danger' is much too strong a word. What we have here is nothing more than a mild annoyance. We can run indefinitely with the current situation; anybody who's talked to me in the past couple of months knows that. Hell, even the three backup scenarios we've got aren't the end of the line. If I had to, I could make activated charcoal and rig filters from the materials and chemicals we have in the supply rooms. I stocked that stuff on your orders when we were outfitting the ship, sir."

He shook his head. "The only danger in this situation is that with all the extra work I'm putting in, I may flunk Dr. Vance's theoretical physics class!"

I thanked him with relief, as most of the crew chuckled. But French cut it short:

"That's garbage! Davidson is nothing but a mouthpiece of the captain. We can't trust his words any more than we can trust the Hexies to keep their promises! If we turn back now, it will cost us only a little time; the solar system will be the same as when we left it. But in two or three weeks, it will be too late! I demand that we take a vote, Captain!"

This was getting out of hand. I was about to order Petrov to escort the man to his quarters—then I noticed that one or two of the concerned looks had come back. Agitated or not, French still knew what emotional buttons to press for maximum effect. I had to defeat him on his own ground, to show him that the crew was not with him. But at the same time, I had to show the crew that only the captain was in control of the ship. This was my first real test in the job.

"Mr. French," I said coldly and clearly, "please take notice that decisions on this vessel are not made by vote. You," I swept the whole crew with my eyes, "are all experts in your respective disciplines. And so am I. My primary discipline is the functioning and safety of this ship. It is my job, and my job alone, to assess the situation and decide on the best course of action. To take a vote on such an action would be exactly analogous to taking a vote on where to drill an oil well, rather than letting Dr. Zyyad examine the geologic data and make a determination."

I let my eyes lock back on French's for a moment. "Therefore, Mr. French, we are under no parliamentary rules here. Your motion is meaningless, and will not be acted upon. What will happen is that, if you continue your current behavior, you will be escorted to your quarters and detained there until this assembly is over."

I returned my gaze to the general audience. "Now you have heard Mr. Davidson's assurances that there is no real danger. I would like to add this: if I believed that there *were* a danger, I would still not consider turning back. The reason is quite simple, and you are all aware of it: for decisions in which trip time remaining is a critical factor, we really passed the halfway point when we were five and a half months onboard the Hexie ship. At that time, we were eighteen and a half months from arrival at the Hexie world, and the same time from arrival back in Earth orbit if we hit the abort switches.

"But at this point in time, there is no doubt about the decision to proceed. We are only twelve and a half months from the Hexie world—but thirty-six and a half from home.

"And if any of you are apprehensive about whether or not the turnaround will come as scheduled two weeks from now—well, I'm sure you're not alone. But the Hexies have a perfect track record so far, and I don't have any reason to think we'll get any surprises." I smiled. "So for the next two weeks—"

"Damn you, Whitedimple! You and your smooth talk! You're nothing but a madman, and you're talking everybody else into going your madman way! You're just making us go on so you can stay on your power trip! You schemed for years to get this job, and now you're bound and determined to keep it, even if it kills us! But I know something you don't: every one of these crew members in his secret heart, wants to turn back before it's too late! And I'm going to make it happen! I'm going out of this ship, over to the Hexie console, and flip that abort switch. And I don't—"

"Be quiet, Mr. French!" I motioned to Prentiss, who was standing to one side of the seated audience, halfway to the back of the theater, on the opposite side from French. "Mike, would you please escort Mr. French to his—"

"You'll do nothing of the sort!" French shouted. And then, God help me, he pulled a gun. My gun. Left lying in a dresser drawer in a room that was never locked because of the Careless Captain's open door policy. "Stay where you are, Prentiss! I mean to go out and throw that switch, and anybody who tries to stop me will get shot!"

"Better do as he says, Mike," I said. "I think Mr. French is quite serious." Prentiss stopped before he got to the back row.

As I talked, I was stepping off the stage and starting slowly down the aisle on the left side of the crew, toward French. I was very bitter with myself. I'd been criminally negligent in not keeping the gun locked up after Chin's warning. Now somebody might pay for that carelessness. We all might pay. No telling what French would do when he got out to the Hexie console and found the abort switch sealed and locked.

I was scared for myself, and for everybody. I remembered to keep at such an angle to French that no one else was in his line of fire. I swallowed dry spit. French, wild-eyed, was also backing, but more slowly than I was advancing.

Out of the corner of my eye to the right, I glanced at Junior, who was starting to get up. He raised his eyebrows minutely at me. I shook my head just as minutely. Then he shook his own, and continued to get up. He slowly started advancing toward French from the other side, across the back of the small theater.

French noticed the movement, and swung the gun furiously toward Junior. "Stand off, Badille!" he said. "You're such good buddies with the captain, you'll join him in hell if you come any closer!"

In the meantime, I'd advanced to within three meters of the sweating French. He swung back toward me and said viciously: "Both of you, stop right there. If either one of you moves again, so help me I'll shoot! I mean it!"

"Stop, Junior," I said quietly. "This man is truly dangerous!"

Junior's voice cracked with fear, but the tone was belligerent: "To hell with that, Admiral. We're close enough so there's no way he can get both of us. Give it up, French!"

French wheeled murderously on the runt, raising the pistol; I knew he was going to shoot. I yelled and started toward him. He began to turn back toward me, pushing the gun away from his body, and I knew that in a fraction of a second, he'd be squeezing the trigger in my direction. I did what I could—dove in a bellyflop toward his feet. In the middle of executing it, I felt a searing burn on the tip of my ear, felt a shock in my buttocks, and simultaneously heard the startlingly loud report of the gun.

Then I struck his legs. The pistol went off again, but the shot must have gone wild; French was on his way down by then. Junior was there, grabbing at the gun, wrenching it from the bigger man's grasp. Then, seemingly without time elapsing, several of the crew members were on the pile, grabbing French's arms and holding him down. The man was struggling and shouting: "Let go! I want to go home! Let me go!"

I was still on my stomach. I twisted toward the main body of the theater, looking for the doctor. He was sitting four seats away, wide-eyed and frozen with terror. "Doctor Korliss!" I tried to speak over the hubbub and French's yelling. "DOCTOR KORLISS!!"

He came to life and looked at me, startled.

"Go get your bag, and bring it in here—quickly!" I said. "Get a sedative into that man right away!" He nodded, arose, and hastened toward his office.

Shouting at Korliss seemed to sap what strength I had; I wondered if I was in shock myself. I felt I had to do something about the confusion in the theater. There were people milling around, and at least three heated conversations taking place; in the background I heard someone crying. Still lying on the floor without the will to get up, I twisted around again. Several people were heading for me, concerned looks on their faces; they seemed to be moving in slow-motion fog. Kari Nunguesser was one of them; but she was intercepted by Korliss, who had returned with his bag. The doctor grabbed her arm, spoke urgent directions into her ear, and pulled her toward the captive French, who was sobbing and still struggling. Then they were blocked from my view by the legs of the people moving in to comfort me.

And then all of a sudden, the fog went away, life speeded back up to normal, and Junior was squatting down beside me holding out a wad of tissue. There were others in a ring around me, walling off most of the noise and confusion; but Junior was the one who counted.

"Here you go, Admiral. Looks like your ear is trying to set the three-minute leak record. Red really isn't your color."

I started to sit up, then winced and stayed on my stomach.

"Don't look now, hero, but that nasty little slug found a resting place farther down on my anatomy."

He looked at my buttocks, then chuckled nastily. "Well, then, Captain. I always did think you were a mite lazy. Do you good to spend a couple of weeks on your feet."

Then I remembered what a chance he'd taken, and got angry. "Damnit, Junior, I told you not to make a move back there. That guy was serious. The officers could have figured something to do when French got outside the ship."

The gnome was the very model of contrition: "That's a bunch of crap, Dimp. French was off his whack. He was bound and determined to shoot somebody or something; you saw that look in his eye as well as I did. When he found that lockbox on the abort switch, he'd have tried to shoot it off. He might even have put a pellet into the Hexie console—then we'd really have been in a fix."

He squinted into my eye. "You knew it, too. There was no way you were going to let him out of *High Boy* without a showdown. So you puffed out your chest and tried to be a one-man hero squad." He reached out and dabbed at the blood slowly trickling down the back of my neck.

"Besides," he added, "I seem to recall the last time you risked your hide by yourself. Told you then you wouldn't go it alone again."

He was looking so defensive and out of character that I had to laugh—then wince because it moved the wrong muscles.

"Wonder Boy," I said, "sometimes you're too smart for your own good. There's something you may not realize: your hide is a hell of a lot more valuable to this expedition than mine. As a scientist, I'm just a hack, but with all the stuff you've got tucked in that oversized brain, you're our best chance to put two and two together and come up with something useful on this trip—especially if the Hexies decide to keep their toys for themselves. So get this through your head: keep yourself intact until we get back to Earth orbit, and you can dump your brains into whatever godawful machines they have by then. There are four of us who can fly this boat, but you are unique."

Junior snorted. "That's cowshit, Admiral. And the hell of it is, you don't even know it. Isn't anybody more important onboard than you. Without you in control of this shindig, chances are four to one against getting back. But with the Admiral in charge, we got at least fifty-fifty. I've been talking with people."

I looked in his eyes and shook my head. He was serious. "Whatever you've been smoking, Junior, has turned your brain to Jello." Then I winced again, and looked around for Korliss. He was just finishing up with French. Petrov and Prentiss were leading the defeated maniac, dopey and staggering, toward the exit.

Korliss bustled over without being asked. He examined me briefly. "We've got to remove a bullet from your gluteus, Captain," he said. "I'll go prepare the operatory, and see you there shortly. Don't try to walk unassisted; you need to keep weight off your left leg. Get two people to lean on." He hurried off.

Then I was being helped up and held up by Edward Allison-White and George Reid. Almost the entire crew was still clustered around, looking on with concern. Petrov and Prentiss were gone; I was the only officer present. I realized then that I couldn't just leave them cold.

"The unfortunate Mr. French," I said to the group, "provided us with a valuable—and, thank God, relatively inexpensive—lesson this afternoon. His fears were no different than the ones we all have in common; his only failing was that he didn't have the motivation or discipline to keep them under control. He wasn't really afraid of an ECLS breakdown—he was afraid of the unknown."

I smiled. "Aren't we all. Perhaps he'll recover when he experiences turnaround with the rest of us. I ask you to

give him every chance. He is, and will remain, a member
of the expedition."

Exit.

My mind raced during the painful walk to Korliss's
sanctum. I had had half a mind to tell the crew gently that
I was going to make a search of the ship for possible
weapons, but I left the order unspoken. I didn't want
anyone to think that the captain was also panicking. If
flipship didn't occur, as advertised, within three weeks,
then it would be time to think of such things.

Before I knew it, I was lying face down on the table in
the small operatory run by Korliss, and he was pushing a
needle into a vein at my wrist. Then I got tired of thinking
and went to sleep.

Thirteen days later, the Hexie vessel stopped accelerating for ten and a half hours, turned over, and began
blasting back. There was a big blow-out that night. I
attended standing.

Chapter 11

In retrospect, perhaps our biggest mistake—or piece of bad luck—was in not having a crackerjack quantum mechanician on the expeditionary crew. I know somewhat of the discipline, as all cosmologists must, but I was out of my league. The Hexies have a depth which has resulted in an entire transportation technology based on localized abrogation of the laws of statistical quantum mechanics. Their maturity can be inferred from a conversation I had with Thiestree . . . finally explained to him the old parable of Schroedinger's Cat, because it is still a valid illustration of our philosophy and leads conveniently to the many-worlds hypothesis of quantum mechanics. His reaction was: "So you have developed an entire physics based on the premise that a sentient observer is required to collapse a wave function? How delightfully egotistical! How amusing!"

—Dinsworth: Hexie White Papers

"Well I think you should have the whole crew lined up facing the Hexies when they come aboard. Then, as they approach, you move out from the line, float forward ten paces, raise your right hand, and say 'HOW.'"

It was Saturday night, Ethanol Ethel's was open for business, and the feeling was high. We were only an estimated three weeks from the time when the Hexie ship would arrive at its home.

I took a sip of raspberry cooler (I was actually beginning to like the stuff) and smiled at Michele Kimberly. "Somehow, I can't see myself in the role."

"What a shame, Captain," she said. "That greeting has a simple dignity which is really quite effective."

Michele's outgoing, friendly manner would be a surprise to her former colleagues on Earth. She was in her mid-forties, with sandy hair and a sprinkling of freckles. She was the leading American cultural anthropologist, and one of the top ten in the world. But she had a reputation for hard aloofness in her social and professional life. The only time she ever seemed to unbend was when she was living with the natives on a field study; then she behaved as they behaved. Either she'd changed considerably in the past two years onboard, or she was engaged in a field study of the entire crew. I suspected the latter, but was grateful either way.

We were sitting at the "Captain's Table." Funny how traditions get started. The captain's table was wherever I chose to sit during the Saturday night party. I had started early in the trip by choosing to sit with someone different every week, and now the habit was so thoroughly ensconced it had become an unspoken law of the ship. If I got to the bar early and took a vacant table, I was inevitably joined by other people—but never anyone who'd sat with me in the past two or three weeks. The exception to this rule was Junior, who sat with me about three times out of four. I was grateful that the crew accepted this without rancor—especially since most of them had lost bets of one kind or another to the gnome.

Everyone had been to the captain's table several times during this second year of the voyage—even Jason French, who had become resigned to the trip and once again avid in his role for SpaceHome. Everyone, that is, except Kari Nunguesser. She had not spoken to me voluntarily for many months—since well before turnaround. The crew ignored the situation, and I had become hardened to it—except for a feeling of emptiness that once in a while started in my abdomen and took over my whole insides.

I still believed that it was for the best that I had alienated her, but over the last year's time, it had seemed to make less and less difference. The crew had come to accept ship's discipline as a matter of course. Several times, I had started to make my way over to sit at her table, but something had always stopped me—maybe the ghost of a habit; maybe because I didn't know what to say.

". . . so how *are* you planning to do it, Captain?"

Hastily, I came back to the present and replayed the last few seconds of dialogue in my mind. "Well, right now, my thinking is to meet them as a committee of three: Edward, Grace, and myself. There's no real reason for me to be along except that rank hath its privilege, and I damn well mean to exercise it."

Michele furrowed her eyebrows for a moment. "Gifts," she said. "You ought to think about presenting token gifts at that first encounter. That's almost a universal formal contact ritual among human tribes, and one that's sure to . . ."

I let my gaze wander to the table on our right, where Kari was talking to Michael Prentiss and Anna-Marie Smith. Michael and Anna had been a twosome for over six months; now I wondered idly if it would become permanent when we got back home. Then, for a brief second, my eyes fell on Kari's. She looked right at me, then slid her gaze past my shoulder so smoothly that I wondered afterward if she'd really seen me. At that moment I made up my mind to get up, step over to the table, and say something to her. Any thin excuse—maybe about the Hexies' postulated longevity; we'd been talking about that earlier.

"Excuse me for just a moment, Michele." I was doing it. As I said the words, I half arose from my chair.

And froze for five seconds as six strident tones sounded over the ship's speakers. Six tones. The ten-and-a-half-hour alert for a change in acceleration. I continued standing and took a count. Everyone was in the bar except Petrov, who was exiting toward the control room.

"Ladies and gentlemen, it seems as if we have one Saturn rotation until something is going to happen. Please remain here while I go up to the control room and find out what. I'll let you know as soon as I can."

By the time I got upstairs, Petrov already had a printout of the message from the translation computer. He handed it to me without a word and I read:

Acceleration will cease 6^6 heconds from final warning tone, and remain off for 1,296 heconds. This will be followed by attitude readjustment and recommencing of acceleration, after the standard warning tones. New acceleration value may be different by a small percentage from that experienced previously.

I read the message to the crew, and added: "It appears as if this is a final attitude update and adjustment of acceleration to pinpoint us into a precise orbit—otherwise, it shouldn't be necessary. As of now, we are on ship's alert. That means all inside and outside airlock doors will be closed, and entries and exits will be made one door at a time, as if a pressure differential existed. No one will exit *High Boy* unless authorized by an officer.

"We'll spend the next two hours preparing our quarters for zero G. After that, common room cleanup assignments will be posted in Mr. Petrov's roster file. I will inspect in six hours, and I want to see all surfaces clean. Too many of us got grit in our eyes during turnaround a year ago. And remember, the zero G could be followed by pitch, roll, and yaw—so items must be secured from acceleration in all axes.

"Mr. Badille, I'd appreciate it if you would go out to the Hexie console and verify the completeness of the message. Please suit up before you exit the ship. That's all for now. Ladies and gentlemen, let's get to work."

The next ten and a quarter hours were filled with hard work and swearing; they went fast. After a year, I'd forgotten how much volume *High Boy* surrounded. It took me over three hours to do the inspection, and I knew I hadn't caught everything. I was back in the control room only a few minutes before the countdown clock jerked its way to zero. The warning countdown started precisely on time; 21 tones later, we were in free fall.

"Ladies and gentlemen, you're free to move around for the next fifteen minutes, but please stay near your seats and strap back in as soon as you hear the warning."

Zero G felt funny after a year. I swallowed and felt the swelling beginning in my neck and face. I glanced over at Petrov's imperturbable countenance. "How do you feel, George—eager, excited, afraid?"

He smiled the faintest of smiles—all he ever allowed himself, really—and said, "Perhaps all of those and more. I believe we have some interesting times ahead, Captain."

Petrov was rigidly old school. In the two and a half years

I'd known him, he'd never called me anything but "Captain" or "Sir." Secretly, I approved. It gave the crew a sense of direction to hear the second most powerful man aboard announce the captain's rank as a matter of habit every time he spoke. I'd come to appreciate more and more the first officer's stolidity and reliability during the long voyage. For the everyday functioning and status of the ship, he was the perfect authority; the facts were always at his fingertips. For entertaining conversation, I could always turn elsewhere.

I wasn't watching the clock, so the first six warning tones caught me by surprise. Within twenty seconds, the countdown was finished. The ship moved minutely—a little yaw and the slightest bit of pitch, I thought—then acceleration built up again to high levels. I glanced at the acceleration readout on the ship's nav computer, although I didn't really trust it. It had drifted steadily down for about half the trip, then climbed slowly back up until it was reading about .98 G just before acceleration cutoff 20 minutes ago. Now it worked its way slowly up to 0.943 G and stayed there.

There was a message on the translation computer's screen. I read it aloud to the crew: " 'Current acceleration will terminate in 2,007,727 heconds, after which ship will perform orbital insertion maneuvers. Following maneuvers, all holds will be depressurized. After depressurization, contact will be made.' That ends the message. That time figure has been punched into the mission countdown clock, ladies and gentlemen. It now reads 18 days, 19 hours, 43 minutes, and 4 seconds. With the best guess we can make at actual acceleration, that puts us about 13 billion kilometers out and 15,000 kilometers per second, relative.

"All right, it's been a long night. Let's secure from acceleration routine and get some sleep. Except for Mr. Badille, who may first check the Hexie console and report back to the control room, if he would be so kind. Captain out."

I turned to Petrov. "George, go get some sleep. I'll take the watch." He nodded and left.

I was staring off into nothing when Junior's voice surprised me from over my shoulder:

"A penny for 'em, Admiral."

"Huh? Oh. I was just wondering what we would see if we could step outside the ship for a second."

"Just a small point of light, from this far out—but I know what you mean. Myself, I would have liked to take a few doppler sightings at mid-trip. Josh had us coasting at a 300,000-to-1 time dilation. Old boy's thick in the head, but there's no way to prove him wrong until we climb out of this cocoon and have a look around."

"Any surprises from the Hexie console?"

"Naw. Same message. You going to hit the hay?"

"No. I'm going to take a watch here until the rest of the crew starts stirring."

"I'll get the cards."

"Get some sleep, Junior. You've got bags under your eyes."

"So what's another bag or two when I can pick up some more gin winnings?" He disappeared for a moment, and returned with a deck. As he sat down in the right seat, I pulled out the sliding table between us.

"How much do I owe you now?"

"Eight thousand four hundred ninety-six dollars, eighty-six cents. Last game was a skunk."

"Just how do you think you're going to collect?"

"Let's find out what the natives use for currency, then I'll figure out a way for you to rob a bank."

"Contact will be made."

"Your mind wanderin' again, Dimp?"

"I was just thinking of the last words of the message: 'Contact will be made.' "

"Yep. We're really doin' it, Admiral. Gonna kick around and have some fun."

"I do believe you're right, Junior."

BOOK III

THE
HEXIE WORLD

THARTHEE

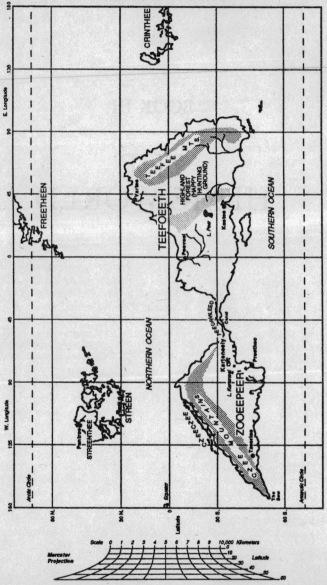

CRINTHEE

E. Longitude

W. Longitude

Arctic Circle

FREETHEEN

NORTHERN OCEAN

STREENTHEE
STREEN

Pentroph

MOUNTAINS

CZEE-CZEE

L. Kepenny Oil

Kepenny

ZOOEEPEER'

Tenntee

CZEE

The Beer

Antarctic Circle

Karjaneely

EURMEED
Canal

Prowtheee

Kenteo

L. Peer

SOUTHERN OCEAN

HIGHLAND
FOREST
(HAPPY
(HUNTING
GROUND)

Peewrod

Vartee

TEEFOEETH

TEEFEE
MTS.

60 N.

30 N.

Latitude

Eq. Equator

30 S.

60 S.

Scale 0 1 2 3 4 5 6 7 8 9 10,000 Kilometers

10

20

30

Mercator
Projection

40

50

60

Latitude

Chapter 12

The Hexies' greater range of audition creates a barrier to mutual communication that should not be ignored. Their ears can quite easily pick up the lowest sounds humans are capable of producing, and the highest. They can listen to our languages with complete comprehension, and speak it with facility. And their linguistic abilities are such that they are able to learn almost all concepts and nuances of human speech. Unfortunately, the reverse is not true. Their everyday speech ranges from 1,500 to 30,000 Hz, and they have vocal cord capability to well over 35,000 Hz.

Their consonants are not too difficult to understand and duplicate: thus, their "P" sound is a cross between the English P and K; their "F" has a V sound added; their "R" is "swallowed" quite like the French, the "TH" is almost a pure theta, and so forth. Any trained human voice can duplicate them with reasonable facility. But the multiple vowels are the real key to their language. These are exceedingly complex, and impossible for humans to hear or reproduce completely. We can only give them a simple "ee" representation on paper or in speaking, when in actuality they may range through several sounds and frequencies.

An excellent example of this are the "Christian names" for every Hexie, which we found out about only by asking them if they had our equivalent of first and last names. They do, but the "first names" are always high-frequency "tags" within the single name complex, and always inaudible to humans. Thus, we have never been able to verbally identify an individual Hexie with anything other than the equivalent of "Smith" or "Gonzales." The consequences of

*this physiologically induced communications barrier should
not be underestimated. . . .*
                              —*Petrov:* The Hexie White Papers

The final tones of the decompression signal counted
down. Then faintly, then with a roar, the atmosphere
whistled out of the hold around *High Boy*. Our big vessel
strained at the tie-downs, but held nicely.

As soon as the sounds died away I made my way back to
High Boy's airlock. Everyone aboard was already suited.
Our plans had been solidified over the past two weeks,
and there remained nothing to do but wait for the Hexies
to show.

I was betting, based on what I'd do in their place, that
the Hexies would want to check us out before allowing the
large cargo door to open and our ship to emerge. I was
also betting that they'd come to us through the small
airlock, rather than wait for us to come out. After all, our
only medium of communication was through that console
in the small hold.

Therefore, Edward Allison-White, Grace Kitigawa and I
waited in *High Boy's* airlock. It faced the small Hexie
hold, and as soon as we could see the aliens enter without
weapons, we'd open our own airlock outer door and go out
to meet them.

But after only a minute or two, I deviated from plan on
an impulse. I opened the outer door without waiting for
them to come in, and we floated there in the open airlock,
waiting for them.

We waited just long enough to be convinced that nothing was going to happen. Then Petrov's voice came over
my private channel:

"Captain, we just received a message that the Hexies
will meet us in the small room of the Hexie ship in 216
heconds."

"Thank you, George. And since it looks as if the Hexies
are going to be talking to us real time, please patch a voice
translation directly into the open suit channel so everyone
can listen; give it general override priority. And give me
private channel three for direct voice input into the computer, with repeat over the open channel."

"Done, Captain."

"Thanks. Stand by." During the conversation, the three of us were making our way clumsily toward the small hold—clumsily because we were carrying gifts we intended to present to the Hexies when we met them.

So we arrived just about the time the outer door was opening.

"Two Hexies are coming in." I began the running commentary to the crew assembled in the theater. After much soul-searching, I had decided not to allow holovision cameras to televise the proceedings—they could be too easily mistaken for laser weapons.

"I see several more waiting outside the hull. Now one more is entering. They must have noticed that there are three of us, and are matching numbers. They appear to have full-pressure suits, rather than micropore. Either they don't have the technology, or have no sweat glands for body heat removal—Dr. Korliss, take note. From what I can see through their visors, they look just as advertised: eyes small and round, with only a vestigial nose. They also appear to be slightly shorter than Edward and I, but slightly taller than Grace.

"Their suit gloves are articulated, with six short digits. I believe Mr. Badille collects three or four wagers on that score." The pictures in the Hexie manual hadn't shown the number of fingers on the beings, and that had been the subject of much friendly debate during the voyage.

I was narrating the contact calmly enough, but my heart was pounding a kilometer a minute. At least my adrenal glands had a sense of history.

"I am now moving forward to present what appears to be the lead Hexie with the first of our gifts. It refused me—at least I think it is a refusal: arm held horizontally, making a forward chopping motion. Now it is going to the console and punching out a message, which ought to be coming over the translation computer any sec—"

"Information: It is proper that you are present in this star system. Interrogative: Atmosphere with partial pressures of 190 millibars oxygen, 802 millibars nitrogen, .1 millibars carbon dioxide, temperature 20 Celsius sufficient to sustain you unprotected."

"Ladies and gentlemen, I believe that we have just been greeted as warmly as possible, considering the limitations of the Hexie artificial language. We will also have no trouble breathing their atmosphere, if that is its composition." I voice-controlled over to channel three and said: "Affirmative. End of message."

Almost immediately, a short message appeared on the console below the message the Hexie had constructed. The Hexie nodded its head once in a remarkably human gesture, then typed more lines onto the console.

"Interrogative: number of personnel aboard your vessel."

I answered with 22. The Hexie came back with another message:

"Information: we are 12 in number. Interrogative: proper to enter, pressurize hold, and inspect your vessel."

The Hexie manual had taken an inordinate amount of space to make sure it presented an understandable definition of the word "microorganism." It then assured us that theirs and ours were incompatible to the point that no deleterious interaction could take place. Humans and Hexies were about to put that to the test. And the humans themselves were to be put to their own test: the inspection of the ship was a prudent measure I would have taken myself before allowing a large vessel loose in our solar system. I hoped they didn't see anything which might be mistaken for a weapon.

"Affirmative," I said to channel three.

The Hexie moved his mouth, perhaps talking to the other members of his party. Nine more entered. Then he punched buttons in rapid succession on the console, which the computer interpreted as untranslatable. But the Hexie personnel airlock doors closed—outer, then inner—and my suit started immediately to de-balloon as the hold was filled with gases.

"Mr. Petrov, please check the composition of the outside atmosphere here and inform us when pressure levels off at 992 millibars. After that, all crew will please remove their helmets unless I tell you otherwise. Also, Mr. Petrov, if you please, equalize pressure across *High Boy*'s airlock when it is safe to do so."

"Affirmative, Captain. We are leveling off now at just

over 990 millibars. Osygen 19.15 percent, nitrogen 80.84 percent, cee-oh-two 0.01 percent. Equalizing pressures now." I heard in back of me the hiss from *High Boy* as the valves were opened.

But I was more entranced by the spectacle in front of me—of a dozen Hexies removing their helmets. I noticed that Grace and Edward were following suit; hastily, I reached up and did likewise. When I got it off and velcroed to my belt, I did a double take. The Hexies were peeling their suits completely off, helping each other with very human movements. They appeared to be articulated much the same as we were.

"They're taking their suits completely off," I said into my throat mike, "so we'll do likewise, crew included." I started to swim over to Edward and Grace, but they weren't having any trouble. They'd worn micropore suits. For prudence' sake, and to show the Hexies both kinds, I'd worn a full pressure suit.

So I struggled with the clumsy thing while the Hexies did the same. Going through my contortions in zero G without specialized hand and foot restraints was uncomfortable, but I managed to see that the Hexies all wore shorts and tunics, and that their bare arms, legs, and faces were covered with short gray hair as expected. What was unexpected was its apparent texture—it seemed to be silky-soft, like that of a short-haired Persian cat. The "fur" on their heads and faces was shorter, and their features were much more mobile than their pictures had led us to believe.

But mainly, I was struck by the ludicrousness of the whole scene. Here we were, undergoing the first minutes of the most momentous occasion in history, and were all busy struggling out of pressure suits! I felt like laughing and swearing at the same time.

I'd turned myself around during the final maneuver of pulling my legs out of the front of the suit; but I was relieved to feel a pair of hands holding the back firmly while I completed the maneuver. Edward or Grace must have finished, and was now giving me a hand.

I finally got my legs out, and turned around to thank whichever one it was—and found myself spinning face to

face with a Hexie. The alien was still holding my suit, and
we were in a slow, synchronized tumble. He (it) had his
mouth halfway open, with his thin lips pulled back. I
could see that an omnivore's teeth were there, but they
were almost entirely concealed. It was like a toothless
gaffer laughing at a senile joke, and somehow I was sure it
was laughter, or at least a smile. I had the feeling that the
Hexie might also be struck by the same ridiculous thought
as I had been earlier.

I grinned acquiescence and said, "Thank you," nodding
my head. "And by the way," I added, "I don't believe
we've been introduced. My name is Whitey." Feeling a
little ridiculous, I touched my chest as I carefully pronounced my name, then stuck out my right hand as we did
a slow tumble together in the weightless environment.

He looked at it for a moment, then took it tentatively in
his own and voiced a single word in a very high voice. As
near as I could make out, it sounded like "Kanteen," with
the vowels sliding up impossibly high, then coming back
down for the "nt" in the middle and the "n" at the end.
The entire effect was something of an ear-piercing aural
roller coaster.

Then he turned and said something rapidly in a complex
multi-toned singsong which ranged from soprano up, and
seemed to cut in and out of the human audible range.
Inwardly I groaned. If they couldn't learn our tongue, we
were in trouble. There was no way humans could master
those high tones.

Back to business. I took my suit from the Hexie, got my
bearings, pushed off a bulkhead, and made my way over to
the series of storage lockers the Hexies had graciously
provided us in the large cargo hold. Passing one marked
"dried feces," I opened another which hadn't been used
yet, and stowed my suit. With gestures, I offered the
Hexie the same opportunity. He took it, speaking again to
his compatriots. They floated by in order and did likewise.
While all this was going on, I spoke through my throat
mike:

"These beings are every bit as cute as they look in their
pictures, but I want to remind you that we know nothing
of their touching habits. We will be coming in shortly, and

I enjoin each of you to refrain from physical contact unless they initiate it. You'll understand what I mean when you see them—their body fur is almost irresistibly pettable."

Then I turned to Grace and Edward, who were holding back, possibly with the thought of taking their suits directly to the airlock suiting room for stowage.

"Please put your suits in with the others. It's probably not necessary, but it might make the Hexies feel just a little safer if we cast our lot with theirs."

They both nodded without speaking and moved to do it—then had to wait while a fascinated Hexie contingent inspected the shiny two-way stretch fabric of their Boyle's law suits. The Hexies obviously had not seen anything like them before. Allison-White did a very credible explanation by wetting his arm with spit, then stretching the suit material over the wet spot and pantomiming the water evaporating through the suit with waving fingers. He kept up a slow, elegant patter while doing it, in keeping with his anthropological training. One or two of the Hexies nodded in that remarkably human way; the others cocked their heads at a peculiar angle, which I took to be the equivalent of furrowing eyebrows in perplexity. Sweat glands might very well be nonexistent on the Hexie world.

At a brief word from "my" Hexie, who seemed to be in charge of the contingent, the others desisted, and the suits were finally stowed. Then the Hexie turned to me and cocked his head in a way somehow different from the way the others had been doing when perplexed over the micropore suits. I took a guess and gestured to *High Boy*'s airlock, then pushed off and floated over to it.

My Hexie and I got there first, and I turned around to see Edward Allison-White happily entrenched in the middle of the main group. Grace Kitigawa was bringing up the rear with two stragglers. Before they got to the airlock, one of the two detached him/herself and made his way over to the supports that held the seven interfaces between the Hexie ship and *High Boy*. He unfastened a pocket on his tunic, pulled out a small flat case the size of a pocket calculator, and began to make rapid comments in that complex singsong as he inspected our handiwork.

Just as I was wondering if we should wait, my Hexie

touched me tentatively on the shoulder, "smiled," and gestured at the airlock. I nodded and opened the outer door, then went through and opened the inner. Making another quick decision, I spoke back to Kitigawa:

"Don't close the doors behind us, Grace. They might get claustrophobic in a strange ship."

"I understand, Captain," she said.

I took them first to the theater. It was a political decision. I was afraid the crew would tear me to pieces if they had to wait an hour or two to see the Hexies face to face.

So before I knew it, I found myself facing the crew with a gaggle of Hexies pouring into the room, not having planned what to do next.

I introduced the crew members, one by one, as if we were meeting at high tea.

Then my Hexie returned the favor, saying unpronounceable names as his contingent waved their arms in a funny circular motion, one by one.

While this was going on, I beat my brains to figure out what to do next. I shouldn't have bothered. After it was all over, there was just the tiniest of pregnant pauses, then Junior floated over to the Hexie nearest him, stuck out his hand, and said with an exquisite sense of propriety:

"Hi. In case you didn't catch my name, it's Junior Badille. You want to see my rock collection?"

The Hexie said something in coloratura, then slowly something that sounded like "Freentree," and by that time Michele Kimberly was already making a move to another Hexie. Then both groups were coming together. In short order, the theater was a free-for-all of individual conversations and pantomiming sessions.

I turned to my Hexie and said: "Sir, would you care to see the control room?" I gestured to the appropriate exit from the common room.

He gave me that gaffer's smile and nodded. Before leaving I raised my voice over the babble: "Ladies and gentlemen, will you please give me your attention for a moment!"

They all quieted, the Hexies with more alacrity than the crew.

"I imagine I'll be spending the next couple of hours

escorting Kanteen, here, around the ship. Outside of that, we seem to have no set format, so please feel free to indulge yourselves as you see fit. Show the Hexies the common rooms, your private quarters, or anything else they might wish to see—but please leave the protective covers on all critical controls. Unless you get further word over the ship's comm, please be back in here in two hours—that's 11:45 ship's time."

Then my Hexie added a paragraph or two, saying God-knows-what, but hopefully something akin. While he was doing it, I spoke softly into my throat mike:

"George, Michael, please be ready. We'll be coming in just a minute."

While introducing my Hexie to Prentiss and Petrov, I picked up a little more on his name, partly from hearing him/her say it again, and partly from listening to how the expert Petrov repeated it to him. It was—with ululating ee's—"Panteen." The first letter was actually a cross between a P and a K, but closer to a P. George learned to pronounce it right away, but I never did. And even Petrov couldn't do the ee's correctly.

In fact, while Panteen was being shown the nav computer by Mike, Petrov said to me quietly:

"Captain, we can forget trying to ever learn to speak this language fully. Either they must learn ours, or we will have to communicate through computers, with all their limitations of innuendo."

I nodded agreement, unhappy to have my fears confirmed.

Panteen was interested in everything, so we did the ship from top to bottom, but I got the distinct impression that he was getting an overview only. The members of the Hexie contingent were another matter. Machine shop, cafeteria, power distribution center, water closets, CRF drive, surgical operatory, ECLS system, observatory—everywhere we went, it seemed there were one or two Hexies peering with great interest into the workings. They were calibrating us. That was okay; I'd want to do the same thing.

And something was happening for which I was very grateful: the Hexies were picking up our language with remarkable rapidity. They were excellent mimics, pronouncing words with high voice but great clarity after hearing them only once or twice. Panteen was no exception to this. Within an hour and a half he was even starting to form crude sentences.

With the two hours nearly gone, we were almost finished. Almost, because I needed to show Panteen something. I felt he was entitled to know.

I took him to my quarters, worked the combination on my personal locker, and took out the gun, which had remained locked up ever since the unfortunate incident with French a year ago.

I put the magazine in, then took it out again, and gave both parts to the Hexie.

"Panteen, this is the only weapon aboard our ship. Please take it with you when you leave." I said it slowly and distinctly, pressing the pieces into his hands.

It was obvious from the way he handled and looked at it that he knew its function. After a brief inspection, he looked at me with his round eyes and "smiled" broadly. Then he tilted his head from side to side in the distinctive Hexie "no" gesture and said:

"No, you take." He held it out.

I nodded, threw it back into the chest, and randomized the lock. My feeling of respect and trust for Panteen had been growing throughout our tour together. Now I knew that he or she had style.

Then we went back to the theater, where the time was past for collecting. All were there, and conversing animatedly. Panteen said a few singsong sentences to the collected group. The Hexies made various gestures of farewell, then headed toward the airlock.

Then Panteen turned to me and said: "We talk." He pantomimed with his fingers the act of inputting to the Hexie console in the small hold.

I nodded, then turned to the crew. "Grace, Edward, would you please accompany us out? Junior, I'd appreciate it if you'd go to the control room and stand by with Mr. Petrov. We're going to be passing more messages back and forth, and they might be complex. I'd like your expertise at the translation computer."

"Aye, aye, Captain," he said.

"And Mr. Petrov, after we leave, please re-establish pressure integrity in the ship. We might be evacuating soon."

Petrov nodded and left with Junior for the control room.

Back outside *High Boy* in the cargo hold, we donned and checked suits, then Panteen made his way to the console and typed:

"Interrogative: proper to depressurize."

I checked with Petrov, then affirmed.

The Hexie made a few more rapid strokes of the keyboard, and after a short series of warning notes, during which we all grabbed hold of something, the air was once again whistling out of the holds.

Almost immediately afterward, one of the Hexies opened the small outer hatch. I was closer this time, and saw that there was a line attached somewhere on the outside of the Hexie vessel, to a much smaller boat alongside. It looked to be about the size of Junior's old *Pandora*.

Panteen floated in the open hatch, facing the vessel, for several seconds; he was obviously communicating with it. Then he turned back and beckoned me over to the console. A complex message was being formed on the screen. Just about that time Petrov's voice sounded in my private channel:

"Captain, there is an extremely detailed message coming through. The computers have not yet started a translation."

"Understand, Mr. Petrov. It is a canned message being sent over from another Hexie ship. If the computer has trouble with it, confer with Mr. Badille, and get the best translation you can. I want it as soon as possible. And go ahead and pipe it to the crew."

"Yes, sir."

Then, after a few more seconds, the flat voice of the computer came over the general channel:

"The functioning of apparatus of your species for transmitting information by sound waves is understood by our species. Your apparatus is not proper for proper transmitting to our species—"

The computer cut off in mid-garble, and the gnome's voice took its place:

"My translation program is making a hash of this message, so I'll interpolate anthropocentrically. From previous studies of our voice patterns—I guess they mean when they visited the solar system before—they deduced that it would be impossible for humans to learn to speak the Hexie language; therefore, Hexies must learn human speech. This will not be difficult for them; they are adept at learning new languages. It will take several weeks—perhaps less if we have brought a usable voice-keyed translation between the artificial language used aboard the vessel, and our current language.

"The next part gets trickier. Apparently, it is most proper for greetings and exchange of artifacts—gifts—to take place after the exchange of languages . . . hell, Admiral, what they're saying is that they'd rather wait to greet us officially until after they've learned our language. In the meantime, if it's convenient, they'd rather we stay in orbit around their planet. They don't seem to be adamant about it, though. If we're uncomfortable in zero G, they'll set up a place for us to live on the planet while they learn our language.

"But wherever we stay, they need to visit with us continually to learn the language properly.

"They understand that we might need some time to talk it over, so they'll wait 1296 heconds, or even longer if we wish, for our answer. And that's the end of the message."

I voice-activated channel three for direct link to the translation computer, and said: "Reply forthcoming in 216 heconds." I had no intention of going into a labored discussion with the crew; I activated the three-way channel set up for the scientific leaders and me to talk privately:

"Grace, Edward, let's hash this out and give them an answer quickly. . . ."

There were advantages and disadvantages to both schemes. We finally decided that the discomfort of a few weeks in zero G would be offset by the chance to make detailed observations of the Hexie world from orbit. And besides, that seemed to be the way they wanted it, and we were the visitors.

And to make it faster, we had much more than a Rosetta Stone for them. We'd taken the entire set of artificial

Hexie words and concept sets, and had made written and voice—male and female—translations. We had a rugged portable PC set up with the appropriate bubble, screen, and speakers. It was complete with the simple operating instructions, and a keyboard in artificial Hexie characters modeled after the one on the ship. There was also an additional bubble with accompanying book which was a 2,000-word primer of the English language, with referent pictures as unbiased as we could make them.

"Mr. Prentiss, would you please bring out the English teacher? And while he's doing that, Mr. Petrov, will you activate a two-way voice link between the theater and control room? And I'd like Anna-Marie Smith and Hagar Zyyad to stand by to advise Mr. Badille: I'm going to need the frequency ranges and transmitted energy densities of all our active observational instruments."

I activated channel three for the first simple part of my message:

"Information: to remain in orbit is acceptable. Stand by for further message." Then I switched back to the general frequency:

"Mr. Badille, I'd like for you to formulate a message telling them that we request a polar orbit, if possible. Work out with the ladies which one would be best for general observation—sun-synchronous or whatever—but don't take a long time. Then give them the specs of our active instruments and ask them which ones we shouldn't use, if any. And ask them as delicately as possible, with that damned artificial language, if we can look outward, observe their solar system and the rest of the galaxy."

"Workin' it, Captain."

The runt had probably started constructing the message while I was discussing it with Edward and Grace. He was perfectly capable of reading my mind from a hundred meters away. It was less than a minute later that I saw the long message begin to emerge on the console screen.

"Transmitting."

Panteen watched the message unfold. He was also undoubtedly listening to a translation from their companion vessel; I hoped it was clear.

"Finished."

Panteen continued to stand there for a while after it finished, then, for a moment, I could see his thin, mobile lips moving inside his suit. Shortly, the translation computer's voice sounded in my helmet:

"Orbit with specified inclination and period is proper. All observations are proper."

Panteen looked at me, visor to visor. I nodded. Then he hooked into a foot restraint and typed a short message on the console.

"It is proper to observe the stars."

I looked back into his visor. Big gaffer's grin. I smiled back, trying not to show too many teeth.

Chapter 13

*Humans have built their technology base over the centu-
ries by literally squandering the natural resources of Earth.
The Hexies seemed to have accomplished the same result
without anywhere near the same magnitude of resource
depletion. I noticed first from orbit, then on the ground,
that the Hexie world was much more "intact" than Earth—
and I knew quite well the signs to look for. Is this striking
difference between our worlds due to the Hexies' smaller
population and longer lives? Can we deduce from it that
their floater technology was developed early so they could
strike a balance between use of planetary and other system resources? Or do they have other lessons to teach
us?*

—Zyyad: Hexie White Papers,
                         Prefatory Notes

Two days later, with *High Boy* firmly ensconced in a
sun-synchronous "mid-morning" orbit, Junior and I were
making the rounds. All systems onboard were functioning
quite well, except for the zero-G plumbing—which never
functioned well enough for anybody.

We'd just come out of the lower decks, where Sean
Davidson was still laboring over the CO_2 removal system.
We were saving the mole sieve units, and had switched
entirely over to LiOH cannisters. The Hexies were sup-
plying us with fresh batches of the chemical, so we didn't
have to bake out the cannisters, vent overboard, and dis-
turb the more sensitive planetary observation instruments.
Sean had already been assured in faltering English that he
would be able to get heating elements built to the specifi-
cations he needed, so he could fix all the mole sieves and

have plenty of spares. The Hexies were friendly and our spirits were high.

I was glad to be able to perform official duties with Junior in attendance now. The runt had been dubbed the "Expedition Omnivore" by the crew, and it was perfectly natural that he sample all the goings-on with me. Our next stop was the nadir observatory, presided over by Anna-Marie Smith and Hagar Zyyad.

As we floated in, we found them monitoring screens, peering at readouts—and talking indiscriminately to computers, each other, and three Hexies in attendance. I noticed that two of the Hexies were female—distinguishable by their coarser body hair.

"Hello, ladies. How go the studies?"

"Wonderful, Captain," answered Hagar. "Come over here and look at this globe Teefeer brought us. Isn't it beautiful!"

Indeed it was. We knew the quality of the Hexies' manufacturing processes from the Saturn artifacts, and this was a beautiful example. It was metallic, multicolored, with an exaggerated relief scale for the mountains, and engraved major latitude and longitude lines and feature names. The detail was exquisite. I'd put the price at more than $10,000 on Earth. But our geologist didn't seem to be interested in the quality.

"Eighty percent water mass," she said. "See the two major continents? The one on the left is Zoeepeer—it's shaped something like South America lying on its side. That's where the world capital is."

She snaked a finger toward a large lake in the southeastern corner of the land mass. "That's Lake Karteneel, and the capital city of Karteneely is on the western shore. Foreefee, here," she gestured over to the male Hexie, "says that the area is very beautiful, and that we will enjoy it."

I glanced over at the Hexie, who was nodding and smiling.

"The other continent is like a giant version of Australia," continued Zyyad, "and the two are connected by a narrow isthmus, here. Foreefee says there's a canal, built many years ago, connecting the northern and southern oceans."

I nodded, looking at the two dominant land masses. They stretched together three-fourths of the way around the globe, and were almost entirely in the southern hemisphere, assuming the globe was right side up. Only the northern quarter of the western continent stuck above it. Outside of the two continents, the globe appeared almost empty. There were only three major archipelagoes to break the monotony.

"Lots of water on this planet," I said.

"Yes," agreed the woman. "But there's still plenty of land on the continents, and the island groups. And look here." Her finger swung up to near the north pole. "There's a major archipelago way to the north that we haven't been able to see visually yet, because of the cloud cover. Teefeer says it has both volcanoes and glaciers."

Junior turned to Anna-Marie Smith and said: "Anna, you got enough data on continental and sea-floor altitudes yet to perform statistical analyses?"

"Yes," she said, nodding. "Even though we've only made forty passes, the data are testing out with a p of less than point oh-two. We've got a preliminary global altitude set that's bimodal about the mean. Mean's about three and a half kilometers below sea level."

The gnome tugged at his ear. "Plate tectonics, then?"

"Looks like it," she said. "Thin oceanic plates and thicker, differentiated continental plates. Oceanic ridges and trenches—a very complex system of them in the northern hemisphere especially. They also have broad continental shelves on the northern side of the western continent, and north and south of the eastern continental lowlands. The largest archipelago—it's called something like 'Streen'—is also surrounded by a shelf."

"You think they're in a geologic high-water phase?" said Junior.

"I believe so," she said.

One of the Hexies had drifted over and was listening intently to the conversation. She said distinctly: "Plate tectonics is very necessary to make intelligent life."

I couldn't help staring at her mouth as she spoke. She wrapped her thin, mobile lips around the words, achieving a result much like a person who has learned to speak very

well without her dentures. The effect was heightened by a
tendency to whistle the "S" sound. I hadn't quite gotten
used to it, even though I'd had several hours of "language
lessons" with Panteen. Then I realized what she'd said,
rather than how she said it.

"Anna, is that a true statement as far as we know?"

"I don't know, Captain. You'll have to ask Edward." She
furrowed her brow. "That's the first time she's volunteered any information."

I nodded. Some of the Hexies had already learned a
remarkable amount of English—certainly enough to converse meaningfully—but none had so far helped to supplement the data we'd been taking. Even the gift of the globe
wasn't a real help. It was obvious that we would get the
relief data anyway—it was probably meant as an instruc-
tional tool so we could learn the native names for the
geographical features.

It looked like the Hexies' attitude was to be friendly,
but see what the humans could do on their own. It was a
good strategy for assessing our technology, perhaps to see
what they'd like to trade for, and what they might offer
that we'd be interested in. But unless they eventually
reciprocated, we'd be at a decided disadvantage in any
dealings with them. If we had something they really wanted
badly, we'd have to know the full gamut of their own
technology in order to drive a fair bargain. That was a
point for serious discussion with Panteen, when he attained enough facility in English.

In the meantime, I smiled at the Hexie and said: "I'm
not sure we have been able to verify that, yet, but I
wouldn't be surprised if you are correct."

Junior and I exited; Peter Dinsworth was next. *High
Boy* was "pointed" in the direction of our orbital velocity
vector. Our next stop was straight through the diameter of
the ship, from the nadir observatory to the zenith. We'd
attached our 1-meter reflector to the outside of *High Boy*'s
hull as one of our first acts upon achieving stable orbit,
and Dinsworth hadn't taken a meal with the rest of us
since.

The scene was quieter in the astronomical observatory.
Carl Dunsworth was assisting Peter, naturally, but their

usual Hexie contingent was absent for the moment. When we arrived, Carl was talking quietly to the computer, and Pete was looking at the Orion Nebula on his monitor.

"Sightseeing, Pete?" I asked.

"It is beautiful, isn't it, Captain," he replied. "But this is all in the line of duty, I'm happy to say. We're done with the globular clusters. Got M13 located as our baseline, then found separation angles to Omega Centauris and NGC 6397 in Ara. From that, the computer," he gestured to Dunsworth's instrument, "put us somewhere on a line from Sol to Orion—about 200-300 light years out, RA just over six hours and declination about seventeen and a half degrees."

Junior screwed up his face. "Not too many G0's or G2's out thataway," he said. Junior had been a star pupil (pun achieved, but not intended) in Dinsworth's class during the outbound voyage. The onboard astronomy computer was naturally a specialist in nearby stars. It had extensive data on all bodies in the 113 million cubic light-year volume in which we expected to find the Hexies. But even Junior had balked at memorizing the locations of a couple of million stars, and had stuck to the high F and low G types—the ones most likely to be stable and have a reasonable zone of life. "Maybe SHC 11035?"

The astronomer nodded his head. "Could be. In fact, we've set up the computer with that assumption, and are checking the angular separation of the stars in the Trapezium." He waved to the console showing the heart of the nebula. "For second check, we'll look at some of the apparent magnitudes of recognizable in-line stars—Betelgeuse should be only ten degrees off line, for instance. Then we'll go backwards through Sol and look for one like Zeta Ophiuchus," he smiled, "and Sol itself, of course. It ought to have a visual magnitude close to eight point nine—and we know its footprint pretty well."

"How long before you have us verified?" I asked.

"A day. Two at the outside," he answered.

"Any chance of placing us in time?"

He shook his head. "Not unless you want to spend a couple of years or more in orbit, Captain. The measurements are way too fussy to do in one shot with this klooge—really need a good specialized instrument for that kind of accuracy. Even then, you'd have to spend quite a while checking to make sure of the identities of the stars with high proper motions, then doing the careful position measurements."

I nodded. I'd taken his course, too (at the 'B' level), and knew the answer already. "Well, in that case, Pete, you're not in a rush. There's more than enough time to verify the Hexie sun, so get some food and sleep." I looked at Dunsworth hovering over the computer. "You too, Carl."

He looked up and said okay.

"It's still hard for me to believe that you and your fellow collaborators have learned our language so rapidly. I compliment you on your diligence, and thank you for troubling yourselves on our account. It has made us feel welcome more than anything else you could have done, Panteen."

It was ten days later, and my Hexie cohort and I were making the rounds of *High Boy*. All of the Hexies were now amazingly fluent. During the first week, they had passed through a stage of constructing the language in a stilted, almost archaic manner, but now were speaking very passable colloquial English.

"That is good, Whitey, because we want you to feel welcome. But like so many of the differences between us, we do not find it hard to believe. To us, the speed at which we learn new languages is not unusual; it is normal. Perhaps the ability to learn languages was more strongly selected in our evolution. I can tell you that it has been our custom from antiquity to maintain and exchange local languages, even though we now possess one which is spoken universally throughout our world. We grow up learning several, just as did your Mr. Petrov."

He gave me that gaffer's smile. "And your 'English Teacher' has been a great help." The Hexies smiled a lot, and were especially fond of words or phrases with double meanings. "English Teacher" was very mild, but they still got a kick out of it when they found out that it was our informal name for the dry official appellation, "Computer Aided Learning System for Basic English." They were very amused, also, when they found out that we called them "Hexies"—so much so that they preferred we use that name rather than the local equivalent of "humans."

"You might also be pleased to know that many more than just we—us?—I get confused sometimes—36 professionals are learning your language. The entire world government, the major representatives—ambassadors, I think you'd call them—from our five 'countries,' and perhaps one third of the general population are attempting to become proficient."

That stunned me for a moment. "I'm overwhelmed, Panteen. Truly overwhelmed."

"Overwhelmed? Above whelmed? On top of whelmed? I do not know this word 'whelmed.' "

I smiled. "Overwhelm is a single word, a verb. The formal meaning is something like 'to defeat by greatly superior force,' but I was using it colloquially to mean 'overcome with emotion that you would do so much for us.' "

He took on a blank look for a moment as he added the word to his large vocabulary, then said: "But you really shouldn't be overwhelmed, Whitey. This occasion is certainly one of great interest for our people. Were our positions reversed, your people would do the same thing, would not they—would they not? How do you say that?"

" 'Would they not' is formal; 'wouldn't they' is colloquial," I answered. "And the answer is yes, in part. If your language were very easy for us to learn, many would do it. But I doubt that a third of our population would participate. It's hard to say because our customs are set by the fact that it is much more difficult and time-consuming for us to learn new languages. In our societies, it is the visitor who is expected to learn the local language. There is no 'exchange.' "

As he thought about that one, we drifted into the lounge. It contained a discussion group consisting of Edward Allison-White, Michele Kimberly, and five Hexies. Chin Wu Lin and Jason French were also there; they were not taking part, but observing with interest.

On standing orders, they ignored us after quick casual greetings. Panteen and I listened for a while. Allison-White and Kimberly were exchanging in-depth information with the Hexies on historical and current cultures. It was the continuation of a session which had been going hot and heavy for half a week. The only thing changed from previous days was that the two "contact specialists" were present. No one addressed them, but once in a while one of the Hexies would shoot a glance their way.

Panteen and I stayed for a few minutes, then left silently.

"Whitey, tell me again the functions of Jason French and Chin Wu Lin. When we spoke of it before, I did not grasp it completely."

I thought for a moment, then decided to approach it sideways. "You have five countries within your world government, do you not?"

"Yes, and these five have further political subdivisions," he said.

This was news to me, but I continued: "And among these five or more countries, you have rivalries—competition—for economic status?"

"That is true, Whitey. Just as it is among individuals, so it is among larger units. We believe that there is a natural law which governs such competition among peoples, and that this law produces optimum results with minimum arbitrary interference from governing bodies."

I nodded. "Well, we have such competition, too. Chin and Jason are representatives of the two economic units which have sponsored this contact between our species. Their function is to make sure that no one unit gains too much of an economic advantage in any possible trade agreements that stem from our visit." I smiled. "We probably have much the same considerations as do your rival units: overlapping economic interests, prevention of monopolies, survival of individual manufacturing companies, and so forth."

He was silent for a long moment, then asked: "Do you not think that the distance and time for travel between our worlds puts a lesser importance on such mundane things as trade agreements?"

I glanced over; he seemed to be looking at me sharply. "Perhaps not," I answered carefully. "Even with a 236-year travel time such as we have, I believe that an exchange of some kind could bring great rewards to both our peoples."

To my knowledge, nobody had yet told the Hexies that we had their star pinpointed; but as of now, they knew.

For a brief moment, his face fell into a type of expression that I couldn't place. Then he nodded and said: "Maybe you are right. In due course, we shall find out what we might exchange. But tell me, what means do you have for resolving conflicts which arise among your competing units?"

That one was complicated. I offered a lengthy explanation, using concepts that I hoped Panteen understood. I tried to be as honest and inclusive as I could. When I finished, his face was screwed up into what I thought of as a frown.

"This word 'war.' Does it mean conflict between units in which individuals are injured or killed?"

"Yes," I said. "It is considered a means of last resort for resolving economic or political differences."

"How many individuals risk their lives in such conflicts?"

"Sometimes only hundreds, sometimes many thousands. In the big wars of the 20th century—150 years ago and more—millions were involved. But for many years now, only the smaller nations have waged wars." I didn't broach the complex subject of controlled nuclear stockpiles and standing armies of the larger countries—or the uneasy, nonformalized agreement among the larger nations not to allow the smaller ones to use nuclear weapons.

Panteen got that frown-look again and said: "We, too, used to engage in these wars—many thousands of years ago. But they are extremely wasteful of resources. Any unit that tried to engage in war would seriously damage its economic base." Then he gave me that gaffer's smile. "Besides, we are—how do you say it?—interested more in our individual affairs than in those in larger political units."

"You are individualistic," I said.

"Individualistic," he repeated. "Yes, we are too individualistic. Violence among individuals or very small groups for economic reasons sometimes may happen. But if any large unit tried to establish a group to make a war, the leader of the unit would be laughed from his position. You say that your large countries no longer engage in these wars. Why don't they prevent the smaller ones from doing so? Surely they must deplore the waste and loss of many lives, and possible danger to their own interests?"

So I started explaining rival interests of larger nations, and how the smaller ones were included in their spheres, and subject to unwritten "hands off" rules. And that got me into international conglomerates and cartels, which were also major players, and only loosely bound to their respective governments—and many times nominally located in smaller countries for economic reasons. The subject was too complex, even for me, to understand completely. I'm afraid I didn't do too well in getting it across.

When I finished—petered out, actually—Panteen screwed up his face for a moment, then broke back into a smile.

"It sounds like your planet could use a little simplifying of relationships."

"I agree most vehemently, Panteen."

"Which of these units or countries are you from, Whitey?"

Before I knew it, I was explaining about SpaceHome and its complex role in the human economic tangle. I was honest enough to tell him of our hopes for total independence from such entanglements, and of Earther hopes to keep us in their spheres because of our place above Earth's gravity well. And I came full circle by telling him that French represented SpaceHome, and Chin a consolidated group of Earther interests.

"But," I finished, "we have strong hopes that our relations with you Hexies will be a spur to resolve and simplify many of these complexities and entanglements."

Panteen rolled his head and smiled—but it was not a full grin. "I hope that you are correct, Whitey."

". . . impossible to speak, of course, but unsurprising in terms of architecture. It is much like the romance languages, in which ideas are expressed as groups of sounds with verbs tending to come first, then nouns, upon which the verbs act. The major difference is that modifiers tend to be contained within the verb or noun as ultrasonic components. That is why so many of their nouns, for instance, have the sound we represent with 'ee.' That is actually a component of the word which might change from use to use, depending on which modifier the speaker attaches. The physical scientists among us will realize that much more information can be transferred per unit time in the higher frequencies than in the lower. Therefore, the language they speak is much denser in information content than we realize. This has strong implications of which we must be aware at all times."

"Thank you, Mr. Petrov. And if you don't mind, I would like to have a written explanation of those implications in the open file for all of us to read as soon as possible. I believe we need to share your thoughts before we enter into extensive dealings with the Hexies."

"Of course, Captain. I'll transfer that section from my private file immediately."

We had been in orbit nearly three weeks by ship's time, or 24 rotations of the planet below us. We were going down to the surface tomorrow to make our formal debut, be received with speeches by the world leaders, and be installed in apartments on the surface. For the past week, I had been gradually matching our "day/night" cycle to the 20.4-hour period of the Hexie world.

"Thank you. Edward, would you give us a few words next?"

The elderly gentleman unstrapped himself and floated to the podium.

"I'm afraid I don't have much to add to Michele Kimberly's masterful summation. The long lifespan and physiologically shared child-rearing responsibilities seem to be the root causes of most of the anthropological disconnects between humans and Hexies. But considering the enormity of those two differences, the similarities between the cultures of our two species is quite amazing. I believe we are going to have to develop entirely new concepts in convergence of global cultures similar to those in evolutionary convergence we reluctantly adopted after first seeing the pictures of the Hexies."

"Thank you, Edward. Mr. Prentiss?"

"Their music is almost nonexistent. What they have appears to be extremely stylized, and used on certain formal occasions only. They don't seem to integrate music and emotionalism together as do humans. I do not understand this, and so far have simply accepted it as one of the few significant cultural differences between our civilizations. After hearing Mr. Petrov's summation, however, I think we might be able to pursue a tentative hypothesis that their speech itself might represent a continuous exposure to the richness that music brings to humans."

"Junior?"

"Nothing significant, since they won't talk for now. But they seem pretty impressed by our computer technology—especially its miniaturization. I think this correlates with the fact that they haven't had to sweat like we have to lift our civilization out of the gravity well. Leads me to believe they developed their molecular technology before they got spaceflight. I'm not giving odds on that yet, though. Too many variables. But overall, I'm going to agree with what Ethel said earlier: I think we've got things to bargain with, but won't find out until they're ready to tell us. They're just naturally good horse traders."

"Grace?"

"Nothing until I am able to converse at length with some of their teachers of mathematics who might have learned English. I have some texts crudely translated by Taigreel, but he is no mathematician, and we are having trouble with symbology. . . ."

"George?"

"This is a combined report for Kari Nunguesser and myself. We have concentrated primarily on . . ."

I repressed a feeling of distaste. Korliss was a heavy flirt—the closest thing to a masher we had onboard. The thought of him working in close daily contact with Kari gave me some feelings I neither understood nor liked. I forced myself to concentrate on what he was saying.

". . . physiological safety factors. The Hexies have not helped us very much, except to assure us that it is safe for both our species to intermix, and that their food would not sustain us. We had to believe them from the start, since their 36 investigators who have worked with us have regularly journeyed back and forth from the planetary surface; they even use pilots who are not part of the team. In other words, they have no quarantine protocol. Three days ago, we discovered the reason when we began to investigate samples of their food: their amino acids are universally dextrorotary, whereas ours are levrorotary. We have therefore evolved totally incompatible protein structures. Our life forms—down to the level of viruses—cannot interact with theirs in any meaningful way. We haven't yet studied the carbohydrates, but their meat will act just like roughage, and we'd best not eat it. In fact, for now, I'm placing a ban on the eating of all Hexie foods, to keep control of our intake. And that ban will probably not lift for our entire stay on the Hexie world. We'll have to continue to eat ship's food."

"Thank you, George. Do you have anything to add, Kari?"

"No, Captain."

"Anna-Marie? You're the last."

"I won't take up the time, since you've been putting all of my useful findings into the read file and everybody seems to know them. One interesting note, though. I finally got around to asking Teefeer what the Hexie name for their own world was. She said: 'Oh, I guess the closest you could come in English is to call it Tharthee.' So now at least we can refer to it with a single conversational referent, instead of—"

Junior's cackle was rudely loud.

"Why are you laughing?"

It took him a few seconds to calm down enough to say: "Anna, you know all the Hexies are studying written English?"

"Of course. In fact, I've given Teefeer several maps of the Earth for the Hexies to study. Whenever she asks for the name of a feature, I pronounce it for her."

"Well, sweetheart, I'm afraid you've been the victim of a runaway anagram."

"I still don't understand. What's an anagram?"

(At that point, a careful listener could have heard a soft slapping sound as I hit myself in the forehead with the palm of my hand.)

"Write out the word Tharthee and rearrange the letters. I'm sure it won't take you very long to discover that one of the combinations turns out to be 'the Earth.' "

"Oh no. I *thought* her smile was wider than usual."

The gnome looked me straight in the eye, grinned, and said: "Captain, you realize, of course, that this means war."

Chapter 14

. . . and after all is said and done, I remain convinced that the Hexies will milk us for every bit of superior technology that we possess, while holding out only the promise of their own. They will try to get everything and give nothing.

> —*French:* Hexie White Papers,
> Monologue of the SpaceHome
> Contact Specialist

Decelerating from orbit without hearing the white noise of a reaction drive was a strange feeling. This was my first trip in a Hexie "floater," and I was looking around like a high school kid, interested in everything. The entire crew of *High Boy* was aboard, along with the 36 Hexie investigators who'd mothered us, and vice versa, for the past three weeks.

Almost everyone was in the passenger compartment strapped into acceleration seats, but Panteen, Junior, and I enjoyed special status—we were in three spare seats in the control room of the vessel. The only other person with us was the pilot, who was doing much the same thing as any pilot would be doing at this time: punching keys and monitoring the progress of the navigation computer to make sure we got down in the right place at the right time. I noticed that she wasn't using voice.

"Do you use voice-activated computers in any of your vessels, Panteen?" I asked.

"Not in small boats such as this one, Whitey," the Hexie responded. "The equipment required is too bulky, and we really do not need it, anyway."

I nodded and thought for a moment. True, voice recog-

nition and control required complex circuitry—but the
hundred or so megabytes could easily be put into a chip,
with backups galore for malfunction protection. Junior may
have been right about the Hexies not bothering with computer miniaturization. In fact, we might be one or two
factors of ten better than them in weight and volume. I
knew the runt would pick up on that without prompting,
so I let it go and turned back to ask another question—but
Junior beat me to the punch.

"Panteen, what the devil makes this boat accelerate?"

Not only did Panteen grin hugely, but he made that
strange choking sound in the back of his throat which was
Hexie laughter.

"K-k-k—Junior, you are wonderfully blunt. Most of us
know only on a very elementary level, because the technology is complex. The exact workings of our floaters have
been closely kept a monopoly by the Tharkee Company
for nearly three sets of 1,296 years—4,000 of your years,
perhaps. But I will tell you what I know, which I learned
as a very young adult: in the floater's drive, there is a large
plate of a special kind of metal. When we want the floater
to accelerate, the drive mechanism persuades the mole-
cules in this metal to move non-randomly in the desired
direction."

Junior rolled his eyes. He'd deduced that much years ago
from the behavior of the dodecahedron retrieved from
Saturn's atmosphere. The only piece of news was that a
metal was involved. Manfully, the gnome girded his loins
and tried another piece of the problem:

"Hmmm. Unless the second law of thermodynamics
doesn't apply in this neck of the woods, you probably have
a hard time getting rid of the net heat generated from
inefficiencies."

Panteen grinned again. "You speak with delightful
phrases, Junior. I do not know about woods having necks,
or thermodynamics having laws. But we do have an extensive technology for heat transfer from the way in which the
floaters work. This technology is just as necessary as the
drive mechanism itself. Our plate of special metal is surrounded by a very large mass of material with very great
ability to absorb heat. This material is also a Tharkee

Company secret; it is manufactured in orbit and is quite expensive. During acceleration, heat is removed from this material. When the drive is turned off, heat returns to it—somewhat more than was removed in the first place."

"So how do you remove this excess heat?"

"Each place where a floater is—housed? garaged?—there is a heat transport system, connected to an extensive world-wide network of plumbing. Ultimately, ocean water absorbs the excess heat."

I frowned, disengaged brain, opened mouth, and inserted foot: "If you have many thousands of floaters, wouldn't you have to worry about global ecological consequences of heating the ocean water?"

"—haw haw!—" "—k-k-k—" The two carried on for some little time before Panteen recovered enough to answer:

"Whitey, my friend, please forgive me, but you have recreated one of the classic jokes of modern times. Indeed, one should be aware of potential consequences of such a network. And when the Tharkee Company first began operating, there were ecologists who raised just such an issue. The company had invested millions of dollars in readying its product for marketing, but were only too happy to accommodate the well-meaning ecologists. They quicky proposed a world law wherein the allowable ocean temperature rise from their product was limited to one-over-six cubed the increment from freezing to boiling—oh, dear, your base ten units are so confusing—"

"Call it half a degree centigrade," Junior cackled.

"Thank you, Junior. Limited to half a degree centigrade per 1,296 years. Even though we do not like laws, this one was passed without debate—it was rushed through under pressure from the new company. K-k-k-k—it turned out to be one of the greatest jokes in our history. The ecologists, and the entire world government, participated unknowingly in a real-life joke play. Most of the government was laughed out of office—without even being assisted by the Frinithee. And as for the ecological group—k-k—they not only disbanded, but each member had to retrain in another discipline, because not one of them could ever get work again in their chosen profession. They had not—how is it?—done their homework."

"I guess I fell into the same trap," I said. "How bad was it?"

"Please, Junior," said Panteen, "you explain. I still have trouble with your units."

The runt was still chuckling. "Kitchen arithmetic, Admiral. Hexie world's about 6,400 klicks in radius. The ocean averages about 4 klicks deep and covers 80 percent of the surface. Takes ten-to-the-twenty-fourth calories to heat it half a degree. That's the equivalent of about 70,000 gigawatts continuous waste power." He pulled an ear. "Assuming any kind of efficiency at all, that means they can run maybe half a million gigawatts useful power continuous average."

"That's a lot of gigawatts," I said lamely.

"Dern tootin'," said Junior; then he turned back to the Hexie. "And thanks for the chuckle, Canteen."

"Canteen?" said the Hexie. "Is this a joke name you're giving me, Junior? A canteen is a place of rest and relaxation, is it not?"

I wondered where he'd heard that word. It was slightly anachronistic—not unknown, but not in general use, either. The Hexies seemed to be omnivorous collectors of language.

". . . not that one I was thinking of. A canteen is something to take along on a trip; it holds water. When you get thirsty, you take a drink from it. Humans are always thirsty for knowledge."

"K-k-k—thank you, Junior, for that nice name. I like it much better than the one given to me recently by my fellows, which is 'Panteenee.' About one in a thousand of our offspring are genetically intractable, and present too much of a problem for the parents to raise. These are sent to a single complex maintained by the world government on the Eastern continent. The person who manages that complex is called the Panteenee. I suppose a quick translation would be 'headmaster for the home of juvenile delinquents.'"

I groaned. "I agree. I like Canteen better."

"You must forgive my fellows, Whitey, but they do like a good joke. And in ways, it is an apt one. To us, even an oldster of your species would seem very young. And as a civilization, you are just coming out of a period of considerable delinquency. In fact, there has already been a great deal of debate about whether or not humans are safe to deal with."

All traces of levity were gone as the Hexie looked into my eyes. "This is something it would be unfair to withhold from you, because you will have to deal with it once you get down on the planet. Many of us are sympathetic toward contact and commerce with you, but many also believe that to accept you with open arms might be a dangerous mistake."

I thought very hard for five seconds. "In your opinion, Panteen, what is the major factor that causes the trend against us?"

"It is something that may be hard for you to understand," he replied. "You people are a fine group, and fascinating as individuals, but to us, you lack a sense of—balance?—in your philosophy of living, and perhaps your whole civilization. You must understand that we, the Hexies," he smiled, "revere a total sense of humor. You are quite good at making jokes, too, but we think that you have a hard time laughing at yourselves. From what little we have been able to gather, it seems as if you pick leaders in almost the opposite way from us. Your great humans all seem to be surrounded with dignity. The more dignified and serious they are, the more likely they are to be considered 'great.'

"Yet we revere leaders who can see the humorous side of things, including themselves. Our world leaders are almost always elected on the wave of a 'joke play.' It may be written by a playwright, but the underlying premise—the humor—is invariably devised by the politician. We believe this gives us a sense of balance—an ability to face a hard world and universe—and even a strong degree of sympathy, that may be lacking in humans."

"Wow," I said, then turned to the gnome. "Junior, do you have the feeling that we've just been called a bunch of stuffed shirts?"

"I do believe so, old pip," he said.

"Canteen," I said, turning back to the Hexie, "I thank you very much for your words of advice. But you were being awfully serious as you said them. Perhaps you have been associating with us humans too long. . . ."

"K-k-k-k—Whitey, I believe there is hope for you." He looked out a window. "And now, we should stop this serious conversation so that you can see one of the most beautiful regions of our planet." He gestured to the viewports. I looked out and the breath went away from me.

The good views of Earth are from low orbit—say 200 kilometers—through as large a viewport as possible, or just floating in a suit. I've never done it, but they say it's quite a sight—much better than through a telescope. The absolute best way, they say, is from a high-altitude hypersonic plane, 20 or 30 kilometers up. The only time I'd been at that altitude was in a shuttle cabin without windows, coming down, and a booster cabin without windows, going up.

As we'd been talking, I'd been watching the pilot and the course of the floater. She'd killed our orbital velocity, which was all north-south, then plane-changed us and matched the planet's rotational speed at about 30 degrees south latitude. At no time did she attempt to establish an orbit. Once matched, she appeared to take us straight down. There was some buffeting from winds, but no frictional heating. We simply slipped into the upper atmosphere and descended at a kilometer or two per minute toward the land below.

When we looked through the generous viewports, the "lake country" was spread out fifty kilometers below and rising, leisurely, toward us. It was a land of green and blue: high rolling hills surrounding valleys, with seemingly a lake in each valley. But dominating all was Lake Karteneel, an irregular polygon measuring two or three hundred kilometers across at its widest point. To the south, the continental coastline ran east-west to a point about three hundred kilometers due south of the lake, then turned south and ran out of sight in the distance. I strained my eyes to follow it over the gentle curve of the planet, but was defeated finally by the distant haze.

"The lake country is known for its clear air and sunshine," said Panteen, "but today seems especially remarkable. Visibility is the best I've seen in several years. This is a good season for you to visit. The early autumn temperature is warm for us, and may even be comfortable for you. Currently, it is well over one-sixth of the way from freezing to boiling.

"Now we are close enough to see the capital city of Karteneely." He pointed a furry finger down through a canted side window. "Look there on the eastern side of the lake—you can see the shadows of the taller buildings."

The city came into plain view as we descended. It was a charming blend of green and color: grass and trees, white glass and earth-colored buildings—with enough pastels thrown in to make it just different from views of Earth. Another noticeable difference was that the buildings weren't laid out with any pattern that I could see. And something was missing. I couldn't place it at first, then it dawned on me: there were no streets. I could now see vehicles—but they must all be floaters. And then something else struck me: the city wasn't nearly large enough to house the millions that must live and work in the world's capital. There was a central core with the tallest buildings looking to be several stories high, and some residences surrounding it, but I estimated that no more than 50 or 60 thousand could possibly live there.

"Panteen, how many people live in Karteneely? It hardly seems large enough to be the seat of the world government."

He smiled. "Yes, I understand you have very large cities on Earth. We also used to have large cities. But for many centuries—millennia?—they have been lessening in size as we have taken advantage of the technology of the floaters. Now, Karteneely here is the largest center we have. Less than six-to-the-sixth people live in or near the city, but 36 times that many work here. Almost all live in the surrounding countryside, within a radius of two or three free."

The Hexie units of measure weren't too difficult to remember, even though based on sixes. The basic unit was the "freel," which was the planetary circumference divided by 6^6. It was very close to 860 meters. The "free" was 1,296 times the freel— about 1,100 kilometers. Therefore, the Hexies commuted to their capital city from as far

away as 3,000 kilometers. Floater technology certainly had
its advantages.

". . . lake country is too beautiful to go to waste, and we
tend to be an independent people—we like to 'get away
from it all,' as you say. And even from three free, the
commute takes just a little less than a tree."

At my insistence, Panteen used Hexie units often, so I
could get used to them, but it was still a little strange to
hear "free" and "tree" and not think of unshackled woods.
It wasn't really difficult. The "tree" was the basic useful
unit of time, and was $\frac{1}{36}$ of a day—almost exactly 34 minutes. And that made the next one down—a "treen," which
was $\frac{1}{36}$ of a tree—very close to one minute. No problem.
The Hexies could therefore commute at the rate of 6,000
kilometers an hour—call it Mach 4—but they must have
very good traffic control near the city, with a million or so
commuters.

". . . control is difficult, and it takes quite a large computer, along with very complex communications and tracking systems."

I looked to the surrounding hills, now "moving up" to
our altitude at a rapid pace. Sure enough, there were large
antennae on almost all of them—and all three types: radar,
ladar, and microwave. I wondered what Panteen meant by
"large." It would only take a couple of gigabytes of RAM,
with maybe another ten in fast memory or ROM.

Now we were really getting down. The city was starting
to take on real character. Except for large fliers just above
the tallest rooftops, there seemed to be no floater traffic
within the city boundaries. The "streets" were footpaths,
with pleasant-looking foliage on all sides. We appeared to
be descending to a large building, which I estimated would
be as large as a city block in an Earth city, and most of the
foot traffic in this part of the city seemed to be moving
toward it. I surmised that our reception would be large
and auspicious.

"Looks like they're going to haul out the fatted calf,"
cackled the gnome from another viewport. "You got a
building that can hold all those people, Canteen?"

"No, Junior," said the Hexie, smiling. "We will be received by the world government in our largest building—it

is our world's largest theater for joke plays—but it holds only six-to-the-fifth. The remainder are here to try to get a live glimpse of your party. After all, you have raised quite a commotion among us. Would it not be the same if we were to visit you on Earth?"

"In spades, Canteen, in spades. Probably even be worse—we'd have ground cars thrown in to add to the confusion."

We landed on top of the block-sized building. Before the roof cut off our view, we could see literally swarms of Hexies gathered around all sides of the structure. Panteen turned to me.

"Whitey, I know it is an imposition, and please feel free to refuse if you are too tired, since this is your first experience with gravity in some weeks—weeks! What a funny concept for a species that loves tens: seven days! —but it would be a good thing for us if you could walk around the edge of the building and show yourselves to the people, who will not get to see you otherwise."

I looked at the gnome. "How are you feeling, Junior?"

"Fiddle fit, Admiral."

We trooped back into the main cabin. I was greeted by a chorus of "What's up?" from the crew.

I held up my hands. "All right, folks. You've been briefed on what's going to happen on stage, but we've just been asked to do an ad lib: to show ourselves to the multitudes first. Their theater only holds about 6,500 people, but it seems there's about ten times that many hanging around to get a glimpse of us. So how about it?"

We trooped around the edge of the building, waving to the throngs, before we descended into the theater. Once inside, we knew what to expect. We would take an elevator down three floors to stage level, and there, so help me, we would become part of a set! It seems that the proper place to hold such an occasion as this was in the world president's large reception office, but since we were so special, they made special concessions to hold it in the theater. However, appearances would be maintained. We would be on a stage—but the stage would be set to mimic the office we should be in. The Hexies had a marvelous sense of theater, and were masters of live theater art.

In the large elevator, Panteen reminded me of it: "I do

not wish to make you uneasy, Whitey, but I would be careful not to be too pompous on stage. There will probably be many 'joke plays' written about this ceremony, and the playwrights will 'take shots' at everything we do and say."

"Thank you, Panteen," I laughed. "I can't think of anything you could have said to make me feel more nervous."

We were ushered into seats onstage. The set was so realistic—furniture, windows with outside views, and so forth—that I had to look at the audience occasionally to remind myself that we were not in a large office.

But when I did, the sight of all those alien faces left me a little wobbly-kneed, and the holo cameras grinding away the whole time didn't help, either. I tried to reassure myself by thinking that our cultures must be different enough so that if I made any faux pas, nobody would know.

Except the crew, of course. From my place on the front row, I sneaked a glance back at Junior, three seats behind and to one side. He caught my eye and winked broadly. I smiled and relaxed. I'd be damned if I was going to let the runt enjoy this alone.

We were introduced back and forth. There were seven Hexies onstage: the five heads of the Hexie "countries," the world president, and the "Frinithee." If I hadn't been briefed, I'd have thought the Frinithee was a vice-president or something equivalent. In fact, he was a figure almost as powerful as the president herself: a world-class ombudsman whose sole duty was to research the important decisions and laws made by the world government, and make fun of them. In this, he was *not* the equivalent of the "opposition party." The post was held for life, or until the incumbent's joke plays became stale.

Thank goodness the Hexies had long ago laughed pompous speeches out of existence. The world president said a few words in both Hexie and English. Her English was very good, with only a trace more of that "whistling" accent than shown by the contact team.

Then I said a few words, uncomfortably conscious that the cameras were grinding, and that fully one-third of the live and holo audiences understood what I was saying. I harped on the trade theme for about a minute, then sat down. My main message was that I thought we had something besides good humor to share with the Hexies. By that time I already knew that they were staunch capitalists, and had more than their share of honest greed for a buck.

There were three gifts to be presented on each side. We didn't know what theirs were, or vice versa. As the "visitors," we were to present our gifts first. I offered up the initial item, which was a model of the Earth-Moon-SpaceHome system, with scales incorrect so that all three bodies could be discerned. Seeing the beautifully detailed model of the Pinwheel, complete with solar parabolas, MMF, and even the partially completed Big Cylinder, gave me a momentary pang of homesickness. I sternly repressed it. Also by custom, I explained the gift as I presented it. It was received with smiles and polite exclamations of pleasure at its beauty.

Our second offering was made by Edward Allison-White. It was originally to have been the "English Teacher," but now that was gone, of course. So on the strong combined advice of Ethel Erickson and Junior, he was presenting an item from our onboard spares supply! It was a standard hundred-megabyte/one gigabyte memory chip—a cube about two centimeters of a side, with interleaved 10-molecule layers of silicon, diamond, and germanium. For our onboard computers we used it in the low-capacity mode, of course. We had no need for a seventh-generation computer with liquid helium cooling to take advantage of the gigabyte capacity.

Under careful instruction, Edward told of its capacity in powers of six, rather than ten. We wanted to obtain the maximum impact on the Hexies.

There was indeed some reaction—perhaps a little sucking in of breath at Edward's mention of six-to-the-thirteenth elements—but it wasn't quite as strong as expected.

The real surprise for us was the final gift, presented by Grace Kitigawa. It was a set of twelve small pieces of the finest of Japanese, Chinese, and Korean pottery art. They were exquisite, with their miniature flower artwork and layers of lacquer, hand-rubbed until they glowed with inner beauty. They'd been intended only as goodwill gifts, but when the holo cameras zoomed in for closeups, the audience sucked in its breath with audible awe.

To continue our surprise, one of the five leaders—the one from the western part of the western continent—completely broke protocol, rose from his seat, and went to the president's side to more closely examine one of the tiny bowls. He bent over it for several long seconds, turning it over in his little hands. Then he straightened up and nodded, keeping an absolutely straight face. That face without even a hint of a smile was a formal one; I'd heard about it from Michele Kimberly. It meant that something was so remarkable that in no way could fun ever be poked at it.

And in a moment, after the western country's leader sat back down, the world president confirmed my guess. She carefully chose three of the pieces and gave the rest back to Grace.

"These are beautiful—lovely. I do not have the words to say of their quality in your language. They are too valuable for me to keep all of them. I will take these three for display in the presidential residence, where there is a collection of such works. The others you should keep, or sell here through an agent who understands their value. They will bring enough money to allow your crew to purchase many luxuries during your stay on our world."

While I chewed that over, the Hexie president got up to give the gifts to us from the world government. She alone did the presenting, explaining the history and site of manufacture of each of the three items.

The very first one was a pleasant surprise. Pleasant, because it would begin to make our job easier right away; surprising, because I don't know how they managed to put it together in so short a time. It was a Hexie-to-English lexicon—written and spoken—with illustrations and phonetic breakdowns of all their sound groups. From it we could begin to build a true Hexie/English software package, as soon as we modified the input and output to handle the higher frequencies. I could almost hear Junior licking his chops behind me as I accepted it gratefully.

The second gift was from the largest "country," the one in which the seat of world government was located. It was an exquisite orrery of the Hexie solar system. We'd known from the Hexie artifacts found in our own system that they had superb manufacturing process control, and the globe they'd given us for study was a further example, but this was some kind of ultimate. I took a quick look at the workmanship as I accepted the gift with profuse thanks. The detail on the various small globes continued down to the limit of my ability to discern fine detail; somehow, I knew that it would take a high-power binocular microscope to resolve all the information it presented. Suddenly, I felt embarrassed at the relative shabbiness of our own similar gift.

The third gift made me feel better, and explained some previous events. It was a set of 18 pieces of handcrafted pottery, mainly miniature china plates and bowls. The president explained that they typified the finest works of art from the western country of Mnierfree, and were the principal export of that area. I looked carefully at several of them. They were nice, but nowhere near the quality of the Eastern pieces we'd given half an hour before. As I thanked the president and passed the pieces around for inspection by our crew, I glanced over at the western country's leader. His face remained absolutely immobile, and did not return my glance.

The ceremony over, the world president made a final short speech.

"Our friends from Earth, we have now exchanged gifts, and we have received you to our world. You have our leave to remain here as long as you wish. We are sorry that we cannot provide you with food, but all other needs will be taken care of for as long as you choose to remain. You will be given apartments in this city in which to dwell. Transportation will be provided to wherever you wish to travel—on the world or off of it. We encourage you to learn about our world, and to teach us of yours. And when you wish finally to depart, you will go with our best wishes, and we will remember Humans as we knew each of you."

I mulled that last sentence over, even as I was standing to make my reply. It sounded like a gentle way of saying that the impression we made was going to weigh heavily in the Hexie decision about what to do with Humans in general—so we'd better be good.

"Thank you, President Czankee—not only for your gifts and generosity, but as a species, for giving us the chance to participate in this great adventure. We intend to remain as long as possible. But even if we were to leave this day, we would carry back stories of the beauty of your world, and the kindness and laughter of your people."

Chapter 15

The Hexies take one sexual partner for life. Period. Monogamy is not a choice; permanent male-female pair bonding is a physiological imperative. Through a process we do not yet understand, the birth of the child somehow stimulates hormonal changes in the male also, and both sexes suckle their young. The survival advantages of this arrangement are obvious; the social consequences are also obvious, upon reflection. . . .

　　　　　　　　　　　　—Kimberly: Hexie White Papers

Our apartments were homelike and unusual at the same time. Sean and Michele had worked closely with the Hexies in charge of housing us on the planet, so the beds, chairs, bathrooms, lights, and so forth were anthropometrically correct, but the stamp of alien manufacture was on all of them. There was a lack of angularity we were not used to, and a blend of colors—pastels, blacks, and whites—a little strange to our eyes.

The site of the apartments was choice: on a hillside right outside the city, overlooking the lake. The setting was quite lovely, and the foliage—all based on chlorophyll conversion of sunlight—was close enough to ours to be positively homelike.

Some of our habits seemed to surprise the Hexies—for instance, the frequency with which we used the water closets. On Tharthee (I might as well call it that) animals tended to use their intake more efficiently, and held their liquid and solid wastes quite a bit longer—Hexies included.

Another surprise to them was our lack of permanent pair-bonding. A Hexie, after attaining adulthood, chose a partner fairly early; the pair then produced a child in short order. The process of giving birth and raising the child bonded them so closely that a permanent lifetime relationship was formed. Consequently, the Hexies were surprised when literally all of us requested separate quarters. They knew we were split equally man and woman, and had a hard time understanding that (with some exceptions) we did not wish to be housed in male-female pairs. When they finally found out that we had habits of occasionally changing sexual partners, some just tilted their heads in that peculiar way that said so eloquently: "we'll never understand."

And for our part, the Hexies' apparent nonconcern with sexual matters was perhaps the most unusual difference between our species. Humans are generally obsessed with *vive la différence*. Much of our own humor, in fact, would be lost on the Hexies because they didn't even comprehend the concept of a "dirty joke."

But for the most part, the more we learned about the Hexies, the more like "fellow travelers" they seemed. There were so many similarities in attitudes and cultures that we found it almost impossible not to accept them as brothers and sisters.

However, we had a mission—a duty to ourselves and humans to perform. During the first few days on the ground, I held serious meetings with the crew, and especially with Edward and Grace. I planned to delegate authority to them, but we had to get straight what we wanted to do.

The Hexie world government had made it clear that we would be observed and studied, just as we would study the Hexies, but we were not to be shackled or kept as "pets" of the government. We would be given freedom to come and go as we pleased, provided we did not break their relatively simple laws of intrusion, bodily harm, or theft. The "contact team" would remain with us. At least one of them would accompany each of us whenever we traveled outside the city. This was partly to keep us out of trouble, partly to keep studying us, and partly to translate, whenever necessary.

We finally settled on using the Hexie contingent as prime sources of information to find out what other sites

and Hexie persons we needed to visit. The objective was to
find out as much about Hexie science, technology, and
culture as possible before our food supply got low enough
that we had to head for home. (The discovery that Hexie
world life was based on right-handed amino acids and
left-handed sugars was quite a blow to our hopes of getting
fresh food on the planet. They refused to let us try to grow
our own anywhere on the planet, and I didn't blame them.
Unlikely as it was to happen, one seed getting out of hand
could cause lots of trouble for their ecology. We were
requested strongly to eat no seed-bearing food on the
planet, and special provisions were set up to dispose of our
wastes, even during trips outside our apartments.)

So we had a little over a Hexie year, if we wanted to
stay that long. I did. Not only did I want us to find out as
much as possible about the Hexies, but I wanted to give
them plenty of time to feel comfortable with us. I felt that
we had a fine group of people, and that the longer we
were on the ground, the more the Hexies would take to
us.

The Hexies made no bones about their nature—they
were individualists and highly capitalistic. The world government was laissez faire by historical and political necessity. It would supply us with all the basics, but the rest
would depend on the individual Hexies with whom we
came in contact. They might give us gifts, or they might
choose to cold-shoulder us. What happened during our
stay here was largely up to us, our individual desires, and
how Hexie individuals perceived us. We might approach
anyone we wished and ask him or her to devote time to
us, or vice versa.

An important consideration in our contact plan was our
possession of the nine remaining Eastern *objets d'art*,
which we came to realize early on that the Hexies coveted
very much. With Panteen's conspirational help, we caused
the word to be spread that we would give all of the pieces
away before we left the planet—but that we would not
decide to whom until our stay was almost over. This was a
transparent device to get everyone to be nice to us, but it
worked like a charm. The Hexies were quite capable of

recognizing an appeal to greed, even while responding to it and laughing at themselves the whole time.

So instead of us having to buy favors, we usually had only to indicate an interest—whereupon gifts and invitations to the homes and offices of scientists, technology experts, and manufacturing moguls would be bestowed with alacrity.

Thus our band spread far and wide into universities, laboratories, observatories, and homes of the well-known and wealthy. I left this hegira in the able hands of Grace and Edward. My only instructions to the crew were:

"Have a good time and be yourselves—and for goodness sake, let them know that you can see the funny side of life. The better your sense of humor, the more likely you are to get along."

Myself, I took on two jobs. The first was as the expedition archaeology guru. I visited the homes, offices, and even the diggings of several of the leading authorities, under the guidance of Panteen and an eager young (227 years) Hexie archaeologist named Grantheer.

The two most important things I learned were: (1) the Hexies had better, more sensitive dating methods than we did. They had better preservation due to a colder climate, longer written-history baselines, and much better availability of cross-checks; and (2) with some differences in flavor, they seemed to have a past just about as warlike as our own—they'd just been civilized longer.

I didn't consider archaeology studies to be my primary endeavor on the Hexie world. The most important function I performed was to kick around, accompany others on their own voyages of discovery, see the sights, and shoot the bull with Panteen. I wanted to get an overall gestalt of the world and the people, to be in the best possible position to judge Hexie intentions toward humans and take that judgment back to the solar system.

All of this let me have a lot of fun, with the excuse that I was doing useful work. Junior said it with his usual fine delicacy:

"What a bunch of crap, Dimp. What it is, you've worked hard for four years and now you're going to lie back on your duff and take a break." Then, cackling: "Of course, I intend to do likewise, since I have the only other job in this crazy outfit that'll allow me to get away with the same crap."

I began by just walking around the city for a couple of weeks, talking to anybody who knew English—and some who didn't, when Panteen was with me—and soaking up the attitudes. I also watched quite a bit of holo, asking any convenient Hexie to translate for me when possible.

I found out some things to think about during that early period. The Hexies' longer lives gave them a perspective we needed to understand more fully. They tended to take a much broader view of things, to put ongoing events into historical perspective even as they were happening. Regarding us, they seemed to be genuinely friendly, but with an undertone of reserve. There was watchfulness, and perhaps a resolution to do whatever was necessary to preserve their own species if we humans turned out to be inimical to their perceived future.

But their reserve was mainly hidden, a "deep background" to a worldwide avid interest in us humans and our doings. The Hexie sense of curiosity was every bit as developed as our own—we created a stir whenever we visited a new place.

The most striking thing about living with the Hexies was feeling their indomitable sense of humor. We'd been exposed to it during our month in orbit, and I'd had stronger hints from Panteen. But the more I experienced the Hexie world, the more I came to realize that their humor was perhaps the most important cultural mind set they possessed.

Joke names were more than commonplace; they were ubiquitous. I soon made a proper transition. The best way to find out how the Hexies truly felt about something was to ask what its joke name was. If the joke name was clever and complimentary, that thing or person was admired; if it was simply funny or innocuous, there was probably general acceptance. If the joke name was bitingly satirical, the person or thing probably had garnered disapproval of the populace.

Animals were most popular for use as joke names, because they had a wide variety of characteristics and habits;

but the Hexies might also add special high-frequency adjectives for special tailoring. Thus, a person who made threats (or promises) that he usually failed in executing might be called "big kalikree with a high, squeaky voice," which is equivalent to our "all bark and no bite." The cleverest joke names were phonetic puns on the person's or thing's true given name.

Junior made joke names a special project. He was most qualified to do this, because he was best equipped to memorize the relevant parts of the Hexie lexicon. He was constantly asking the Hexie names for people and things, and bestowing his own joke names on them for practice.

In this way and others Junior was the first of us to get a real "reputation" among the Hexies. He was popular wherever he went, and always drew a crowd. Both his size and sense of humor set him apart from the rest of us in the Hexies' minds. He was easily recognizable, and always likely to say something that would make the Hexies laugh delightedly.

I tried my best to imitate the runt in my own way, but I was a tyro by comparison. He was everywhere and into everything. He wore out more than one contact team escort, and when he was with me, his "watchdogs" seemed more than willing to leave him to Panteen. That was an arrangement which suited me just fine, as we were able to sneak more time alone that way. Panteen was sensitive enough to our moods to realize when we wanted to talk together for a while without someone else listening in.

Another thing I found out early was just how pervasive the Hexie "joke play" system was. There seemed to be at least one shown on holo every day. (I found out from Panteen that some were reruns, and some were classics revered by the public.) And about once a week there seemed to be an important new debut. Some of the plays were stylized, and some obviously informal. Many had slapstick I could enjoy even without knowledge of the language. A universal ground rule seemed to be that a live audience must be present at the taping, and that the camera move to it once in a while to show closeups of the audience reaction.

I was watching the holo one afternoon, waiting for Junior

and Panteen to show up at my apartment. We were going to take a trip to the far northern archipelago of Freetheen. A new show started, and I was surprised to see the world president appear on the screen. She talked for several mintues before the action started. Her speech was punctuated by grins and laughs in such a way that I knew what was coming. When she got off, a joke play began immediately.

It was a very high-quality production, judging from the others I'd seen—and I thought those had been excellent! The set was so realistic that at first I thought it was more like a movie. Then the first audience shot proved it was a stage: the camera panned 180 degrees and zoomed in on the audience members, never breaking continuity, before it panned back to stage center. No chance for a faked reaction there.

And then, much to my astonishment, a human entered stage right. And even more astonishing, it was obviously me! The makeup and characterization were superb, down to the lift shoes the Hexie must have been wearing to get my height. The rest of the crew followed. The scene was obviously meant to represent our welcoming ceremony. I wished I could understand what was being said, because I could hear laughter from the audience quite often.

I turned the holo down when I heard the multitoned doorbell of my apartment.

"Come in, Panteen!"

The Hexie entered, with a look on his face that I took for puzzlement. "Whitey, how did you surmise that it was me? Sometimes you do things I still cannot understand."

"Everyone else is gone, so it had to be either you or Junior—and Junior never bothers to ring."

"But I thought that humans revered privacy, even as much as we do."

"True enough, Panteen. But Junior is not one to respect convention."

"K-k-k—I have noticed that, and so have my fellows. We now call him Kreekree. That is a small wild animal, both charming and annoying, which inhabits both continents. It is very cunning, and can enter the most tightly closed homes. It gets into everything, and eats any food left out. A couple visited by a kreekree will have two or

three days of work to get their house back in order. Yet we
admire the kreekree because it is so clever."

I smiled. "That's Junior, all right." Then I changed the
subject by gesturing to the holo screen.

"There's a joke play being broadcast, which involves our
crew. What's it all about?"

Panteen smiled. "I was in the audience for the first live
performance last night," he said. "It was amusing, but not
an especially great one. Its live run will certainly be less
than six days."

"But why did President Czankee introduce the play?"

The Hexie looked at me from 600-year-old-eyes. "Whitey,
I think you still do not appreciate the force of the joke play
in the politics of our countries and the world government.
Since Teenteel became the first world president many
generations ago, then retired to take the office of Frinithee
for the remainder of his life, the play has been the prime
factor in important decision-making. Unless a decision or
policy is so clear-cut that it is obvious to a large majority of
the population, there are bound to be one or more joke
plays to try to corner opinion. If a decision is ill-advised
and a subsequent joke play well-done, it is quite likely to
force a change of leadership."

He smiled. "Naturally, there are bound to be joke plays
with humans involved."

"Is this the first joke play involving us?"

"No, this is the third. As you might expect, two opposing factions exist outside the government. One wants to
welcome you without reservation. They wish to establish
immediate unlimited trade, bring our technologies to the
same level, and proceed together to new discoveries and
techniques possible with our combined skills and outlooks.
This faction believes that we may not be the only species
who have, ahh, begun to extend ourselves beyond their
local system, and that it is only a matter of time before we
encounter another which may not be nearly as friendly as
yourselves."

I smiled without showing teeth. "I must say that I find
myself completely in agreement with that faction."

"K-k-k—I do not blame you, Whitey. In fact, I must
confess that I find myself, for all my conservatism, leaning

toward that faction also. Being close to you day by day tends to make me much more sympathetic toward your aspirations. But unfortunately," he continued, "that faction is smaller than its opponents. They believe that humans are basically too repressive and warlike, and likely to be unstable partners in such a relationship. They think there is even a possibility that humans would do everything they could to gain the upper hand in such a partnership."

He looked me in the eye without smiling. "This faction believes that we should dismiss you for good, and close communications with you altogether. In fact, they are distressed that you have been permitted to learn the location of our solar system with respect to your own."

He continued without smiling, which I took seriously. When the twinkle left Panteen's eyes, it was time to listen.

"And now, most of the people of the country of Mnierfree side with this faction." He allowed a small smile to play briefly on his face. "I'm afraid that your gift of handcrafted pottery to the world government had something to do with this. It is something which we can poke fun of, but it will remain a real force nonetheless."

"The views of the government command a majority which is still much larger than either faction," he continued. "That is to wait to pass judgment until events mature—to get more information before we decide what to do."

I thought about everything for a moment.

"It seems to me," I finally said, "that the 'wait and see' attitude is the only one which makes sense right now. No matter how much I sympathize with the first group, I cannot believe that Hexies have had enough time to truly evaluate humans yet. After all, you've known us for only just over a preeleen." (The Hexie year contains 483.73 of their short days. They break this down into 12 preeleen— "months"—of 36 days each. At the end of the year there is a longer period called the "preelee," which lasts either 51 or 52 days, according to a formula much more complex than Earth's leap year scheme.)

Panteen moved his head in a nod which had become

almost human during the past few weeks. "And neither
have you had time to evaluate us. The world government—
and probably even the Frinithee, if the truth be known—
believes that 'wait and see' is the best strategy.

"But," he said with the twinkle back in full force, "if
there is one area in which none of us are conservative, it is
the expression of our views through joke plays. Each faction knows its duty lies in trying to capture the sympathy
of the general populace by making them laugh at the
others.

"And so, quite early on, the 'make them go home'
faction presented a play. This was followed several days
later by one produced by the 'welcome them with open
arms' faction."

Panteen smiled. "In the first, I regret to say that you
humans were not shown in such a good light. The 'juvenile
delinquent' theme was played strongly. And I must confess that some of my own reports added some material for
their story. We understand fairly well the roles of Jason
French and Chin Wu Lin, and these were artfully exaggerated in the play." He winked in a gesture he'd picked
up from humans. "Those two gentlemen themselves have
added to the picture. They seem to expend much energy
trying to negotiate commercial advantages in which the
other is left out."

I nodded and winked a wink of my own. "This seems to
be an activity well understood by Hexies."

"Yes," smiled Panteen, "and one of which we are quite
fond of mocking among ourselves."

"Well," I said with a sigh, "how did the other faction
fare in their production?"

"Not quite so well, I'm afraid," responded the Hexie.
"Unfortunately, their cause is more philosophical than personal, and is more difficult to present in a joke play.
Humor is much more solid when individual personalities
can be characterized. They were able to portray Junior
quite sympathetically, and Grace and Ethel were also
good subjects. But you, my friend," he pointed a finger at
the middle of my chest, "have not become a memorable
character. Hardly anyone on the planet realizes that you

have an excellent sense of humor, because you have not shown it in your behavior."

That was a bitter pill to swallow, especially after my lecture to the crew.

Panteen saw my face and smiled. "*I* know your wit, because I have worked with you closely. In fact, I was called in as a professional advisor by the producer, and I gave them several examples of your humor. But alas, they were incidents that only I knew of, and did not create a wide feeling of believability among the viewers."

I expressed mock anguish. "So here I am, a total failure—and not even six-cubed years of age yet."

"K-k-k—you illustrate my point, Whitey. Your wit is sharp, but you save it for the few. You must spread yourself around, my friend."

I smiled but shook my head. "I won't go out of my way to get into politics, Panteen. Not yet, anyway. So what about this play that's going on right now?" I gestured to the screen where Hexies and humans were still cavorting.

"As you have probably guessed, this is the government's answering play. In the productions of both other factions, the world government was pictured as wringing its hands and blithering—dithering?—about making a decision, not knowing what to do. This play attempts to turn the tables on both 'act now' factions by portraying them as hasty juveniles."

He smiled. "Even though she lost some timing, President Czankee was smart to delay her own play. She gained much by waiting to see what material was in the other plays, then capitalizing on their mistakes. And also, by taking her time, she was able to put together a superior production."

Panteen waved a hand at the holo. "We Hexies love good theater, and this is an excellent example. Of course, the president commands top playwrights and facilities, but taking her time for a good production was a strong factor in the superiority of her effort."

He looked at the ongoing action on the screen for a moment before continuing: "I found it entertaining—much more so than the previous two. And by the finish, I found myself moving back from the 'open arms' faction to the 'wait and see' group, so the play had its desired effect."

"Will the Frinithee produce a play now?" I asked.

"I do not think so," answerd Panteen. "He may eventually do so—but not right away. The Frinithee's primary function is not to make decisions, but to criticize them. He best serves his office by staying in the background, continuing to gather information, and remaining in a posture to ridicule the president if she makes a hasty or incorrect decision. If the Frinithee acts too quickly—"

"Hey, you guys, you look awfully serious! The president's play that bad?" Junior entered stage left and put an end to our conversation. "I think the likeness of me is pretty good—the actor doesn't even have to wear elevator shoes. And that's a great joke name—Kreekree. I'm going to do my damnedest to live up to it."

Panteen smiled fondly at the gnome. "You have already lived up to it, Junior—that is why it was given."

The gnome cackled, delighted as a kid with a new toy.

"Okay," I said, "let's get this show on the road before the Boy Wonder, here, gets his head swelled too large to get out the door."

The Hexies were avid lovers of the natural beauty of their world, and floater technology allowed them to indulge their sightseeing proclivities to the full. All the spots of great wonder were well-attended.

One of the greatest was the northernmost island of the archipelago called Freetheen. This chain of islands had been formed the same way as Hawaii on Earth. Its origin was an active point in the planetary mantle, which regularly broke through the overriding plate to build an island from fresh magma. But there were two major differences that set Freetheen apart from Hawaii. The first was that Freetheen's underlying plate was moving more slowly, and the activity had been ongoing for a much longer time; therefore, the island chain was longer, and its islands larger, than Hawaii. Second, instead of being tropical, it was arctic. In fact, the newest island—the one with the active volcanoes—was within ten degrees of the pole.

And that was the reason for its attraction. When the

molten lava met the 80-below-zero ice, it put on quite a show.

While we were walking to the floater, Junior got down to business:

"So, Canteen, what's the joke name for this island?"

Panteen smiled. "It is 'Plaqueer,' which you would translate as 'Pile number 8.' "

"There's got to be more."

"No. But the joke is what is understood among us, rather than actually said in the name. In this case, the word 'pile' is understood to mean 'pile of dung from the pranikee.' "

The gnome cackled. "That's pretty high-class for a joke name, Panteen. Didn't think you guys had it in you."

It seemed pretty low-class to me. I asumed my "eyebrows raised politely while Junior and Panteen are sharing a private joke" pose and waited patiently. Junior finally relented.

"Admiral, you know the Hexie fauna are pretty good at holding in their feces, but the pranikee is the champion anal retentive of all time. It's about the size of a small bear, and lives in the far north, on a few of the islands of Streen. Hibernates a lot, and with one thing and another, it only takes a dump once a year. I haven't seen it, but it must be a godawful event. Anyway, the pile is large, and incredibly fertile. Turns out that fifteen or sixteen species of Hexie plants and insects depend on the once-a-year cycle for their own existence."

He turned to Panteen. "You must have laid that name on it within the past few generations."

I understood what he meant. It took a sophisticated knowledge of plate tectonics to get the point. Without having taken Anna-Marie Smith's classes aboard ship, I would've still been lost.

"Correct as usual, Kreekree," said the Hexie. "In fact, we did not even know of Freetheen's existence until we started exploring the world with floaters."

The trip from the capital city of Karteneely to Freetheenee, the northernmost island, was just over 15,000 kilometers. We planned to do it in an hour and a half by taking the floater up out of the atmosphere, killing most of our eastward velocity, and simply moving north. Junior and I were both under instruction as floater pilots, so I took the con for the trip north, and Junior would take it coming back.

I enjoyed flying a new machine, and the exhilarating feeling of controlling a craft relative to a planetary surface. I was helped by the fact that the Hexies didn't use voice control in their floaters and that—outside of the vicinity of the big cities—they were accustomed to flying manually, trusting their collision radar to keep them out of serious trouble. The controls were set up with visual displays that I could use with some coaching, and I didn't have to learn too much Hexiese to work the console keyboard. Mostly it was stick control. It was fun.

We went straight up 20 kilometers, after which Pintee, our instructor pilot, gave me control. I had a pleasant session, and at its end I was mildly proud of having successfully battled the arctic winds and brought the floater to rest on the southern rim of the island's most active volcano.

The scene spread out in front of the forward viewports was awe-inspiring. The crater was filled almost entirely with snow and ice—not surprising, since the temperature here at 80 degrees north latitude averaged far below zero. But where the volcano was active, we could see a lake of lava glowing in the half-light of spring; the sun was not far below the horizon. I saw where the lava flow must go over the lip when the volcano erupted. It was almost directly across the rim from us—a large notch with smooth edges. There was a breeze blowing directly from our position toward the north. The steam from the lava dissipated quickly, leaving the whole sight open to our view.

"We have excellent conditions for seeing," said Panteen. "And the volcano has been very active for the past sixday. I hope we have luck and see an eruption." He turned and headed for the airlock. "Come. Let us go outside. It is unsporting to watch the volcano from behind glass."

Junior and I knew about the Hexie custom of getting outside to see the sights, even if they traveled there in comfort. We approved, but this would be a cold one. We donned heated suits, then full-body parkas with hoods.

Even Panteen and the pilot put on plenty of clothes. Frostbite was rare among the Hexies, but not impossible.

We stepped out into seventy below, and needed every bit of our protection. At Panteen's insistence we stood silently for a while on the lip, listening to the ice in the caldera shift and crack. It was eerie.

Finally it got too cold to stand still, and it looked as if the mountain would not cooperate to put on a bigger show for us, but I was still glad we'd come. Earth did not hold a comparable sight—and certainly not SpaceHome.

Before we headed back to the floater, Pintee turned to me and said: "That was a good job of flying, Whitey, and your landing was quite nice for a beginning pilot. It is difficult to choose between yourself and the Kreekree as to expertise in handling a floater."

Her voice startled me from a reverie. I'd been thinking back in time to the rim of another crater many years ago—Mons Gargantua on Titan. I'd done some pretty fancy piloting there, too. I wondered if the Hexies were occasionally telepathic like humans.

"Thank you, Pintee," I said. "But your excellent ladar had a lot to do with the landing. I depended on it in this twilight."

Then Junior turned to Panteen with another apparently irrelevant question: "Canteen, have you Hexies come up with a joke name for the Admiral, here, yet?"

"No, Junior. Whitey is not yet well-known enough to have a joke name given by the general populace." In the quiet icy air I detected what might have been just a touch of regret in the Hexie's voice.

"Pity," said the runt. "If he doesn't get one soon, we'll have to start one ourselves." Junior was fully aware of Hexie politics, and the need to have the human leader well-known and well thought of. The best way to accomplish this was for me to have the right kind of joke name.

"That is possible, Junior. The manufacturing of joke names has been done before—especially by young politicians who wish to appear well known before their time has really come." I could picture the Hexie grinning toothlessly in the shadow of his hood. "But if we do that, we must be very careful. If we are found out, and the name is not appropriate, we could be laughed off the planet."

As I watched Panteen's breath steam out into the air above the caldera, I became aware that the red glow kilometers below was increasing in intensity. Looking down, I saw new magma forcing its way up through the crust on the lava. Steam rose fiercely from the pool's edges, where it was expanding onto untouched ice. Then suddenly, the lake burst into violent action. Red-hot liquid boiled, then exploded upward in a fountain of glowing lava. The pool rose and spilled over the notch in the southern rim—great steams arising where the liquid rock ran over snow and ice. It was magnificent.

"Ahhh," said Panteen. "Our irrelevant talk has brought the volcano to life. We have goaded it into expressing displeasure with our inattention."

We watched it for a full tree, risking frostbite gladly, before climbing back into the floater. Then Junior took us out over the center of the caldera for a spectacular closeup before he rose up out of the atmosphere for the trip back home.

Chapter 16

. . . detailed study of Hexie physiology and histology will be a task of many years. For instance, do they have a Krebs cycle nearly equivalent to ours, in which adenosine triphosphate is the body energy transport molecule? Do calcium, sodium, and magnesium play the same crucial roles? And so forth. We are just beginning the monumental task of translating the physiology primers and advanced texts . . . limited discussions and studies on Tharthee, there appear to be some major differences. Their building blocks are dextrorotary amino acids and levrorotary sugars. They utilize their intake, both liquids and solids, much more efficiently than we do. And so forth. Whether or not we shall be able to ferret from these differences the basis of their longevity is unknown at this time.

> *—Korliss:* Hexie White Papers

. . . computer controlled, of course, and their standards are exacting. Whitey, they could teach us a thing or two about high-G manufacturing, especially at the micro level."

It was Ethel Erickson doing the talking, giving me her second briefing. She'd been a busy bee, both on the planet and off.

"How about microgravity?" asked Junior. He sat in with me during briefings if he wasn't busy elsewhere. Usually, either Grace or Edward was also present, but today they were both gone. I preferred to have the gnome over anybody else. He asked smarter questions and made me look good.

"They ain't so hot there," she said. " 'Fact, we might teach them a thing or two." She scratched at a wrinkle in the corner of her mouth. "Can't quite figure it, either.

With the tonnage they can put into orbit, they should be doing shit-hot—have it all over us."

Junior tugged an ear. "Been kind of interested in that myself, old girl. I think it's economic. Humans pay about 20 bucks a pound to lift surface material into Earth orbit, since we can't use CRF in the atmosphere. Hexies pay at least a couple of orders of magnitude less. I think that gives them a couple orders of magnitude less motivation to make the most of what they've got once they get up there. Essentially the same gig as their computers being so much larger than ours."

"Yeah," said the woman, "so how does that square with their fine control of microprocessing on the planet? It was the high cost of lifting hardware into orbit that gave us the initial motivation to go micro—and yet it turns out that the Hexies actually have better control than we do on Earth. Doesn't make sense. And don't call me 'old girl,' you little squirt. I'm young enough to be your grandmother."

"Three gets you two that it has something to do with their floater technology," said the runt, ignoring Ethel's diatribe. "I'll bet that if you look into it, you'll find that they developed their quantum molecular technology before they went into space, and that the technology requires some pretty fancy control of miniature manufacturing processes."

He wrinkled up his wizened face. "In fact, I'd be willing to bet that they got floater technology even before computers. That might be a clue we could use, since the Tharkee Company doesn't seem anxious to talk a lot about the origins of its proprietary knowledge. Maybe there's something obvious that Fermi, or Schroedinger, or one of those other old farts missed and got us off on the wrong foot."

"Ethel," I asked, "do you see any doors at all that we could get a foot into? Do we have things they really want?"

"I think so, Whitey," she replied. "They've got depth and maturity in what they make and use—but not nearly as much variety as us humans. I think they're soft from too many monopolies or near-monopolies in large, important technology spheres. We humans tend to create markets for products that aren't always useful—but I think the Hexies go too far in the other direction. As long as a monopoly doesn't charge too high a price for its item, the Hexies seem content to let it flourish."

She pulled out an old-fashioned handkerchief and blew her nose. "We might be heading in that direction, but we ain't there yet by a long sight. We flood ourselves with new and different ways of doing things, and lots of times, we get improved products out of it. We've got a selection of consumer and technological hardware that'd make their heads swim. All we've got to do is find out what they might be interested in. Not deodorants, that's for damn sure."

She put the handkerchief back into her coat pocket. She always wore a coat, even indoors. She claimed that the planet was so cold that even the 25 degrees inside our complex seemed like 15.

"Hmmm," I said intelligently. "Tell you what: tomorrow you and Junior go into a huddle and figure out how you might work on those bright little hunches he's been throwing out. Then develop an action plan with decision points, and get your Hexie counterparts to take you to the right people to try to get to square two. Check it out with Grace or Edward first, of course."

"Good thing you asked me nicely," said the woman. "Otherwise, I wouldn't dream of working with this little pipsqueak, here."

"I love you, too, Grandma, old girl," said the pipsqueak.

I beamed fondly at the pair. They worked well together. I had high hopes they might dig up something useful.

For the hundredth time since climbing into the big sailboat, I took a deep breath of salt air and looked around delightedly. "I could really fall in love with this, Panteen."

"So you have said several times, my friend," smiled the Hexie. "We, too, feel a strong attraction for the sea, even though it is no longer an important commercial avenue of transport. That is why we still build and sail these boats—just for the love of it. And that is also why the government assists the Kircheeth Company in keeping the canal open. It is expensive, but every year, thousands pay the tolls to sail through it and feel in our own lungs and bodies how it used to be."

We were just at the southern portal of the Hexie equivalent of the Panama Canal, built before the advent of floater technology. We were going to sail through. There were seven of us—all from SpaceHome except for Dick Gates, who'd never been asea on Earth and wanted to give it a try.

The eastern and western continents were pulling away from each other, sedately but inexorably, at a rate of about half a centimeter a year. The part that was stretching was the connecting isthmus, called Teeurvileed. It was narrow, tortuous, and had a high mountainous spine running almost its entire length. It had been crossed twice: once by the Hexie forerunner species several million years ago, when it first spread across both continents; the second time by the advanced species that arose on the eastern continent after a cold spell of a hundred millennia had decimated the original population almost to the point of extinction.

The canal itself, and the territory on which it was situated, were for generations bones of contention between the two territories occupying the proximal ends of the continents. In fact, it created the political situation that resulted in the rise of Teenteel to power and the beginning of the modern political system.

I lurched my way to the bow of the boat to get an unimpeded view of the headlands as we entered the canal. Panteen came with me. The opening was natural. It appeared to be just an inlet, like several we'd already passed on our way here. I said so to Panteen.

"That is because it is indeed just an inlet, Whitey. It has been several sixes of years since I have been here, but as I remember, this inlet bends to the west, before finally coming to an end. There the canal proper begins."

I looked past the headlands to the interior. The rugged mountains, through which we'd be sailing shortly, lifted their shoulders haughtily. I breathed deeply again and was glad to be alive, and glad to be seeing things that no human had seen.

I waved my hand at the scene in general and said to

Panteen: "What is the joke name for this magnificent property?"

He grinned toothless. "Teeurvileed, the isthmus, we call 'Theend Leetcha,' for a species of fish that remains connected for a long while after mating. They actually have to struggle to disengage the male's sexual member from the female.

"The canal itself we call 'Phrifeer.' The closest English equivalent is 'an expensive-to-maintain item of which one is too stubbornly fond to discard.' Perhaps a close translation would be 'white elephant,' which is an English expression I understand only from context."

I shook my head in chagrin and admiration. "You truly have a joke name for everything, don't you, Panteen?"

All of a sudden he was possessed by one of his rare, serious moods.

"Not everything, Whitey. Once we discovered another species that was truly bad, and out of fear we destroyed their civilization. We have no joke names for them, or anything associated with our actions. Some things are too serious even for us to joke about. It is a pity, because if we could ever bring ourselves to laugh about it, perhaps the pain would go away."

I thought hard for a moment, then chose my words carefully: "What was so bad about them that you had to destroy them?"

"They were intelligent, and almost to the point where they would travel off-world for the first time. They had almost ruined their planet with wars and waste. They seemed to be motivated solely by power and avarice. It seemed likely that they would turn everything in the universe to their own ends, if they could. They were truly vicious, by our standards and yours, Whitey. But we did not kill most of them; we simply destroyed their civilization."

I looked at the Hexie, then said: "How did you do it?"

He shook his head. "Please, my friend, let us not pursue this further. It is truly too painful for us to talk about still, even after several generations. I should not have mentioned it, so let us pretend that I did not." He smiled again, and the light came back into his face. "Let us continue to enjoy this day, as we sail through the penis of Theend Leetcha."

I smiled back. "You're the boss, Panteen."

But I didn't enjoy the day for a long time afterward.

". . . so I want you to find out everything you can about this other species. Edward, Grace, this is important. From what I could determine, the Hexies hated doing what they did—but it didn't stop them, in the final analysis. We need to find out what they did, and why, and when—hell, we need to find every detail we can dig up. Spread the word. Ask questions discreetly, but ask them."

"I got the word yesterday, Captain. Those mole sieve heater elements are now a nonproblem. They made us up a few dozen, no sweat, as soon as they got the specs and translated them."

"That's good to hear, Sean. How's the overhaul coming?"

"Slow but sure. I figure we'll be ready in a few weeks."

"Good. Don't overdo it, but keep your hand in. I'll be up for inspection as soon as you give the word."

". . . don't keep a 24-hour day in SpaceHome just to do business with Earth, Captain. We do it because it's healthy. We've evolved that way, and deep down inside we're unhappy with anything else."

"I haven't noticed any unusual behavior among the crew, George. Are you telling me there's trouble brewing?"

"Maybe not for a while yet. Humans have proved to be remarkably adaptable. And so far, the signs are minimal. A slight lack of energy for some; a few more headaches than normal; a higher incidence of constipation and diarrhea; irregular menses among the women. Nothing to get excited about right away."

"So when should I get excited?" Korliss's worry worried me. I'd been constipated a couple of times myself; it was tough trying to train the bowels to a new length of day.

"I wish I knew. It's hard to be an M.D. and still keep up with the physiological literature. I know there've been studies done for well over a century, but they aren't common. It's very inconvenient to keep research subjects shut off from the world for months at a time on an artificial day/night cycle. I haven't read anything with a long enough baseline to really tell. We'll just have to play it by ear."

"All right, doctor. Keep me informed. I'd like regular reports. How about once every preeleen?"

"That's a Hexie month—36 days—isn't it?"

"Yeah."

Jason French and Chin Wu Lin came in and sat down without a word when I gestured them into chairs. I could tell from their faces that it was going to be a difficult session.

"Gentlemen, I can't say that I'm entirely pleased by your collective activities during the months we've been on the planet."

I waited for a moment. When no comment was forthcoming, I stared at French until he squirmed and broke:

"I haven't done anything contrary to any directives, Captain—either yours or the scientific leaders'."

I put my fingertips together—a nervous habit from years gone by that I still hadn't completely lost.

"That is true, Mr. French. The general orders are to get out, snoop around, see what you can see. And you have both done that. My problem—our problem—is the way in which you've been doing it. It seems you're both a little too eager to try to make commercial arrangements with the Hexies, before we even have a chance to assess what might constitute a reasonable trading arrangement. To the best of my knowledge, this expedition is not empowered to bind any human group to any kind of commercial agreement with the Hexies."

"That's to the best of *your* knowledge, Captain." French's tone was polite, but with a hint of subliminal sneer.

I stared at him until his eyes dropped, then looked at Chin. His face remained immobile. If he were enjoying our byplay, he'd never show it.

"It's true that I don't know the full scope of your instructions," I said. "And since you have not appeared to be endangering the expedition's goals, I haven't said anything so far. But now that we are coming to understand the Hexie culture better, I think it's time to issue a warning. You are going overboard, and it's being noticed by the Hexies."

"What boots it, Captain?" Chin now chose to enter the conversation with an earnest question. "If there is one thing about the Hexies we can be sure of at this point, it is that they have economic, ahh, motivations fully as strong or stronger than our own. They appear to react favorably to possibilities of profit from our visit. So why should you now be cautioning us?" He appeared to be genuinely curious.

"The answer to that is complex," I began carefully. "One factor is that the Hexies are very rapidly learning the nuances of our behavior. They now have a strong appreciation for the fact that you two are quite differently motivated from the rest of the crew. They are aware that you represent strongly conflicting interests among humans, and stand ready to play you off one against the other."

I looked directly at the man from Hong Kong. "Mr. Chin, you have found out that your attempts to trade precious stones were useless. The Hexies apparently do not value diamonds and the like except as industrial commodities. They are quite rare here, so what they need, they manufacture."

Chin remained passive during my revelation of his recent activities, but I noticed that French grinned evilly. I turned to the second man.

"And you, Mr. French, have discovered that the Hexies possess only CRF technology, rather than the hoped-for matter/antimatter propulsion." Now he was discomfited; I smiled sweetly. "This was something you could have found out quite openly from George Reid two months ago. Not only did he get the information in a straightforward manner, but the Hexies allowed him a thorough inspection of one of their vessels."

I added an afterthought: "By the way, their technology is much the same as ours—perhaps five percent more efficient. That is a fact that we can use in open and legitimate bargaining activities."

Now I tried to put as much sincerity in my voice as possible. "Gentlemen, the fact that I know of your activities isn't important; it's how I learned of them. It was through the Hexies themselves. They weren't particularly upset—they didn't even think your efforts were very important, but they did find them amusing. I was told about your endeavors as a joke on humans."

I looked back at the Easterner. "Mr. Chin, what are your beliefs about the importance of the Hexies' sense of humor?"

He folded his hands over his stomach. "I find it, ahhh, rather interesting, especially in light of their true natures, which seem to be quite mercenary."

I nodded and turned to the other. "What about you, Mr. French? What do you think about humor in the Hexie culture?"

"I think they're like a lot of people I know," replied Ogumi's former stooge. "They smile to your face, then stab you in the back."

A fox is always first to smell his own hole. I glanced at Chin. The slightest of smiles played at the corners of his mouth.

"Well, let me tell you something that is a definite fact and no joke: the Hexies run their world with humor. They use it as a political and economic weapon. A person who cannot see the humorous side of things—and who cannot laugh at himself—does not succeed in either business or politics. I told you this at our first briefing, when we'd been on the surface for only a month. Apparently both of you have discounted or forgotten what I said.

"And that makes both of you people to be looked down on by the Hexies. Surely they are mercenary. But they also know how to laugh at their own natures—an ability which neither of you seem to share. Therefore, you have become two of the most famous humans—famous because of your sense of self-importance, your rivalry, and most of all, because you are 'easy marks' to be made fun of by the Hexies. You are the butt of most of the jokes that they tell on us humans, and you'd better believe that has a bearing on how all Hexies treat your overtures. You are both in danger of being laughed off the block."

I looked Chin in the eye. "I'm especially surprised at you. I would have thought that your business dealings on Earth would have made you more sensitive to your surroundings—even granted that you have dealt most of your career with people it would be death to laugh at."

The Chinaman had at least gone from impassive to thoughtful. I continued while I had him: "Thus, Mr. Chin, you wasted three weeks finding out that your private jewelry collection was relatively worthless in trade. Quite frankly, you were given the runaround. And Mr. French, you spent over a month pursuing the ghost of the matter/antimatter drive. The Hexies had great fun at your expense—and, I might add, somewhat to the detriment of the image of the expedition."

"I can live with that," I continued, "but only if you'll finally take the point: if you take yourselves too seriously, the Hexies will never take you seriously."

I smiled as tightly as I could. "That was the first part of your warning; it was more for your personal sakes than anything else. And now comes the second part."

I hardened my face. "Your strong independent activities are giving the appearance of a split-authority expedition. The Hexies are much too astute not to notice this, and I will not have it any more. This is one expedition, with one purpose. I will not allow it to become fragmented."

I flicked my eyes back and forth between them. "When you were assigned to this expedition over my objections, I was given orders relating to your conduct. I was not to impede your activities so long as you did not threaten the success of the mission. I have tried to give you as much leeway in your dealings as possible, pursuant to those orders.

"But it is now my judgment that your conduct has gone over the line. Therefore, having consulted with the scientific leaders, I am giving you both the following instructions: from now on you will declare, to either Allison-White or Kitigawa, your intentions to visit or talk to any Hexie other than your regular contact team escorts. You will give at least one day's notice, and your counterpart will be notified of your intentions. If one of you wishes to accompany the other, he will be allowed to do so without impedance.

"Whoever breaks this rule will be confined to quarters for the remainder of our stay on this world. That is all."

Chin paused at the door before exiting.

"If all of what you have said is true, Captain, then any punitive action against either of us is likely to draw a disparaging laugh and itself threaten the expedition."

"Very astute, Mr. Chin. And quite true. But such action has now become the lesser of two evils, in my judgment. And to overcome the possible bad effects, I will have to laugh at my own ineptitude to show proper perspective in the Hexies' eyes. I shall portray you and Mr. French as wayward children, whom I have let get out of hand by not being firm enough, and whom I have had to spank as a deplorable consequence of my own incompetence."

He looked at me searchingly through epicanthic folds. I returned his gaze blandly.

"I can see, Captain, that you have given this matter some thought."

"That is my job, Mr. Chin."

"So it is." He closed the door quietly behind him.

"It's magnificent, Panteen."

We were standing on top of the tallest point of a small island bordering the sea enclosed by the Streen archipelago. Two thousand kilometers to the northwest, across the widest part of the sea, was the largest island, called Streenthree. From our vantage point we could see at least three dozen other islands, ranging in size from a hectare or less to several square kilometers.

"Well, I would certainly say that it is a beautiful sight," replied the Hexie, "but 'magnificent' I would reserve for the Bow of Zoeepeer. You will understand when you finally see it."

Panteen was developing a fine sense of nuance.

"You're giving the Bow quite a buildup. I hope it lives up to it."

"It does, my friend. It is spring in the southwest part of the western continent now. When summer comes, we shall see it. And with luck, the icebergs, too, shall come."

I stared to the north, over the multitude of tiny islands dotting the inland sea. We'd been two seasons on the Hexie world now. We had two left, at the most.

"You are thoughtful, Whitey."

"I was wondering what the future holds for us. Where do we stand, truthfully, in the eyes of the people? We've been here for half a year now. We have technologies and items of trade I believe you want, and you certainly have things we would find useful. Yet it seems that no serious overtures have been made. What is our status?"

He said: "The early flurry of joke plays has run out; there were only two during the winter and early spring. The factions who portray the world government as a bunch of 'little old ladies' have much truth on their side, but the government has no trouble laughing at itself about this and so shrugging off the insults. It is really unheard of for us to make big decisions such as this in a single season, or even a single year, unless there is a strong urgency."

"Or to answer a tough question, perhaps," I said finally, "like the one you just dodged. Truthfully, where do we stand?" I smiled to remove barbs.

"Now it is my turn to be the little old lady," he said, laughing at himself. "All right, I shall tell you straight. The 'wait and see' faction is still the largest, but the 'send them packing' group is gaining ground. They have been amassing evidence that there is much unhealthy competition on Earth, and between Earth and SpaceHome."

I suppressed a few butterflies and willed my heart to slow down. "But our competition is economic at the root. Don't you have such competition, too?"

"True, my friend. But it does not carry such serious overtones as yours seems to foster. Sometimes your people get involved to the point of mass slaughter on one or both sides."

I stayed silent for a moment, then took another tack.

"You have many monopolies here, don't you, Panteen? Do you ever find yourself wishing you had a broader choice of manufacturers of critical products?"

"Sometimes,'" he answered, "but not as often as you might think. Pure monopolies are not allowed to flourish unless they have a unique patent, and do not charge unreasonable prices or restrict their output to drive up the market."

He smiled. "We do not have mass interest in organized sports such as you humans, but the populace spends much time in a game called 'monopoly watching.' Companies must prove themselves continuously, or they might get laughed out of business."

"But," I continued, "what if a monopoly holds a process as a closely guarded secret, so no one else can duplicate it—yet it has become necessary to your economy, such as floater technology?"

He smiled. "Somehow, if such a monopoly attempts to enrich itself beyond reason, the secret process manages to get stolen. It has happened in the past. If prices become too high compared with manufacturing costs, the economic incentives for industrial theft become greater and greater. Bolder and bolder attempts are made, until the deed is finally done. There have even been cases of violence and injury to persons, even death. This is uncommon, but not unknown."

He grinned me a gaffer's grin. "Even as you do, we also carry the genes of primitive ancestors, and we have also crawled up to civilization from a demanding environment."

"If your economic competition sometimes involves violence, as does ours," I said carefully, "then aren't you putting yourselves in the position of children passing judgment on other children?" I used the metaphor deliberately. Hexie children were born with only half the brain capacity of adults, and required a century of nurturing and training before they began to take their place in society.

"K-k-k—you make a strong point, Whitey. Let us say that we might be children who are nearly come of age, while you still have several years of growth yet to accomplish."

"Yet we humans mature rapidly," I countered. "And perhaps this contact will be an important catalyst in pushing us to adulthood."

"Perhaps," he smiled. "Yet for the moment, there are two joke plays running which depict your crew members wearing smiling faces, but concealing a violent nature. These pictures seem to us to contain a strong element of truth, but thankfully are received with a grain of salt, for the most part. After all, we still feel that we may be close brothers under the skin, no matter what our outward differences."

He then spoke to me intently: "Your greatest opportunity lies in that fact, my friend. You should exploit it to the utmost."

"It would be a great shame," I sighed, "if your people deliberately isolated themselves from us. Six-cubed light-years of separation makes it very simple to do, unfortunately."

Panteen took so long to reply that I finally took my gaze from the island vista and looked to his face. He was staring at me with his mouth open about to speak. Then he seemed to change his mind, and smiled—somewhat ruefully, if I read his expression aright.

"It is a shame," he said finally, "that you humans are so short-lived that you must attach so much importance to that small a distance. . . ."

"The pilots are now back in business." I was in conference with Petrov, Prentiss, and Badille. "The overhaul is completed, checkout and service tests finished, and it's time to get *High Boy* back into harness. Therefore," I smiled, "we four will now take on extra duty. George, would you please work us up a schedule so that we each put in three days per preeleen to regain our proficiency? Autonav and manual procedures both. I want us to fly in pairs."

The Russian nodded. He remained taciturn, but I could tell that he was pleased to have a chance to get out away from the Hexies for a change. He'd done stevedore's work in studying the Hexie language, but he was not at home with the Hexie culture. The idea of a lot of people actually laughing at themselves as a way of life, rather than on rare occasions, was alien to him. He tried, and at least managed to convey a neutral impression to the Hexies, but he never really did get into the swing of things on Tharthee.

"And George."

"Yes, Captain?"

"Don't spend all your time aboard *High Boy*. Keep mingling and learning all you can. And when the word comes for us to go to the Bow, I'd like you to come with everybody else. It's a sight I don't want any of us to miss."

"Certainly, Captain."

Three seasons. I don't know where they went.

Chapter 17

The dominance of humor in the Hexie culture seems an established fact. Equally established is the candidly mercenary nature of their civilization and its individuals. I believe that we must understand both of these facets thoroughly before we attempt to do business with them. If their abilities at clever circumlocution are any guide, they will use their humor shrewdly at the bargaining table.

—Chin: Hexie White Papers,
Monologue of the Earth
Contact Specialist

"They tell me that conditions are perfect—as good as they've been for several years. There was an unseasonable warm spell last month that calved hundreds of icebergs off the antarctic glacial mass, and they're arriving at the Bow in full force. The weather at the western tip of the continent is cool, breezy, and crystal clear—perfect viewing conditions."

I smiled and looked over the collected crew. Most were grinning and eager for the outing. It was good to have us all doing something together for a change.

"Before we leave, a caution. To any of you who have even a touch of acrophobia, stay away from the edge. The ledge we're going to be on is not very large, the winds are fluky, and the sheer drop is three freel—two and a half kilometers—down to the water."

Panteen came in briskly. "Captain, if you're ready, the floater has arrived."

"All right, ladies and gentlemen, let's go!"

The big floater took us 5,000 kilometers to the outpost harbor city of Tzeerlee. We didn't go directly to the Bow for two reasons: (1) space on the ledge was strictly limited, and the concession was run by the Klanpree Company, based in that town in the country of Mnierfree; and (2) the winds were so treacherous around the Bow that it was much safer for an experienced pilot to take us in.

When we got out to change floaters—we'd be making the trip in a specially designed tourist model with lots of window area—I looked around at the "city." It was somehow rough-hewn, even though it had much the same look as many of the cities we'd seen in other less civilized parts of the world. I wondered what the people here did for a living.

"This is the third largest city of Mnierfree," said Panteen, reading my mind as he was wont to do of late. "And they subsist on much the same economy as the rest of the country. They sell specialty foods to the rest of the world, which are particularly delicious and do not grow so well elsewhere. They also export furs from the cold-weather animals they raise. These are much prized because the artificial imitations are not nearly so beautiful or functional."

He smiled. "And of course they have an extensive cottage industry in producing handcrafted pottery art, which is the best this planet produces. Some of these pieces are in your possession. The largest remaining industry is ferrying visitors to the Bow and its environs."

I turned to the Hexie. "There are many times when you seem to know exactly what I'm thinking, Panteen."

"We are much alike, Whitey, my friend, underneath these unimportant exteriors," he said.

The pilot was a rather young male, judging from the dark color of the body fur. And he was—if I read him right—very nervous. When Panteen introduced him to me, he grinned rapidly and said something high and squeaky in Hexie.

"He says he is very honored to meet you, Whitey, and admits that he has never had so famous a group on one of his tours."

"He is quite young, isn't he?" I said, smiling toothlessly at the Hexie in case he'd been making a joke on himself.

"Yes. Somewhere between four and five times six-squared,

I would guess. But the Klanpree Company has assured me that he is the best pilot they have."

"Tell him that we are quite nervous at being flown to the Bow by the most renowned pilot in the Klanpree Company," I said.

"K-k-k—with pleasure, Whitey." Panteen turned and did the deed, whereupon the young Hexie laughed and seemed to relax somewhat. But he did not altogether lose his nervousness. I forgave him.

From Tzeerlee to the Bow was another 3,000 kilometers. The pilot took us up to thin atmosphere and did the trip in less than an hour. For most of the flight, we paralleled the Czee Mountains—the magnificent cordillera that ran 10,000 kilometers along the northwestern coast of the western continent. From our altitude of thirty kilometers, we could see nothing of the terrain below; for almost the whole voyage we were above a thick layer of stratus clouds that hid everything below.

"Whose deal, Admiral?"

I looked up from my thoughts to see Junior standing beside me with a deck of cards and cribbage board.

"Why in the world did you bring those along?" I asked the runt.

"Checked the weather for the western continent before we left," he said smugly. "Knew we'd be socked in most of the way there. Besides," he added, "I want to sharpen my game for the trip home and I thought I'd start with the easiest competition available."

"What makes you think we're leaving soon?" I asked.

"Nothing in particular. A lot of little things. Mainly, we've been here just about long enough. We know them pretty well; they know us pretty well. I think we're almost done."

I took the cards and looked for a place to play. All the tables were occupied. "How much do I owe you so far?"

"Eight thousand seven hundred thirty-three dollars, sixteen cents. In Hexie kleeree that's about 6,982—maybe a fourth of the value of a small lacquered bowl from our dwindling supply."

"Tell you what," I said. "Let's hold off until we get

back. I'll sell one of the bowls and pay you off in kleeree; then we can start even on the trip home."

He looked at me shrewdly. "So you're feelin' that it's time to hit the road, too."

"Yeah, except that the government hasn't made any kind of a decision—and it doesn't seem bloody likely that they're going to before our food runs out. I hate to leave with things up in the air. There must be *something* we can do to swing things solidly our way."

"Tell me what, Admiral. We've done about all we can to convince these puppies that we can laugh at a good joke, too. We can't stop being ourselves—and I guess we can't help it that the Hexies are a little bit nicer than us. They've just had a little more time to get civilized."

"That doesn't count."

"I know. I wouldn't let it count if I were in their shoes, either. They've got to judge us on what we are, not what we're going to be."

"I think their decision is even harder than that, Junior. They've got to judge us on what we'll become if our association continues. Even I have a hard time with that one."

"Crystal balls are hard to come by for any species, Captain. I've never noticed any guarantees associated with life."

"Yeah, I—hey, look. We're coming to the front."

Junior gazed with me through the downward viewing windows. The clouds stopped abruptly, and we could see the mountains at last. But the view was much more than just mountains. We were less than a hundred kilometers from the Bow. The continent was narrowing down to where the southern and northwestern shorelines came together at the very southwestern tip of the huge continent. On the right side of the now-descending floater, we could see the central ocean; out the left side, the southern. The Czee Mountains pushed right out to the shores on both sides without compromise.

Here near the Bow there was not a trace of continental shelf. Anna-Marie Smith had told me that the massif plunged more than a kilometer straight down into the sea. Needless to say, the coastline on both sides was rugged. "It's kind of like the Na Pali coast on the northern side of Kauai," she'd said, "only much more so!"

Now we were approaching the longitude of the Bow, and had descended far enough to start feeling some turbulence. The pilot gave the signal for everyone to take their seats and strap in. I moved forward to take my chair directly behind the control section.

At my request the pilot took us out over the ocean, ten kilometers beyond the cape, for his final descent. I wanted plenty of time for the photography buffs to get pictures.

"Look, there's an iceberg!" That was Hagar Zyyad's voice from the back of the cabin.

"And there's another one—and a third!" That sounded like the normally unexcitable Dick Gates.

As we descended through ten kilometers I could now see at least a dozen icebergs of various sizes. It was an amazing collection. Then I turned back to look at the Bow, and was overwhelmed.

There at the continent's end the Czee Mountains threw a sheer cliff four kilometers straight down into the ocean. Right at the land's very apex it ran for half a kilometer before trailing back to start the southern and northwestern shorelines. It was as if the cordillera had shaped itself into a gargantuan arrowhead with its very tip filed flat.

A fluke of the strong antarctic current turned it directly into this bastion, so that the cliff actually split the stream into northern and southern forks. And when the seas were high and setting westerly as they were today, they broke with tremendous force against the flat, four-kilometer wall that was directly in their path.

As I watched, stunned, a wave broke squarely against the cliff. The spume seemed to rise forever before it finally dissipated in the winds.

The Hexies paid homage to this wonder in the best way they knew: they refused to give it a joke name. It had a proper name, but that was not used either, and could only be found on maps. It was universally called Thanreel: the Bow of the Ship—or, simply, The Bow.

Somehow, it didn't seem majestic enough.

The pilot cruised back and forth along the cliff from

about three kilometers out, halfway up. Then, after five minutes, he edged in toward the wall. For the life of me, I could not see where he was going to land. It was only late morning in the brilliant sunlight, and the entire face was still in shadow.

The pilot said something to Panteen, which he translated for me to relay to the crew:

"The pilot says we'll stay on the ledge until past noon, then hover out here again on the way back so you can see the cliff in full sunlight."

We were now about two-thirds of the way up the cliff and edging toward a spot I still couldn't discern. Then suddenly the wall cut off the sunlight and I saw the ledge. It looked about the size of a postage stamp from 500 meters out.

As we got closer, it began to look larger, but by then, the air currents were playing with us and I was glad to have a local boy at the controls. At the last minute he deployed the sturdy tripod landing gear, then dropped us with commendable skill on the ledge, as far away from the dropoff as possible.

Before he gave us the signal to unstrap, the pilot spoke again to Panteen, who then raised his hands to quiet the crew and said to us:

"The winds are not too bad today, ladies and gentlemen, but the pilot asks me to tell you the safe way to see the view from the ledge: Do not walk closer than two body lengths to the edge. Past that, it is highly advisable to lie down on your stomachs and crawl until you can put your heads over the edge and look straight down. He asks me to tell you that if you follow these rules, you will not be in any danger."

I was the last one out. By the time I exited the floater, most of the crew were already on their stomachs and crawling to the edge. Although it was summer here, I was glad that we'd worn warm clothing. The Hexie global temperature averaged only a degree or so less than Earth's, but down here at 55 degrees south latitude, with the wind blowing off the icebergs, it was 10 Celsius at the most. I stuck my hands inside my jacket pockets and looked around.

The ledge was not very big. Perhaps 80 meters in total length, its widest point—where the floater had landed—was no more than 15 meters. The floater itself was eight meters wide, with its special tripod landing gear extending out another meter from the left and right sides to give it extra stability on the ground. That left only five meters to spare between the outboard landing skid and the sheer edge. I looked at the slim margin and shook my head, glad once more that I didn't have to do the piloting.

The young Hexie looked at me looking. I smiled at him and said: "Better you than me, brother." Panteen, who had stayed beside me, translated in squeaky tones.

The pilot didn't smile. He just said something and sauntered toward the cliff, not bothering to drop to his knees until he was less than a mater from the edge.

"All he said was, 'Of course,' " translated Panteen. "He seems to be unusually serious."

"That's all right with me," I said fervently.

Panteen started toward the edge, but I lingered to look up. Above us the cliff rose more than a kilometer in a sheer climb. I had no clue as to what was beyond that, because we were tucked so tightly up against it. The little ledge we were on was absolutely clean; there was not even a boulder to hide behind. If anyone were caught here in a storm with the wind blowing wrong, it would be all over.

I walked slowly toward the edge. When I got to the line of feet, I got down on my belly and crawled forward until my head was hanging over the lip. I looked down and fought vertigo for ten heartbeats before I could focus on the sea, 2,500 meters below. A huge wave crashed into the Bow, and even from that high up I could hear it—almost *feel* it—in the fabric of the rock. The white foam took five seconds to dissipate.

There were three icebergs close by. Two were too far to the north; it was obvious that they'd sweep by without impacting the Bow. But the third one, only a kilometer out, looked to be coming straight for a point directly beneath us.

The pilot, on the other side of Panteen from me, spoke briefly to my friend.

"He says we are lucky," said Panteen. "Even on a good

day such as this, only five or six icebergs actually strike the
Bow. This one should hit in less than half a tree!"

Junior was immediately to my left. I turned to him and
said: "Fifteen minutes until it hits."

He nodded without speaking, then, after half a minute,
he said: "That puppy's got to be 300 meters high, anyway.
I wouldn't be surprised if we could feel it strike."

The floating mountain was brilliant white in the late-
morning sun; it actually hurt the eyes to look at it very
long. Then, majestically, it sailed into the shadow line,
and within a few seconds, was swallowed in shade. Twenty-
four pairs of eyes strained to watch it as it closed inexorably with the Bow.

"Ought to hit in a minute or two!" said George Reid
from several bodies away.

"Remember," added Georgiana Krebbs, "the submerged
part will strike, rather than what we can see above the
water."

The Hexie pilot backed himself away from the edge and
got up carefully. Then, with a brief word to Panteen, he
headed back toward the floater. Panteen nodded without
turning away from the spectacle below; the collision was
imminent.

To this day I have no idea why I was uneasy about that
seemingly innocent act. At first I thought he was just
going back to check something he might have forgotten on
the floater. Then I began to wonder why he'd do it right at
that point, when even he should be interested in the rare
strike.

Without any volition I backed up onto my knees, stood
up, and said to Panteen and Junior: "Be back in a second."

The runt half turned his head. "Where you going, Capt'n?
She's going to hit any second."

"Just want to get my camera," I said, standing fully up
and starting quickly back toward the floater, about 30
meters away along the ledge. The pilot was halfway there,
and hadn't seen me yet. Again without knowing why, I
quickened my pace to close on him, doing it as silently as I
could to avoid attracting his attention.

"What the devil are you talking about, Admiral?" The

gnome's voice was clear enough so that I knew he'd turned his head toward me to speak. "You don't even *have* a—" He shut up all of a sudden. I knew he was getting up, then.

Hurrying, almost tiptoeing, I continued toward the floater and the pilot, who was now almost at the door. And then a feeling of ridiculousness came over me. There was absolutely no reason for me to be acting like I was. I slowed down and was about to turn around when the young Hexie reached the steps leading up to the door.

He started up, and as he was doing so, looked back and saw me for the first time. Then all of a sudden he dashed up the steps and threw open the door.

I was already in action—had been ever since I'd seen the look on his face. I closed the ten meters between us in less than two seconds, and was up the steps in another two, but I was almost too late at that. By the time I got there he was inside and slamming the door shut.

I put my hand straight into the rapidly vanishing crack between the door's edge and the jamb. I was just starting to form a protective fist when the high-speed vise hit. I bellowed with pain and fell halfway back down the steps, but the sacrifice had done its job. The door was swinging back open, and the pilot had vanished.

Even as I stopped myself and hurtled my body back up toward the open door, the craft came to life and lifted up and toward the edge. I had only made it halfway inside.

"Junior!" I shouted, knowing the runt would be close behind. "Hit the deck! Watch out for the landing sk—" Then about two gees of acceleration hit, and I struggled with mad strength to get the lower half of my body into the cabin.

I'd barely gotten my feet in and away from the opening when the floater suddenly tilted so that the door became a hole in the bottom. I hung on for dear life and said a short prayer of thanks: one second earlier, and I would have been dumped straight down onto the iceberg below. We were now fifty meters out from the Bow. Then the floater leveled off again and I was thrown around with my head sticking out the door looking back at the ledge. A gaggle of startled faces were looking at me with open mouths. Kari was on her feet only a meter from the lip, her face frozen in horror. Insanely, I yelled at her to get away from the edge.

The craft went into a shallow dive, then pitched up suddenly, rolling back onto its side. The pilot was still trying to dump me out the open door. I let the floater's motion put me into a controlled lurch around the bottom of the opening, then I grabbed the door with a free hand and savagely slammed it shut. The decisive click of the latch mechanism was music to my ears.

I started toward the pilot's chair, looking forward the five meters to the Hexie for the first time since crawling aboard. He hadn't had time to strap in, which accounted for the fact that his maneuvers hadn't been violent up to now. I intended to get him before he could do it.

He took a quick look and saw me coming, then did the only thing he could do: tipped the craft almost straight up on its tail. He was hoping that I'd fall to the back of the passenger cabin, while his pilot's chair kept his own body in place.

I was ready for that. I'd closed a third of the distance while he was assessing the situation. As soon as he began to flip the nose up, I went face down in the narrow aisle between the seats and braced my feet against the chair legs on either side. Then I grabbed two forward chair legs with my hands, and began to use both hands and feet to move forward. It was like climbing up the side of a building with convenient projections every half meter. We were under almost two G, but pumped up with adrenaline as I was, I knew I could make the remaining distance in a short time.

"I'm coming after you, boy!" I shouted, more to try to shake him up than anything else.

He decided to chance buckling himself in. He put the floater back down to a 45-degree pitch and eased a bit on the acceleration—just enough so that when he reached for the straps, he'd keep control of his arms.

He'd just clicked the buckle into place across his shoulders when my good hand slammed against the side of his head with all the force I could put behind it.

He fell forward and sideways against the stick. The
floater nosed down, began a sharp turn to the right, and
threw me up against the back of the pilot's chair. Hurriedly, I grabbed the unconscious pilot's body, pushed it
back, and took the stick in my other hand. I leveled off
and headed the floater away from the Bow, then let go of
the stick long enough to punch the three-symbol code
sequence that told the craft to maintain speed, altitude,
and heading. We were safe.

I unstrapped the youngster, wondering if he'd stay out
long enough for me to get back to the ledge and get help.
Then I saw blood trickling out of an ear and hoped I hadn't
permanently damaged him. I contented myself with listening to his breathing, and feeling his heart beating strongly
against his chest wall. I strapped him into one of the
passenger seats, found some general-purpose tape, and
used it to secure his upper torso and arms to the chair.
Then I returned to the controls.

By that time the floater was several kilometers away
from the Bow. The people on the ledge were probably
more than a little apprehensive, and so was I. I didn't
fancy trying to land on that little platform in those fluky
drafts. Besides, I was starting to get the shakes. My body
and psyche had mulled over what I had done to them and
decided they didn't like it.

I took psyche firmly in hand, along with the control
stick, released the auto control with the proper two-key
sequence, turned the floater 180, and began to lower it
back down to the proper altitude. I didn't increase speed
going back, because I needed time to still my beating
heart and get the feel of the controls.

My landing was shaky, to say the least. First I flew
slowly in toward the ledge, nose first, waving my free
hand so they'd know everything was all right. Everyone
was huddled back against the cliff wall until they saw it
was me. Then I saw George taking charge. In short order
he had them herded well away from the widest part of the
ledge, giving me plenty of room to set the floater down.

I did it very badly, once letting a fluke get hold of it and
push it back out over the edge, another time banging the
inboard landing skid against the cliff about five meters up

off the deck. Finally I set it down, hard. The outboard skid was a comfortable three meters away from the edge, thank goodness.

I slumped in the chair and just sat there, breathing.

"Damnit, Admiral! There you go again, taking a joy ride without inviting me along!"

"Could've used you this time, Junior." I opened my eyes and looked into the concerned face of the gnome. "Sometimes I wish you weren't so slow on the uptake."

"I'm gettin' old, Admiral. Time was, I wouldn't let a fat and lazy year turn me all soft in the brain. Well, no time for regrets now. We got to get out of here, fast!"

"What are you talking abou—oh, oh. I see. You're absolutely right. I guess I'm slowing down a little myself."

I turned around to start shouting orders, but saw that Petrov and Prentiss were rapidly herding the crew into the floater. Panteen was already taking his seat on the right side, directly in back of the control seat. He spoke to me as he was doing so:

"Whitey, my friend, I do not know how to tell you how chagrined I am that—"

"Excuse me, Panteen. We'll talk later." I got out of the pilot's seat and turned to Junior. "Wonder boy, can you pilot this thing out of here? I've got a hurting hand, and I'm a little shaky."

"Sure thing, Captain," he said, inserting himself into the driver's seat and looking over the controls. "Where to?"

I thought hard for a moment. "Along the northern coast. Keep as low to the water and as close to the cliffs as possible without killing us. And go as fast as you can without pushing through mach. I don't want a shock wave pointing to the floater."

"Don't teach your Grandma, old son." He turned back toward the crew and shouted: "All right you turkeys, strap in tight! We've got a bumpy hour ahead of us!"

He moved the craft slowly but firmly up and away from the ledge. Admittedly, taking off was easier than landing, but the runt did it more smoothly than I could have. He still had the best touch. He punched four keys on the console and the landing gear motors came to life, retracting the skids.

Then my breath caught in my throat as he spun the craft 180 and dove us in a controlled fall toward the water below, picking up northward velocity at the same time. Before we were halfway down, we came to the northern border of the Bow. Junior, one eye on the ladar and the other on the blurring cliff to the right, swung us toward the northwest, hugging the wall to keep the floater constantly in shadow.

The water rose to meet us. Still contour-following the cliffs to the right, the gnome pulled about three G to level us off 50 or 60 meters above the wave tops. He locked the altitude into the keyboard, then pushed the speed up, carefully watching the water below. We were still under Mach 1 when I began to see the beginnings of a disturbance wake starting to form. The runt nodded his head, cut the speed back five percent, then locked it in. Then he proceeded to relax somewhat. All he had to do now was hug the terrain to the right with the lateral direction control. The ride was bumpy, but not intolerable.

"We're having some fun now, Admiral."

"Just steer the boat, hotshot. I'll take care of the one-liners."

I twisted around and assessed the condition of the crew. It wasn't great. Many were gripping their chair arms until their neck muscles stood rigid. A lot of the faces were white, and some had a tinge of green. I did my duty:

"Listen up, folks! I believe we are out of the worst danger now. If they had somebody watching closely, they would probably have been down on us by now. Our unconscious friend here," I pointed to the young Hexie, "did not have time to use his radio—that I guarantee!" Nervous chuckles.

"And as for the stunt flyer now at the controls of this here vehicle," I swiveled my pointing finger back over my shoulder to the gnome, "perhaps some of you have heard—possibly even from his own mouth, though I know he is quite a modest fellow—that Junior Badille is the best pilot among us. I would like to grudgingly admit at this time that there is some truth to that rumor. That is why he is at the controls rather than someone else."

Now they were relaxing, even showing smiles of relief.

"We'll probably stay down here on the deck for an hour or so, just to be absolutely sure of our safety, so let's all relax and enjoy the scenery. It'll stay bumpy, so keep the belts fastened. The flight attendants will be around shortly with drinks and dinner. In the meantime, just press your call button if you need a pillow or blanket."

I turned back around to a chorus of mild chuckles.

"How's it handling, Junior?"

"No problem, Admiral. I could steer this buggy with my feet."

"Don't get fancy—you'll scare the yokels."

He cackled without taking his eyes from the front viewports. "So what's the plan?"

"Let's put about six-to-the-fourth freel between us and the Bow, then let Panteen punch a message up to the relay satellite and back down to Karteneely. If we get the complete message off and get a confirmation from the world government without interference, I think we can take it up and head for home without much danger."

I turned to my Hexie friend. "Panteen, is there a private code you can contact the world government with, so that if you get a reply you'll know it's from Karteneely and nowhere else?"

He thought for a moment. "Yes. There is a person I can call."

"Good. Let's compose a message. I'd like to relay the essential details of what has happened in the shortest time possible."

The Hexie looked me in the eyes for a long moment. "My friend, I do not understand what you are doing. Surely, the country of Mnierfree has attempted a savage coup, and might have gotten away with it if we'd all been killed. But surely, as you say, the game is up now."

I shook my head. "Not if they can get us before we get enough of a message out to pin it on them."

"I do not understand."

I spoke earnestly: "Panteen, I think we both understand the motivation behind this incident. It was to have been a

regrettable accident, setting back many years the cause of
Human/Hexie intercourse. It might even have given the 'send
them packing' faction enough time to convince the people
that maybe you shouldn't reinstitute contact at all.

"But for this to work, it had to be an accident—completely
above suspicion. So tell me: why didn't the pilot just crash
us all into the side of the cliff? It would have been simple,
clean, and convincing."

The Hexie was silent for a long moment before answering.

"I understand that such self-sacrifice is common among
humans, but it is not so with us. To protect our families
from danger, yes; but for an abstract cause, it is hard to
generate the motivation. We would be willing to *risk* our
lives, certainly; but to coldly and deliberately take one's
own life. . . ." He shook his head. "Perhaps you do not
understand."

I smiled without humor. "Ah, but I do understand, my
Hexie friend—and almost all humans feel exactly as you
do. Perhaps only one in six-to-the-fourth, or even less,
would be able to steel himself to take his own life for an
abstract cause. I understand, all right. So what then was
their plan? They still had to make it look like an accident."

He thought for a while. "I see. The floater would still
have to be crashed, even if we were all killed outside of it.
Perhaps some of us would have been put inside before the
crash was done by automatic control, and some just thrown
down to the sea, with door open or windows broken to
explain missing bodies. . . ."

"Yes," I said. "And one of those missing bodies would
be that of the pilot, who would need another floater to get
away after doing his job. A grisly job, Panteen. He'd have
to use the floater's landing skids to kill us on the ledge, or
push us off into the ocean. Could the youngster have been
callous enough to do it?"

"I do not believe so," he answered. "Taking life is quite
difficult for us. I believe it would have to be someone older,
better balanced, with a thorough belief in the justness of
his cause. And even then, he or she would probably have
to retreat to the Happy Hunting Ground for many years
thereafter." The "Happy Hunting Ground" was a human
joke name for a smart Hexie institution. They kept a huge

tract of the eastern continent as a wilderness area, with no technology beyond bow and arrow allowed. Any Hexie could live there for as long as he wished. Married couples went together, if they felt the need to drop out.

"I thought that might be the case," I said. "Our young pilot was quite nervous. He was certainly inexperienced in matters of intrigue. I believe it was his job simply to take the floater, leaving us on the ledge, and rendezvous with another floater which had followed us. Another person or persons in the second floater would then do whatever was necessary to finish the job, then together, they'd crash our floater and take the young pilot back secretly with them."

I looked at him grimly. "So we can surmise that somewhere nearby is another floater with at least one callous, determined citizen inside. What do you think that citizen would do if he decided that the original plan had failed?"

"I do not know." Panteen had become very thoughtful.

"Neither do I," I said. "And I am a stranger in a strange land. I do not know how well another floater or tracking network can pinpoint us. I do not know what weapons might be brought to bear. I do not know how fast we can be located and attacked once we start to send a message."

I waved a hand back in the direction of the crew. "This is my family. It is my duty to protect them from harm to the best of my ability. Can you help me in this? Is there anything else I can do to assure the safety of my children?"

Panteen thought for half a minute, then shook his head. "I believe that you are taking the correct course of action."

"Good. Now let's get busy and compose that message."

A long time later, lying back with my eyes closed, I felt Panteen's gaze hold on me for a long time. I opened my eyes and looked over to find him considering me with an unreadable expression.

"I thought I knew you quite well, Whitey, but you have qualities and depth that I did not appreciate. Now I know the true meaning of your expression, 'to rise to the occasion.' Tell me, are all humans blessed with this ability?"

"Why certainly, Panteen. Given the right circumstances—"

"Don't you believe him for a second, Panteen!" The gnome rudely butted in without taking his eyes from the forward windows. "The Admiral's one of a kind. That's why he's the Admiral."

"Shut up and soldier, soldier," I said. "And save your lies for the bleacher crowd."

"K-k-k—I still do not understand half of what you and Junior say to each other. But I believe him, and not you."

Time passed. The Hexie pilot woke up, struggled against the tape, then quieted down after Panteen talked firmly to him for several seconds. About a thousand kilometers from the Bow, we sent our message. It was short, to the point, and received and answered in Karteneely without interference. That being the case, several more messages were passed back and forth between our craft and the world government.

Then, feeling much safer, we rose to 100 kilometers and took a semi-ballistic course toward the big lake we had come to regard as home for the past three seasons.

I slept while Junior and Panteen conversed quietly. The change of motion of the craft brought me back awake. We were dropping through darkness. Infinitely far below were the barely discernible lights of the big city. Junior's hands were off the controls; apparently, we were now being brought in by computer.

My hands were both swollen—one from stopping the door, the other from hitting the pilot. All in all, it had been a hell of a day. I looked over to find Panteen regarding me in the dim cabin light.

"Whitey, my friend, I do not know how to tell you how badly I feel about what has happened today."

"I feel pretty bad myself, Panteen."

"I suppose you will wish to depart for your home system now. I deeply regret that you will be taking this final memory back with—"

"We will not be going back for a while, Panteen," I interrupted gently. "First, there is something very important we must do. It will take some time."

"Do you mean to prosecute the country of Mnierfree? That would be very difficult. The evidences are very slight—slim? I do not know how to say it."

"No, Panteen. I have no intention of trying to do that. Tell me, what would *you* do if you had a fairly large sum of money at your disposal and felt that you had been unjustly used by a large and powerful group?"

"Why, I'd . . ." His face lit up like a Christmas tree. ". . . of course! You are going to—"

"Produce a joke play," I finished firmly.

The gnome cackled gleefully from the control chair.

Chapter 18

Stalin once said, publicly and quite candidly, that the only thing he feared from the people was their laughter. Perhaps if he had worked to laugh his opponents out of power, rather than murdering them, he might have started something that would have caught on. But of course that would have made him, too, vulnerable to being laughed out of power. Joe Stalin was a shrewd one, all right. . . .

—Krebbs: Hexie White Papers,
Informal Prefatory Notes

"Captain Whitedimple, please meet Vronczee. For nearly six-cubed years she has been the leader among playwrights on our world." Panteen said the formula words, then tactfully disappeared, leaving us alone in the Hexie's office.

"I'm very pleased to meet you at last, Vronczee. Several of my crew have spoken highly of you."

"And I have found them quite charming myself, Captain White—"

"Please, call me Whitey."

"Whitey? A joke name?"

"No, just a nickname. I'm much too important a person to have a joke name."

"K-k-k—you have a fast wit, Whitey."

"And you a glib tongue, Vronczee. You have an excellent command of English for one who has not spent all her time with the humans. I am especially gratified at your command of subtlety—and that is not a joke."

"Language and subtlety are two of my most important tools, Whitey. As I was saying, I have found most of your crew so charming that I feel more than a little guilty at

having recently written a play somewhat deprecatory to
their character."

"We shall certainly try to survive in spite of that, Madam."

"Indeed you shall, especially since the play was not
particularly well received. In it, I portrayed humans as
somewhat villainous, if harmless, and the world government as a vacillating body of nincompoops unable to decide what to do with them. It was the most forgettable
play I have written for many years."

"It sounds like your heart was not in it. Why did you do
it?"

"That is a question which requires a complex answer.
Part of it is that I am a professional. I accepted a fee, and
did the best job of which I was capable. Part of it is that I
am the Frinithee's chief playwright, and am strongly obligated to support his beliefs. Right now, he leans toward a
policy of noninvolvement with humans. He believes they
do not have enough balance or stability to be completely
safe partners in civilization. I try to support him in that
belief."

She smiled faintly. "So he requested me to accept the
job of writing a play for the group that wishes immediate
action taken to break off relations with humans. He is not
ready to produce a play himself yet, but the fact that I
wrote the play is a strong message to the world government."

"It's a pity that your play was not a success, Vronczee.
But perhaps that is an indication that the government's
policy is still widely accepted among the populace." I
smiled without teeth.

She returned the smile. "I hope you are right, Whitey.
That way I could believe that my art is not growing stale."

I looked her over surreptitiously, but carefully. The
coarseness and color of her body fur showed that she was
old, quite old—but certainly not slow. She showed a great
wit, and a superb command of English.

"A penny for your thoughts, Whitey. Are you judging
me?"

"Quite frankly, Vronczee, I am busy being amazed at
your intellect. I am a learned man, yet I believe that your
command of my language is nearly as good as my own."

"It might surprise you how shallow my command really is, sir. For instance, what is a 'penny'?"

"A very small unit of money," I laughed. "And I take your point. Let's say, then, that you have the best command of any Hexie I have met."

"That is true," she said complacently.

"And I'm going to have a hard time, I see, trying to figure out exactly when you are laughing at yourself," I added.

"That is also true," she said. "I am very subtle."

"And quite modest," I smiled.

"That, too, is true."

"Vronczee, would you consider taking on a job as playwright for the humans?"

"I don't know, Whitey. There are two reasons to say no. The first is my natural leaning toward the policies of the Frinithee. No matter how strong my professionalism, I would feel at least a pang of guilt if I enlisted with you. The second is the fact that no joke play concerning humans has yet been successful. If I read the expression right, you are the 'kiss of death' when it comes to playwrights."

She smiled—wryly? "I thought I could be the exception to that rule, by getting to know your crew—or at least some of them—well enough to find good material. But I failed."

"You won't fail this time, Vronczee."

"How can you be sure?"

"Because Junior Badille and I are going to be behind you all the way, feeding you gags and plot material. We'll also make sure that you talk to everybody on the crew for as long as you need to characterize them in your own mind."

"Ah, yes, Junior Badille—the little Kreekree." She smiled delightedly. "We now add another adjective to his name that you humans cannot hear. It means highly elusive— you think you have your hands on him, and find only that he has gotten away again. You might translate it as 'the quicksilver Kreekree.' I would look forward to spending more time with him than the few minutes I had before he flitted off to something else."

"The association would certainly be more rewarding for

your craft than the many days you spent with George Petrov and Edward Allison-White."

"George was an enormous help to me in learning your language," she said without smiling.

"You are too kind," I said.

"I know."

Then she stopped smiling and looked at me seriously. "Tell me, Whitey. What happened at the Bow? Even the Frinithee's spies have not been able to find out for certain, yet the whole world is buzzing with outrageous stories. The only thing certain is that a great harm has been done to your crew, and that Mnierfree is probably behind it."

My quick moves and strong request to the government to suppress the whole story had paid off, then. I wanted tension and interest to remain high to guarantee a large audience for the play. It looked like I was going to get it.

"If I tell you, Vronczee, it will be in strict professional confidence, and only because you have agreed to become our playwright."

The toothless smile came back. "It might be worth it, just to know something the Frinithee doesn't. You understand, don't you, that my services are very expensive. How will you pay me?"

"If you will come to my apartment, I'll show you."

"Etchings, Captain? I warn you that I am a married woman."

I laughed delightedly. "You know us so well, then, to make that kind of joke?" I had never known a Hexie to indulge in sexual humor, or to understand the human propensity toward such jokes.

"Yes," she smiled, "but what is a penny?"

"An amount insufficient to purchase an etching!" I laughed.

When we got there I didn't waste any time. I went to my locker and pulled out an exquisite Korean piece. I unwrapped it and set it on the table in front of the Hexie.

"We have three of these left, and I can think of no better way to use them. If you would take our commission, this will be your payment. I am sorry that I am not able to give you the other two, but I understand that I will need them to pay for the production."

She just looked at the tiny vase and nodded absently. I misinterpreted her silence. "If you do not like this type of art, you can sell it with no fear of hurting my pride. I am told that it will bring a respectable sum of money to the seller."

"That is not funny." She continued to stare at it for several minutes. Then, with infinite care, she picked it up and held it, turning it over carefully in her hands, before setting it back down on the table.

"This explains much," she said finally. "Though my friends have urged me, I have been very busy and have not found time to go to the presidential home to see the pieces on display." Then she took her gaze reluctantly from the artifact and looked into my eyes.

"I have a collection of the finest pieces from Mnierfree. I am a wealthy woman, and can afford them. But I will have to display this in a separate room, so as not to make those others appear shoddy. Yes," she nodded, "I will take the job. Now tell me what happened at the Bow."

I told her without the frills. As she listened, her face got very serious.

"Mnierfree has taken much too much upon itself. This is a very serious business, Whitey. I do not know if we can incorporate it into the play. We consider murder not to be a joking matter."

"But we must try, Vronczee. In fact, that is the crux of the play: to make small of Mnierfree's efforts, and to show all Hexies that we are close enough brothers under the skin to understand and forgive. And not only that, but to find a solution based on communication and commerce, rather than violence and alienation."

"Are those the messages you wish to convey with the play, Whitey?"

"Yes. In the play, I want the solution to be that one or a group of artisans from Mnierfree go to Earth to learn the craft which has threatened them. In fact," I smiled, "I would even welcome that as a true solution. With your lifespans, it should be a relatively simple matter to master those arts and bring them back to this world for good."

"Wouldn't that defeat the purpose of trade? You'd be giving up your monopoly."

"By that time, Vronczee, if we haven't found plenty of other things to trade profitably, then our brotherhood isn't as strong as I think it is." I grinned. "In fact, I know of several already. My crew has not been idle these past months.

"And," I added, "we could also profit from a trade of cultural knowledge. I believe humans have much to learn of individual and cultural balance from the Hexies—but I also believe that you can learn much about competitive methods of technological improvement and increased productivity."

"You are a dreamer, too, Whitey." She smiled and put a small hand on my arm. "Now tell me, do you have a story line worked out for us to begin with? If this is to be a true political joke play, the story must be yours. I cannot and will not supply an outline for you. Both my reputation and yours require us to observe this rule."

"So I understand," I said, while she fiddled in her pocket, brought out the local equivalent of a Kleenex, and sneezed into it—the highest, squeakiest sneeze I'd ever heard.

"Pardon me," she said. "But whenever I'm around a human for longer than a tree or so, I have to do this every once in a while. I believe that I actually have a reaction to human hair. It is a—an—how do you say it?"

"Allergy!" I answered, amazed.

"This is a joke word?" She smiled tentatively.

"No," I said, still shaking my head. "It's just that it's so—so human! Many of us have allergies, and sometimes to animals, just as you seem to have."

"Why, that is true," she said. "I also have allergy to some small animals. We cannot keep a pet in the house because of this."

"Astounding," I shook my head. Then, thinking of the possible consequences: "But can you tolerate this? Perhaps you will find it too distressing to work with humans. I know that some people get into serious difficulty if their allergies are too strong."

"That is certainly not the case, Whitey. For me it is only the mildest of inconveniences to be with humans. I shall just have to—how do you say it?" She waved the tissue.

"Sneeze."

"Yes, to sneeze, every once in a while." She put the tissue away and got back down to business. "Now, tell me your story line."

Junior and I had worked it out in some detail during the week since we'd gotten back from the Bow. I laid it out for her, lightheartedly. She began to smile shortly into it, and even laughed twice. When I was finished, she was more respectful and enthusiastic than she'd been before.

"That is quite good, Whitey! And you have conceived the play correctly as vaudeville, rather than high comedy. Reliance on strong sight gags will be much more convincing, since it would be highly unbelievable to portray humans as having mastered our language sufficiently to engage in subtle bantering. . . ."

"Vaudeville?" I looked at her in amazement. How in the world did she have command of words that I had to dig back into my distant past to even remember? Vaudeville, indeed!

She was puzzled for a moment, then finally seemed to figure out why I was stunned. She smiled broadly. "As I gracefully admitted a while ago, Whitey, I have the best command of English of any Hexie you have met. Does it surprise you that I have paid special attention to the words and expressions of my own craft?"

"Vronczee," I said reverently, "believe me, it is most pleasurable to be surprised in such a manner. You are truly a professional."

"That is correct."

She began work immediately. This was to be a rush job, since I wanted to produce the play while tension over the Mnierfree incident was still high. She did double duty for us, setting up the production organization while she began to work filling in the background and gags for the play. She used her best producer for the job, and after a while let him have his head when she was sure he understood the requirements.

It was a good thing the Eastern pieces were so valuable— the talent and production values for the play were to be of the highest caliber, and they didn't come cheap.

The very first thing Vronczee insisted on was an extensive interview with each member of the crew. She got them to tell stories not only about themselves and the Hexies they'd met, but also about each other. Junior called it "digging dirt with license." The runt also gave the playwright a joke name of "Sneeczee," which was a prairie animal having a high bark sounding much like the laugh of a Hexie. He also had to explain to Vronczee about Snow White and the seven dwarfs to make her understand the double pun on her name.

The Hexies were past masters at putting on rush productions to catch the issues while they were fresh. So help me, they actually did the scripting and rehearsing in parallel, polishing the scenes as they went. It was an amazing process.

Which I didn't get to see much of. I was busy most of the time doing something absolutely necessary for the ultimate success of our cause: getting myself a public reputation as a real, approachable, witty, etc., member of the human expedition. I held public and private sessions with the world and state governments (except Mnierfree. Even though I had earnest messages for them, I wanted to keep world tension high, so I conspicuously avoided them.). I met and talked with large groups of both factions opposing the government. I spoke to the leaders of the largest companies. I attended, and spoke at, the equivalent of Rotary luncheons and Shriners conventions all over the world. The only thing I didn't do was tell the story of what happened on the Bow. I answered all such questions with repartee that ended with, "See it in the play."

I worked hard to establish a reputation as a properly witty leader, able to laugh at myself and others with equal gusto. I used information from any source I could get—the diaries and white paper notes of the crew, the recorded conversations with technological and industrial big shots, and even Junior's listing of Hexie animals and joke names—to establish the theme of human-Hexie brotherhood, and to espouse the cause for continued intercourse.

In the meantime, the production of the play proceeded apace. After interviewing the crew, Vronczee set up a "tiger team" of humans and sympathetic Hexies to work with her. Panteen was on it, as well as two other members of the Hexie contact brigade. She also demanded and got Junior, and then together they selected two other crew members: Grace Kitigawa and Dick Gates. The selection of Grace didn't surprise me—she had a twinkle in her eye much of the time, and Junior respected her wit. But the taciturn Gates was another story. The gnome set me straight:

"Guy's got a beautiful, droll sense of humor, Dimp, but for some reason he freezes up when he's around you. One price of being the Admiral, old son—hard to get to know what the commoners are really like."

Compared to a similar production on Earth or in SpaceHome, the process here was incredibly time-efficient. First the play was story-boarded, then written and rehearsed in parallel. Vronczee would write a scene, either alone or in consultation with one or more of the team. Then the full tiger team would go over it line by line and put teeth into it. Then Vronczee would give it a final polish and send it off to the producer, who would schedule it through the director and cast while the next scene was being written (I'm using human equivalent concepts here. The actual functions were somewhat different among the Hexies.).

The cast would memorize the scene, then play it with full dress and set for the tiger team. At that time, it got the final changes before being incorporated into the full script—but by then the cast had it pretty much down pat anyway, and needed very little time to give it final stage polish.

Vronczee claimed that the cast was drawn from the best in the world, but even Gates, who was an inveterate theatergoer on Earth, was amazed by their ability.

"These people are an order of magnitude better than any show people I've ever heard of," he said. "They pick up the words and characterizations like they were born to the parts. And the stage hands, spotlighters, set projectionists—the whole production crew—are fantastic! They could teach us a thing or two about the art."

I tried to get down to see one of the scene showings, but both Vronczee and Junior nixed the idea.

"No dice, Captain, sir," said the runt gleefully. "You're one of the 'fresh reaction' audience. Can't have you spoiling your first enjoyment of this masterpiece. We only have nineteen humans for the taping as it is, and we want to keep it that way. Besides," he snickered, "you might be tempted to write out some of the juicy stuff we put in about the ol' Admiral."

And in exactly 42 days from the time I had my first talk with Vronczee, the play was ready to tape. Amazing.

The play would run live in Karteneely for as long as the audiences came to see it, but the first performance would be holoed, with audience reaction, for worldwide distribution the following day.

This taping was to have an added twist, because I had insisted on it from the start. There was to be an English version, for viewing by the crew and a few dozen proficient Hexies. I wanted the audience reaction shots to cut back and forth from Hexie to human, showing them both laughing at the same gags. It was a basic part of my strategy, and a major theme of the production. The English version would run only once, but nevertheless, an entire second cast was used to present it in parallel with the main Hexie production.

"The English version cast is the 'second team,'" Vronczee told me, "but they are accomplished actors all. And they all understand English quite well enough to give a highly satisfactory performance. You will not be disappointed, I think."

I wasn't. The only apprehension I felt during the whole night was when the crew and I were being ushered into the small theater with its large stage, lights, and holo cameras. Then, as the play started, I forgot about everything. I just enjoyed.

What made me relax was the first minute of the opening scene. The humans, just before disembarking from the transport floater to be welcomed by the government, all attached large signs to themselves which read "GOOD GUY." For that first instant, I laughed wryly and wondered just how sympathetic the play was going to be.

Then the humans walked into the reception—there to see the world president, the Frinithee, and all the heads of state wearing "GOOD GUY" signs on their chests. I laughed delightedly and all tension left me. I'd been set up, but not as hard as the Hexies must have been.

The signs became a running gag throughout the play, with various characters changing the signs on the chests of others when they did something they didn't like, or surreptitiously turning their backs to change their own signs back to "good guy" when a convenient moment presented itself.

The "you-ain't-got-nuthin'-to-point-your-finger-at" theme began in that first scene also. While the humans were presenting their gifts, the cameras and spotlight zoomed in on the backs of French and Chin standing together. They were holding knives at each other's backs so that no one else could see.

But the spotlight kept moving on, to the table on which the gifts were set. Grace had already presented her exquisite art. The Mnierfree leader sneaked a piece off the table and looked at it with dismay, picking up a similar sample from his own country and comparing it with the other. He stage-whispered "Oh, shit!" Then he pulled a small bomb from his pocket, lit its old-fashioned fuse, and put it in a vase from his own country. He finished the action with perfect comedy timing, placing it in the hand of the world president, who was groping for it behind her back while still talking to me.

There followed a classic suspense bit, with the vase being passed with the rest of the gifts from human to human—with smoke still dribbling out the open end. Chin finally ended up with it. He carefully compared it with one of the similar Earth pieces which had been given back to the humans. Then, in an obvious critical commentary, he wrinkled his nose at the inferior Mnierfree vase, looked around, and tossed it out a convenient window when nobody was looking. The play forged ahead, with nobody noticing the explosion from below the window a few seconds later.

The comic intensity of the play was sustained wonderfully, as the months of our visit were compressed artfully into a few hours. I laughed sometimes until my sides hurt. Even when the joke was on me, it was delightfully fresh.

There was a repeated gag with French and Chin. Several scenes opened with one of them trying to persuade a disinterested Hexie that his particular faction—Earth, or SpaceHome—was the road of the angels, and the way to increased Hexie prosperity. The particular Hexie who'd been cornered always rolled his head in assent, but did it with a peculiar twist that made the gesture a cynical one—unbeknownst to the human. Just when the Hexie was getting fed up with the chauvinistic harangue, a "real" crew member would come into the lab or office, elbow Chin or French aside, and begin to ask eager, earnest questions about some aspect of Hexie culture or technology. The bored Hexie would immediately perk up, begin to talk animatedly, and walk offstage with the crew member, leaving the "contact specialist" in the lurch.

There was also a delightful running gag—always started by me, and always finished by Junior. I was forever trying to figure out whether or not a given Hexie was really a good guy or a bad guy. I was always frustrated, first trying out one sign, then another, shaking my head and finally pinning on one which read "in-between guy." Junior would then come onstage and slap over that a sign with a joke name on it—and it was always the appropriate joke name for that particular Hexie.

Junior eventually got carried away with the gag. He ended up doing it to every member of the human crew also—sometimes not even in context with the ongoing scene. He would just enter stage right or left, slap on a joke name sign, then exit without fanfare. Finally, at the end of the play, with the crew just about to leave for Earth, the whole cast ganged up on the runt: they plastered him all over with signs—and every one of them read "SMART ASS." I wondered what the sign said in the Hexie version, even through my laughter.

The scene on the Bow wasn't vicious, but it didn't have much comedy, either. The script made it very plain exactly what happened, and the probable reason. The play didn't show what went on inside the floater, even though Vronczee had finally dragged it out of me in some detail. What showed onstage was the floater buffeting around, then swerving to avoid the cliff and ledge (the special effects were superbly staged), then landing clumsily. After

I dragged the unconscious pilot out, all the crew members pinned a "HERO" sign on me, then shook their fists at the young Hexie on the ground. But I wasn't so sure. I tried a "VILLAIN" sign on his body. Then I stepped back to survey my handiwork, thought for a moment with chin in hand, and finally shook my head and changed the sign to a "???."

The last scene was a superbly artful combination of humor and message, typifying the whole play. As we were finally ready to leave, I got positive about at least one Hexie: Panteen. I embraced him and pinned a "FRIEND" sign on his chest. On all the other Hexies I pinned signs reading: "HUMAN-LIKE," except for the leader of Mnierfree. On him, I put a sign saying "DANGER." Then it was the world president's turn to become judgmental. She went around putting signs on all the humans reading: "HEXIE-LIKE," except for French and Chin, who got "DANGER" signs.

At this point the spotlight moved to Junior and the Frinithee, standing together off to one side. Junior took in the scene with his hands on his hips, shook his head, and looked at the Frinithee. They rolled their eyes together, circulated rapidly among the cast, ripped off the signs the president and I had placed, and put joke names back on everybody. The message was clear.

Then everybody ganged up to pin the "SMART ASS" signs on Junior, after which the crew began to file off into the transport floater. While they were doing it, the spot moved to the leader of Mnierfree, who was becoming more and more agitated. Finally, he tore at his hair and ran over to Grace, who was hanging back, and said: "I can't stand it anymore! How do you do it? How do you make them so beautiful?" She replied: "Come back with us, and we will teach you." He looked tormentedly at her for a moment, then reluctantly shook his head and went back to stand by the world president.

The rest of the crew filed into the floater. Then, just as the airlock was beginning to close, the Mnierfree leader yelled: "Wait for me!" He ran to the floater and slipped inside just as the door shut for good. Then the floater took off and the curtain rang down.

Chapter 19

The Hexies have a more spectacular technology than we do, but ours seems to drive toward improvement more strongly than theirs. For instance, even though their space-age tech predates ours by thousands of years, our computer science is more advanced, and I think we'll get "never-break" technology before they do.

Discussions with Badille and others have convinced me that this disparity is due to the fact that they had floater technology early—so early that the ability to get easily out of their planetary gravity well has spoiled them. They have been able to tap their system resources and the zero-G environment almost from the beginnings of high-tech civilization. But the whole Human philosophy is still dominated by the mass economy and limited resource-thinking of our old Earth-trapped society. What we manufacture and how we manufacture it is still driven by this philosophy.

Therefore, it might be a mistake to think that the Hexies will be avidly interested in our mass-conservative high tech. What they might be looking for even more is friends.

—Erickson: Hexie White Papers, *Post-Correlation Addendum*

I sat there nursing my aching sides for several minutes after the play was over. It had been a wonderful catharsis—a release from more than three years of the tensions of command. And I wasn't alone. The crew had been laughing just as hard—maybe even harder—than I. French might have been an exception, but even he had gotten a few chuckles out of it. And Chin Wu Lin had been a pleasant surprise: the running gags with the signs had somehow tickled his Oriental fancy and gotten him right into the spirit of it. He'd even laughed at himself once or twice.

The Hexies watching the play with us—about 40 in all—had been delighted. They'd laughed indiscriminately at the humans and themselves, so the holo cameras had plenty of material from our small audience to demonstrate the humans' abilities to laugh at the same things Hexies laughed at, including themselves.

I finally got up and went with some of the Hexies and a few of the crew to the large theater two blocks away. It was the first building we'd set foot on when we landed on the Hexie globe, and now it was replaying that scene to another large audience. We made our way to the "playwright's box" up on the right wall of the theater, overlooking stage and audience, and looked for the seats which had been promised us.

We needn't have bothered to be quiet. When we entered the play had already begun. It was in the middle of the second act, and the all-Hexie audience was rocking stiffly back and forth in its seats and laughing with high barking coughs that drowned out everything else in the theater. The onstage cast was in the middle of one of its many artful pauses to let the noise subside before carrying on.

Junior and Vronczee were sitting together. They'd saved a seat for me, which I grabbed gratefully. Some had to stand.

I took advantage of the pause to congratulate Vronczee. "It was superb, madam; you had us in stitches." I waved a hand out over the audience. "But I see that I don't need to tell you that."

The laughter was finally quieting down, so she had to whisper her thanks. Then she added: "But I had an excellent book to work from, thanks to you, Whitey. And Grace, Dick and the Kreekree here," she patted Junior's head, "were invaluable."

"Nevertheless, Vronczee," I whispered back, then raised my voice as the audience broke into fresh laughter, "the fact is that none of us are playwrights. This success is yours, and we're all grateful."

"Thank you, but say no more, Whitey," she responded, "because the audience is giving me enough thanks already to raise my ego to heights it has not seen for many years."

We watched the play run its course. There were many artistic pauses, which both actors and producers love. I was able to follow the action pretty well, having just seen the translated version. I laughed all over again during the burlesque gags, and I noticed the Hexie audience laughing raucously at some parts I couldn't remember as side-splitters.

"The Hexie language version," explained Vronczee during one of these laugh breaks, "has some subtleties lacking in the all-English production—allusions to local politics or situations humans might not understand. 'In jokes,' I believe you would call them."

During the scene on the Bow, there was a lot of commotion mixed with the few chuckles provided. This was the first time most of the viewers were exposed to the true facts. I saw a lot of faces swivel up to look at me in the box. My entry there had apparently not gone unnoticed.

Then, during the last scene, while the audience was rocking and coughing at the spectacle of Junior and the Frinithee repinning the proper joke names on the cast, Vronczee leaned over and said:

"I showed the script to the Frinithee, and he approved with almost no reservations."

I was a little startled. "That's good, but I thought you wanted to keep the details of the play a complete secret until this showing."

"Yes, but I had to do it for two reasons. The first was this scene. It has the effect of setting policy for him—even though I know that the policy of individualism versus chauvinism is one of which he approves. And as his chief playwright, I had to consult him to maintain my reputation for integrity. The second reason was emotional. I need to keep faith with him—after all, he is my husband."

I laughed with the audience, but for an entirely different reason. Junior cackled from the other side.

After it was over, the gnome summed it up: "Looks like we've got a winner, kids." Then he twisted around to give a thumbs up to Dick Gates and Grace Kitigawa, sitting near the back of the box. Dick was grinning. Grace's eyes were twinkling merrily over her smile.

The play was an enormous success. It ran live for two performances a day, right through the time we finally departed the planet—and who knows how much longer. Hexies who'd seen the taped version came from all over the world, day after day, to sit in the audience and laugh again. Such a run was very unusual, and indicated almost overwhelming acceptance of the humor and the message.

The day after the premiere, the taped version was quickly cut, edited, and whatever else, and broadcast that very evening. Panteen, Junior, and I sat in my apartment and commented as we watched it again on the holo.

"You have produced a great success," said Panteen about halfway through. "This is quite enjoyable, even though I saw it last night from the box. I believe it will become a classic."

"That would be nice," I answered. "Especially for Vronczee. She deserves it."

"Perhaps," said the Hexie, "but she has let it be known throughout the city and the world that the play was entirely conceived, roughed out, and produced by you." He smiled. "She could do no less, since it is true. Her own integrity would be diminished if she did not spread the word."

"Don't worry, Admiral," cackled the gnome. "She'll get lots of glory; there's plenty to go around."

"I'm sorry we won't be around for the run of the show," I said.

Junior raised an eyebrow. "Time to punch out, Captain?"

"Yes," I said, and turned to the Hexie. "Panteen, can you arrange a meeting with President Czankee some time in the near future?"

"Considering the certain success of your play," smiled the Hexie, "I'm nearly positive that I can get you one or two tree with the president tomorrow. She is, after all, a politician."

I got an appointment for the afternoon.

When I entered her office, the president wasted no time in congratulating me on the excellence of the play.

"I have not laughed so hard since I first saw the holo of

the play that put Geerthee into office six-to-the-fourth
years ago," she said.

I blushed modestly.

"And I also took its points, along with the many millions
on the continents and archipelagoes." She looked me in
the eye and smiled. "Whitey, you have—I don't know how
to say it right—accomplished an excellent thing for your
cause."

"Pulled off a coup?" I suggested, smiling without teeth.

"Perhaps. I do not know that phrase. But it will now be
very difficult for the government to make any decision
against continued involvement with humans. The sentiment you have created will remain for many years, and I
believe it will still be a force even some six-cubes from
now. I would not be surprised if this play became a
classic."

"Thank you for your words of praise," I said with a
straight face. "And my entire human crew is gratified that
the Hexie people are sufficiently civilized to laugh at
themselves."

"K-k-k—Whitey, perhaps you actually deserve the joke
name which is now beginning to circulate around Karteneely:
Thitee."

I raised my eyebrows. My joke name for the play's
purposes had been "Feenkree," which translated very
loosely as "a mother opossum who has too many offspring
and spends all her energy scurrying around trying to keep
them out of trouble."

"I thought you were still having trouble finding one that
everyone could agree on."

"No longer," she said. "Your recent talks among high
officials and others on the planets laid the groundwork,
and now, with your authorship of the joke play, and your
behavior on the Bow being known, the new name is
circulating with great speed among the people. There is
even strong speculation that the play will be changed to
reflect the new name. Do you know what it means?"

I didn't.

"As you hear it," she explained, "thitee is an animal
which lives in the mountains of the Eastern continent. It is
noted for its bravery and courage, especially when protect-

ing its young." She gave me a toothless grin. "The part you can't hear is a modifier which normally does not apply to this animal. It means 'having a subtle sense of humor which can surprise you if you do not watch out for it.' . . ."

I reflected, not for the first time, that the Hexies could say a lot with a short supersonic burst.

" . . . Panteen, upon which he told me that the closest he could come in English was perhaps 'lion with a twinkle in his eye.' "

I was mildly embarrassed, even while realizing that such a benign joke name could help our cause with the Hexies.

"I could think of many names closer to the truth which would not be quite so complimentary," I said weakly.

"Do not underestimate your achievements here, Thitee," she replied seriously, then smiled again. "In fact, I am glad we do not compete for office. I think you would make a strong opponent if you believed in what you were doing."

"With my luck," I said wryly, "if I were president, Junior would end up as Frinithee."

"K-k-k—the Kreekree would make a superb Frinithee. If only he could keep interest in the job for two or three six-squares."

For many months now, I had never heard a Hexie refer to the gnome by his human name. It was always Kreekree. And that was good, too. I smiled.

"Perhaps when we depart, I should leave him here as a nuisance to the government."

She smiled, but took the point. "You are planning on leaving soon, then?"

"Yes," I said. "For better or worse, we have accomplished all that we can, and I think it is time to go. We would like to depart as soon as it is convenient, if you would be so gracious."

"I anticipated that, Whitey—especially after the acknowledged success of your play. It is good theater for you to exit now. The starship will be ready within six days."

"Thank you."

"And what news of us will you carry back to Earth? Do you think you will decide to engage in further commerce with us?"

"For our part," I answered, "there is no question. We think that it would be very stupid not to continue the relationship we have established. I do not see that anything but good can come of it for both our species."

She gave a slight nod, but her words weren't so encouraging: "For our part, I am afraid that we still remain undecided. Even with the success of your play, there are still many of us who have doubts about humans, but I made a decision last night after seeing your play. It is frankly less harsh than the one I had been considering beforehand. I have decided that we shall hold contact in abeyance for six-squared years after you depart. Then we shall come to your system to reassess the situation. I feel that this decision is in the best interests of all factions. The time is not too long, considering the importance of the decision to merge two species into a single trading and technology partnership."

"The Frinithee might portray you in an embarrassing light if you continue to put off the final decision," I suggested hopefully.

"Perhaps," she said, smiling. "But I do not think it will come to anything. After all, six-squared years is only a fraction of a generation—quite a short time for us, really."

I switched from politicking to intelligence-gathering: "What will you look for when you return?"

Her smile broadened. "Whitey, you have already told us what to look for, in your play: whether or not the individual people of your civilization are able to pursue their own goals within their society. We realize that such ventures as travel between stars are expensive, and must probably be aided by government. But we also believe that for a government to wield too much control is bad. Too much control can lead to a people's energy being wasted on fulfilling the needs of a small group."

By now the smile had faded. "We suspect from what we have learned that your species has a greater tendency toward this behavior than ours. And if we see that this is the probable direction of your evolution, we will shun you. If we believe it to be dangerous to us, we will have to make a very hard decision about whether or not to attempt drastic action. After all, you now know the location of our system; we have made ourselves vulnerable to you. You may think we are harsh for this, but we must not allow ourselves to believe totally that humans will behave their best toward us."

She smiled again, but only slightly. "You and your crew have shown us that you have individual maturity remarkable for your short life spans. We have enjoyed the company of nearly every one of you. On the other hand, it is difficult to believe that you are a true cross-section of humans. We have yet to see that you are mature enough as a species. And remember, it is not your intelligence that is most important. It is your tolerance, your ability to laugh at yourselves—which you have certainly demonstrated here as individuals!—and your willingness to accept us as friends and partners, not just a source of technology."

This woman was astute. I realized then that I had to put the incident on the Bow and the joke play in perspective. They had been important—had probably turned public opinion around, in fact—but they were not enough to get us anything but a respite. I was thinking that in the next 40 years, we'd better make some positive improvements on Earth, and not blow it in SpaceHome, either. But that made me remember that I didn't have the slightest inkling of what to expect when we got back.

"The light-years which separate us have an effect other than distance," I said. "When we get back to our own system, we will have been gone so long that even I don't really know what to expect—but I cannot believe that the idea of permanent contact will be greeted with anything but enthusiasm."

The president looked at me for a long moment, then said: "Perhaps you might be surprised at how little things will have changed." Then, as I raised my eyebrows, she continued: "You have just finished a period of territorial expansion within your solar system. And if our own history is any guide, you will spend a considerable length of time consolidating that expansion and developing your system's resources."

This woman was no slouch for brains—and she'd done

her homework, too. Just how well was evident as she continued:

"You do not have floater technology, of course—at least, you did not have it when you departed your system. But your establishment of orbital basing and your mastery of the fusion drive are adequate economic substitutes. After all, even we do not use floaters for long-distance travel because they cannot compete economically with fusion.

"But of course," she added, surprising me even further, "your growing pains are evident in the unhealthy economic competition between Earth and SpaceHome, and these need resolution. If the split between your factions becomes too antagonistic, we will certainly have a difficult decision to make when we visit you again."

I smiled ruefully and shook my head in admiration. "Hearing you speak, Czankee, is enlightening. I now have no doubts that you have learned as much about us as we have about you. And when you return, we shall see what we shall see!"

She raised her hand in the formal Hexie gesture of handshake and farewell. "I am very sorry that we cannot talk longer, Whitey. Though I have not been able to spend much time with you, I have come to regard you as a friend. Many of us feel that way about many of you. I think it is a good sign. If it is all right with you, I will arrange a short ceremony for the day of your departure. Can your crew be ready in six days?"

"Yes," I answered. "And thank you—from me, and from all of us. The hospitality you have shown has been wonderful. This year has been the highlight of all our lives. I cannot believe that its promise will not be fulfilled." I raised my own hand and exited.

"Kreekree," said Panteen with feeling, "when you are gone, many of us will feel a lessening of interest and liveliness in our affairs." The Hexie raised his hand, then took the gnome's gloved hand in his own and shook it.

We were in the transport floater. The rest of the crew had already transferred into the Hexie starship, then into *High Boy* inside. Long goodbyes were not in vogue among the Hexies, but this time, they'd made an exception to the rule. The entire Hexie contact brigade had come along to see us into the ship, and farewells had been lingering.

But now it was down to just Junior and me. I watched with a lump in my throat as Panteen helped the runt put his helmet on, then slapped it affectionately with a furry hand. Junior must have felt it, too, because he didn't offer his usual sly remark. He just stepped into the airlock, leaving Panteen and me alone in the anteroom.

Then Panteen took my hand in his. "Whitey, my friend, our Thitee, whose name will be remembered for the years to come. It has truly been a memorable year."

"Too true, Canteen." I gripped his small hand, smiling very slightly.

The friendly face looked up into mine inquisitively. "I still see one last twinkle in your eye, Thitee. Perhaps a final question to add to the six-to-the-sixth you have already asked?"

"Yes. One which comes to mind every once in a while, but that I've forgotten to ask until now: What would have happened if we'd accidentally destroyed the 'little bird' nesting in the artifact you placed on our sixth planet?"

He gave me a final gaffer's grin. "Why, you wouldn't be here right now—and we would be missing one of the finest and freshest joke plays ever to come to the world."

"Goodbye, Panteen."

"So long, Whitey, my friend. I think we might meet again."

"That's a good thought, Panteen. I'll keep it with me."

Then he helped me on with my helmet, and I joined Junior in the airlock. *High Boy* and the starship were waiting.

BOOK IV

HOMEWARD

Chapter 20

I found out early in our residence on the Hexie world that the "Tharthee" anagram joke on us had been repeated in one of the first joke plays about Humans, and quickly became a minor classic around the planet. Therefore, I coached the crew to call the Hexie world every anagramic variation of "Tharthee" they could think of when talking to Hexies. Dialogue was supposed to go something like this: ". . . here on Ratheeth—Artheeth?—Theethar?—I'm sorry, what did you say the name of this planet was?" I'd overheard only Junior, Edward, and Anna actually work the gag, but they'd all done it well. They sounded spontaneous, and had gotten big grins from the Hexies who knew English.

The actual Hexie name for their planet is Preef, but I have instructed the crew to continue to use Tharthee in their writings, and in their dialogues with other humans when we return to the solar system. Eventually, someone will discover the anagram, and then we'll have a good object lesson for the serious folks back home who might have a hard time believing that an entire culture can be built around a sophisticated sense of humor.

—Whitedimple: Hexie White Papers,
Appendix D—Captain's Journal

. . . *beep-beep-beep . . . beep-beep . . . beep . . .*
"Acceleration commencing. Point three G . . . point five . . . point seven . . . point nine . . . point nine five . . . one point oh-oh . . . one point oh-two . . . one point oh-two-three . . . repeat . . . repeat. Ladies and gentlemen, we are leveled off at 1.023 G, and now back on ship's routine. To compensate you for this inconvenience, we

will change back to a 24-hour day incrementally, to give
your sleep habits and bowels a chance to catch up. In case
you don't remember, duty assignments are to be found in
Mr. Petrov's roster file. Crew duties will begin immediately.

"People, we did a good job and I'm proud of all of us.
We've got two years of confinement remaining, but with
what we've been through already, I think we can do it
standing on our heads. We've got plenty of food, a completely overhauled life support system, enough work to
keep us busy for several years, and glory at the end of the
road.

"And since the ship's clock tells me that today is Thurs-
day, and since we have 43 percent of our original alcohol
ration remaining, I am announcing that day after tomorrow evening, Ethanol Ethel's will be open for business.
That's all for now."

". . . continue with classes, of course. They have been a
mainstay of our activities, and will continue—albeit now as
a secondary pursuit. Our primary activity shall be the
consolidation of our findings and the recording of said
consolidation in the Hexie White Papers. We find ourselves now in the enviable position of Charles Darwin
after his epic voyage on the *Beagle*: we have enough data
to keep us occupied for a long while, and actually possess
the leisure time to devote to its reduction and collation.
Grace?"

"Thank you, Edward. We do not wish to dictate a highly
structured course. Each of us has a different experience
base and a unique data set, which will require individual
treatment. However, we are suggesting a general order of
business: first, organize your data and record your observations into your white paper file without consultation, as
a single-blind exercise. This will strengthen the statistical
validity of nearly identical observations from different people. When this stage has been accomplished by the majority, we should begin to discuss our findings across disciplines.
The results of such seminars should be added as a marked
set of afternotes to your sections of the white papers.

"There will be one exception to relegating our educa-
tional classes to a secondary status: we must learn the

Hexie language—at least the written word—as well as we possibly can. We all have books and other written material we have collected from our contacts. I believe that we will find computer translations unsatisfactory for many purposes, and prefer to use our own. It will be the responsibility of George, with help from Junior, to provide the necessary instruction. George has learned much of the structure, the formal and informal phraseology, and the colloquial subsets of the Hexie global language. He also has a large collection of dictionaries and encyclopediae. Junior has mastered many of the words and phrases used for humor and allegory, which appear to creep into even their 'hard' scientific writing. He is also responsible for the translation software, on which all of us will be dependent for the reduction of taped conversations in the Hexie language.

"Classes will begin immediately, and all will be expected to attend.

"And I would like to remind all of you forcefully that you must retain a humorous viewpoint throughout your labors. Junior has told me in no uncertain terms that a significant percentage of our data cannot be interpreted intelligently without taking humor into account." She looked over the gathered crew and let a small smile play at the corners of her mouth. "Even though our own notes and papers—which must be read by our peers on Earth and in SpaceHome—may not be as lighthearted as the original data sources."

"Damn shame, too!"

"Thank you for your candid opinion, Junior."

"Well, I, for one, don't see any reason for continuing with classes at all." That was Jason French speaking. We were at the captain's table, an institution which had been re-established almost immediately upon leaving the Hexie system. This was his first visit. Perhaps it had taken him this long to forgive me for the honesty with which we'd portrayed him in the joke play. At the moment, though, he was busy being morose and contrary.

". . . 500 years of progress, there's not going to be any resemblance to sciences we know now." He took a sip of "raspberry lightning" and frowned. "I have no doubt that when we get back, ninth or tenth or whatever-generation computers will have taken over all of our technology jobs, including," he eyed Junior sitting to his left, "programming."

The gnome cackled. "Jason, if you weren't so serious, you'd be funny. I'll lay you ten to one, right now, that when we get back there'll be just as many scientists and technicians hanging around as when we left. What do you think the human race is going to do with itself—lie on the couch and eat bonbons, for Chrissake?"

"I didn't say that," French backpedalled. He wasn't about to take a bet with the little man. "But you have to admit that the pool of knowledge here onboard *High Boy* is going to be hopelessly out of date. . . ."

I let French ramble as I looked casually around the lounge. None of the faces seemed to reflect what he was saying; I saw only enthusiasm. We'd been accelerating six months now, and the time had literally flown, compared to the outbound voyage. I had a motivated crew who had stood all tests and learned to work and play together. I looked forward to relaxing for the next 18 months, with tension perhaps only at the end for our uncertain future. But these people had grown the confidence to face that with equanimity.

My eyes were stopped suddenly by those of the only person who hadn't visited the captain's table: Kari Nunguesser. She was sitting two tables away with Dinsworth and Dunsworth, and looking right at me. I smiled. She didn't, but continued to look into my eyes for two seconds before returning to the conversation.

At that moment, I resolved to do something about our situation, and thereby sealed my fate.

I looked into the exercise room before entering. Kari was alone. Perhaps a dozen times on the outbound trip I'd seen her alone there when I'd been about to enter—and had turned away. This time I wasn't going to turn away. In fact, I had carefully watched and waited for this very chance.

I had the kind of nervousness that makes the legs wobble, but at least I wobbled in the right direction. I pushed open the door to the gym and went over to the treadmill, where she was walking up a gentle slope and watching a holo. I turned the machine off. She'd seen me coming, of course, but she didn't say a word through the whole performance. I looked her in the eye.

"Dr. Nunguesser, you have a ridiculous name."

"You should talk, Dr. Whitedimple," she said with a straight face. This lady was not slow on the uptake.

Then she cocked her head and said: "Are you sure you want to go back that far?"

"I need to," I answered, "because right after that I should have smiled and mentioned your brains and beauty. The problem is, you're *too* beautiful. The cargo handlers were all drooling, and I was too proud to class myself with them. If the truth be known, I still haven't stopped drooling. It's downright disgusting. Every time I see you smile, my mouth waters and my knees go bad on me."

"Like this?" She smiled and blinked twice. She didn't have a single bit of makeup on, and smelled like sweat and Kari.

I let my knees buckle for effect; they didn't take much encouraging.

"That's the one."

"I'm getting older, Whitey. It's been six years."

"Closer to seven," I said, "give or take 450. You're over forty, and by the time this trip is over I'll be on the back side of fifty. But you're still the sexiest thing ever to fill out a jump suit."

"That won't last, Whitey."

"If you live in SpaceHome, you can fake it for another 30 years or so. After that we can settle down and spoil our grandchildren."

"Mister, if that's a proposition, I'm going to have to think it over. After all, you have behaved like a perfect ass for the past three years."

"I disagree," I said vehemently. "There's nothing perfect about me. And if it makes any difference, I love you, Kari. I have loved you for many years. At first I didn't know it, because I'd never really experienced it before and thought it was just some new kind of infatuation. But it got worse instead of going away. And then it got all mixed up with worrying about how Junior felt about you, then with my feeling of responsibility to the expedition. But no matter how much I tried to ignore it, no matter how dumb I acted—"

She reached over the railing of the treadmill and put a finger to my lips. The touch made me go hot and cold, then hot again.

"Hush. I've had time to think it over now. I accept your proposition. It's the best one I'm likely to get in my waning years. And if it makes any difference, I love you, Whitey. I've loved you ever since you sent that hundred kilos of cauliflower to Junior. I pictured you traveling all the way over to the farm and doing something special for a friend you cared about, and then I fell in love with you."

She leaned down and kissed me firmly, with salt. I helped my knees out by holding on to the railing.

"Kari?"

"Mmmm?"

"I hate to start asking favors right away, but could we wait to get married until we get back home?"

"Depends. Can we mess around?"

"Discreetly, but yes!"

"How often does 'discreetly' mean?"

"I don't want to be blatant. Say, two, three times a day, max."

"I like your style, Whitey. You have enough juice for that?"

"I'm a mutant. Got an internal storage pouch. I've saved up about ten kilos over the past seven years."

"Egad. We've got to get you on a weight loss program right away."

I followed her into the shower. It was a long shower. . . .

"Better do something quick—you're running out of fuel."

"I'll let it fall until I get close to the surface, then give it all I've got."

"You're the pilot. But right now would be the time to abort and light the CRF. You could still get a D-minus that way."

"I'll take my chances."

I was giving Josh Vance piloting lessons. We were simu-

lating a manual landing of a tug on Iapetus with limited
RCS mass. Josh was not a threat to the piloting profession.
He had plenty of guts, but not much feel for thrust and
inertia in a gravity well.

"Damn. Hit at 30 meters per second." He looked up
from the impact figures. "Could I have walked away from
it?"

"Yes," I said, "if you'd had your suit sealed, been well
strapped in, could get the airlock open, and had some-
place to walk to." I smiled. "But you lost about fifteen
million dollars worth of tug on a bad decision, and you get
an F for the run. Josh, you move a space vessel like you're
trying to tack a sailboat or fly a plane—and you should
know better. You don't have any fluid to react against.
Now, I'm going to run it again and I want you to—"

"This is an all-hands announcement. I say again, all
hands."

That was Michele Kimberly's voice, and I knew what to
expect.

"A come-as-you-are party is now in effect. Last one to
the lounge is a rotten egg!"

I threw up my hands, then smiled. "Come-as-you-are"
parties had been started by Junior, and had become an
institution. One night about five months into the voyage,
we'd all been awakened at three A.M. by the runt's cackling
voice over the intercom, announcing an immediate all-
hands meeting in the rec room. The voice said that it was
a "come-as-you-are" affair, and promised dire and long-
lasting punishment for the last person or persons to meet
the muster.

Besides the ship's officers, Junior was perhaps the only
person onboard who could have gotten away with it. Within
ten minutes, everyone was gathered. The runt proceeded
to harangue all of us about getting too serious about ourselves again, and didn't we learn anything at all from the
Hexies? He then proceeded to award fancy certificates to
every crew member, which listed his or her accomplish-
ments on the Hexie world—tongue in cheek, of course—
and featured that person's joke name in written Hexie,
with free translation in English and that person's native

language, if different. He'd also set up refreshments for a midnight snack.

The gnome had spent a tremendous amount of work in making the certificates and planning for the party; it was a wonderful surprise for everyone. The event was completed the next day, upon the posting of a large announcement on the rec room wall. It stated that George Reid had come in last, closely preceded by Hagar Zyyad. It listed possible reasons for them being so late, speculated as to their past and present relationship, and made suggestions about what they might do to avoid holding up meetings in the future.

Thus were established the rules of the game: "come-as-you-are" parties could be called any time, night or day; they were called for a universal purpose from which everyone would derive enjoyment or benefit; they entailed hard work and self-sacrifice by the person calling them; and the last person or persons to arrive were liable to public slander. And since they required hard work, they weren't held often enough to get tiresome. Once every five or six weeks was the average.

I approved of them wholeheartedly—even though one caught Kari and I *in flagrante delicto*, and we had to hustle our butts to avoid getting caught. They added a delightful note of randomness to our lives.

". . . better get our rear ends down to the lounge, or Michele will post an announcement that we were holding hands in the control room," Vance grinned. That grin had been unusual at the start of the outbound voyage; it wasn't any more.

I told the computer to shut down. "Let's go."

Even though I was somewhat put out at interrupting the training schedule, I was looking forward to what Michele might have for us. For the past four weeks she'd been spending two hours a day locked up in the "hobby shop," and she'd been using the kiln a lot. I knew that because I had to okay the power requests.

Josh and I beat three people to the lounge.

The fact that our gifts were pottery wasn't the surprise—the workmanship was. There was a heavy, glazed coffee mug for each of us, with our names in small block letters. But our Hexie joke names were prominent, in fancy script

with gilded initial caps. And she'd gone to the extra effort
to do a picture of the Hexie animal or thing represented
by the joke name, on the opposite side from the name.
The pictures were high-grade art. Mine showed a prowl-
ing thitee with a sly grin on its face, and one eye closed in
an obvious wink. It was good commercial quality.

Michele presented each one with a little speech about
the person, making anthropological observations in connection with their joke names—in many instances, finding
hidden meanings that the Hexies hadn't even dreamed of.
She beamed at the exclamations of delight as each person
showed his or her mug to the others with pride of
ownership.

I watched her basking in the glow of accomplishment,
and felt good for her—for all of us. Michele had come from
Earth as a cold, taciturn individual. Now she was returning free and easy, as part of a group that had grown close
with the toils of years. I was glad for our closeness; we'd
need it perhaps, marooned together in a future surrounded
by an unfamiliar civilization and hearing an unfamiliar
language. A wave of sadness and premonition passed over
me, even as I smiled at Kari across the room. She was at
my side in a flash.

"A smile on the outside and sadness beneath," she said
quietly so no one else could hear. "What is it, my love?"

"Just thinking a little too much for my own good," I
said, still smiling. "Wondering what we'll all be doing two
years from now. I've really gotten fond of this gang; I hate
to have to take us into the unknown again. We've paid our
dues already."

"Maybe they'll make a 'Happy Hunting Ground' for us
until we can learn the new ways," she said. Her face was
serious and beautiful and I wanted to take her into my
arms and forget everything else for the rest of my life.

"That may not be so far from the truth," I said. "Something like that might be necessary to preserve us from
cultural shock."

"What's up, kids—why the faces?" Junior had noticed
our group of two, come over, and put his arms around
both of us. He'd known without being told the day after
Kari and I had first come together. Since then, he'd acted

the part of a matchmaker who'd finally been successful after a long and trying effort.

I told him what we'd been talking about.

"We'll kill 'em dead, Admiral. No matter what year it is, class will out."

"We'll come through it all right," Kari agreed with conviction. I hoped she was right. That last six months wouldn't be easy. There was too much time to think about it as the trip was drawing to an end.

. . . *beep-beep-beep* . . . *beep-beep* . . . *beep* . . .

"Acceleration commencing . . . all right, ladies and gentlemen, we're leveled off. Secure from zero-G condition. Folks, we're backing down toward home."

A month after turnover I was propped up on one elbow in bed, looking at Kari lying on her back beside me. Her eyes were open, focused on nothing in particular. I was filled with wonder, that we had just made love and I still ached for her. I reached out and traced a vein on her breast, just barely visible in the dim light.

"A farthing for your thoughts, sweetheart."

"Mmm? Oh, I was just thinking about that time on the Bow. You'll never know how afraid I was, seeing you half in and half out of that floater, your life hanging on a chance."

I laughed quietly. "Funny you should mention that. The one distinct memory I have of that whole thing is looking out the door and seeing you stand up near the edge of the cliff. I was really angry at you for risking your life that way."

I leaned down and kissed her shoulder, then we both got quiet again for a while. I wasn't thinking about anything in particular, but she must have been following a distinct line of thought, because after a minute she said:

"Funny that Mnierfree should take such a terrible chance. I can understand the basic motive, but so much time will have passed by the time we get back to the solar system, we can't even be sure that those Eastern art forms will still be practiced, even."

"But the Hexies knew that our Eastern artisans have

been making that stuff for thousands of years," I said lazily, going back over well-hashed ground. "So there wasn't much doubt, at least in the minds of the Mnierfree leaders, that we'd go on making them. The lines of competition are set: cottage industry against cott—" All of a sudden, about six-squared bits and pieces of information came together in my head. I sat bolt upright and blinked three times.

"What is it?" Kari sat up beside me. Even in my excitement, I admired the wonderful display of skin in the half-light of the cabin.

"Get dressed. We're going to pay Ethel a visit."

"God, she'll be furious. It's two-thirty in the morning." But she was slipping into the captain's water closet, even as I sat down at my console and spoke Ethel's private number.

"Whoever it is, whaddaya want?"

"Ethel, this is Whitey. Get your clothes on and warm up your computer. I'll be over in about five minutes."

"Boss, this better be good, or I'm gonna eat you alive."

"Trust me, Ethel."

I slipped into my jump suit. Kari was coming out of the WC fully dressed as I zipped up.

Ethel didn't even blink when she saw Kari and me together. She just laid into me.

"Boss, if this isn't important, I'm gonna cut off your alcohol ration for the rest of the trip. I'm an old woman and I need my sleep." But she *smiled* at Kari. "Hi, sweetheart. Couldn't you keep this madman in bed where he belongs?"

"Don't look at me, Ethel. He popped up and was calling you before I could get a rope on him."

"Listen, Ethel," I said. "Why should the country of Mnierfree have risked everything to try to wipe us out? We've assumed that it was because we threatened their industry of valuable small pottery pieces. But could we really threaten them with a cottage industry that requires a four- or five-century round trip to take payment?"

"I don't know, boss. We hurt their pride, too."

I shook my head. "That's not a factor," I said firmly. "The Hexies might risk such a crime for economic reasons, but never for pride. I want an economic answer—is our Eastern art an economic threat to Mnierfree?"

She sat down at her desk console, rubbed her eyes, put her chin in her hands for about ten seconds, then said: "All right, I'll need to talk to Sakaguchi, Chin, and Kitagawa."

I raised my eyebrows.

"Listen, Boss. I know the approximate software the Hexies used to figure the economic threat, but I've got to know what inputs they fed it. They must have asked our own Easterners those questions to get their data. For instance, what's our yearly output of those artifacts that caused the trouble? Is it worthwhile for the Eastern countries to hoard their output for 500 years at a crack, just to make one big killing by loading up a ship to the gills? Can they even *make* a killing at all? What's the price on Earth versus Tharthee? How many man-months goes into one of those little buggers? And then, how many Hexie-months goes into one of theirs? What's the yearly Mnierfree output, and what do *they* get for their good stuff? Come to think of it, I already have the answers to some of those. . . ."

She keyed up her section of the Hexie White Papers, began scanning it, and was soon lost to the world.

Before half an hour was up, the party began to get out of hand, so I had to move our operations to the rec room computer. Kari and I made coffee while Ethel conferred with Hong Kong and Japan and kept her fingers flying on the console. Junior appeared and asked what the hell.

I told him, then suggested he could get the mugs off their display cabinet on the wall while Kari and I started on some cocoa for the non-coffee drinkers. He pulled an ear, grinned, nodded, and went to do it. Peter Dinsworth came in about then. The runt grabbed him by the arm and pushed him toward the mugs, talking him into the picture.

By the time Ethel came up with her first rough estimate, there were 14 crew members standing in a circle around the computer console. The old dame looked up into my eyes; her own were wide open.

"We'll only pick up one-half of one percent of their gross market," she said wonderingly, "give or take a tenth of a percent."

I nodded. "Now run it assuming a five-year round trip."

It took her about 15 seconds to make the changes and read the output.

"We'd take 57 percent of the market, plus or minus 11 percent. Boss, I do believe you might be right. We're no threat unless they've got FTL."

I looked at the gnome, who was shaking his head and muttering under his breath. I grinned at him, wickedly. "Cheer up, Wonder Boy. It was only a matter of time until senility set in. It's probably all this high-G living you've been doing."

"Jesus, Admiral," he said, scratching his nose. "We had so many clues. . . ."

"Actually, I'm always glad to know you're human, once in a while. Now, speaking of high-G living, why don't you spend a while finding out what our acceleration really is, as opposed to the 1.023 G we've been so relativistically assuming? Find out what our time dilation really has been, if anything. Share the job with Josh. Since he's still asleep, we'll get him up now."

I turned to the wall comm and punched code into the simple keyboard there so that my voice would carry everywhere onboard:

"Attention all crew members. This is the captain. I'm calling a 'come-as-you-are' party, and you'd better hurry up and get to the rec room. Half of us are already here!"

I looked over to Junior, who was grinning and nodding his head.

"How about it, Wonder Boy—you think you can get me a wag within an hour or so?"

"That going to be your present to the crew?"

"Yes. I hope so."

He pulled at his chin. "You got the tapes of the daily nav computer acceleration readouts since we started the trip?"

"Bet your ass."

"Then I think I can get you a rough answer. It won't be very good until we get a longer baseline, but it ought to be enough to tell us whether we're really a time capsule, or just Marco Polo."

"That's what I want. Commandeer whatever you need. I'm going to the kitchen to rustle up some food for the troops." That was my duty as a caller of the party, now that it was official.

I put on another thirty cups of coffee, made another dozen of cocoa, and a dozen of tea. Then I nuked four dozen sweet rolls I found in the "ready" freezer, no doubt ruining part of Georgiana's plan for breakfast later that morning.

By the time I was able to bring the first half of the rolls out, the gaggle had already moved to the main stairwell connecting the five pressurized levels of *High Boy*. I set the rolls down and moved to the landing on the common-room level, gently elbowing Hagar and Carl out of the way. Down one level, in the maintenance bay, Sean Davidson had rigged an LED/photocathode setup to shine across the weight attached to the bottom end of a make-shift plumb-bob. Now he was setting up a small laser surveyor to point back up along the line.

He looked up and said: "Okay, pull her back up! Watch your head, Captain."

I ducked back from the opening while the weight moved up through my field of vision. Then I stuck my head back in and looked up to see Junior pulling the line up through an opening in a jury-rigged contraption three levels up. As I watched, he finished and slid a flat plate across the opening.

"Okay, plate in place!" the gnome shouted down.

"Laser light warning!" shouted Sean back up the stairwell. "Everybody get your eyes out of here!"

The surveyor laser wasn't powerful enough to do any damage, but I obeyed the safety injunction anyway.

"Activating! . . . Okay, laser off! Junior, I got 17.64 meters!"

"Thanks, Sean. Stand by. We'll be another 15 minutes finishing the setup. Rig some padding down there on the deck so the ball won't make a racket when it hits!"

"Will do!"

I took advantage of the relative quiet that followed to announce that the first batch of sweet rolls was hot and ready; then I hurried back to the kitchen to fetch the remainder. I didn't want to be late for the finale.

I took the second batch of rolls up to the control room

by way of back stairs so I wouldn't interfere with the goings-on.

"Admiral! You're just in time for the grand finish." Junior waved his hand at a large ball bearing sitting on a small trap-door in the middle of a platform suspended at waist level over the open stairwell. The steel marble was interrupting another light beam—and would continue to interrupt it until it was removed. Wires ran from the photodetector to a data interface on the deck.

I stuck my head below the contraption and looked into the stairwell. The rungs spiraled down through the airlock level, the living quarters, the common level, and to the maintenance bay, where I saw Sean's head looking back up at me from 15 meters.

"Oh, hello, Captain! Tell Junior that I'm ready any time here!"

"I heard you, Sean!" yelled the runt. "We'll be dropping in a few seconds! Everybody clear the stairwell and quit moving around!" He turned to Prentiss at the ship's main control board. "Okay Mike, cut the fans."

The air circulation system stopped its gentle whirring as the second officer punched a button.

"Admiral?"

I stood up and looked at the runt. He offered me one end of a string attached to the bottom of the trapdoor.

"This is your game. You want to serve the ball?"

I shook my head. "You go ahead. You did the work. Besides, if it doesn't fall straight enough to trip the bottom beam, I want *you* to take the hit."

He grinned and yanked hard on the string. A couple of seconds later a dull "thunk" drifted up the stairwell.

"That was a good one!" Sean's voice came from below. "One point nine-seven-seven-oh-six seconds!"

The gnome took one eyeblink to do the calculation, then looked at me, grinned hugely, and stuck out his hand. I took it with raised eyebrows.

"Point nine-two-one G. All your hunches were right, Admiral. Fifty to one we're in an FTL ship. Hell, a hundred to one. No time dilation to speak of; maybe a few months on each leg, maybe not. We'll see when we get a better baseline."

About that time I heard a ragged cheer from the common room level. Apparently someone with a calculator had heard Sean's numbers and had done their own math.

I went to the controls and thumbed the intercom mike.

"Ladies and gentlemen, I believe that I can now announce with some confidence that the year of our return to the solar system will be 2103. We're really going home!"

Chapter 21

The human drive for wealth and power has been con-
ceded by our psychological scientists to be linked to the
genetic survival mechanism. However, for many years a
debate has raged: is this drive secondary, linked directly
to survival—or tertiary, linked through the sex drive? Our
studies of the Hexies may have answered this. The Hexies
obviously seek wealth and power. Equally obviously they
do not seek it, even subconsciously, to attract members of
the opposite sex. Therefore, it is a secondary drive, and
linked directly to survival. We now believe that this is also
the case for humans. Our observational correlations are
quite strong. . . .

    —Edward Allison-White & Michele Kimberly: Hexie
                      White Papers,
                      Post-Correlative Addendum

As the data from many acceleration tests came in, and
were correlated with the behavior of the onboard navigation accelerometer readings, it became mathematically certain that we'd not undergone any serious time dilation
during the voyage. The extrapolation back to turnover had
us at 0.89 G, plus or minus .05. Now, as we slowed down,
the true readings were heading back up toward (presumably) 1.023 again.

"It's a bitter pill to swallow, Admiral," the runt had said
at the captain's table the first Saturday night after we
found out. ". . . so damn many clues strewn all over the
place, but when it came right down to it, I couldn't throw
out a few simple rules of physics and put two and two
together. . . ."

"Just goes to show," Ethel had broken in from behind

the bar, "even a smart-aleck pipsqueak know-it-all can miss the nose in front of his face once in a while!"

Mayumi was sitting with us that night, and inserted a new thought: "Perhaps they didn't have FTL when we made the outbound trip. That first ship might really have been there for 4,000 years, and been an older technology."

"Naw," said the gnome, polite as usual, "Hexies would have to have 'never-break' technology to pull off that stunt—and I guarantee you they don't. Would have shown up on everything we saw on and off the planet." He sipped and grimaced. "Just another clue I missed."

"Vaudeville!" I said suddenly. They looked at me strangely for a second. "Vronczee casually used the word 'vaudeville' the first time she talked to me. I had to dig back in my memory to figure out what she was talking about. I'll bet she never heard that word from any of the crew."

"Wouldn't be surprised but what you're right," said Junior. "We can all probably dig up anachronisms from our conversations with the Hexies. My guess is they've been watching us and listening for a long time."

I nodded. Really thinking about it, I could remember several times when Panteen had almost let the cat out of the bag. And right before we'd left, even the world president may have been on the verge of telling me.

". . . artifacts in the Saturn system and the starship probably haven't been there more'n forty, fifty years at the most." The runt grimaced again. "Damn physicists back home'll want to crucify us for upsetting their apple cart. Serves 'em right for canalizing our thinking. What're you smiling about, Cap'n?"

"When we did so well with the joke play," I answered, "I thought we had the last laugh. But I guess the joke was on us after all."

"That might not turn out to be a bad thing," said Mayumi. "The fact that we didn't know about FTL technology, but still wanted partnership with the Hexies, might speak well for our motives. It may have gained us points."

"You might be right, Yumi," I said. "In fact, I'm sure you are. It would have the effect of adding depth to the tests we'd already passed just to volunteer to make the trip in the first place."

"Yeah," Junior said sourly, "but I still feel like the country yokel who's been sold the Brooklyn Bridge. . . ."

The next ten months swept by like wildfire. Sometimes I thought we were in our own little pocket of time compression, no matter what physics was doing in the space around us. Classes were attended with renewed vigor. Conferences were held to correlate notes for the white papers and write combined appendices. Each member of the crew dug back into memory and tape recordings to try to pick more clues out of what had been said by the Hexies. More notes were appended to individual sections of the papers.

French began to lick his chops visibly. Ogumi might very well still be in power, and his stooge had that promised Board seat to look forward to. Even Chin, who'd been secretly disappointed to find that the Hexies' long lives were natural, rather than technological, seemed to come out of his shell. His almost-inscrutable face took on a subtle resolve as we drew closer in time to the solar system.

"Acceleration will cease 6^6 heconds from the final warning tone, and remain off for 1,296 heconds. This will be followed by attitude readjustment and recommencing of acceleration, after the standard warning tones. New acceleration value may be different by a small percentage from that experienced previously."

"All right, crew, we've got ten hours to get shipshape for zero G. You know the drill, and we've been expecting this. Captain's inspection in six hours. Go to it!"

. . . *beep-beep-beep* . . . *beep-beep* . . . *beep*. The attitude maneuvers were small, but detectable, then acceleration began almost immediately. It went back up to 1.018 G, according to the now accurate accelerometer of the navigation computer. I read the subsequent message to the crew, who were still strapped into their seats in the theater.

"Current acceleration will terminate in 18 days, 8 hours, 7 minutes and 16 seconds, after which the ship will be in final orbit. Following the standard 6^6-hecond warning for orbital insertion, an important final message will be delivered."

I looked at the readout and pursed my lips thoughtfully. Then, before turning the intercom mike off, I added an unnecessary: "Less then three weeks, folks!"

My private call buzzer woke Kari and me unexpectedly in the middle of the night, less than three days from journey's end.

"Go back to sleep, darling." I kissed her forehead, got up, and crossed over to my desk.

"What is it?" I was a little testy.

It turned out to be Peter Dinsworth. Surprise. That was the first time he'd ever given me a private call.

"Captain, I'm awfully sorry to bother you in the middle of the night, but I'd like to talk to you in private, if I could. I'd rather nobody knew about it."

I put my fuzzy brain into gear. "I'll come to your room. Leave the door open a crack and I'll let myself in."

"Thank you, Captain."

I closed Dinsworth's door quietly behind me. The astronomer was sitting on the edge of his bed with his head in his hands. When he looked up to speak, I could see he was very worried.

"Captain, what I'm going to tell you might sound silly. Hell, it even sounds silly to me, but I couldn't sleep thinking about it—and I'm not going to rest until I get it off my chest." He paused and ran a hand through his tousled hair, then looked up at me as if uncertain about how to begin.

"Go ahead, Pete," I smiled. "If it's silly, then you'll just owe me one. But I don't think it will be."

"Well, you know Carl and I are pretty good friends . . ."

I nodded. That was an understatement. They'd hung out together from before the start of the voyage five years ago. They were almost as tight as Junior and I.

"Well, Carl's been acting real nervous for the past couple of days. It's not something anyone else would notice, but I know him pretty well."

I nodded without speaking.

"Tonight we sat together for the party in Ethanol Ethel's, like we usually do. And when you authorized a double ration for everybody who wanted it, Carl got a little tipsy . . ."

"He wasn't the only one," I said. It had been a pretty rowdy party.

"Yeah, I know," he smiled quickly, then got serious again immediately. "But Carl wasn't in a good mood at all. In fact, I thought he was going to cry a couple of times. He kept putting his arm around me, saying that I was the best friend he'd ever had, and that he'd miss me terribly—once he even said he was sorry. When I asked him what he was sorry for, he just shook his head and said: 'Nothing, I didn't mean that.' "

The man looked at me earnestly. "Captain, I know Carl. He was lying when he said 'nothing.' I know it doesn't sound like much, but the whole thing worried me enough so that I couldn't sleep. I just lay in bed for three hours with my eyes wide open. Then I called you."

He looked defensive, but determined. "I hope it doesn't mean anything, and that I'm just acting like a little old lady, but I know Carl. What I'm afraid of, I guess, is that he's going to do something that he's already regretting in advance. What it might be, I haven't a clue."

I cudgeled my memory hard, all the way back to when the crew first assembled as a group in SpaceHome. He'd been such a pussycat for the past several years that I'd almost forgotten: he began as a staunch advocate of Earth. In fact, at first he'd hated SpaceHome and everyone in it—with the mindless hatred of a spoiled child who'd been denied a piece of candy. In his case the candy was an energy-boosting modification to his pride and joy, the old CERN accelerator. The cynical grant administrators had told Dunsworth that SpaceHome was the cause, because they pulled out of the Saturn Retrieval agreement and now Earth had to go it alone and needed to divert his funds to do so. The physicist was completely naive, and had believed without question. I remembered his undisguised contempt for all SpaceHomers when we first met, and my complete surprise when I finally found out the reason. But by then, the lucky friendship with Pete Dinsworth had begun—along with the maturing process.

But before he got to SpaceHome—yes. Dunsworth could have been subverted. Could he carry out a plot against the expedition, even after all he'd changed, and all we'd been through together? On his own, I didn't think so. But if he were being watched . . . after all, if he could be subverted, so could others. I didn't like to think that my command might be in danger, after all this time and being almost home again—but I couldn't discount the possibility. I trusted Dinsworth's judgment.

The astronomer was patient, letting me think it through. "I hope it doesn't mean anything either, Petey," I said finally. "But you were right to tell me about it, and I think you were also right to tell me in private. If something is going to happen involving Carl, he may not be in it alone."

"That's what I thought, Captain. Carl can be pretty determined when he sets his mind to something, but it isn't like him to, to—instigate something like we both might be thinking of."

I thought hard for another minute, then said: "Okay, Pete. We only have a couple of days until we're out of the Hexie ship and can send a message back to Earth system. If something's going to happen, I think it'll be before then. I'm going to tell Junior about this, but no one else. We'll all keep our eyes open, but still hope that it's a false alarm. Now, you get some sleep, and I'm going to make the rounds of the ship."

I looked him in the eye. "And for God's sake, Petey, don't start acting suspiciously yourself. Watch Carl, but do it casually."

"Right, Captain."

I took a quick turn around the ship, ending back up in my quarters. Kari was wide awake.

"What's happening, Whitey?"

I told her.

"Oh, God. Now I've got a sinking feeling in the pit of my stomach."

"Don't feel like the Lone Ranger."

"Why don't you just call a meeting of the crew and tell them to be on the lookout? Nobody would dare try anything then."

I shook my head. "Can't do it, sweetheart. In the first place, it could turn out to be a false alarm—in which case, I'd destroy the unity of the expedition and maybe lose everything we've worked for the past five years. And if it's not a false alarm, whoever's behind it might go to plan B, which takes into account the fact that everybody's alert—and plan B might be even worse or more desperate than the original."

"Damn it, Whitey!" So help me, there were tears in those beautiful eyes. "It was bad enough seeing you throw your life on the line twice, when you didn't know it was coming! But to have to stand by and watch you put yourself in harm's way—"

I put my finger to her cheek and caught some of the wetness there. I found it amazing and wonderful that someone could care so much for me.

"Comes with the job, Kari." I kissed the cheek and tasted sweet salt.

"To hell with the job."

I held her for a while. A long while.

"Whitey?"

"Hmmm?"

"Do me a favor?"

"Speak."

"When this job's over, go into something safe and sedentary, like archaeology."

"They tried to kill me twice when I was an archaeology professor. That's why I got out of that line of work."

"Well, something else, then."

"How about politics?"

She pulled out of my arms and looked up into my face. "Are you serious?"

"Been thinking about it."

"My darling, you don't know the first thing about politics. And besides, most of the politicians are owned by the cartels and consortia."

I laughed. "I'm not talking about Earth politics. I'm talking about the only kind of politics that SpaceHome has to offer: the politics of the Corporation itself."

"You'd put yourself up against Ogumi?"

"Maybe. I don't know."

There was silence between us for a long while, then she spoke again: "Mightn't that be dangerous, too?"

"Not physically, darling. SpaceHome isn't quite like the power structures on Earth, with an entrenched upper echelon doing away with ambitious underlings. Ogumi is certainly powerful, and enjoys his power, but in orbit we're much more constrained by our small physical size and our need for each other.

"SpaceHome is as good a pocket of rugged individualists as you'll find anywhere. The president of the Corporation can't get away with too much; anything he does is subject to close scrutiny by 80,000 people, upon whom he depends for food and breathing air."

She nodded. She'd lived in SpaceHome long enough to understand the realities. "Okay, I give you that you'll be safe, compared to what might happen on Earth. But politics is a lot of hard work—long hours, worrisome days, and sleepless nights. Why would you want to bring that on yourself—on us?"

"I don't, really. I'd be perfectly happy continuing to do what I was doing when we first met—teaching youngsters how to pilot and doing guest shots at the university and business clubs."

I took a break to kiss her lightly on the lips.

"But if I just go back to what I was doing before, I may not be able to live with myself."

"You have to go on to bigger and better things?"

"That's not it." I took her by the shoulders and looked at her. "Tell me something: Do you think the rest of the human race is going to believe—I mean really, deep down inside believe—what the Hexies are all about?"

We'd talked about that before as a crew together, and we'd decided that the outlook was none too rosy, so she knew the answer:

"Probably not. Certainly not on Earth." She thought about it for another moment. "And so you're telling me that SpaceHome might be the place to start, and you're going to try to do something on your own?"

"Maybe on my own, but I'm hoping to get help—and SpaceHome has other advantages than just being full of individualists. It has the high ground, and not only for physical resources; it's an electronic high ground, too. A broadcast from SpaceHome reaches half the Earth—all of it, if you count the fact that we can see almost all the geostationary transmitters at any time."

She worked that one over for about six-squared seconds, then spoke with a catch in her voice: "Whitey, it sounds like you're talking revolution, in a half-assed kind of way. Worldwide joke play broadcasts?"

"Something like that isn't beyond the bounds of possibility."

She hugged me tightly. "Now I'm getting scared all over again. You could have the Earth cartels ganging up on you before you're done."

"Not if I do it right."

She shuddered in my arms. "I don't like the way you're talking. Revolutionaries always die young. Say something to make me feel good again."

"I love you. I will never leave your side. It's all a long shot. I don't really have the temperament for politics. Ogumi's probably firmly entrenched, and likely to stay that way for a long time. Junior wants us to kick around the solar system with him and have a good time. We have enough money from our crew pay to buy a house in the Big Cylinder and settle down and raise kids. I'm basically lazy, and I've done enough already to last me the rest of my life."

"That's better."

"Now let's get dressed and go talk to Junior. We've still got a possible situation here to think about."

"Thanks a lot. The sinking feeling is back."

I kissed her again. "We've got to take care of business now, so we can take care of business later. Besides, just being with you makes me feel good, and confident. When Junior hears about it, we'll see what odds he gives that it's all a false alarm."

"Three to one you got trouble, Admiral," said the gnome sourly, still rubbing his eyes from the four A.M. wakeup. "You don't have your gun anymore, do you?"

I shook my head. I'd taken it from my room and deorbited it on one of the training flights after *High Boy* had been refurbished. The trusting soul. "What makes the odds so high?"

"Petey knows Dunsworth like the back of his hand. And I know Petey. Never heard of that man losing a night's sleep over anything. He worships his bed."

"Okay, then. Looks like we've got a three-day job on our hands."

"You going to tell anyone else?"

"No. In fact, I wish I could give Pete a pill to make him forget the whole thing."

He looked thoughtful for a second, then nodded. "Check. So it's just us, then."

Kari couldn't stand it. She had to give it one more shot: "I can't believe it, Junior! You're actually agreeing with this kamikazi hero! What's the matter with spreading the word?"

The runt was awake enough to cackle. "Kari, my love, when the Admiral makes a leadership decision, it's the right one. Sometimes he does it on instinct, sometimes by plain common sense, but I've never known him to be wrong. That's why he's the Admiral, and the rest of us are just peasants."

It started the next day, right before lunch. Petrov's voice came commandingly over the intercom on the "all hands" circuit:

"All right, everybody, this is a 'come-as-you-are' party. I've saved the best for last. And if you're late getting to the lounge, remember who controls the duty roster."

It was quite out of character; I'd be willing to bet he wrote it on a slip of paper and read it. Then it hit me. I shivered with fear and my heart rate went up 30 beats. Petrov! A man with superb reflexes, and possibly in the best physical condition of anybody in the crew. Hard as a rock, and as unyielding.

Petrov and Dunsworth. What could they do? There were no arms of any kind aboard; of that I was sure. I'd done a thorough search of the *High Boy* and the entire accessible volume of the Hexie ship the first day of the homeward voyage. Ironically, my reason was that I didn't want to take the slightest chance that Mnierfree might still try to pull a coup by sabotage as a last-ditch effort. I'd gone through everything, even crew quarters and baggage.

Petrov and Dunsworth. What was the connection between those two? They were both Earthers, of course, but there was something else—something that I felt I already knew. In the back of my mind, there was a clue waiting to click into place. I knew it was critical for me to remember it, but it just tickled my subconscious without coming out into the open. As I hurried toward the corridor containing Junior and Kari's apartments, I cudgeled my memory without success.

They were waiting for me in Kari's room.

"C'mon, let's go."

As we hurried toward the lounge I made assignments. "Junior, Dunsworth's yours—Pete'll be watching him, too. I need to be able to concentrate my full attention on Petrov."

The gnome grunted as I continued: "And for God's sake, be careful. I don't know what they're going to do, but whatever it is, if Dunsworth screws himself up to do it, he'll carry it through."

"You just worry about Petrov, Admiral. I'll cover your back."

As soon as he said that, my tickle returned for a brief instant, then went away again. There wasn't time to think about it now; we were almost to the lounge.

"Kari," I said, "I want you to stay as far away from both Petrov and Dunsworth as you can."

"Screw you, Kurious Whitedimple." She was white-faced and tight-lipped. There was no time to say anything else, because we were coming into the lounge.

Out of habit, and to keep up appearances, we stopped by the wall rack on the way in and got our personal mugs. As usual, there were refreshments provided, and people were lined up at the coffee urn. As I was standing, waiting for Kari to fill her mug, I looked casually around the lounge. I let my eyes rest on Dunsworth no more and no less than anyone else. The whole crew was gathered now, after the late arrival of George Reid.

Dunsworth was wearing common garb: a lab coat buttoned down the front, but he wasn't drinking coffee. He had both hands jammed into the large pockets in the front of the coat.

I completed my turn. Kari had finished getting her coffee, and I stepped up to the urn, frowning. A coat like that was perfect for concealing a small weapon—but what kind of weapon? I glanced up at Petrov, standing at one end of the lounge on a pair of upturned boxes. He was also wearing common garb: a jump suit, with the short officer's tunic on top—also possible to hide a weapon underneath. What weapon? The tickle was back.

I began another turn to see who else might possibly be dressed to conceal a weapon. As I started it, my eyes rested for the briefest moment on the ship's clock on the wall.

Clock. *Click!* In one flash of recall, I knew that all but three of us were in the deadliest of danger. I completed my turn with a jerk and saw the enemy behind me, standing at the far end of the lounge from Petrov in perfect tactical position. His hands were tucked into the voluminous sleeves of his Oriental robe. Prentiss was only two meters away from him, praise be. The old Chinaman saw my face and realized instantly that the game was up. He began to pull his hands out of his sleeves.

"Mike!" I shouted. "Get Chin! He's got a gun!"

I whirled back around, beginning to bull my way toward Petrov at the same time. The Russian had reached underneath his tunic and was pulling out a metallic object. I saw that it was going to be too late; I'd never get to him in time. A shot rang out from behind and to the left, but I ignored it. I'd probably die from Petrov's hand, anyway.

But even as the shot was fired, a mug came sailing from somewhere to my right. It went in a flat arc toward Petrov, trailing coffee in the air behind it. Kari had gotten into the act.

It didn't put him out of commission, but those mugs were heavy, and Petrov's reflexes knew it. He ducked instinctively and threw up an elbow to ward off the missile. That gave my brain, now working in high gear, time to decide that mug-throwing was a good idea—and let fly with my own. This new missile once again put the first officer off balance before he could recover.

I was now halfway to the man, and everything was running in super-slow motion. I was passing French and grabbing the mug out of his hand when Kari let fly with another one, which distracted Petrov just long enough for me to get my throwing arm in position.

From three meters away, and running toward him, I sailed the missile as hard as I could, right at Petrov's head. He started to duck, but it caught him a glancing blow on the temple and stunned him momentarily.

I arrived as he was recovering. He was bringing the gun up past waist level, just where my head was. For a terrifying instant, the funny-looking barrel swung up right toward my face. Then I was twisting aside and grabbing it with both hands, pushing the barrel away from me and jerking it downward with desperate strength. I heard the snap of his trigger finger breaking just before the gun went off.

The bullet ricocheted from the deck, but I never found out where it went. Petrov came down on me. Half-stunned, broken finger and all, he was still bound and determined to get the gun back. I was now half-stunned myself, with 80 kilograms of Russian on top of me and wrenching my gun arm.

Then Kari, my avenging angel, arrived with a third mug in her hand. According to Gates, who told me later, she swung it over her head and down onto Petrov's with enough force to knock out a mastodon.

I struggled out from underneath the limp body, still holding onto the strange weapon, and looked anxiously around the room. Prentiss had Chin's gun and was covering him with it. Dunsworth was down with Michele Kimberly and Peter Dinsworth sitting on top of him; he was crying. The battle of the lounge was over.

Though the action seemed to have lasted hours, my objective time sense told me that it had been no more than 20 seconds since the moment I glimpsed the wall clock and started it all.

The wall clock had reminded me of the "crazy clock" Chin had shown me four years ago—quite deliberately, I was sure, to allay suspicions in case I decided to search the rooms on the outbound voyage. The "crazy clocks" given to Chin, Petrov, and Dunsworth by the so-called "Society for the Preservation of Space for Earth"—which could be conveniently taken apart and reassembled into lethal weapons, with small bullets no doubt concealed somewhere inside the base.

I was just catching my breath and getting up a good anger when Sean Davidson stepped aside to let Dr. Korliss by. Then I saw what Korliss was heading for and my knees almost gave way from fear. Junior was lying face down on the deck two meters from Dunsworth. There was a little trickle of blood coming from under his body.

I walked forward, stiff with horror. Kari came with me, holding my hand tightly. Korliss had turned him over by the time we got there. Blood was all over his chest. He was unconscious, breathing raggedly with a gurgling sound.

Mayumi came in and set Korliss's bag down at his side. The doctor quickly opened it, got out a pair of scissors, and cut open Junior's jump suit. There was a hole on the right side of his chest. Whenever his chest moved, blood bubbled in it. I got sick to my stomach, but stayed there while Korliss examined the wound quickly.

"Pneumothorax," he said. "Collapsed lung. Shattered rib. Some internal bleeding. How much, I won't know until we get him on the table."

"What's the prognosis, George?" Kari asked in a husky voice. She was in better shape than I was.

"I'll let you know when we open him up," he said. "Lucky that was a small-caliber bullet, or he'd probably never have had a chance." Then he got down to business.

"I need two assistants in surgery. Nunguesser to work inside with me, and Gates to pass instruments. We won't be able to scrub until I get him stabilized."

Even in my sickness and fear, I knew that Korliss had made the right choice for assistants. Kari and Dick were the only ones who'd held surgical instruments of any kind in their hands since school days. But I didn't envy them the job—especially Kari, who would have to help the doctor cut into the flesh of a man we both loved.

". . . okay, lift!" Korliss had six of the crew moving Junior in a field carry toward his office. They passed out of the lounge in the direction of the small operatory. I wanted to go with them, but I couldn't. I had duties, important duties, still to perform in the lounge.

I convened an inquiry immediately, while Junior's life was still on the table 20 meters away. I wanted to face them while I was still angry, and they could feel my anger.

"You three," I said immediately as soon as they were placed in front of me, "are not on trial. As sole judicial authority aboard this vessel, I find you guilty of mutiny and attempted murder. Both of these crimes make you liable to immediate capital punishment. If Mr. Badille dies, murder will be added to the list. Pending the outcome of events in the operatory, I will withhold sentencing."

I looked the three men over. Petrov was still groggy from the blow on his head. He was sitting on a chair between the other two, his trigger finger held stiffly out from his hand. I knew this man would never willingly tell me what I now desperately needed to know to ensure the safety of my crew when we arrived in the solar system.

Dunsworth was still sweating from effort and fear. His face kept working the whole time, as if he were about to break down crying again. Even though he'd been the one to shoot Junior, I felt a flash of sympathy for him. I suspected that he'd been recruited into this coup as a completely naive dupe. His qualifications were that he'd aggressively disliked SpaceHome before leaving Earth. I suspected that whoever was behind this also held a threat of some kind over his head back home to make him keep his original pledge. He probably didn't know very much.

Chin was calm, if a little white in the face. He had the air of a man who'd lost an expensive throw at the gaming tables, but no more than that. He probably figured that I would not have them put to death, unless perhaps Junior died. It galled me that he was right.

"What I'm interested in now," I told them finally, "is the reason for your actions. I will take every measure necessary to find out before we come to orbit in the solar system."

"Torture, Captain?" said the Oriental, mockingly.

"I'm not in the mood for your sophomoric word games, Chin. If necessary, I will use the onboard store of drugs to elicit answers. It will be a slow process, but we have two days to work in."

"Then I will tell you what you wish to know, Captain. I do not wish to subject this old body to chemical punishment."

I studied him carefully. I knew that in my present condition, he could probably lie rings around me.

"Mr. Davidson."

"Sir?"

"Do we have enough equipment aboard to make a good polygraph?"

"I doubt it, Captain. I can rummage around if you like. Some of the stuff'll be in the doctor's office."

"Forget it." I looked over the crew remaining in the lounge. "Grace, Ethel, would you please come up here and seat yourselves in front of Chin?"

When they'd done so, with mildly inquisitive looks on their faces, I said: "While Chin talks and answers questions, I want you to watch him carefully. If at any time you think he's lying or holding something back, please let me know immediately. Don't be shy about it."

I focused my attention back on Earth's "contact specialist" and made sure the portable recorder Davidson had set up for the occasion was still running. "Very well, Mr. Chin. You may start by telling us why you are volunteering this information, rather than having us drug you to get it."

"Because I believe that you are determined to have the information, even if it causes us physical harm. And since our coup has failed, you will guess much of it in any case."

Grace and Ethel both opened their mouths immediately and began to speak together. I held up my hand to stop them. "You first, Grace."

"He is holding something back," she said.

"He's also testing us, Boss," said Ethel.

Chin looked discomfited for the briefest of moments, then smiled thinly.

"You have chosen excellent polygraphs, Captain. I spoke the truth incompletely. I also wished to try to protect the interests of my clients as much as possible during this inquisition. I still hope to do so."

"I warn you, Mr. Chin, that if I feel your answers are

not satisfactory, I will commence alternative questioning methods as soon as possible. Now, what was the purpose of this attempted takeover of the ship?"

"To give a technological advantage to Earth, if possible, in case the Hexies possessed faster-than-light travel," he answered matter-of-factly. "Our best computers quoted odds of approximately 10,000-to-1 against, but even on that small chance, they felt it worthwhile to plan for the eventuality. . . ."

It turned out after careful questioning that it was not Earth that backed the plan. Even though SpaceHomers tend to categorize that way, Earth rarely does anything as a planet. In this case, it was a coalition of five powerful consortia who'd approached Chin, and Chin himself had made most of the arrangements, including the disguised guns and the final plan to use them, based on ship's routine. Chin was also behind the last-minute Earth demand for a "contact specialist," which had gotten him aboard. Chin personally hoped that Hexie technology might be able to prolong his life—but that was not the only motivation for his coming along. Much greater wealth and power were to be his, too, if FTL turned out to be a reality. And if he were exceptionally lucky, he'd end up with all three.

"But now it has turned out to be none," he said. "I continued to underestimate your abilties, Captain, right up to the end. Even with Mr. Petrov's sole assignment being to neutralize you, you still succeeded in—"

"Cut the crap, Chin, and tell me the rest of the plan."

They were to render the crew helpless for the short time remaining to the voyage. Then, when they were out of the Hexie ship, they would take High Boy in secret to the Earth base on Callisto. They assumed that the Hexie ship would be unavailable for study.

Once on Callisto, there would be two courses of action possible: If the Hexies had openly given FTL technology to humans, it would simply be transferred directly to Earth—or rather, the coalition of consortia. If not, then the crew would be subjected to hypnotics and other drugs to drain them of as many clues as possible to add to the onboard data base, in hopes of gaining eventual insight into the Hexie secret. In either case, the crew would be interned on Callisto or some remote spot on Earth for the remainder of their lives.

"He's lying, Boss," said Ethel at that point. Grace nodded her head sadly.

"Truthfully," admitted Chin, "I do not know what would have happened to the crew. We discussed many possibilities, from internment to death. We did not make a final decision, but agreed to let it rest upon events as we saw them when we returned. Death was the highest probability."

"And how did you plan to keep yourself from being killed or incarcerated on your return?" I asked acidly. "Your presence back on Earth would be an embarrassment, too."

He opened his mouth, but I held up a hand. "Never mind. I'm sure you worked up a foolproof scheme to assure your own safety, and I'm not really interested in the details right now. What did you plan to say to the Hexies when they returned in 40 years?"

"We also took that into account. If the Hexies accompanied us back, the plan would never have been activated. If the Hexies were to follow later, the plan could be put into effect, and both Earth and SpaceHome would swear the ship never returned."

I nodded disgustedly. The bastard had done a thorough job of thinking it out. I opened my mouth to make another sarcastic remark, but was saved from looking small by the arrival of a gowned and messy-looking Dick Gates. His smile lifted my heart.

"We thought you'd like to know right away, Captain. Junior's going to make it all right. George and Kari are just finishing up. They sent me on ahead with the news."

I took about ten seconds to collect myself. I told myself sternly that I was conducting a serious court of inquiry. Leaping up and down and shouting for joy was improper behavior.

"Thank you, Mr. Gates. We're very happy to have that news."

I turned back to the three conspirators. I really had all the information I needed to conduct the ship after separation from the Hexie vessel. "You three will be confined to quarters for the remainder of the trip." I looked again over the assembled crew. "Mr. Davidson."

"Captain?"

"Rig the doors on their rooms so they can be closed and locked from the outside only. Use whoever you need and get it done as soon as you can."

"Yes, sir." He grabbed George Reid by the arm and led him out of the lounge.

"Mr. Prentiss, please form a detail to search and strip their rooms. Use the women. I want the rest of the men to stay here. Everything that could possibly be used in any way conceivable as a weapon is to be removed. That includes the computers and other electronics. When you're finished, do the same for the west hall water closet—that's the only one they'll be allowed to use. Tell me when you're finished and I'll inspect."

I looked at my dwindling crew after Prentiss left with three women.

"Josh, Dick, Pete, Jason—you are now bodyguards. Jason is assigned to Chin, Dick to Dunsworth, and Pete and Josh to Petrov. Beginning now, it is your sole duty to restrain them from making any movement not specifically authorized by me. Use immediate force if necessary, and yell for help. You'll be on duty until they are safely tucked away in their quarters. Ethel, go get a roll of strong tape—enough to strap their arms and legs to the chairs they're sitting in."

"On the way, Boss."

I began to dismantle the three homemade guns still lying beside me. "Grace, would you please go to the tool chest and bring me a small vise and a ball peen hammer?"

"Certainly, Captain." She left quietly.

"Aren't you being overly cautious, Captain? After all, it is quite improbable that any further attempt at a coup would succeed at this point."

"Shut your mouth, Chin. If I want your advice on a 10,000-to-1 shot, I'll ask for it."

On time a day and a half later, the 36 tones sounded to give us our ten-and-a-half-hour warning for orbital insertion and zero G. The message that followed said that after the ship stopped, we would be free to activate both small and large cargo doors at our leisure. But 6^5 heconds (less than two hours) after the first time a hatch was opened, the ship would close up and depart—and its acceleration would be 6.14 G, so watch out for the plume.

Then there was a personal message to me from Panteen:

My dear friend Thitee,

If you have not guessed by now, you will know in a short while that our starships travel many times the speed of light in a vacuum. We were all amazed that you did not know this by the time you arrived. And then (you will pardon us for this, I hope) we did not tell you while you were here. This was partly out of love for a good joke, I admit, but also to continue testing your wish to have us as friends and not just a convenient source of technology. You will be pleased to know that your continued desire for permanent contact, still not knowing, acted in your favor. It was very difficult for us to keep the secret until you departed.

For many, many years we have watched your civilization grow. We have had to retreat farther and farther from your planet as you expanded your own technology, of course. We suffered with you through your great wars, and still suffer with you through your now smaller ones. We suffer for ourselves at the same time, because we feel the need to have you as friends. In many ways, you seem so much like us, yet there is this great difference: your people slay themselves in great numbers with frightening regularity. And in many of your individuals, there seems to be an ability to treat other individuals with deliberate cruelty. We do not fully understand this. Do you?

Yet you grow. You take six steps forward, then five back, but you grow nonetheless. When you began to make plans to put a base on Iapetus about a six-squared ago, we finally decided to take a chance, and so we planted the five artifacts in the Saturn system, and the sixth on Saturn itself, to test your resolve and desire for initial contact. When you found them, we placed the starship in orbit. I myself was in charge of this project. I developed the artificial languages to make you believe that it had been several six-to-the-fourths since we had visited you, and

*that we did not understand how to travel faster than light.
I also had much fun in "giving you the runaround," even
though it was part of my duty and made the task much
more expensive.*

*And so you passed all the tests of resolve. And yet, even
the way you passed them showed the unhealthy side of your
nature as a species. You were in violent competition, seemingly, in all phases of the retrieval of the artifacts.*

*We certainly share some of your genetic tendency toward
violence, as you found out to our mutual chagrin on the
Bow of Zoeepeer. However, your species seems to have
gone beyond the evolutionary necessities in this tendency,
and so is more dangerous than ours.*

*And yet you showed remarkable maturity in the way
you finally handled the incident on the Bow. Your for-
bearance, and your production of the joke play, were
masterful displays of the kind of behavior we hold in
highest esteem. And thus you brought us to the point
where we will show ourselves to your solar system in a
short six-squared. In this, you are to be congratulated,
Whitey, for I did not think it would happen even in my
lifetime, let alone yours.*

*Please give my regards, and those of all the peoples they
have met and talked to, to all of your crew. And especially
say a thanks to your Kreekree for me, and for all of us. He
brought joy to the lives of everyone, and taught us all over
again how to laugh at ourselves, and at life.*

*Now I will say goodbye, Thitee. Until our species meet
again. I shall be there, and I hope you will, too, because
you are a fine friend.*

I took it down to sick bay and read it to the Kreekree
before posting it on the bulletin board.

"Okay, we're clear of the ship. Mike, get the antenna
pointed at the Sun and start sending the message. The
sooner we can punch out a few reps, the better I'll feel."
The message to the solar system was short, sweet, and in
plain, nonencrypted English: we'd been to the Hexie world
and were back; they had FTL, but wouldn't share the
secret. And we were heading for home along the direction
of our beam.

I reflected briefly that sending a fast message as an insurance policy was an occupation I could do without—even if it happened only once every other year.

"First rep sent, Captain."

I bent to the computer, talked to it, punched keys, and played with the mouse. Our nose slewed to point directly at Sol, now only a pinpoint of brilliant light, but soon to grow large and warm.

"Second rep sent."

I thumbed the intercom mike. "Acceleration commencing in five seconds. One G. Stand by . . . three . . . two . . . one . . . commencing." The force built up smoothly. It was nice to see 1.000 on the nav accelerometer again.

"Third rep."

"Okay, folks, we're headed home!"

EPILOGUE

. . . almost two centuries ago that Fermi said, "Where are they?" and eventually touched off the great philosophical debate of the last half of the 20th century.

The anthropic protagonists were Tipler and his camp; they expanded on Fermi's plaintive question, and proved to their satisfaction that if just one advanced civilization in this galaxy had, any time up to a couple of million years ago, risen to a level of technology just a hair above our own, their von Neumann machines—robotic replicators— would now have overrun every solar system and we'd see the evidence. Such evidence being absent, humans were alone.

The "we are not alone" camp was informally led by the man after whom this series of lectures is named. He'd grown up thoroughly schooled in the principle of mediocrity, and simply couldn't believe—given our completely mundane place in the cosmos—that the human species was unique in possessing intelligence and civilization. He put forth strong philosophical arguments that no intelligent species would create von Neumann machines; they were too likely to become Frankenstein monsters and turn on their own makers. And he backed year after year of fruitless SETI efforts with his famous "Absence of evidence is not evidence of absence."

With all due respect to the late Dr. Sagan, his war cry was not a theory, but just an axiom—not even testable. It lacked flavor, and soon became trite. In the battle to possess Occam's razor, Tipler's following used the old thesis that eventually won them the day: "If they were here, they'd be here by now." Sagan's camp had to put forth weaker offerings such as: "They're so far beyond us we wouldn't even know it if they were trying to communicate."

And as the SETI projects covered more and more ground in the electromagnetic spectrum—then the gravity wave spectrum—without results, the mediocrity argument dribbled away into dust. And for that matter, so did the debate. Because shortly the 21st century ushered in the more robust activities of establishing our own solar system as an economic base—activities which are still ongoing . . .

. . . answer to Fermi's question was simple after all: "They're here, and watching us." It was the old zoo theory—one of the weaker ones that failed to win a prize during the debates . . .

. . . think that Sagan's ashes are doing a Brownian dance of laughter in their orbit around the sun? Think again. What are the facts? Mediocrity is established: not only is the development of life a robust process—but with Hexie data, it seems that so are the development of eukaryotes, the Gaia turnover, and manipulative intelligence. We must accept the statistical fact that intelligence abounds; there are almost certainly thousands—possibly millions—of planets in this galaxy alone which harbor intelligent life. And we also know that faster-than-light travel is a technological fact.

All of which takes us right back to Fermi: Where the hell are they? Do you accept the thesis that the Hexies are the first species, give or take a million years, ever to develop FTL travel? If so, you don't belong here; you need to be in a school for the retarded. Do you accept the thesis that many other civilizations developed FTL travel—and all destroyed themselves and each other before they got to us? Go to the same school. And if you think I have a simple thesis of my own, you're wrong. Sir William's razor is now dulling itself trying to shave a pickle.

What I am going to do is put forth an idea. And even though it will eventually be proven or disproven (providing we keep ourselves alive), I won't dignify it by calling it a theory. . . .

> —Badille: Excerpts from the Sagan Memorial
> Lecture of 2105—the "Plateaus
> of Technology" speech—
> delivered by holocast to the
> assembled students and faculty
> of Cornell University

Of course, it's been over three years since we came back. So what am I doing now? Politicking for a place on the SpaceHome Corporation board of directors, of course. I'm trying something new: to be a member who takes a combined interest in the profits and well-being of the corporation, but at the same time looks out for the interests of all the other citizens of the Colonies, too.

This isn't radical; after all, SpaceHome is a tight ecological society, and the continued existence of the corporation depends strongly on the labors of everyone in the habitats. But I want to make sure the Board never forgets that. It might also be a model for some of the Earth combines to think about.

The radical step will come if I ever get to be president. I'll establish the position of ombudsman and make it as powerful as I can while I'm still in office. If I can get away with that, we'll see what the next step might be.

My advisors (Kari, Junior, Grace, and Maggie O'Malley) have told me in no uncertain terms that a memoir such as this would help enormously if it were published. And it would go a long way toward fixing in the public mind exactly what the Hexies are all about.

That last part I agree with wholeheartedly. We made quite a splash when we returned, but I'm certain still that few people on- or off-planet really understand the importance of humor in the Hexie culture—and how it might balance our own. I'd be amazed if more than a handful of humans have bothered to wade through the lengthy analyses of the Hexie civilization and the "joke play" system.

I've tried in my lectures and public appearances to drive the point home, but the message is barely getting around SpaceHome, let alone Earth. The White Papers run to a gigabyte or more—so how many people have actually read them?

For the purposes of further education, I've decided to try to spice up this manuscript with excerpts from the papers and their various addenda. Maybe that will also make amends to some of the crew members who have not appeared in detail in this memoir. It's not that they weren't important, but I've had to cut large sections as a matter (firmly drilled into me by the publisher) of literary expedience. All of them worked their tails off to make our expedition a success.

Kari? She's teaching graduate molecular biology at SHU— and still fighting off horny young students and horny old professors. We're married, of course. Two children have not done anything at all to her luscious figure, and her smile and eyes can still melt the teeth out of a Cenozoic fossil. She's sexier than ever.

At the birth of our first child, she suggested that I take hormones so we could be like the Hexies and both suckle the brat. I countersuggested that it wouldn't particularly help my public image to appear at the lecturn with beard and tits. We compromised: she suckled, I changed diapers. Such a deal.

The three conspirators? I let them go, of course. The crew was outraged, but I beat them down in a no-holds-barred debate on the long trip down-system to Earth orbit. What good would it do, in the final analysis, to bring them publicly to account—or to charge the five consortia that backed the scheme? For my money, the only possible outcomes would have been bad—for Earth, for SpaceHome, for the species.

So during that trip home, we hammered out our own plan. It included placing our individual testimonies, along with Chin's, in a few safe places on Earth and in SpaceHome, to be brought forth only if someone started bumping off the crew in a suspicious manner. And we made a very solemn pact to disavow anyone who tried to spill the beans otherwise.

Then we called in the three, the day before final docking at SpaceHome, and told them what we'd done. We instructed them as to how they'd save their own skins in light of their failure: they would tell their backers that they never executed the plan because they were certain that none of the crew had been given the slightest hint of how FTL technology worked. The truth—that we didn't even know the Hexies *had* FTL until we were off planet— would help make this believable.

And so the villains shared in the glory of homecoming. They were even invited to our triennial reunion earlier this year. None of them showed up, which gladdened our hearts.

So why am I revealing all of this in my memoir, only a few years later? I'll tell you: I'm playing a joke on my slave-driving advisors, who have nagged me for the past 18 months to spend my "leisure" time organizing notes and dictating words into the computer. I hope they sweat until they get way down to this part. Don't worry, kids; I'm going to edit that whole incident out, including the earlier clues that didn't hit me until almost too late! After all, this is only a draft.

The rest of the crew? Almost universally, they went back to work with higher status. At our reunion, we reaffirmed the need to push the maturation of our species as hard as we could before the Hexies return. If I ever get into office high enough to do any good, I plan to call in a few nickels on them. After all, I did save their bacon a couple of times, and they owe me. And if any of them get to high office—well, I'll be glad to spend a nickel or two to help them out, too.

Except maybe Jason French. Ogumi's still the SpaceHome Corporation president—and he paid up and got Jason on the Board. French smiles a lot, but he doesn't like me very much. That's all right. If I have to put up with him—well, he's got to put up with me, too. It evens out.

Junior? He was up and around well before we hit Earth orbit. Right after turnover I altered the nav program to hold us down to point three G for a few hours, and then we threw a blowout in his honor.

It turned out that Dunsworth had been the first one to get his gun out of his pocket. He might have still turned the whole thing back around even though Mike, Kari, and I had stopped the other two. But Junior sailed right at him, took his first bullet, then knocked him flat on his butt with a flying body already in shock from the wound. The gnome saved us all.

Michele, who'd made new mugs to replace the ones

broken in the battle of the lounge, made a special one,
which we presented to the runt that night. It had a picture
of a hairy-chested hero on it, with the words "MACHO
MAN" boldly running around the body of the cup.

Junior was rude and sarcastic through the whole thing.
But he ate it up.

So what's the gnome doing now? Two things, mainly: (1)
trying to build an FTL ship on paper, and (2) putting
outrageous ideas into the heads of the Whitedimple tod-
dlers. Number one is a lot tougher, of course. "The problem is," he keeps mumbling over and over, "how much
physics do we keep, and how much do we throw away?"

Poor guy's only got two real clues. First is that we kept
accelerating the whole trip. The Hexies wouldn't have
built the ship that large and wasted all that CRF fuel just
to keep us fooled—that would have been too expensive to
put up with. Second is that the hull appeared to be at least
partly organic material, and to have gotten noticeably thin-
ner during the two-year voyage. Even though the runt was
incapacitated when we departed the ship for the last time,
he had George Reid make estimates of the hull thickness
to compare with measurements he'd taken before the outbound voyage.

None of it makes any sense whatever to me—and maybe
it never will to Junior, either. But he keeps plugging
away. He's grown a lot, and is not afraid of failing.

Before we had our first child, Kari and I squandered
some bucks we had left over from buying our house in the
Big Cylinder, and we took a trip with the gnome to
Saturn. We stayed with Mom and Pop in SOS for a while.
And I finally did a polar traverse over the winter half of
Saturn, fulfilling an invitation Junior had extended to me
many years ago: to see the backlighted rings in all their
glory. But it turned out that we'd waited so long to do it,
we had to go over the north pole just like we did the first
time, when the rings were front-lighted.

Junior makes extra spending money teaching Sam Sebastian's kids how to become hotshot pilots. He took over
my job, in fact. I had to quit because of a booked-up
schedule of public appearance commitments.

The runt had plenty of offers from research and technology outfits—both in SpaceHome and on Earth—but he'd taken a solemn oath never to punch a clock. Said he'd rather sponge off Kari and me for the rest of his life.

But he's holding, not hurting. Instead of blowing his crew pay on a plot in the Big Cylinder, he invested it, settled down in an apartment in 'Home III, and now clips coupons every month. He spends a lot of time teaching his own brand of physics to a very smart computer he's built in his pad. He's also got some special deal going with SHU's Department of Computer Sciences. Every once in a while, he does some work for them of some kind or other: networking, or architectural analysis, or whatever—I don't speak that language very well. And in return, he gets an hour a month core time on their seventh-generation cryogenic thinker. I wonder what will come of it all.

Addendum 2138: "Eureka!" cackled the gnome.

The Hexie White Papers
Combined Discipline Appendices

Appendix A: THE HEXIE WORLD

By Dinsworth, Gates, Smith, and Zyyad

(Supplemental material by Badille,
Sakaguchi, and Whitedimple)

Executive Summary

Planetography

The world of the Hexies lies in a solar system 238 light years from Earth. Its primary is a G0 star, seen from Earth as an object of apparent visual magnitude 8.97; it is one of a visual pair at RA 6hr 5.7min, Dec 17deg 25min, listed as SHC 11035 (087 Orionis) in the SpaceHome general sky survey of 2078 [N.B.: This pair was originally listed incorrectly as a binary double, # 849, in the F.G.W. Struve Catalogue].

The Hexie primary has been of no historic interest to humans, except for being targeted by the Earth-based SETI Society in 2055 AD as a "primary search" star, it being of such an age and composition to have a reasonably large and stable zone of life.

The Hexie system contains seven major planets. Three are gas giants; one is slightly larger than Jupiter, one slightly smaller, and one almost identical in mass to Saturn. There are four terrestrial (rocky) planets, all in-system from the three giants. Two are inboard of the Hexie planet (named Tharthee) and one outboard. There are two thinly populated asteroid belts occupying the principal resonance gaps formed by the primary and the two largest giants.

Tharthee is 162 million kilometers from the primary in an orbit of very low eccentricity. Its period of revolution is 412.38 days [N.B.: All units in this appendix are converted to standard metric, including time in standard sidereal days and years, except where otherwise noted].

Tharthee is slightly less dense, and slightly larger (radius 6443 km), than Earth. Surface gravity is 1.023 standard G. The planetary surface is 21 percent land and 79 percent salt ocean, including north and south polar ice covering a combined 6 percent of the water. The planet is currently in a geologic high-water era.

Classic plate tectonics dominate the crust-mantle interface. The two continental land masses account for 92 percent of the dry land; they are close together, but in the process of separating. They remain connected by a thin isthmus which is very mountainous. The reason for this is that two oceanic plates are coming together where the continental plates are separating; the subduction of the southern plate tends to elevate and widen the isthmus. However, the separation is proceeding faster than the mountain-building process. Therefore the two land masses will disconnect within another 100,000 years. (From their own determinations of plate boundaries and crustal movements, the Hexies estimate that the separation will occur within a few kilometers of the ancient canal crossing the isthmus.)

Tharthee's rotational period is 20.4 hours, and subject to a lesser degree of dynamic braking because its single moon, although closer than Earth's at 140,000 kilometers, is only 502 km in diameter. The axial tilt of 26.8 degrees trends the globe toward more severe seasons; but this is ameliorated by the oceanic expanse and configuration, which fosters greater north-south energy exchange than on Earth.

The climatic consequences of the slightly brighter primary, the larger orbital radius, smaller orbital eccentricity, greater axial tilt, the smaller moon, and the current continental configuration are summarized as follows: (1) the mean planetary surface temperature is 1.5 degrees lower than Earth's; (2) the climate is overall slightly less moderate, but local effects over the land masses make this effect almost unnoticeable compared to Earth; (3) the tides are less in magnitude than on Earth, but oceanic currents are more pronounced; and (4) the generally larger ocean expanses create a measurably greater interhemispheric thermal energy transfer.

A major consequence of (4) above is that severe coriolis storms are more common than on Earth. The major destruc-

tive effects of these are experienced in the southern part of
the Streen Archipelago, the far northwestern coast of the
eastern continent, and the southern islands of the Czeeczee
Archipelago.

Geography

The two joined continents comprise 92 percent of Tharthee's
land mass, and stretch together two-thirds of the way around
the globe. The remaining 8 percent is concentrated almost
entirely in four major archipelagoes and the isthmus joining
the two continents. The main features of each of these land
masses are described below.

Eastern Continent—Teefoeeth. This is shaped roughly like
an equilateral triangle, with one apex at the isthmus. Each
side of the triangle is about 10,000 kilometers long. The
northern part strides the equator and is tropical; but the
southern half is temperate. The mountains of the great eastern range (Teefee) are quite tall, the highest peaks being
6000-7500 meters.

The Teefee range is paralleled to the west by a much
older formation of high rolling hills, geologically similar to
the Appalachians of the United States of North America, but
more evolved.

The two massifs are separated by 2000 kilometers of highlands. A large portion of this highland, stretching from 10 to
35 degrees south latitude, is forested. This area teems with
wildlife, and was the cradle of emergence of the first intelligent species during a period of geologically rapid fluctuation
in weather between 5 and 6 million years ago (see Appendix
B). Currently it is cool, mild and pleasant. This tract of
14,000,000 square kilometers is called Vazteer. It is the
technology-restricted zone, joke-named "Paczeer" ("the huge
womb") by the Hexies and "The Happy Hunting Ground" by
the human expeditionary crew members (Appendix B).

The western lowlands comprise the "civilized" part of the
continent. This is the third of the triangle to the west of the
older massif. It contains a great inland lake (Peer) 800 km in
length. The large river system has spawned a series of river-
port cities in the northern part of the lowlands.

Most of the eastern continent lowlands is devoted to farming and farming towns. There is a great underground aquifer
system to supply irrigation water. The system is maintained

by a well-distributed rainfall pattern. There is only one crop cycle per year; but the soil is rich and the crops healthy.

The Isthmus—Teeurvileed. The land bridge between the continents is somewhat analogous to Central America on Earth, but there are major differences: it thins out much more quickly, is somewhat longer at 4000 kilometers, and is dominated by a temperate climate. Its name in the universal Hexie tongue, like many of the land feature names, is retained from one of the multitudinous older languages. The joke name is "Theend-Leetcha" (a species of salt-water fish).

The isthmus was, and is, formidable to travel. It is dominated by rugged mountains and active volcanoes with peaks in the 2000-4000 meter range. There are many stretches where the mountains slope directly to the sea, making passage extremely difficult. The ancient roadway between the two continents (what remains of it after hundreds of earthquakes and volcanic eruptions since it was last repaired 4000 years ago) wanders incessantly back and forth between the northern and southern shores, seeking the path of least resistance. It crosses the divide some 278 times.

The older Hexie species made the journey across the isthmus some 4.2 million years ago when it was wider and less rugged. The more advanced species negotiated it with considerably more difficulty just over a million years ago (Appendix B).

The canal was built some 6,000 years ago in a rare, narrow section of coast-to-coast lowlands, which crosses the divide at an altitude of only 143 meters. Since the advent of floater technology, it has been maintained privately (with some government subsidy) as a combination historical monument and tourist attraction.

Western Continent—Zoeepeer. This is smaller than the eastern by 20 percent. It bears a strong resemblance, both in shape and size, to South America rotated 60 degrees clockwise.

The major mountain chain, Czee, occupies 40 percent of the land area; its tallest peaks range from 2500 meters in the east to 6000 meters in the west. The massif lies close to the northern coast and parallel to it. The mountains become younger, taller, and more rugged toward the southwest, finally tapering to a continental keel with an extremely sharp drop to the open sea below. This keel area, comprising the

westernmost 3000 kilometers of the continent, is so rugged
and treacherous that it was totally unexplored before the
advent of floater technology. The shoreline was mapped only
by boat, an undertaking treacherous in itself because of the
local currents and weather in the high southern latitudes. The
southwestern continental tip, nicknamed "The Bow," is a
prized tourist attraction because of its spectacular topography
and placement to intercept calved icebergs from the south
polar fields (see the body of this Appendix for a complete
description and analysis).

The belt of inhabited land south of the Czee massif is
composed of 3 regions. The westernmost has a wide summer-
winter temperature swing; it fosters deciduous trees bearing
high-quality "fruit," and fauna bearing luxurious winter fur.
The central region is characterized by rolling hills and lakes in
the south; this is the highly-prized residential region known
as the "Lake Country," dominated by Lake Karteneel with
the world government seat Karteneely on its eastern shores.
Rich farmlands dominate the country to the north of the
Capital. The easternmost region is a small area with extremely productive farmland extending to within 500 kilometers of the canal.

North of the Czee mountains between west longitude 100
and 135 is a narrow belt of land on which are many coastal
resort towns. East of this is a much wider belt of rain forest
and jungle lowlands.

The largest archipelago—Streen. This contains some dozen
major islands and hundreds of smaller ones—thousands, if the
very smallest are counted. It actually constitutes a small continental plate, which happens to be 55 percent submerged in
this geologic era.

The archipelago is about the same overall size as Australia,
with narrow channels between the many islands and a large,
shallow inner sea. The group is situated due north of the
widest part of the western continent. It lies in the mid-
northern latitudes, between 30 and 50. The largest island is
Streenthree.

The topography is much like that of New Zealand's North
Island: hilly, with few trees. The climate is cool and relatively
mild, and the grassy foliage makes an ideal grazing ground for
herds of wild and domesticated herbivores. These herds provide a large portion of the protein in the Hexie diet.

The second largest archipelago—Crinthee. This has somewhat less than half the land area of Streen. It sits astride the equator approximately 8000 kilometers east of Teefoeeth. It has a discontinuous, ancient mountain chain running as a theme through the islands. The mountains were raised by the collision of the archipelago with Zoeepeer during the most recent Pangea phase of the planetary tectonic process, some 270 million years ago.

The tallest island mountain is 2400 meters, just high enough to be out of the heavy air of the tropics, and almost exactly on the equator. On the top of this mountain is a hotel which features a large telescope (mirror of nearly 3 meters' diameter) moved from the city of Peeveel after the advent of floater technology, and kept in good working order as a tourist attraction. (The view of the Orion Nebula is spectacular, and a tourist favorite.)

The third archipelago—Freetheen. This is an island chain tectonically similar to that of Hawaii. It has been formed by movement of the north polar plate over an active spot in the underlying mantle. The island chain is therefore primarily a series of extinct volcanoes. The only active ones are three on the youngest island. There is a major difference between Freetheen and Hawaii: the geographical placement. Instead of being near the equator, Freetheen is in the far north.

The chain runs north-south; the active point where the magma erupts is at 78 degrees north latitude. The plate drift is southward, so the older islands are south of the newer ones.

There are 8 principal islands in the chain, stretching from 54 to 78 degress north latitude. Those above 65 degrees exhibit glaciation, including the one with active volcanoes. When the red-hot magma erupts, it is often through a covering of snow or ice. This is truly spectacular, and one of the wonders of the world.

Only the northernmost island is a tourist attraction. The two southernmost islands grow a species of long-haired herbivore (kolczeer) whose coat is sheared, woven into luxurious rugs, and coveted by well-to-do Hexies. The rugs are expensive because these two islands are the only places where the beasts will flourish, mate, and grow proper fur.

The smallest archipelago—Czeeczee. This chain consists of 14 major islands, and stretches 5000 kilometers, parallel to the northern coast of Zoeepeer and some 200-400 km off-shore. Geologically, it is the top of a coastal mountain range resting on a submerged continental shelf.

The 8 western islands are a refuge for some 160 species of poikilothermic fauna which began to differentiate from mainland species upon geologic isolation some 22 million years ago. Some adaptations to the frequent hurricanes experienced in this part of the archipelago are quite interesting. Tourists may observe only; they are permitted to land their floaters at 3 designated spots on each island.

The 6 eastern islands are resorts, with spectacular surf on the northwestern shores.

Appendix B: THE HEXIE CULTURE

By Allison-White, Badille, Dinsworth,
Dunsworth, Erickson, Kimberly, Kitigawa,
Reid, and Whitedimple

(Supplemental material by Smith,
Vance, and Zyyad)

Executive Summary

Prehistoric Hexipology

Six million years ago during the down-side fluctuations of
the current ice age, the first Hexies emerged as semi-intelligent
bipeds with approximately 50% of their current brain capacity. The cradle of emergence was in the forested highlands of
the eastern continent called Vazteer, which is joke-named
"Paczeer" ("the huge womb") by the Hexipologists, "Vatheel"
("the resort hotel") by Hexie non-professionals, and "the Happy
Hunting Ground" by humans.

After another 1.5 million years of stressed development,
during which brain size increased another 20 percent (to 60%
of current size), the climate ameliorated and glaciers retreated
southward and up into the mountains. There followed 1500
generations of mild weather. During this period of nearly half
a million years there was explosive continental spreading. The
eastern continent was overrun, and the isthmus (then broader
and not quite as rugged as today) was crossed 4.2 million
years ago. By 4 million years ago, the western continent's
habitable sections were also completely settled. Brain size did
not increase appreciably during this period.

For several hundred thousand years thereafter, the climate
went from 'mild' to 'normal,' which was sufficiently severe to
isolate the various groups spread over the continents and
force further development. But now the widespread groups
began to differentiate somewhat; it is speculated that the most
strongly differentiated groups would no longer have been able
to interbreed by the end of this period 3.2 million years ago.
Brain sizes increased to 65-70 percent of current value.

Then for 1.7 million years the climate regressed and the ice
came again. Weather conditions became worse than they'd
been for several million years. The only groups which sur-

vived were those in the northern lowlands of both continents. There was one exception to this generalized extinction: in the central region of Vazteer three or four groups, at least two of which were moderately differentiated, consolidated their numbers. From this union in adversity, the modern Hexie species emerged. Over these several thousand generations, this emergent species developed fire and advanced tools. The ontological evidence implies that during this period the dual auditory centers were neurally integrated. [It is also speculated that the modern species strategies of dual suckling and care for the young, and delayed three-stage brain growth of the children, evolved during this period. See Appendix C for full physiological description of the "carapace phenomenon" and the cyclic climatological correlates of the 180-200 year delay of sexual maturity after reaching full brain and body growth.]

Then a million and a half years ago the ice started to recede again, and the modern Hexie species began to expand territory. The expansion was not explosive this time, being paced by weather, food supply, and competition with the isolated groups which had survived in the northern plains. The other groups may have slowed the expansion, but the final outcome was never in doubt: the new species' brain capacity was 50% greater than that of their remote cousins; their communications were better, their hands were more dextrous, and their tools were superior. Over a period of several hundreds of thousands of years, the eastern continent was once again populated—this time by a truly intelligent species which would never again threaten to differentiate to the point of not being able to interbreed.

For the next several hundred thousand years a relatively static condition prevailed, in which the Hexies jostled with each other for dominance in their now enlarged ecological niche. The limiting factor for the still-nomadic species was always the food supply. Feast and famine reigned with the vagaries of global climate; the total population of the Hexies fluctuated sharply, but was never in danger of zeroing out. The intelligent animals were now much too non-specialized for the vicissitudes of nature to kill them off; they made tools and weapons and invented diverse high-pitched languages of increasing complexity.

During this period the western continent was once again invaded. The route was more difficult by then; but the invaders had a lot more ingenuity and were able to finally cross the isthmus a little over a million years ago. They encountered the direct descendants of the older species, living in the northern plains and beginning to expand; but once again there was no contest in the final analysis. The newcomers prevailed utterly, and totally supplanted their slower-witted forebearers.

Then sixty thousand years ago the climate ameliorated to the current mild conditions. Within a few thousand years, farming was invented in the great river valley of the eastern continent. Before ten thousand more years had passed, city culture began and spread over both continents. Written language and the beginning of recorded history commenced about 35,000 years ago.

As a final note, it is both an irony and a blessing that the only large region of the world which did not wholly adopt the city culture and move into the civilized mainstream was Vazteer, the cradle of emergence of both Hexie species.

Recorded Political History

The archaeological and written records make it quite clear that the similarities between Hexie and Earth political histories are abundant. [This may not be so remarkable from a teleological standpoint; it is unlikely that a species with few similarities would ever get close enough to the Hexies to be allowed intimate study of the record in the first place.] From the earliest days of civilization, the concentration of wealth in the cities time and time again attracted the nomadic looters. Standing civil defense forces rose in abundance as the culturally-nurtured thinkers and doers dreamed up ways of combating the wild rovers. Small armies and weapons sprinkled themselves liberally over the continents—in artifact and, later, the written record.

However, there appear to be two significant differences between the historical violence of Earth and Hexie cultures. First is that the Hexies never seemed to indulge in deliberate cruelty or wanton slaughter. Kill they did, and in some quantity; but the killing was always for immediate economic gain—either easy food or wealth. After the victory was won, there was apparently little or no practice of the human habits of rape, baby-killing, population genocide, etc. Second was that the Hexies never appeared to develop a drive for empire. Political units seemed to be limited to spheres of relatively homogeneous economic interests. Again, there were conflicts—even wars—but always on a relatively limited scale, and because of immediate economic conflict. [For complete discussion of possible physiological correlates—species monogamy, male-female physical and social equality, lifespans, etc.—see Appendix C, and section 2 of the body of this appendix. Also, section 3 contains relevant material on the contribution of the ancient six-family system to independence from strong central government.]

Apart from these differences from human history, growth proceeded in a quite familiar pattern—wars and weapons, victories and defeats, admixings of culture, syntheses of ideas, and nurturing of geniuses in the various cultural cradles. As transportation and communications improved, political units expanded slowly. During the previous several hundred thousand years, languages had developed in extremely diverse fashion among the members of this auditorily sophisticated species. Now, during a period of 20,000 years after farming and city culture were firmly established as the new way of life, there was a consolidation from several hundred distinctly different languages to five. This consolidation paralleled the rise of the five major political units—which we shall call "countries" for lack of a better name—on the two continents, which remain to this day.

The countries developed, and remain today, as loose confederations of Hexies with similar economic interests, with elected governments dedicated to preserve those interests from encroachment by neighbors. Perhaps a more accurate title for these units would be "politico-economic co-operatives." There are two in the western continent, splitting it about 60/40, with the westernmost country being the smaller. Of the three in the eastern continent, the largest encompasses the entire eastern half, from the highland forest to the eastern coast. The other two are smaller, but much more densely populated: one is in the northern part of the lowland plains, taking in the entire large river drainage system and the northern coast 20 degrees of longitude on either side of the zero meridian; the other takes in the entire southern coast west of meridian 45 E, the isthmus to within 300 kilometers of the canal, and the northern coast west of 20 W. [The island continent of Streen has also developed separate status in the past few millennia since the advent of floater technology, but is not considered a major economic force. They call themselves "the sixth country," but are joke-named "the wet upstarts" by the others. Nevertheless, they have produced some excellent joke plays which have been successful in preserving their interests. For complete descriptions of all political units, see section 3 of the body of this appendix.]

The five "countries" grew and stabilized themselves in size and power until technology began to make itself felt uncomfortably. Then about six thousand years ago the first political jokester gained ascendancy and defeated the enemy of a neighboring state by making the entire population of his nation laugh him out of office.

Modern Political History

To understand this subject it is necessary to understand the importance of humor in Hexie cultural history. The Hexies have had a more highly developed sense of humor than Earth cultures from antiquity. Even as far back as 30,000 years ago, they had begun to develop the practical joke into something more than just crude kick-'em-in-the-seat-of-the-pants humor. They also by then had a history of joke and pun names for things—something akin to, but more communicative than human nicknames. They used (and still use) joke names for both fun and social comment. And plays—especially humorous plays—have been a universal entertainment from the beginnings of recorded history.

Aside from this, by 6000 years ago the Hexies had a high civilization, and were cursed and blessed with many of the socio-political-economic symptoms that visit Earth and Colonies today. Science and technology were on the steep portion of the curve and flooding civilization with new products. Increasingly sophisticated transportation and communication were causing the countries to realize more and more that they had overlapping economic interests—with the concomitant potential for conflict; the habitable part of the planet was getting a little overcrowded and some of the countries were experimenting with birth control measures [not as difficult a task as on Earth—see Appendix C, and section 4 of this appendix for physiological correlates]; nuclear technology had arrived, with its benefits and frightening potentials; and the first experiments with spaceflight had begun, opening the door for economic exploitation of the Hexie solar system—and also adding potential new arenas of conflict.

But the Hexie tradition of laughing at themselves was widespread. Will Rogers types were highly respected in all the countries. Political humor was routinely practiced during campaigning by many candidates, and rarely was one elected who had no sense of humor. The stage was set, then, for the "joke revolution."

At the time in question 6000 years ago, a true politico-humorist genius came on the scene. By the time he was just 370, he'd achieved the highest office in his country by producing on holovision a campaign based on a series of comedy plays in which the political history and decisions of his opponent were dissected in hilarious fashion. The population went to the polls laughing; the incumbent was laughed right out of office, and the genius—Teenteel—took the reins.

At the time Teenteel took office, his country was in the middle of a border dispute with the country directly across the isthmus. Teenteel's country was in the western continent, and occupied approximately half the isthmus (the half with the canal); the opposing country was on the eastern continent, and occupied the other half of the isthmus. The dispute was over the boundary, of course. The eastern country wanted enough of the choice rare lowland portion so they could build their own canal (the western country had built the one already there, and charged very stiff tariffs to use it); they claimed it as their ancient right, and were threatening military action to take it over.

But Teenteel, through a brilliant campaign of holovision, articles, and word-of-mouth jokes, put the leader of the opposing country in such a bad state that she, too, was laughed out of office. By the time she left, nobody would have fought the war for her anyway; it was made to seem too ridiculous in the eyes of the populace. The final outcome of ten years of effort by Teenteel was the loose unification of the two countries and the beginning of truly modern political civilization. Within another century all the countries were united by a watchdog world government. Each country retained relative independence, kept its languages intact, passed its local laws and so forth; but the world plebiscite held power in the matter of international decisions and intercourse.

Teenteel, naturally, was the first president of the planetary government—and the last one ever to have held high office in his own country. He gained the absolute trust of most of the world's population, and thus had great powers to wield for the unification of the two continents. During his three-hundred year tenure, he managed to (1) dismantle the arsenals of all the countries of the world, (2) establish a moderate value-added tax to run the world government and create a small neutral world police force, (3) institute a common language for global communications, and (4) perpetuate his office via an election scheme in which the entire world took part.

Teenteel consolidated his power to make the tough decisions regarding the course of world politics. But he was also a staunch supporter of the natural Hexie urge for individual independence. He therefore established many institutions of importance which had the effect of putting checks and balances on the world government. One of the most important posts he created was that of the Frineethee, whose sole function was to ridicule any ill-considered or selfish decisions made by the world government.

It was the Frineethee's job to research every important issue just as thoroughly—or even more so—than did the President. But the research was legislated as being entirely divorced from the government in power. The Frineethee under no circumstances could be consulted by the president on any matter whatsoever, nor could the Frineethee have any dealings with officialdom. Thus, for every important decision made by the President, there was an "independent audit" whose results were likely to be in the form of a holovision comedy skit or a series of political jokes carefully spread around the globe. If a world president made too many bad decisions, he was thus subject to being laughed out of office within a few years.

Upon becoming Frinithee, a Hexie was required to renounce any nationalistic ties and dispose of any large holdings or interests in any company. The Frinithee held office either for life, or until his jokes started to fall flat and he was yawned out of the post by his political peers.

After consolidating the power of the presidency and firmly establishing the world government, Teenteel did a remarkable thing: he retired and arranged to be appointed as the next Frineethee. By the time he died in that post after several hundred more years, Teenteel had endowed the office of Frineethee with a power which was a close second to that of the presidency.

Many institutions grew up around the office of Frineethee. Being a playwright working for the Frineethee was a high honor; many schools of comedy existed, and many a comic playwright aspired to the world's capital to ply his profession in the hopes of being "discovered." Many sayings also grew up around the office—e.g., "yeah, but let's see what the Frineethee says," "as hard as being President with a Teenteel Frineethee," and so forth.

Humoculture

The Hexies' sense of humor pervades everything. The species tendency was always there; and the advent of communications technology and the world government under Teenteel solidified it into a ubiquitous global culture. The clever jokester is held in high esteem, and everybody who wants to succeed tries to live the appropriate lifestyle. To be sure, there is a place also for average-to-dour types—but they are rarely economic successes, and never social ones. Thus, the trait of quick-wittedness is being strengthened in the species, and the Hexie who "can't take a joke" is slowly being bred out of existence. [The Hexies' long lives give them a natural breeding advantage over humans in this wise: the mating process is much less frenetic and much more considered than is the case for the human species. This quality tends to select for socially or physically desirable traits in a shorter time, even though humans go through ten generations to the Hexies' one. See Appendix C.]

Thus, humor and quick-wittedness pervade every aspect of Hexie culture. The more cleverly a product is introduced, the more likely it is to sell. The more cleverly a research grant is presented, the more likely the solicitor to receive it. And so forth. But one should never underestimate the Hexies because of their sense of humor. A ne'er-do-well "good time Charlie" or a boorish practical jokester are appreciated just as little on the Hexie world as on our own.

The Hexies, above all, have used humor to establish a sense of balance. They recognize and respond to serious matters in quite appropriate ways; but their ability to laugh at themselves and the universe holds down their tendencies toward neuroses—personal, national, or global. And that is the crucial difference between their culture and ours. We do not yet have that sense of balance—that humor-driven empathy for the feelings of others and ourselves—which would unify the peoples of the human species and allow them to compromise disputes without disastrous political or military action.

So humor pervades all on the Hexie world. Science, technology, industry, politics, the arts, family relationships, crime, law. And all in all, it does not detract. Every profession has its slackers who are actually better at turning a quip than doing their job—but it's no worse than the traditional Earth statistic of 90 percent of the work being done by 10 percent of the people. In fact, it may be considerably better; one of us (Badille) estimates that on the Hexie world 80 percent of the work is done by 20 percent of the people. Thus, the Hexies are productive, and they flourish.

Floater Technology and Space Exploitation

The Hexies state that the flow of science and technology seem to be much the same in any given civilization—though admittedly this theory has been tested on only three cultures. The laws of physics appear to be identical everywhere in this local region of space-time; and they dictate a certain order to discovery and exploitation. New discoveries must be based on technology developed previously, and so forth.

So painfully, plagued initially by famine, fighting, and other setbacks, a civilization progresses finally to the steep portion of the "S" curve of technological growth. At about that time, energy resources and ecology become serious problems, driving the civilization out into space to keep from glutting its home planet.

But particulars may vary slightly within this framework. The Hexie variation was to discover early how to make quantum mechanics work for technology in more spectacular ways than tunnel diodes and the like.

It happened through the auspices of a Hexie genius named Keertee. On our world, she would have been raised as a contemporary of Fermi and Schroedinger. She worked for about a hundred years in the discipline of quantum molecular technology, finally solving the dual problems of collapsing randomly distributed wave functions in a non-stochastic fashion, and handling the heat loads of the resultant thermodynamic inefficiencies.

She worked for a transportation company, which still holds a proprietary monopoly on her discoveries after 4700 years. Details of the theoretical underpinnings and manufacturing processes are guarded very carefully, and were not made available to the human expeditionary crew. Even the Hexie public knows nothing of them; all floaters and similar devices are built with extremely effective safeguards. (The transportation company keeps their books open to the public to show that their profit margin remains well within the bounds of propriety; thus industrial espionage is discouraged by the Hexie customs of fair play in the economic arena.)

The development of floater technology occurred very early in the space exploration era. It therefore supplanted chemical-powered rockets completely for achieving Tharthee orbit from the ground. The Hexies within a short time combined molecular technology and fusion power to enable them to completely exploit their system from a home-planet base. This created a different economic setup than exists for humans, and obviated the need for an equivalent of the SpaceHome Colonies.

In fact, the only orbiting structures possessed by the Hexies are for manufacturing, some research, and entertainment. The manufacturing facilities require an environment as close to true zero G as possible, and so are situated at the Tharthee/moon L4 point in a non-corrected orbit. Also at L4 is one habitat spun at approximately 0.5 G in which the workers and researchers live during their on-orbit shifts. The microgravity entertainment establishments are all in low orbits for protection from cosmics; they accept the periodic re-boost penalty for this advantage.

The Hexies like low gravity even less than humans, and have not established any permanent bases equivalent to those on Iapetus. Where it is necessary to mine resources from a fixed system location, they pay the economic penalties of higher-G CRF travel, shorter durations of shift-crews, and bringing back raw materials for refinement in Tharthee orbit or on the ground. The Hexies love their home planet, and willingly pay higher prices for staying attached to it. They have not developed the "high ground" chauvinism extant among the current-day SpaceHome colonists.

About the Author

Grant David Callin brings strong credentials to the "hard" science fiction field. He graduated from the Air Force Academy in 1963 and retired from service in 1984. His bachelor's degree is in basic sciences; he has advanced degrees in space physics, and physiology & biophysics. He is also an amateur astronomer who has built his own 8-inch telescope, and dabbles in astrophotography.

He is now a research analyst for Boeing Aerospace Company, heavily involved with Boeing's role in the NASA Space Station Program. "Working the Space Station," he says with a gleam in his eye, "is like a childhood wish come true. It's something I've dreamed about ever since I read *Between Planets* in the early '50's. But," he cautions, "the Space Station won't get built by dreamers. It takes a bunch of hard-headed professionals who worry about systems engineering and integration, design margins, interface control documentation, test and verification, logistics and operations, and a thousand other things."

Callin's background is tailor-made for portrayal of the future SpaceHome society in which his novels *SaturnAlia* and *A Lion on Tharthee* are set. He has a working knowledge of almost every facet of life in microgravity, from orbital dynamics to manufacturing to closed-cycle life support. He combines this background with a natural talent for strong plotting, humor, and depth of characterization. In sum, he is a complete writer of science fiction.

"Everybody is asking: How do we knock out ICBM's? That's the wrong question. How do you design a system that allows a nation to defend itself, that can be used, even by accident, without destroying mankind, indeed, must be used every day, and is so effective that nuclear weapons cannot compete with it in the marketplace? That's the right question."

THE MOON GODDESS AND THE SON

DONALD KINGSBURY

The great illusion of the Nuclear Peace is that there will be no war as long as neither side wants war. We have neglected to find a defense against nuclear weaponry—but we cannot guarantee that a military accident will not happen. We argue that defense is impossible and disarmament the only solution—but we know no more about how to disarm than we know how to shoot down rocket-powered warheads.

Exploring these situations is what science fiction does best, and author Donald Kingsbury is one of its stricter players. Every detail is considered and every ramification explored. His first novel, *Courtship Rite*—set in the far future—received critical acclaim. His new novel takes place during the next thirty years.

In the 1990s the Soviets, building on their solid achievements in Earth orbit, surge into ascendancy by launching the space station Mir. Mir in time becomes Mirograd, a Russian "city" orbiting only a few hundred miles above North America. Now the U.S. plays desperate catch-up in the space race they are trailing.

THE MOON GODDESS AND THE SON is the story of the men and women who will make America great again. "Kingsbury interweaves [his] subplots with great skill, carrying his large cast of characters forward over 30-odd years. Neither his narrative and characterization nor his eye for the telling detail fall short. . . . An original mind and superior skill have combined to produce an excellent book."—*Chicago Sun-Times*

416 pp. • 55958-3 • $15.95

TRAVIS SHELTON
LIKES BAEN BOOKS
BECAUSE THEY TASTE GOOD

Recently we received this letter from Travis Shelton of Dayton, Texas:

I have come to associate Baen Books with Del Monte. Now what is that supposed to mean? Well, if you're in a strange store with a lot of different labels, you pick Del Monte because the product will be consistent and will not disappoint.

Something I have noticed about Baen Books is that the stories are always fast-paced, exciting, action-filled and seem to be published because of content instead of who wrote the book. I now find myself glancing to see who published the book instead of reading the back or intro. If it's a Baen Book it's going to be good and exciting and will capture your spare reading moments.

Another discovery I have recently made is that I don't have any Baen Books in my unread stacks—and I read four to seven books a week, so that in itself is a meaningful statistic.

Why do *you* like Baen Books? Drop us a letter like Travis did. The person who best tells us what we're doing right—and where we could do better—will receive a Baen Books gift certificate worth $100. Entries must be received by December 31, 1987. Send to Baen Books, 260 Fifth Avenue, New York, N.Y. 10001. And ask for our free catalog!